He had to get up.

But there appeared to be a little problem with him just leaping from bed and facing the day. And that problem was the naked female sprawled across his chest.

Uncaring about the brutal pain it would cause, Crush opened his eyes and looked down. Yep. That was a female all right. A—he took a sniff—feline female. Crush's lip curled. Another feline. The most untrustworthy of species in his opinion. And since he was naked, too, he could only assume that they'd . . . well . . . you know.

Christ, what was wrong with him? This wasn't like him. Crush didn't get drunk and sleep with random people. He just didn't. It wasn't in his DNA. It wasn't just the NYPD who called him "By the Book" Crushek, either. He had classmates from junior high, high school, and college who called him that as well.

Yet a little depression, a few too many Jell-O shots to drink at a house party, and here Lou Crushek was. Naked. With a feline.

Who was this female anyway? Anyone he knew? Crush didn't think so. He knew lots of felines, but he didn't spend time around them because they were, as he'd already stated and everyone knew, totally untrustworthy. It was a fact. Look it up!

Don't miss any of Shelly Laurenston's Pride Series

BEAR MEETS GIRL

SHELLY LAURENSTON

KENSINGTON PUBLISHING CORP.
http://www.kensingtonbooks.com

KENSINGTON BOOKS are published by

Kensington Publishing Corp.
119 West 40th Street
New York, New York 10018

All Kensington Titles, Imprints, and Distributed Lines are available at special quantity discounts for bulk purchases for sales promotions, premiums, fund-raising, and educational or institutional use. Special book excerpts or customized printings can also be created to fit specific needs. For details, write or phone the office of the Kensington special sales manager: Kensington Publishing Corp., 119 West 40th Street, New York, NY 10018, attn: Special Sales Department, Phone 1-800-221-2647.

Kensington and the K logo are Reg. U.S. Pat. & TM Off.

ISBN-13: 978-0-7582-6521-0
ISBN-10: 0-7582-6521-2
First Kensington Trade Paperback Edition: April 2012
First Kensington Mass Market Edition: October 2015

eISBN-13: 978-1-4967-0434-4
eISBN-10: 1-4967-0434-7
Kensington Electronic Edition: October 2015

10 9 8 7 6 5 4 3 2 1

Printed in the United States of America

ACKNOWLEDGMENTS

Big thanks to all the hardworking people of Polar Bears International for their invaluable assistance on my research and specifically to Barbara Nielsen for answering my goofy questions and leading me in the right direction without laughing at me once.

Please note that any instance of my hero veering wildly from normal polar bear behavior is completely down to me and my edgy, barely-leave-my-house-to-walk-the-dog author lifestyle.

Smith Wolf Pack
New York
(including friends & known associates)

Bobby Ray "Smitty"
Alpha Male Wolf
Mate: Jessie Ann Ward
(of the Kuznetsov Wild Dog Pack)

Sissy Mae
Alpha Female Wolf
(Sister to Smitty)
Mate: Mitch O'Neill Shaw, Lion

Ronnie Lee Reed
Beta Smith Wolf
Mate: Brendan Shaw, Lion
(Brother to Mitch)

Dee-Ann Smith
Beta Smith Wolf
Mate: Ulrich "Ric" Van Holtz
(Beta Wolf in Van Holtz Pack)

Mason "Mace" Llewellyn
(Lion, Business partner w/Smitty)
Mate: Detective Dez MacDermot, full-human

Gwen O'Neill
(Tigon, Sister to Mitch Shaw)
Mate: Lachlan "Lock" MacRyrie, Grizzly Bear

Blayne Thorpe
(Wolfdog, Best friend to Gwen)
Mate: Bo "The Marauder" Novikov, Lion-Bear Hybrid

Cella "Bare Knuckles" Malone
She-Tiger of the Malone Family
(Friend/sometime partner to Dee-Ann Smith
and Dez MacDermot)
Mate: Lou "Crush" Crushek, NYPD Detective, Polar Bear

For more information on the Pack, Prides, and Clans associated with the Pride series, go to www.shellylaurenston.com.

CHAPTER ONE

B rutal, undeniable pain. The kind of pain that could kill a man. Maybe it had. Maybe the pain throbbing in his head right at this moment had killed him and he'd have to spend eternity feeling like this. Like warmed-over shit melting in the hot desert sun.

The worst part about all this? It was *his* fault. He had no one to blame for this but himself—and those damn Jell-O shots. He should have stayed away from them. He knew better. All that alcohol in those delectable little jiggly squares . . . what was he thinking? And now he could barely move without pain. Brutal, undeniable pain.

Lou "Crush" Crushek tried to open his eyes, but that only made things worse. It was morning and that light coming through the window was destroying any brain activity he had left. If he were home, he'd simply go back to sleep for a few more hours, but he wasn't home. He could tell. The scent was different. He smelled feline. Everywhere he smelled feline.

Crush snarled a little. That's whose fault this was. That damn cat. Male lions. Never trust a male lion! Sure, this particular male lion was married to a fellow NYPD detective and was from one of the wealthiest Prides in Manhattan, but he was also the asshole who'd brought the tray of Jell-O shots around, in their innocuous-looking little cups, and said, with that feline grin, "Go on. Try one."

So . . . Crush had tried one. Then another. And another. After the eighth . . . well, he didn't remember much of anything after the eighth.

What Crush did remember was making the mistake of going over to Detective Dez MacDermot's house for a "small get-together with some friends" that turned into anything but. Normally, when parties or events became something he didn't want to deal with, Crush would find the first exit and head on home to his TV and his quiet life. At least the quiet life he had when he wasn't working undercover, pretending to be a merciless drug dealer, biker, and occasional hit man. But honestly, Crush didn't leave the stupid party because he was, for lack of a better, manlier word, depressed.

A word he rarely used about himself. He wasn't much for sitting around, feeling sorry about his life. He was a bear, after all. A polar bear specifically. No, not one of those guys who insisted on swimming in the Atlantic during the middle of winter to prove how virile he was. But a guy who could swim in the Atlantic during the middle of winter and never worry about dying of hypothermia. A guy who could shift into an eight-foot, twelve-hundred-pound polar bear anytime he wanted to. And, as a polar bear, sitting around being depressed wasn't really his thing. Instead, Crush lived like most of his kind. Being curious. Asking too many questions. Staring blankly at people until they became terrified and ran away. Eating whenever he was even slightly hungry. The usual.

Too bad, though, Crush had discovered something that all bears found distressing. He'd discovered there would be change. Change was coming Crush's way and he hated change. He liked to know things were going along as they should, and when that didn't happen, he became depressed. He still hadn't recovered from the closing down of his favorite deli five years ago. Or that six years ago they'd moved his favorite shoe store—needless to say that as a six-nine, three-hundred-pound guy, he couldn't exactly pick up his boots and sneakers from the local sports store—and Crush still walked to where the old shoe store had stood, gazing into the window, wishing things were like they once were, until the customers inside the tea shop called police about the "crazed meth dealer lurking outside the door."

So no, Crush didn't handle change well, but he didn't see that there was anything he could do to prevent this change from happening. Not after one of his old partners had called him and given him a heads-up. The man wouldn't have called unless he was sure. So now Crush was just waiting for the anvil to drop.

Unfortunately, it felt like that anvil had already dropped right on his head.

He couldn't do this. He couldn't sit here in a coworker's house, waiting for the hangover and migraine he had to go away. No, he just needed to get a move on. He had to get up. He had to deal with the pain. He had plans anyway for the afternoon and he wasn't about to miss out on them. So he had to get up.

But there appeared to be a little problem with him just leaping from bed and facing the day. And that problem was the naked female sprawled across his chest.

Uncaring about the brutal pain it would cause, Crush opened his eyes and looked down. Yep. That was a female all right. A—he took a sniff—feline female. Crush's lip curled. Another feline. The most untrustworthy of species in his opinion. And since he was naked, too, he could only assume that they'd . . . well . . . you know.

Christ, what was wrong with him? This wasn't like him. Crush didn't get drunk and sleep with random people. He just didn't. It wasn't in his DNA. It wasn't just the NYPD who called him "By the Book" Crushek, either. He had classmates from junior high, high school, and college who called him that as well.

Yet a little depression, a few too many Jell-O shots to

drink at a house party, and here Lou Crushek was. Naked. With a feline.

Who was this female anyway? Anyone he knew? Crush didn't think so. He knew lots of felines, but he didn't spend time around them because they were, as he'd already stated and everyone knew, totally untrustworthy. It was a fact. Look it up!

Too bad Crush couldn't be one of those guys who drunkenly slept with a woman only to sneak out before she woke up. It would definitely make his life a whole lot easier, but that would bring him to a new level of tacky he couldn't handle. Just because he felt his life falling apart around him—he hated change!—didn't mean he'd allow it to actually fall apart. And part of keeping his life together was doing the morally right thing.

Man, it sucked being a good guy all the time.

"Uh . . . miss?" Jeez! His voice sounded like gravel. He cleared his throat and tried again. "Miss? Excuse me?" He couldn't see her very clearly with all that black hair, with strands of white and red throughout, covering her face and his chest. He recognized that hair color, though. She was a She-tiger.

Hating to wake her up, Crush tapped her shoulder. "Miss?"

"Hmmh?"

"Uh . . . yeah, sorry. I . . . uh . . ." This was so hard. How did he tell a woman he'd possibly had sex with that he didn't know her name? Couldn't even remember having sex with her? This was getting worse and worse. When the hell did he become a frat boy?

Suddenly she stretched, her long body briefly writhing on his. Crush ignored how good that felt and said, "Miss?"

She lifted her head and gold-green eyes blinked up at him.

Damn, she was pretty. He didn't remember having sex with her? Really? How drunk had he been last night?

She blinked at him in confusion; then she smiled. "Oh. Hi."

Oh, hi?

Yawning and slapping her hand against his chest, she levered herself up and looked around the room, giving him a monumental peek at her breasts and, wow, those were freakin' nice. "What time is it?" she asked.

"No idea. Early."

She nodded and settled back onto his chest, eyes closing, arms tightening around his chest. "Good. I'm still so tired."

Wait. What just happened?

"I have to get up."

"Another hour," she bargained. "Maybe two. Just relax."

Completely confused, Crush said, "Look—"

Her head snapped up, those eyes locking on him. "Are you going to keep talking? 'Cause it's irritating. I'm trying to sleep, and I'm extremely hungover."

Crush's eyes narrowed. *He* was irritating? "Tell me we didn't have sex last night."

"As drunk as you were?" She yawned, already bored with him, it seemed. "I don't think you could have gotten it up with a crane."

"Thanks."

"Wait. Is that what you think? That we fucked?"

"We're in bed together. What was I supposed to think?"

"That I was tired and needed someplace to sleep."

"But we're both . . ." He shrugged a little. "Naked."

"Yeah, I was really drunk, too, so I just took my clothes off."

"Wasn't there somewhere else you could have slept?"

"Most of the people who crashed here last night were either full-humans or canines. Have you ever tried to sleep with a canine? They yip in their sleep. And run. It's annoying. And Mace wouldn't take the couch so I could sleep with his wife so—"

"You asked a lion male to move out of his bed for you?"

"Why wouldn't I? Because he's the majestic lion male, king of the jungle? Or because he's a rich Llewellyn of the Llewellyn Pride?"

"Because it's the man's house."

"It's his *wife's* house. MacDermot just allows him to stay here with her and those giant, useless dogs she owns. And I know she'd pick those ridiculous rotties over that lion in a hot second." She sat up. "Well . . . now I'm awake."

"How annoying for you." Crush struggled to sit up, too, ignoring the screaming in his head.

"What are you so cranky about?"

"You basically just told me you used me like a giant pillow."

"You were comfortable. And didn't yip once. I hate the yipping. Let me tell ya, you don't know hell until you've been trapped in a rainy, miserable jungle during monsoon season with a bunch of canines. Everyone wet and miserable and goddamn yipping."

Crush tried to ignore his migraine and asked, "Why would you be sitting in a miserable jungle with canines?"

"For lots of reasons."

"Name two. No. Just name one. I challenge you."

"You challenge me?" She laughed, her almost muzzlelike nose crinkling a little as she looked him over. "Aren't you cute?"

Finally, Crush had to ask, "Who *are* you?"

"If I wasn't still hungover, I'd give you my most sultry smile and tell you 'your dream come to life.' But, eh. I'm just too tired to bother and, honestly, does one have to really put in that much effort for a *bear*?"

"Are you always this insulting?"

"Insulting? This is me being nice. I even complimented you."

"Yes. Apparently I'm as comfortable as a pillow."

"Yeah. But one of those full-body ones. Or like one of those giant stuffed bears you get when you're a kid. My dad used to get me those and then he'd teach me how to maul 'em."

"I am not—"

She held up her finger. "Hold that." Then the insane female stretched out across his lap and reached down to the floor, grabbing a phone out of her jeans.

Annoyed and disgustingly turned on, Crush snarled, "Woman, get off me."

"Ssssh," she said, settling her butt onto his lap. "Business call."

Did she just shush him? She did, didn't she?

"Yep?" she said into the phone, clearly uncaring that they were *still* both naked and there was absolutely *nothing* separating her ass from his cock. "Now? 'Cause I gotta get home to the kid."

Kid? The woman had a child, but she was hanging out and getting drunk at house parties and torturing him with her butt on his cock?

Thinking about all the shitty parents he had been forced to deal with over the years as a cop, Crush hissed, "You have a child?"

She nodded and while someone kept talking on the other end of her phone, she whispered, "Have to get home. Still breastfeeding." Then, when Crush thought his head might explode, she silently laughed and mouthed, "Just kidding."

Holy hell, who was this woman?

"All right. All right. I'll get Smith on it. You know she loves morning jobs. I know she doesn't work for you, but think of it as outsourcing. We both know she can do the damn job. Besides, she has to realize that not everything can be the close-up kill." Not knowing what she was talking about, Crush was relieved when she winked at him. Good. She was kidding. Because it would be really hard to arrest a naked woman sitting in his lap. "Okay. Good. I'll take care of it."

She disconnected the call and tossed the phone back on her jeans. "I've gotta go."

"Yes. You need to get home to your *child*."

"Yeah. Her, too." She shrugged. "She's pretty self-sufficient. She can almost reach the stove."

Unable to take any more, Crush pushed her off his lap. Not as hard as he'd like—damn his morals—but at least he got her off him and he could move away from her.

Grabbing his clothes, Crush stalked to the door.

"Don't you want my number?" she asked him. "Maybe the next time we could get drunk and then actually have sex. If you're worried about the kid, I can put a little brandy in her milk bottle and she'll be out like a light."

Crush began to speak, but realized he would only say something completely inappropriate and mean, something he simply couldn't bring himself to do. So instead he stormed out, slamming the door behind him.

Tragically, however, Desiree MacDermott stood there in her hallway, her green eyes growing wide as her gaze moved down the length of his naked body while he lollygagged in the middle of her hallway.

His fellow detective finally looked up into his face. "Hi, uh . . . Crushek. How's it going?"

"Fine. Thank you for inviting me to your party."

"Anytime."

"Okay." They stood in the hallway another second, then Crush said, " 'Bye."

" 'Bye."

And, with as much dignity as he could muster at six in the morning while naked in a coworker's house, and still sporting a hangover and a semi hard-on—because even degenerates could be sexy as hell in the morning—Crush headed to his truck and absolute freedom.

Marcella "Bare Knuckles" Malone—She-tiger, feline nation protection contractor for KZS, pro hockey player for the championship shifter team the Carnivores, and the Malone family's bare-knuckles fighting champion—heard the bedroom door open again, but she simply couldn't stop her hysterical, wheezing laughter. No one could! Why? Because that had been the best!

"Cella?"

She heard MacDermot, but Cella couldn't answer her. She was too busy laughing and trying to figure out who that guy was. It wasn't every day Cella got to meet guys who looked like biker gang meth dealers, but had the moral fortitude of Martin Luther. All that indignant outrage over her untended daughter while sporting long, white polar bear hair that reached past his shoulders, a perpetual scowl, a scar on his neck, and pitch-black eyes that probably terrified lots of people. Of course, if all that didn't scare someone, she was pretty sure that what had to be about six feet and nine inches and about three hundred pounds or so of hard muscle probably did the trick. Man, had that body been like a thousand levels of perfect or what?

Yet even though the guy was really scary looking, Cella just found all that intimidating scowling and raging anger so cute. Like teddy bear cute. Plus, he was so damn uptight! She didn't know bears could be so uptight. Unless they were startled into a rage, bears were usually the most laid-back of all shifters, except lion males. Although Cella felt there was a huge difference between laid-back and just plain lazy.

Even worse for that poor bear was how all that uptightness brought out Cella's worst feline qualities. Honestly, the more uptight the bear became, the more she playfully swatted at him. She couldn't help herself. He was just so cute in his moral outrage!

"Cella!" MacDermot demanded, also now laughing. "What the hell did you do to the poor guy? I've never seen him look like that before. He was about to blow a vein in that big bear head of his!"

It was more than she could take. Cella rolled off the bed, hitting the floor, which miraculously made her hangover go far, far away.

CHAPTER TWO

Crush was dreaming about breaking through thick ice, pounding on it with his front legs, the seal under the ice giving him the flipper. *Little bastard*. But then the seal tapped at the ice. Once. Twice. Okay, so now he was taunting him?

"Crushek!"

Crush opened his eyes, looked around. *Shit*.

He turned the truck's ignition key to get enough power to roll down the window. "MacDermot."

She scowled and at first he thought she was angry. Then he realized she was just making fun of him. "Crushek," she said, imitating his voice, then laughed, and rested her arms on the sill. "How long have we known each other, Crushek?"

"I don't know." He thought a minute. "Since the Evans case?"

"Wow. The guys were right."

"Right about what?"

"That you mark time by cases, not by years."

"Yeah, well . . . I guess." Crush heard another knock and looked forward. "There's a cub on my hood."

"We were going for a walk so that his father could get a

little more sleep. When my boy's up, he wants *everyone* up. And gets mighty vocal when they're not."

Smiling at the baby male lion, Crush asked, "Already roaring, is he?"

MacDermot sighed. "Pretty much."

"We're here, Miss Malone."

Cella opened her eyes and looked around. Yep. She was here. "Here" being the Long Island town where she'd grown up surrounded by her family. To most people growing up "surrounded by family" probably meant they'd grown up with a mother, father, maybe a couple of siblings. If they had an extended family, perhaps a grandparent, a sickly aunt, or an orphaned cousin. But that's most people. Cella wasn't most people. She was a Malone. Not any Malone, either, but one of *the* Malones.

Sitting up and yawning, Cella pushed open the car door and stepped out. "Thanks, Mario." Katzenhaus Securities, KZS, was the international feline protection agency she'd worked for since she'd been discharged from the Marines. And of all KZS's perks (and there were many), Cella's favorite was the KZS car service. They used the best and fastest vehicles in the world and manned them with armed and well-trained felines. It was perhaps one of the best limo jobs one could find, paying an incredible salary, but it was also one of the most deadly. Cella didn't like to think about the number of times she'd run back to her car after she'd taken care of a contract, only to find her driver dead in the front seat. This scenario especially sucked when she was in unfamiliar or foreign territory.

Waving once more at Mario and holding her high heels and her purse in her hands, she walked down the street toward her parents' house. Mario could have driven her all the way to her house, but no one who knew the truth about this block would come down it. And the driver, a bobcat from Massapequa, knew about her street.

"Morning, Cella!" cheery voices called out.

"Hey, Aunt Kathleen, Aunt Marie, Aunt Karen."

It must have snowed last night, but not hard. Still, the cold felt good against her bare feet. This was her kind's time of year. The lions and cheetahs could have their summers because the Siberian tigers had the winter. Snow, bracing cold, harsh winds. Lovely.

"Morning to you, little Marcella."

"Morning, Uncle Aidan, Uncle Ennis, Uncle Tommy."

Cella reached her parents' home and went through the side gate into the yard. She walked around the side of the five-bedroom house and into the back. As comfortable with the freezing cold as Cella, her daughter was outside at one of the patio tables by herself, a tall glass of milk nearby, crayons all over the top along with coloring books. Cella sat down next to her, leaned over, and pinched her beautiful child's cheek.

"How's my little baby girl?"

Gold eyes just like her own looked Cella over before asking in a decidedly non-childlike voice, "Nice dress, Ma. Still working the docks?"

Smart. Ass.

Crush leaned out the window a bit, looking down at Mac-Dermot's feet. Sitting quietly there were her four dogs. Waiting. For her. "*That's* impressive."

"It's a skill. I'll admit."

Crush settled back. "So you just happened to be passing?"

"No. We usually walk the other way. But one of my neighbors called. She knows I'm a cop. Apparently there's a meth dealer hanging around, *threatening* everyone. A big, old scary guy in a blue pickup."

"I am *not* old. I'm not even forty. Unlike others."

"Discuss my true age at your own risk, buddy. But I'm sure it's the hair. Although they got the 'big scary' part right."

"Thanks."

She laughed and handed him something wrapped in a paper towel. "A corn muffin?"

"I didn't have any honeybuns."

"I am not a grizzly, MacDermot. I'm a polar, and I am not a fan of honey."

"Okay. Well, I didn't have any walrus blubber hanging around, either."

God, he was being an ass. "Mac—"

"I just figured youse might be hungry."

Uh-oh. He knew what the appearance of that Bronx accent meant. Of course, he only noticed it because MacDermot's time away from New York when she was a Marine had given her some kind of weird, flat accent. But when she got pissed . . . look out. Even worse, she'd started pointing a gloved finger at him.

"I was just trying to be fuckin' nice. Next time I won't fuckin' bother!"

MacDermot's dogs snarled at him, and the cub slashed at his window while giving what could only be called a baby-roar.

Crush turned to the full-human and raised a brow. "You have quite the control of the wild kingdom here, MacDermot."

She snorted, and they both laughed. Okay. He did like MacDermot. She was one of the few people—full-human or shifter—who didn't get on his nerves.

"I'm sorry," Crush finally admitted. "Jell-O shots are not my friend."

"I told Mace not to have those. I was like, 'What are we? A frat?' Hey, do you want to come in for breakfast?"

"Nah. I actually need to get going. Gotta game today."

"God, are you still playing on that shitty hockey team?"

He wanted to argue with her about the level of skill his NYPD shifter team had, but the reality was . . . they really did suck. The shifter firefighters and EMT guys kicked their asses constantly.

She patted his arm. "Are you okay?"

"I'm just hungover. When I got out here, I just meant to close my eyes for a few minutes and before I knew it—"

"No, no. I mean . . . when you got here last night. You weren't your usual scowling, non-talkative self. You seemed a more depressed scowling, non-talkative self. Anything I can help you with?"

Crush locked gazes with her, let out a breath. "Not unless you can get me out of this."

"Get you out of . . . oh." She smirked. "Heard about the transfer, huh?"

"Yeah. I heard about it. I have very good connections. Now can you get me out or not?"

"What makes you think I can get you out?"

"Heard you had some pull."

"Crushek, in the NYPD's shifter division, I'm just the crazy full-human that apparently smells like cat and that everybody steers clear of when I get pissed off."

He had to laugh. "Predators always know when to run, MacDermot."

Cella sat back, smirking at her nearly eighteen-year-old daughter, Meghan. Okay. So Cella had lied to the bear. She couldn't help it. Watching the look of horror on his face when he'd thought she'd left her toddler daughter all by herself while she went out partying kind of made her morning.

Well, actually . . . waking up with all that delicious naked bear flesh had made her morning. The rest of it was really just the icing on top of that cake.

Examining the coloring book her daughter was working

on, Cella stated, "I see they're really challenging you in that private school I'm paying for."

"I was watching the kids this morning," Meghan said about her young cousins, her attention still locked on what she was doing, "and we were coloring."

"But the kids are gone."

"I don't like to start things and not finish." She carefully added a little orange to the sun at the top of the page, of course making sure to not go outside the lines. Cella fondly remembered her own coloring books. *Nothing* had been in the lines. She hated lines. Hated limits. Amazing since Cella had done so well in the Marines. No one thought she would, especially her family. They were so certain she'd wash out during Basic that they didn't even complain when she said she'd signed up. In fact . . . they'd all laughed at her. "*Our* Cella Malone? A Marine? Yeah. Right." But the Marines had given Cella the freedom she couldn't have gotten anywhere else. Freedom from her family. From the Malones. At least for a little while.

"There." Her daughter pushed the coloring book away. "Done." She placed the crayon on the table. When Cella was gone, Meghan would come back and put all the crayons back in the box—in their original order. "Did you have breakfast?"

"Well—"

"I'll make you something."

"Why do you bother asking me when you're going to make me something anyway?"

"It's polite." Meghan leaned in and kissed Cella on the cheek. "Did you have a good time last night at your party?"

"Eh. It was okay. Mostly full-human cops and their full-human wives."

"Your cat killer friends and that dog didn't come?"

"First off, they, *we*, are not cat killers. If you want to be accurate, we're killer cats. And that dog has saved my life a few times. Respect that."

"I don't know why you still do that job. You don't need the money anymore."

"What? You think Boston University is going to pay for itself? Speaking of which, did you get that paperwork in?"

"Yeah. Sure."

"I do *not* want to pay for an apartment in that area, Meghan. Make sure you get a dorm room."

"Can we talk about this later?"

"Why are you getting so cranky?" Cella frowned. "You have been so cranky lately."

"I haven't been cranky."

"You've been totally cranky. At least to me."

"I don't mean to be. It's just very stressful right now."

"It's your final semester, Meghan. You've already been accepted to college and you're doing great in school. You shouldn't be stressing about anything. Just relax. Try and have a good time. I honestly don't know where you get this intensity from. It's definitely not a Malone thing. And you didn't get it from your father. I remember him when he was seventeen."

"You're not going to tell me another Dad-and-hash story are you? Because I don't want to think about my father as some loser."

"Your father was never a loser. Besides, he grew out of that phase. Look at him now. A responsible accountant about to marry the feline of his dreams."

As always when Cella mentioned Brian's upcoming wedding, their daughter got the strangest expression on her face. Cella had begun to think she was upset about the whole event. Seemed typical for a teenager to feel that way but . . . but Meghan was far from typical. And she had to know this didn't change anything. Not between her and her dad.

Cella tossed her shoes up on the table and caught hold of her daughter's hands. "Talk to me, Meghan."

"About what?"

"I mention your dad, you get weird." Cella tilted her head to the side, studying the beautiful girl she adored. "Is it the wedding?"

"No, of course not."

"You know this doesn't change anything between you and your dad. He loves you, Meghan, and so does Rivka."

"You just like Rivka because she's another cat killer."

"You love Rivka and we are *not* cat killers. Stop calling us that. We are protectors of the cat nation. Like the Marines or—"

"The C.I.A.?"

"Well, you don't have to get nasty." Tired of this same damn argument—Meghan, like Cella's mother, Barb, was not a fan of Cella's career as a Katzenhaus contractor—Cella released her daughter's hands and grabbed her shoes. "You know, Meghan, I'm just trying to be helpful and let you know I'm here for you."

Meghan rolled her eyes. "Ma . . . is there anything about me—or you, for that matter—that screams let's sit down and talk about our feelings?"

"I'm trying a different approach. I'm trying to be . . . ya know . . . a proper mother. Thoughtful and caring and . . . and all that other shit."

"Ma, being a hockey enforcer for a guy nicknamed the Marauder, killing on order from a thousand yards away, and being the kind of mom I don't want my male friends around because all they do is stare at your breasts and drool . . . these are your strengths. Let's not stray too far from that. Okay? Great. Now I'm going to make you some waffles. You'll eat, and then you can go upstairs and shower off that funk of . . . of . . . ?"

"Bear," Cella admitted.

"Right. Bear. Yeah, you can go wash that off and you and I will pretend we never had this discussion, okay? Great. Thanks!"

Cella watched her daughter head back into the house they shared with Cella's parents. Cella had known all those years ago when she headed off to the Marines that she was taking a risk. The risk of losing her daughter. But what was she supposed to do? Raise *another* Malone She-tiger? So the kid could end up sitting around all day with all the other "aunts," plotting and planning?

"Just a few more months, Malone," she reminded herself. Just a few more months and the kid would be out of here and off to college, to do whatever she wanted. Meghan's whole world was open in front of her with absolutely no limitations. And that's why Cella had risked everything. Some days she *still* risked everything. And she'd keep risking everything until her kid had everything she'd ever dreamed of.

Picking up her shoes, Cella headed into the house. Her mother, rushing out the side door attached to the garage to handle some rich full-human's wedding, quickly kissed her on the cheek.

"I might be late," she said. "Make sure your father eats."

"I will."

Cella came around the corner and met her daughter in the hallway. The two felines stared at each other until Cella said, "I love you, you trifling little heifer."

"I love you, too, Ma. Even when you're dressed like a high-priced hooker."

"I'd have to be high priced to pay for these shoes."

Crush sat on the bench and waited. He was grateful that MacDermot had gotten him up when she did. Most Sundays during the winter were game days for him and he hated missing even one. He played hockey with a bunch of local Queens and Long Island shifters from different precincts and firehouses because he wasn't good enough for pro . . . or even semipro. He was, to be honest, barely good enough for weekend hockey with his friends and thankfully he'd given up his childhood dream of being one of the "greatest players of all time" long before he reached junior high. He actually left that particular dream to those who had real talent. Instead, Crush played on the weekends with people who didn't care how bad he was, and the rest of the time he was a diehard fan of the pros, shifter *and* human.

"So how was MacDermot's party?" his partner Conway asked.

Crush winced. "I don't wanna talk about it."

"That good, huh? I'm surprised you went."

"Why?"

"You're not exactly known for going to parties that don't end with you arresting everybody at some later date."

"I know you've heard," Crush accused when Conway fell silent. "About the transfer."

"Yeah. I have. Although I've only heard about it for you. Not for me."

"Miller has been wanting to get rid of me for years," Crush complained about his captain.

"You terrify the man, but he has no idea why. You can't exactly blame him, though."

"Yes. I can."

The coyote shook his head. "Look, don't be an idiot, Crushek. This is your chance to make some *real* money. Do you know how much that division pays their detectives?"

"I don't care. God knows I'm not into this shit for the money."

"You're into it to be a badass."

"I *am* a badass."

"But you can still be a badass and make money to help you pay the mortgage on your new place. In fact, you get this job and you might actually be able to *live* in your house rather than in that rat hole you've been using for your cover."

"I do live in my—"

"You can have friends that are actually friends rather than just people you plan to eventually arrest."

"I get your—"

"Maybe a girlfriend. Someone who wasn't once a stripper with a sob story."

"*Okay*." Crush studied his ex-partner. "This is your wife talking to me, isn't it? Through you."

"You know she worries about you."

"And I didn't date the stripper; I just bought bus tickets for her and her kids."

"Sucker."

Annoyed, Crush snarled and looked back at the game. "I'm not wearing a suit."

Conway snorted. "No one in that division wears a suit. And maybe you'll get to work with MacDermot now. You two seem to strangely get along. Of course, with her living with that male cat, you must be like a breath of fresh air."

"But what am I going to do there? Kill on command?"

"They don't do that . . . I don't think."

"Yeah. *That's* comforting."

"God, Crushek, get over it already," Conway snapped. "Nothing's worse than a whiny bear. Especially a whiny bear that's going to be making a lot more money than I will."

Crush didn't say anything, just skated out onto the ice with his fellow players when it was time. Conway was with him, a few minutes later, going for a puck. That's when Crush coldcocked him with his stick.

The coyote, eyes crossing, went out like a light, crashing to the ice, and their team captain yelled, "Jesus, Crushek! I thought we told you no more hitting Conway!"

Crush shrugged. "He called me whiny."

Freshly showered and wearing sweatpants, tank top, and sneakers, Cella walked into the family kitchen, but immediately stopped right at the threshold.

It was her father, brothers, and several of her aunts around the kitchen table. Normally nothing weird. The kitchen table was where they always met to talk, argue, and occasionally eat. The dining room was for holiday dinners or, as her mom put it, "fancy meals." But what really worried her was that as soon as Cella walked in, they all *stopped* talking and faced her, gazing at her. Her family didn't stop talking for anything. Malones were not known for being a quiet breed of feline.

"Hi," she said, wondering what the hell was going on.

Cella's father, Butch "Nice Guy" Malone, walked over to her and gave Cella a big hug, softly murmuring, "Don't ever forget, baby, we'll always love you."

"Okay," Cella said, pulling away from her father and nodding at her family before walking out.

She went across the backyard, around the Olympic-size family pool, and into the connected backyard of her best friend's family. Cella hadn't met Jai Davis, a mountain lion originally from Valley Stream, Long Island, until they were both seventeen and very pregnant. But they'd become friends quickly with both of them being feline and teen moms. As soon as the girls were born, the pair had teamed up, sharing responsibilities when they could, and covering for each other when necessary. It wasn't normal for Malones to allow outsiders into their world, but her father had accepted the Davises without question, which meant all the Malone males accepted them without question. And when Cella's third cousins moved out, returning to a Malone campsite in Boston and leaving the house next door available, the Davises had moved in.

Although, how Cella's father had talked not only Juen Davis, Jai's mom, into making the move, but had convinced his sisters to allow outsiders onto their street, Cella still didn't know. But her father did have a way.

Yet Cella had never been more grateful for her father's smooth-talking ways as she was the moment she walked into the Davis kitchen and asked, "Am I dying?"

Jai Davis, working on paperwork at the kitchen table, didn't even look up as she replied, "Yes. Although to be accurate we all are."

Cella rolled her eyes. That was the only downside of the Davis family. They were intellectuals. Juen Davis was a lawyer, Jai's father had been a heart surgeon before his death five years ago, and Jai was an orthopedic surgeon with a side specialty in artery repair. Necessary for her job as head of the entire medical staff of the Sports Center, where most shifter games, pro and minor, for the tri-state area were played—and where many arteries were severely damaged.

"Well," Cella pushed, "am I *literally* dying? You know. This moment. From a tumor or something you haven't told me about?"

Jai finally raised her head and studied Cella. They had similarly colored eyes: bright gold, although there was no green in Jai's. Otherwise, they couldn't look more different. Jai was black and Asian while Cella couldn't be more Irish if she'd come from Ellis Island with the word "Irish" stamped across her forehead. "Why would you think you are?"

"Because my family just met me in the kitchen to tell me they love me. *My* family."

"My mother tells me that all the time."

"My mother wasn't there, and your mother is a well-balanced, normal woman who can shift into animal form. She's not descended from gypsies. Nor was your father."

"Nope. Third generation Chinese me mum, and daddy was good ol' Jamaican. And I thought Malones preferred 'Traveller' to gypsy."

"I can call my damn family whatever I want to. Does it look like I give a shit about any of that right now?"

"I'm still not clear on why you think you're dying."

"Because"—Cella rubbed her forehead, still hungover and beginning to panic—"when the Malones come at ya, and are nice . . . *someone's dying!*"

* * *

After dinner with his team to celebrate another devastating loss to shifters in the Long Island Fire Department, Crush got home, tossed his equipment and clothes into a corner, and took a quick shower. Once clean, he sat on his bed, a towel around his waist, his sidearm within easy reach. He shook his hair out to dry it before dropping back on the bed, letting out a breath, and smiling.

"Hello, sexy," he said. "You lucked out tonight. No other females to keep me from you." He crooked a finger. "Now come over here and keep me company."

Lola moved in, snuggling up against his side. At least tomorrow morning Crush wouldn't be waking up with any unknown felines wrapped around him. It was kind of a relief really . . . while at the same time strangely disappointing.

"Don't drool on me tonight," he warned Lola, the English Bulldog. "You know I hate that."

She snorted, as always completely ignoring what he'd just told her, and rolled to her back, belly exposed. Like most animals, Lola knew what Crush was, but she trusted him. Knew he'd never hurt her.

With Crush rubbing her pink-and-white exposed belly, Lola fell asleep almost immediately, but it took Crush another hour, even though he was exhausted down to his bones. But he knew the following week his life would change—and he still wasn't happy about it.

Chapter Three

After four solid days of waiting and not wanting to spend another day—or even worse, an entire weekend—anticipating the anvil about to drop on his head, Crush went to his boss's office and stood silently in the man's doorway. Miller had his back to him, going through his files, when he suddenly tensed, his entire body going rigid. His reaction didn't shock Crush, though; the man had the same reaction every time the polar was around.

Slowly, Miller lifted his head and looked over his shoulder, then swallowed. "Crushek."

"Cap."

"Uh, yeah . . ." He went to his desk, but didn't sit down. He never sat down around Crush. Instead, he always looked like he was about to make a run for it. Good luck with that. Crush was an incredibly fast runner. Great swimmer, too.

"You've been transferred."

"So I heard."

"Sorry about the delay. I was just waiting for the final paperwork to come in." And he'd been working up the guts, too. Wuss.

Already knowing the answer, Crush still asked, "And Conway?"

"Stays here."

The captain picked up a folder from his desk and handed it over to Crush. His hand shook.

Crush didn't take the folder, simply looked at it and back at his captain.

"The . . . the transfer is effective immediately"—and the man looked relieved by that—"so feel free to, um . . . go."

"I think we should discuss—"

"This isn't up for discussion, Crushek. It's from the top. You gotta beef, take it up with them. Just leave your case notes and Conway will take care of the rest."

The captain sounded tough until Crush growled a little. He couldn't help it. He was annoyed. Really, truly annoyed.

The captain looked moments from shitting himself right then, but Crush took the folder before he had to see that.

Yet, before walking out, Crush still chuffed. A big one, the power of it sending his ex-boss stumbling back a bit. It was a shit move, but still kind of satisfying.

Cella was doing pull-ups in the gym when her phone went off. She dropped to the ground and pulled it out of the pocket of the hoodie she had lying on the floor. "Yeah?" she said around the panting.

"It's Smith."

"Yeah?"

"You busy?"

"Working out. Home game tomorrow night."

"So is that a yes or a no to my question?"

"What do you want, Smith?"

Dee-Ann Smith was the She-wolf Cella had trained with when she'd joined the shifter-only Marine Unit. And, at the time, she'd hated her. But years later, after they'd been forced to work together—Smith was part of the nationally based Group, an organization that protected all species and breeds—the wolf had managed to grow on her. Still, some days, Smith still got on Cella's last Irish nerve.

"Meet me in Brooklyn."

When the wolf didn't give an address before disconnecting the call, Cella knew that Smith wanted to meet at the NYPD precinct in Brooklyn for the shifter division. Of course, the difficult She-wolf could have just said that.

Cella pulled on her hoodie, zipped it up, and grabbed a towel. She was heading for the stairs to the lower level of the gym, wiping sweat off her face, when a big male stepped in front of her, blocking her path.

Cella looked at the wolf in front of her, waiting for him to say something.

"Darlin'."

"Hillbilly."

He grinned. "Cella Malone, are you flirtin' with me?"

"What d'ya want, Reed?" Reece Lee Reed of the New York Smith Pack had made the hard-won leap from the minors to the majors back when they'd signed Bo Novikov. And the pair had been at each other ever since. Reed, the more personable of the two, had the loyalty of the team. Novikov, the more ruthless, had no problem beating the living shit out of Reed anytime the kid annoyed him. And Reed annoyed Novikov constantly. The grey wolf knew it, too. That was the thing about the Smith Pack wolves. They seemed to enjoy fucking with people as much as the felines did.

"You need to handle him," he replied.

"Handle him? Novikov?"

"Yeah."

She glanced around. "Why me?"

"What do you mean why you? You're the only one on the team who can hold a conversation with the man."

God, that country accent. So irritating. Not so bad on Dee-Ann Smith, also of the Smith Pack, because she wasn't much of a talker, so Cella didn't have to hear that annoying accent more than was necessary. Reed, however . . . *chatty*.

"Look—"

"I'm asking you, darlin', to help us out."

"Us?"

"Yeah. Us. The rookies."

"You've been on the team a little long to be called a rookie. In fact, you've been on longer than I have."

"Exactly. And yet you're considered one of the gang by Lordship Pain in the Ass, and the rest of us are considered worthless scum."

"That's not true. I'm sure that, um . . . did you know you're bleeding from the head?"

"I can feel it drippin'. Do you know *why* I'm bleeding from the head?"

"Because you were hit there?"

"With a row of bleachers from the training rink."

"A row of . . . you mean actual bleachers?"

"Yeah. Actual bleachers. That homicidal maniac"—and that could only be Novikov—"pried *actual* bleachers from their steel moorings and threw them at us."

"Did he perhaps give you a reason why he thought that was okay?"

"I was minding my own business, gettin' ready for tomorrow night's game."

"Uh-huh."

"But Hammond, that new kid, decided to rally the boys and go to Novikov to ask for some tips so they could perform at their best and not let him down."

Cella cringed, easily imagining exactly what happened because she knew all the idiot males involved so well. "Uh-huh."

"So Novikov starts yellin' at 'em, but Hammond wouldn't back down. Kept pushin', kept nippin', as them little foxes are wont to do, which is why they're not allowed on Smith territory."

"And?" she pushed.

"I tried to get Hammond to let it go. Move on. He wouldn't. Next thing I know, I hear metal being ripped away from concrete and by the time I look up, *bleachers are flying at my head!*"

"Okay, okay. Calm down. Take a breath." Cella patted his shoulder. "I'll talk to Novikov."

"Do something, Cella, because I'm this close to callin' in all the Reeds to come here and start kicking some mutt ass."

"Now, now. Let's not get nasty. That's my job." She reached up and touched Reed's forehead, the wolf shying away from her. "Go see Jai about that. She should be in her office."

"It'll heal."

"If that gets infected, you'll get the fever, and she'll pull you from tomorrow's game and then Novikov has more ammo against you. Don't give it to him."

"Yeah. You're right." He smirked, his anger slipping away, the cute, flirty wolf quickly returning. "Think Dr. D. will let me cuddle if I ask her nice?"

"No."

"What about you? Wanna cuddle? Help me *heeeeal*?"

Rolling her eyes, Cella turned and headed to the stairs.

"That ain't real friendly, Malone," Reed called after her.

Division director, unit commander, and black bear sow Lynsey Gentry looked up from the files on her desk and smiled at the polar bear taking up a lot of her doorway. Although, thankfully, this building had been created with shifters in mind, so the doorways were taller and wider and the chairs sturdier.

She motioned to one of those sturdy chairs in front of her desk. "Sit."

With a heavy sigh, the polar walked into her office.

"Well, I'd like to say welcome," she began once he'd dropped down across from her, but when Crushek only scowled—more—and kind of grunted, she knew the man wouldn't be making this easy on her. He was one of the few shifters on the force who'd never asked for a transfer into her "Division with No Name" as Dez MacDermot liked to call it. The man loved what he did, but things had changed and he would have to roll with it. Especially now.

"Let's lay this on the table," Lynsey said, deciding to cut straight through the bullshit. "You didn't ask to be here. I know that. I know you like working undercover. I get it. But you're needed here. There's no getting around that. So, and I say this with kindness, suck it up and get over it already."

The scowl worsened, only now it was tinged with confusion. "How is that with kindness?"

"When you get to know me, you'll realize that it really is." She briefly tossed up her hands. "I demanded your transfer, because you're needed here."

"Needed for what? I don't kill on order."

"Neither do we." When he scoffed, she added, "I don't speak for The Group or KZS. They have their own agendas."

"Then why do you work with them?"

"Because they get shit done while we keep order."

"Keep order? Don't you mean we cover their tracks?"

"If necessary."

"I'm not a trashman, Captain. I don't clean up after killers."

"It's *Chief* Gentry." Lynsey leaned back. "And are you comfortable up there on your high horse, Crushek?"

"I just mean—"

"You sit there in your safe little world—"

"With drug dealers and gun-running biker gangs?"

"—and you're completely unaware of what's going on with your own."

Crushek nodded. "Right. We're being hunted. But we're always being hunted."

"That shit's only part of it, and that's really what The Group and KZS are for. They handle the big-game hunters and the lowlife dogfighters. Sometimes we step in and clean up to protect ourselves, and other times—"

"And other times what?'

"And other times we've got our own troubles among our own kind."

"You want me to arrest—"

"When they're doing something illegal, yes, I want you to arrest our own kind. Let's face it. Our kind can get away with a lot of shit because they're big, mean, and will *eat* the witnesses. Or, at the very least, get the hyenas to eat the witnesses." She picked up a stack of folders she hadn't managed to go through yet. "We've got meth dealers, bookies, hitters, leg breakers." She dropped the folders. "And do you think we can really send in a bunch of full-humans to take down a hyena-run meth ring? Or bear-run bookmakers?"

"We've never got in their way before."

"Of course we have, but in this day and age, it's harder to protect all our kind unless we can get there first. Unless we deal with it first."

The polar, agitated, folded his arms over his chest. "So you didn't hire me to . . ."

"To what?"

Crush shook his head. "Nothing. What *do* you need me for exactly?"

"I brought you here because of your stellar record. You're good, Crushek. And I was tired of waiting for you to get off your ass and see it was time for you to move to the next level. Okay?"

"Yeah." The polar's big arms loosened and he gazed directly at her. "So . . . who am I going to be partnered with now?"

"Well . . . you get along with MacDermot, don't you?"

Cella met Smith at the front door of the Brooklyn precinct. As always, being cat and dog, they sized each other up.

"My, my, someone looks casual," Smith remarked, looking over Cella's seen-better-days sweats.

"And I thought Levi stopped making that particular style of jeans in 1976," she shot back.

Grinning, they walked into the precinct and Chuck, the guard manning the front desk, glared at both of them. "No fighting on the elevator," he warned them.

"Who? Us?" Cella asked before the doors closed.

And once the doors closed . . . ?

Cella swung first, connecting with Smith's shoulder. The She-wolf growled and swung back. The pair quickly put each other in headlocks and stayed that way until the elevator stopped at the eighth floor. The doors slid open and Dez MacDermot was there with a cardboard box in her hands.

She gave an annoyed sigh. "Both of you cut it out!"

She stepped into the elevator, forcing her way between the pair. "Honestly. Can't take you bitches anywhere."

"The dog started it," Cella quickly stated.

MacDermot stared at her. "Really? Chuck?" she called out.

"It was the feline," the guard said over the elevator's speaker.

Smith laughed and Cella rolled her eyes. "Everybody's a goddamn rat. . . ."

The elevator doors opened again and the trio stepped out on the ninth floor. On each floor of this building the cops handled different crimes or research, mostly specific to shifters. But the ninth floor housed the elite team members and detectives. MacDermot had proved she belonged on this floor a long time ago.

"What's all that?" Smith asked MacDermot, gesturing to what she held in her hands.

"Just some research. I'm not finished yet, but Gentry wanted me in her office. Figured I could drop these off at my desk." MacDermot gave Cella a once-over. "You look very . . . casual."

"I've got a game tomorrow."

"Okay, if you feel that's really a good enough excuse."

"Both of you are such bitches."

MacDermot walked to her desk, dropping the papers and folders off there, before smiling and winking at the male now sitting at the desk across from hers.

Cella barely glanced at the man, noticing the surprise on his face when she passed, but he looked away so quickly that she didn't think much about it. Until she stepped into Gentry's office and stopped.

"What?" Smith asked her when Cella went stiff.

Lifting her head, Cella sniffed the air. "Hey . . . hey! Isn't that . . . ?"

"Leave it alone, Malone," MacDermot warned her.

"Come on, Desiree." Smith shook her head. "You must know her by now."

Jesus Christ, what was she doing here? Of course, if she'd been at MacDermot's party, they must be friends, but there was no way that woman was a cop. In fact, Crush had just assumed she was some rich feline that MacDermot had met through her husband. The Llewellyn Pride were very wealthy lions and knew lots of other wealthy cats. But no self-respecting rich New York feline would be caught dead in those sweat clothes with those rips, holes, and bleach stains; or those battered sneakers, no makeup, and her hair in a sloppy ponytail at the top of her head. Yeah, okay, she'd come from the gym, but she didn't have time for a quick shower either? Instead, she was offending everyone with her overwhelming scent. The scent that part of him wanted to roll around in until he was completely saturated with it.

Dammit! That was not what he meant!

See? This was the problem. The woman was completely throwing him off. Damn her.

And who the hell was she exactly and why was she *here* in what Crush now considered "his" house?

Calm down, he told himself. She hadn't even recognized him. Mother of the Year had barely glanced at him, so it was nothing. Apparently, she woke up with a lot of naked men she didn't know, so how could she remember just one? So he wouldn't even think about it. Nope. He wouldn't think about it . . . or her. It was not a big deal that feline was here. He wasn't sure why he was freaking out at all.

Calmer, Crush sat back and, wondering if they had a soda machine somewhere on this floor, heard feet running just before the feline leaped into his lap with her ratty sweats and delicious scent.

"Hi!" she chirped loudly, her arms loose around Crush's neck, her tight butt wiggling on his cock. "So how's my boyfriend? My cute, adorable boyfriend."

Boyfriend? Crush stared at the woman. "What are you talking about?"

"Don't you remember Sunday morning? You. Me." Her voice dropped lower. "Alone?"

"Yes. I remember. I'm also trying to forget."

"You are so cute. Just as cute as . . . something." She paused a moment, glancing off. "Hhmmh. What is worthy of your level of cuteness?"

"I am not cute."

"You *are* cute." She pinched his cheek. "Just adorable with that vicious scowl. Bet you scare all the bad guys."

"Now you're being condescending."

"Can't help it. It's in my DNA. Like my stripes."

A She-wolf with cold yellow eyes stepped up to the desk. "Ain't ya gonna introduce us?" she asked the feline, and what backwoods did they dig this chick up from?

The feline wrapped her arms around his chest and snuggled close, making him want to toss her off and pull her closer. Should he be having two emotions at once? That didn't seem normal or a good idea. At all.

"Can't introduce ya," the feline admitted.

"Why not?"

"Don't know his name."

"Snuggling up to a man y'all don't know. My momma was right. Yankees are whores."

"Well, I know him," MacDermot volunteered.

The She-wolf stared at her. "So?"

"You said y'all."

"I didn't say 'all y'all.' So I wasn't talking to you."

"I don't understand your country-speak," MacDermot complained, dropping into the desk chair across from Crush.

"Can you get off me now?" Crush asked the feline, trying not to flip out completely. Not easy with his cock beginning to twitch. How dare it twitch! He *controlled* every organ on his body, but especially that one!

"But I'm comfortable." The feline stuck her nose against his neck and he felt that touch all the way to his toes. "You smell nice," she murmured.

The She-wolf snorted and MacDermot cringed.

"So"—the feline leaned back and gazed up into his face—"when are we going out?"

Now? "Never. Never's a good time to go out."

She rolled her eyes, annoyed. "Well, I can't marry you until we go out. Duh."

Duh? Did she just say "duh" during the course of an adult conversation?

"We are not going—"

"Because we both know you adore me."

"I don't adore anyone. And I blame you for this, MacDermot."

"*Me?* What did I do?"

"You married that goddamn cat who gave me those goddamn Jell-O shots."

"You didn't have to take them."

"But they were tasty," the feline confirmed. "Especially the black cherry one."

"Well, well," the She-wolf said. "I can't believe me and Ric missed those fancy Jell-O shots."

"You don't come to my party," MacDermot snapped, "and then you make fun of it?"

"Yep."

"Would someone," Crush barked, when the feline began to rub her nose against his neck, "remove this feline?"

"Just toss her off," MacDermot suggested.

Appalled, he said, "I can't just throw off a woman."

"Awww," all three females sighed, which made Crush snarl.

"Isn't he cute when he snarls and scowls like that?" the She-tiger asked the others. "I think he is just so adorable!"

"Not really," the She-wolf answered. "Looks kinda mean . . . and angry."

"No," the feline argued. "That's grizzlies. Grizzlies are mean and angry. He's a polar. They mostly look placid . . . and adorable!" She nodded. "We're dating!"

"We are not dating."

"He's just shy."

"I am not shy."

MacDermot shook her head. "He ain't shy."

"You three get back in here!" Gentry yelled from her office. "And leave the new polar alone!"

"But I'm comfortable," the feline whined.

Thankfully the She-wolf took pity on him and grabbed the feline by the hair, yanking her off Crush's lap. The feline roared and swung her fist, hitting the She-wolf in the chest. The She-wolf hit her back and Crush could tell by the sounds of contact that these two females were not, in any way, holding back with each other. And something about the mini-brawl looked familiar to him, but he didn't know why and was too annoyed to even bother thinking about it.

The pair fought their way back to Gentry's office and Mac-Dermot stopped by his side. "Don't mind Cella. That was the one on your lap. Dee-Ann was the one with the accent."

"MacDermot, I don't care."

"Whatever. I'm out tomorrow, so we'll start working together on Monday." She started to walk off but stopped. "And
are you really going to keep going with that biker look?"

"Excuse me?"

"You're not working vice anymore, Crushek. You have to
look a little less . . . terrifying. You don't have to wear a suit
or anything but . . ." She picked up a handful of his hair, running it through her fingers. "At least get this mess cut."

When Crush growled, she held her hands up, palms out.
"Not a buzz cut or anything. Just look a little less threatening."

"I don't want to cut my hair."

"We're not in a rock band, chico," she snapped. "Cut your
hair."

Yeah, he'd completely forgotten what a ball-busting female MacDermot could be when you had to work with her.

She walked off and Crush stared at his desk. He was so
miserable at the moment, his cock easily settled back down.
"A haircut," he muttered, making the detective sitting at the
desk near him chuckle.

Crush locked his eyes on the leopard. "What's so fucking
funny?" he demanded.

The leopard pointed behind him. "That."

Looking over his shoulder at Gentry's office, he saw the feline standing by the big glass window—staring at him. She
breathed on the glass and drew a heart in the condensation, then
placed a kiss inside the heart. She winked at him, scrunched up
her nose, and mouthed "later" before turning away.

Gritting his teeth, Crush faced forward again.

"Dude—" the leopard began.

"*I won't discuss it!*"

Cella sat down on the other side of Gentry's desk and
laughed so hard she had to rest her head against it.

"Don't pick on Crushek," Gentry told her.

Lifting her head and wiping the tears, Cella explained, "I'm not picking on him. I'm trying to get him to loosen up. He's so damn uptight."

"He's also—should it work out—MacDermot's new partner, so give him respect."

"Yet another partner, eh, MacDermot?" Cella teased.

"Don't blame me. It's you two. You guys get involved and my partners can't run from me fast enough." MacDermot pointed at Cella. "And you're doing it again!"

"It was your Jell-O shots, lady!"

"No one told you or Crushek to suck down a vat of them! And who gets naked and crawls into bed with some guy she doesn't even know?"

Smith raised her hand, only lowering it when they all gawked at her. "Well, I don't do it anymore."

"Wow, talk about a coyote ugly morning for some poor guy," Cella laughed, but no one else joined in, so she stopped.

"Mighta been funny," Smith muttered, "if I'd been an actual coyote."

"Like there's a difference."

"Can we discuss why you're all here?" Gentry snapped.

"Why *are* we all here?" Cella asked, pulling out a pack of gum from her sweatshirt pocket.

Smith took a piece of paper from her back pocket, unfolded it, and handed it to Cella.

Cella looked at the one-page ad, MacDermot leaning over to see as well.

Finally, Cella had to know, "Wouldn't cremation be a better idea? I mean would your mate want you stuffed and just standing around his house when you die?"

"It's not for me," the She-wolf snarled.

"The Group thinks," Gentry cut in, "and I think I agree, that this taxidermist is stuffing our kind and turning us into trophies after we've been hunted down. Although the real problem is, of course, that he's completely *aware* that he's stuffing shifters."

"Oh. Okay." Cella took hold of MacDermot's arm and turned it so she could see the giant Breitling man's wristwatch the woman always wore. It was a real one, too. She could tell, because as a great-aunt once told Cella, "Gotta know the real ones if you're going to sell the fake."

She checked the hour and said, "I've got time tonight. I can take him out."

"Or," Gentry suggested, "rather than you killing anyone you just don't like, you could let me finish."

"See," Cella shot back, "that's a ridiculous thing to say because I don't even know this guy or whether I like him or not. I was just going to kill him."

When the women all stared at her, Cella pointed an accusing finger at Smith. "I was just going to kill him because of her. It's the dog's fault!"

Gentry leaned back in her chair, fingers to her temples.

"Am I causing one of your headaches again?" Cella asked.

"Yes."

"Why are we having this meeting?" MacDermot asked. "As much as I love to see you guys, I have to kind of agree with Cella here. Other than just taking this guy out, I don't know what we need to discuss. And I'm off tomorrow, so that better not be changing," she also felt the need to add.

"When I found out about this place," Smith said, "I was just going to go on in there, cut the guy's throat, and leave—"

"What is *wrong* with you three?" Gentry sighed.

"—but I noticed something when I was hanging around in the woods across the street. There was already a team watching the place."

"What team?"

The She-wolf smirked. "BPC."

BPC, or the Bear Preservation Council, was a Brooklyn-based organization that raised money for the care, research, and protection of full-blood bears worldwide. They were also the cover for the agency that protected shifter bears in the tri-state area. And unlike KZS, the Group, and the NYPD's shifter division, BPC refused to work with the rest of them on anything. They made it very clear that what happened to other species was not their problem and the bears that had jobs with NYPD and the Group were simply foolish.

Gentry's hands dropped to her desk. "BPC was watching the place? Are you sure?"

"Recognized one of the team."

"Recognized him how?" Cella had to know.

"Broke his spine during a fight once."

And that was why Cella "had to know," because she knew she'd be entertained!

"Y'all can stop staring at me like that. He's clearly walkin' . . . *now*."

"You gotta wonder why BPC wouldn't just move on a place like that, too," MacDermot said, her gaze out the window. "From what I hear, they handle shit the way Cella and Dee do."

"They do," Gentry confirmed. "Which makes me very curious about what they're doing."

MacDermot looked at her boss. "You want me to put surveillance on it?"

"I do."

"Okay, but if BPC is already on it, why do we need to get involved?"

"BPC is run by Peg Baissier. And has been for the last twenty years. It's believed that she's become a bit of a problem. There are some of us in the bear community that have been looking for a way to . . ."

"Force her into retirement?"

"Something like that."

"Just because you don't like her?"

"No. Because she's dangerous to her own."

"How do you figure that?" Smith asked.

Gentry moved around in her chair, her hands tugging the jacket of her suit down.

MacDermot glanced at Cella and Smith before saying, "Chief?"

The sow cleared her throat. "Besides his stellar record, there's another reason I had Crushek—the polar bear"—she clarified for Cella and Smith—"pulled into this division as quickly as I could manage without setting off major alarms and a massive investigation by the full-humans of NYPD."

"What reason?"

"There's a rumor his cover was blown."

"By Baissier?"

"Most likely."

"Did you tell his C.O.? Chief of D's?" MacDermot asked.

"I didn't tell anyone."

"Why not?"

"Because this is shifter business and the last thing we need is the NYPD looking into the BPC." She sighed. "And . . ."

"And?" MacDermot pushed. "And what?"

"And . . ." Gentry looked at them all before finally admitting, "Peg Baissier was Crushek's foster mother."

Sick of hearing Conway laugh at him about having to get his hair cut, Crush slammed his phone down.

He hated change. Change was bad. Change sucked. Change . . .

Crush looked around the room, realizing that everyone was staring in his direction, but they weren't really looking at him.

Slowly, he swiveled his office chair around and looked at Gentry's office. MacDermot, the She-wolf, and that damn feline were all standing on the other side of that big window . . . watching him. Even worse—they all looked sad. Devastated. What the fuck was going on?

"That's it." Crush stood, officially unable to take any more of this. "I'm out of here."

CHAPTER FOUR

With MacDermot out on Friday, Lynsey had Lou Crushek spend most of the day going through files and acquainting himself with some of the current open cases. When he said he was leaving early because he had something to do in Manhattan, Lynsey called him in. She knew she couldn't keep hiding the truth about Baissier and what the sow had done or, at the very least, was rumored to have done.

But the polar's reaction to the news . . . not exactly what Lynsey had been expecting.

Crush stared at her, nodded, and replied, "Uh-huh."

Lynsey blinked and looked around her office, concerned she hadn't actually said the words out loud. She finally settled her gaze back on him and asked, "I did just tell you that—"

"My cover was blown? Yeah. You just told me."

"And that it was—"

"My former foster mother? Yeah. Yeah. You told me."

"Uhhhhh, okay. I . . . I guess I just expected more of a panicked, 'Oh, my God! The guys I was trying to put away are going to come kill me' kind of thing."

"Well, they can *try*."

"Okay. Uh . . . perhaps some devastation at the betrayal of the woman who raised you?"

"Have you *met* Peg Baissier?" he asked flatly. "I wouldn't exactly call what she did 'raising me' in the traditional sense. Her leaving me alone this long is really surprising. Which kind of makes me wonder why blow my cover now? What's the benefit? Because she always has a benefit. But other than thinking that, I'm not really shocked."

"All right then."

"If it helps, I'm kind of pissed she ruined my career."

"Well, she didn't ruin your career. I mean, you're out of undercover, but you're still a cop. And now that you're with my division, you'll be making more money and have great people to work with. So, ya know, all good. Right?"

"Sure. Why not?" He glanced around, shrugged, and asked, "Anything else?"

"Not really."

"Okay. Well, like I said this morning, I'm leaving early."

"Okay. Have a good weekend."

"Yeah. Thanks. You, too."

She watched him walk out. Jesus, what had Peg Baissier done to the boy Lou Crushek once was? Hearing the news, it was like he'd just shut down, and honestly, she had to wonder . . . if what she had just told him didn't get a reaction out of him, what exactly would?

Crush scrambled out of the barber's chair, shaking his head. "Forget it."

Conway, who'd dragged him to this shifter-friendly barbershop, laughed. "I can't believe what a baby you're being. Just get the damn haircut."

At the time, it had seemed like a good idea. Late lunch with his old partner and then he could head over to the Sports Center for tonight's game. But Crush had had no idea that Conway would get such a bug up his ass about Crush getting a goddamn haircut. A haircut he didn't even want!

"No way. MacDermot will just have to deal with my long

hair." He tugged at the strands. "This is polar hair. It's not like everyone else's. It just can't be randomly butchered." And, to be honest, Crush kind of knew he would never look good with a buzz cut, which was apparently all this particular barber could handle. In fact, Crush was pretty certain that with a buzz cut, he'd go from looking like a lowlife biker to looking just like a serial killer. Especially with what a full-human date once called his "soulless black eyes." He didn't think they were soulless, but his eyes were black. Like most polar bears' eyes.

The sun bear barber let out a sigh. "Get your ass in the seat."

"No way. You're not just cutting it off."

"All done!" a cheerful voice chirped. And from a back room, a pretty black woman walked out. She was definitely canine, but Crush couldn't tell if she was wolf, wild dog, coyote, or some other canine, which made him think she was a mutt. "Hybrid" being the less offensive term. "I cleaned out your pipes and they should be flowing just perfect now."

Crush and Conway looked at each other, trying not to laugh. To them, "cleaning out your pipes" usually meant a blow job, but since she was dressed in grimy khaki pants and a Philadelphia Eagles football jersey while carrying a tool bag in her hand and had a tool belt around her waist, Crush would guess she was actually a plumber.

"You're a lifesaver, Blayne," the barber said. "And I appreciate you coming over here so fast."

"No problem, Mr. P. Anyway, I gotta go. I got practice in a couple of hours. Gotta meet Gwenie."

"How much do I owe ya, sweetie?"

"We'll bill you. But don't forget you get the neighbor discount." She suddenly focused on Crush and Conway, grinned, waved, and said with an alarming amount of cheer, "Hi!"

Crush jumped a little. Wow. She sure was perky. "Hi."

"What's going on? Everyone looks very tense. Like this." She made a frown that had Conway chuckling.

"This wuss"—the sun bear motioned to Crush—"won't let me cut off his hair."

"Because it's cool!" She walked over and took a closer look. "Wow. So very cool!" Then she sniffed him. "Are you a polar?"

"Uh—"

"How cool!"

"You need the cut, dude," Conway reminded him. "There's no getting around it. He needs it for work," Conway explained to the hybrid. Although why he felt that was necessary . . .

"Well, there's a cut," the canine explained to them, "and then there's butchering." She shrugged at the sun bear. "Sorry, Mr. Peterson, but you're kind of a butcher. You should come with me," she told Crush.

"Why?"

"I know someone who can cut your hair but give you, like, a *great* cut. That way you'll look more handsome bear and less . . ."

She dropped her tool kit on the floor, dragged a chair over, and stood on the seat. Then she put her hands into his hair and pushed the strands off his face. Why did women keep touching him? Was he releasing pheromones or something?

"Oh, God. Yeah," she said. "You lose all this hair it's totally serial killer time." She frowned, leaned back a little. "You're not, though, right? A serial killer?"

What an odd question . . . "No. I'm not."

Her grin was blindingly bright. "Cool! Then come with me. I'm heading back to the office anyway. We'll totally get you fixed up."

"Well—"

But she was dragging him out of the barbershop and down the street, Conway laughing and following them.

* * *

Cella cut through the training rink to get to the team's locker room. She'd spent most of the afternoon with her KZS bosses. She was afraid they wouldn't want anything to do with BPC, considering KZS's history with that organization, but it seemed that like Gentry and the Group chief, Niles Van Holtz, out of Washington state, they wanted Baissier out. Now. So Cella would be again working with MacDermot and Smith. Although what anyone really expected to find at a damn taxidermist's storefront, Cella didn't know. But she was well aware that she was the muscle to their little team. She left the obsessing over every little detail to the canine and the canine-lover.

Of course, none of that mattered right now. She had a game tonight and just enough time to get in a warm-up. She had to be ready. Her father would be meeting up with his old buddies and watching the game from the owner's box. She had to make sure that, at the very least, she didn't embarrass herself in front of him.

Cella reached for the rink entrance door, but she heard the sounds coming through it. Knew what those sounds meant. Growling, she snatched the door open and rushed through.

"Unbelievable." She dropped her bag and charged across the rink and right into the middle of the brawl, pushing the males back and away from Novikov. Because, as always, he was at the center of the fight. But what surprised Cella was that the one fighting him was Ulrich Van Holtz, the wolf the entire league referred to as "The Gentleman." He was also the Carnivore team's captain, goalie, and goddamn owner.

"I control this team!" Van Holtz shouted at Novikov. "Not you! *Not ever!*"

Blue eyes shifting to gold, the longest fangs she'd ever seen exploding from his gums, the hybrid roared, *"Then you can take your goddamn team and—"*

Cella punched Novikov, her fist slamming into his nose, shutting him up. Shocked and bleeding, he stumbled back, gawking down at her.

She pointed a finger at him. "Do not say anything you're going to regret." She spun, pointed that same finger at Van Holtz. "You either." Cella looked around at the rest of her teammates. Well, at least the male ones. The females were sitting in the bleachers, eating popcorn. Useless. These people were useless!

"We have a game in less than two hours," she reminded them. "Let's get ready."

The males skated out, leaving Cella with Van Holtz and Novikov. She motioned to the three females watching them from the bleachers. But they only motioned back. Realizing it would be a waste of time to try to force those bitches to do anything, she walked over to Van Holtz first. "I'll meet you in your office in about ten. Okay?"

When Van Holtz just stood there, scowling at Novikov, Cella turned him and shoved. "Ten minutes."

She went back to Novikov and grabbed his arm, yanking him across the ice toward one of the exits. Without saying a word, she led him to Jai's office.

"Maybe I could just—"

"Trust me!" the hybrid promised, practically skipping down the street like a little kid, but holding on to Crush like a linebacker while Conway followed behind them. *Still* laughing.

She dragged him into an office building, past the front desk, around a pillar, and into a small office. A feline sat at the desk, frowning when she saw what her friend was dragging in.

"We need your help, Gwenie."

"Another stray, Blayne?"

"No."

"Really?" She sat back in her desk chair. "What's his name?"

The canine chewed on her bottom lip, finally eking out, "Big handsome bear?"

Shaking her head, the friend began to turn away but the canine quickly explained, "He needs your help, Gwenie. He was at Mr. Peterson's about to get a buzz cut!"

The feline turned back around, her frown worsening as she looked Crush over. "He'll look like a mass murderer."

"I was thinking more serial killer." The canine looked up at him. "There's actually a difference."

"Yes, I know," Crush responded. "Look, I can just go to one of those Quick Cut places—"

"Bite your tongue," the one called Blayne gasped. "We don't discuss those places here."

The feline rolled her eyes. "I swear. The drama with you sometimes, Blayne."

"Come on, Gwenie. Please? Help a bear-brother out."

Finally laughing, a smile lighting up that pretty face, the feline stood. "All right, all right." She pointed at herself. "Hi. Gwen O'Neill."

"Oh! And I'm Blayne Thorpe. Sorry."

Now it was Crush's turn to frown. "Why do I know that name?" His frown deepened. "You're not a criminal, are you?"

"Here or in Philadelphia?"

Confused and a little alarmed, Crush asked, "Does that matter?"

"Yes," both females answered at the same time.

"Hey." Conway, who'd been lounging against the doorway, enjoying every moment of Crush's nightmare, stood straight, pointed at framed pictures on the office wall, and asked, "Do you guys know him?"

Crush stepped forward and leaned in to study the pictures, shock ripping through his system. "Holy . . . *do* you know him?"

"Hockey fan?" the one named Gwen asked, grinning.

"Hockey stalker, more like it," Conway joked.

"I don't stalk. I just attend every home game. Religiously. Without question. Which is why I can't worry about fancy cuts right now. Gotta get to the Sports Center. Game tonight." The New York Carnivores, his home team, against the Alabama Slammers.

Still, Crush had to know . . . "So *do* you guys really know Bo Novikov?"

The canine grinned. "A little."

Hhhhm. Probably a hockey groupie. But her name still sounded familiar; Crush just couldn't remember why.

"Where are you sitting?" Blayne asked.

"Nosebleed seats. But they're *my* nosebleed seats."

"You didn't invite me to the game," Conway complained.

"I didn't think your mate let you out of the house after dark."

The feline took a handful of Crush's hair and examined it closely. "Weird."

"Do you mind not calling my hair weird? It gives me a complex."

"It's like hair, but different."

"I'm leaving." Crush started to walk out, but the feline hybrid yanked him back.

"Calm down. It was just an observation." She dismissed all that with a wave of her hand. "Come on." She grabbed a case from beside her desk. "Let me get to work. This might take some time."

"Now you're just trying to hurt my feelings."

"Maybe." She smirked. "But just a little."

Jai Davis smiled at the e-mail her daughter had sent her. She had no idea how on God's green earth she *and* Cella Malone had managed to have the sweetest, most reliable daughters on the planet, but somehow they had. Maybe the old adage "it takes a village to raise a child" was true. Because the Malones were definitely a village. In the beginning, the big cats had scared Jai. There were so many of them, all with their black hair and gold eyes and Irish names.

And then there were the campers and RVs. When Jai met Cella, Butch Malone was still playing hockey and when he traveled, the entire family went with him. They'd all pack up their RVs and off they'd go.

It seemed so strange to Jai, so far outside what she considered normal life for a mountain lion from a very small family. Except for the fact that they could shift into another species, the Davises were very average. Nothing exciting about them at all. But the Malones . . . well, excitement seemed to follow them around.

And, if things had been different, Jai probably wouldn't have been friends with Cella, the overwhelming She-tiger with the mean right hook. She was loud; Jai tried not to be. Cella was wild; Jai didn't know how to be. But the day she'd met Cella at the doctor's office, both of them eight months pregnant and miserable, Jai was completely alone except for her parents. Her "friends" had spent more time talking shit about her and her pregnancy than actually supporting her.

Desperate to be away from her disapproving mother's glare, which she'd have to see if she were to return home after her ob/gyn appointment, Jai had accepted Cella's offer to hit Friendly's Restaurant for a plate of fries and a chocolate shake. Of course, the timing had been perfect as Jai's ex-boyfriend, Frost, had walked in with what Jai thought was her best friend. Even worse? They'd come over to say "hi" like that was somehow completely normal. At first, Cella had just sat there, observing. Then, before the new and awfully affectionate full-human couple had walked away, Cella had asked, "Is this the guy who knocked you up?"

"And my best friend," Jai had replied, so angry she wasn't really thinking clearly. And not really expecting that particular information to set Cella Malone off. But man, did it set the girl off. Cella Malone had hauled her sizable bulk out of the seat and proceeded to yell in Laura's face about loyalty and how she was a "whore bitch" for betraying her friend for some piece of cock. That's around the time the shoving match started and Frost, always kind of stupid, had gotten between the two women. When Cella wouldn't back down at his command, he'd pushed her. Just once. But it was enough for a Malone. Especially a pregnant Malone. Cella had laid out the all-star fullback with one punch.

"Come on, Jai," Cella had said casually, picking up the giant Chanel purse that she'd been proud to get for practically nothing off the back of a truck. "We'll go to my house and hang out."

Although Frost had some involvement in Josie's life now, he still hated Cella, wouldn't speak to her or about her. But Jai would eternally adore Marcella Malone because up until then no one but her parents had ever fought for her like that.

Even better, Jai and Cella's daughters were best friends, watching each other's backs and supporting each other over the years. They'd turned out to be lovely, amazing young women who Jai had no doubt would do well in the world.

So, yeah, Jai was a single mom in a world where that was never easy, but she wasn't alone. She had the Malones.

Jai e-mailed her daughter back and had just hit send when there was a knock at the door and Cella walked in with a bleeding Bo Novikov.

"What happened?" Jai asked, coming around her desk. Although she could guess. Another team fight.

"She broke my nose," Novikov accused.

Jai stopped, surprised by that answer because Cella was always the one trying to stop the fights between her teammates. "You did?"

"He was fighting again." Cella pushed the hybrid into a chair. "And he wouldn't back off. What did you expect me to do?"

Jai grabbed the leather satchel where she kept emergency supplies. She could take Novikov downstairs to be treated by one of her technicians, but that would only cause more problems than it would solve since all the techs were afraid of Novikov. "You'll have to cut her some slack, Bo. Cella only knows how to handle her brothers and uncles one way. And she hits them."

"The Malone Bare Knuckle champ five years straight," Cella bragged. It was an honest brag. There were several breeds and species of shifter Travellers who roamed the states and Cella had been named champ at their annual summer get-together five years in a row.

"I didn't do anything wrong," Novikov complained, snarling a little when Jai began to examine his nose with her fingers. "I was just trying to help."

"And how did you do that?" Cella asked.

"I told Van Holtz who he needs to fire and provided a helpful list."

"Oh, really? Let me see." He pulled the list out of his sock and handed it to Cella. Without looking at it, Cella ripped the sheet of paper into pieces and threw it in Novikov's face.

He stared at her before calmly saying, "I made several copies."

Jai stood back with a laugh and asked, "Why?"

"Blayne," he said, speaking of his fiancée.

"What about her?"

"She does the same thing to my lists, so I always make multiple copies."

Wow, Jai mouthed at Cella before she went to get a towel to help control and clean up the bleeding.

"I tried to help," Bo insisted, "and once again Van Holtz was being an asshole."

"I personally think you're both fighting for that title," Cella shot back.

"He's unreasonable."

"And you're a dick. You know you're a dick. And you wear your dickness proudly."

"I know. But we're not going to make the play-offs this year if—"

"Play-offs are out. I know that."

"And that doesn't bother you?"

"It's not going to keep me up nights. I'm definitely not making lists because the play-offs are out."

Jai frowned at Cella's statement, glancing at her friend. She'd admit she didn't actually follow sports beyond the health and welfare of her patients. The money was great and she didn't have to worry about her less-than-acceptable bedside manner—apparently she could be cold and standoffish. But she'd thought the team was doing well this year.

"Too many new guys," Cella explained at Jai's unspoken question about the play-offs. "Not enough focus. We've been all over the place this season."

"And I'm trying to help," Bo insisted.

"By throwing bleachers at Reed?"

Jai quickly looked down at her bag as the hybrid growled, "I hate that guy."

"Because you don't think he can play or because he flirts with Blayne?"

Bo scratched the back of his neck. "Both. But," he quickly added, "Reed needs to work harder."

"I agree with that, but when he asks for help for him or the guys, *you throw things at him!*"

"I'm here to play and to win, not handhold. That's Coach's job, but he's weak. So I went to Van Holtz with my suggestions, since he fucking owns the team, and he hit me."

"All right. All right." Cella pressed her hands to her eyes. "Let me deal with Reed and the rookies."

"Why? So Reed can hit on you more than he already does?"

"Reed is a whore," Cella admitted—and boy, was he—there was not a pussy that man didn't seem to take an interest in. "We know that, we've all accepted it. Besides, I'm beautiful. *Everyone* hits on me. They can't help themselves." Cella smiled, then winked at Jai. "I'm captivating. How's his nose?"

Jai carefully wiped up the blood. It was beginning to clot. "It'll be fine. It's not broken. Just bloody."

"It's not broken?" Cella looked at her knuckles. "I'm losing my touch." Apparently deciding to worry about it later, Cella said, "Novikov, you worry about you. I'll take care of everybody else."

"Do you want my list?"

"If you give me any more lists, I will beat you to death with a baseball bat. Or a two-by-four. Whatever's handy."

Bo stared at Cella. "That seems unreasonable to me." And Jai loved how he said that with almost a professorial air, like he was observing bacteria developing in a petri dish.

Cella clenched her fists, definitely trying to control her annoyance, and faced Jai. "Clean him up and have him ready for the game."

"You got it."

Cella walked to the office door. She had it open when Bo said, "Malone?"

She looked at him over her shoulder, but he just stared at her. Jai, having spent many hours cleaning up Bo Novikov and his victims, knew what he *wanted* to say and knew how much it would help at the moment. So Jai pushed his shoulder, urging him on. Finally, after a few seconds, he muttered, "Thank you."

"Yeah, yeah," Cella said with a smile. "But will you still love me in the morning?" Then she walked out, closing the door behind her.

"I never know what she's talking about," Bo admitted.

"It's all right," Jai promised. "I can assure you it's rarely anything very serious."

After "styling" Crush's hair—okay, he'd admit it, it didn't look *too* bad; at least he didn't look like a serial killer—the two females insisted on walking with him to the Sports Center while Conway headed on home.

"So you're both going to the game, too?" he asked.

"Later. We've got practice first."

"Practice?"

"Derby!" the wolfdog cheered.

Yeah, he'd seen that picture of the Carnivores with what he was now guessing was Blayne's derby team. That explained how the two women knew Bo Novikov and Crush's other favorite players from the current roster. At least, that's what he hoped. He'd heard about Novikov's reputation with women and he'd hate to think the man was using these two. They were just so damn sweet.

They arrived at the Sports Center and Crush headed for the front doors, but Blayne caught his hand. "This way," she said, pulling him.

"Yeah, but—"

"With us."

Blayne dragged him into the restricted, underground parking area of the center and to a set of elevator doors. They stepped into one and went down several levels. Although all of the shifter activities took place underground, Crush knew the floor they were heading to wasn't the one he used to get to his season ticket holders' nosebleed seats.

"Uh . . . Blayne?"

The doors opened. "Come on." She dragged him out, the feline following—and grinning.

"You might as well just go along," Gwen told him.

"That sounds wrong."

Blayne pulled him down a long hallway filled with shifters on the move, getting ready for the upcoming game.

Blayne suddenly stopped. "Wait here."

"Yeah, but—" Blayne was gone so he looked at the feline. "I should grab my seat. The lines are usually long."

"I promise it'll be worth the wait. And"—she looked him over—"I did an amazing job with your hair. You need to show off your sexy new look."

"Yeah. Thanks for that." Christ, it was just a haircut. From what he could tell he still looked like your average biker meth dealer. Only now it was like he was heading to the funeral of an aged relative.

Cella walked down the hall that held all the owners' offices until she reached Van Holtz's. Like his office with the Group, it was big but sparse. Except for occasional meetings, Van Holtz wasn't big on using offices. He loved working in his kitchen, at home or at his restaurant. That was always the best place to talk to him. But today, Cella didn't have that kind of time.

The wolf sat in his chair, his head on his desk, his eyes staring out the window. She hated seeing him so miserable. Although, she must admit, she preferred this to the time she'd walked in and found Smith under the desk giving him a hummer. But hey, they were in love. Cella couldn't argue with anyone being in love.

"He drives me nuts, Cella," Van Holtz admitted before she'd even said a word. "Just the sight of him makes me want to smash his face in."

"Just out of curiosity . . . how come?"

"He's just so sure he's right." Van Holtz lifted his head, planted his elbows on the desk, and rested his chin on his raised fists. "He never listens to anyone else." Pretty brown eyes narrowed on her. Actually, all of the man was pretty. Just damn pretty. "Except you. He listens to you."

"Only because he finds me completely nonthreatening."

"No. He respects you."

"Wrong. He respects my dad. Everyone respects Nice Guy Malone."

"I want him to quit. I want him out."

Cella had been afraid this was coming. There was only so far a man's unbeatable talent could go to make up for his annoying OCD tendencies, and few shifters had patience for OCD anything.

"I know you do. But . . . let me handle him."

"You? Why would you want to do that?"

"It's like you said. He listens to me. He trusts me. I'm his enforcer. He knows I have his back on the ice and off. And you know I have the *team's* back."

"I can't ask you—"

"Yes, you can." She closed his door and stepped farther into the office. "I do this shit all the time with my own family. The Malones band together against outsiders, but inside, they fight constantly. My father alone has eighteen siblings."

Van Holtz sat up straight. "Not with the same . . ."

"Oh, God, no." Cella laughed. "No way. It took my grandmother ages to settle down with one male."

The wolf's eyes grew wide. "Wait . . . are you saying that *all* your father's siblings are from the same—"

"Mother. Yeah. Grammy Malone. The Malones are matriarchal and the females only settle down when we're ready to or when the women of the family feel it's 'time,' " Cella said with air quotes. "Although, they don't do much matchmaking these days. Thank God."

Van Holtz shook his head. "I'm sorry. I can't let it go. Your grandmother had—"

"Eighteen children. Yes. Happily, too. She loves her kids."

"She's still around?"

"Yeah. She retired from KZS about—"

"She was in KZS?"

"Who do you think taught me to be a sniper?"

"The Marines."

"Nah. It was Grammy Malone."

"But when did she have time?"

"She made time. Plus, she had the entire Malone family to help raise her kids. And the last eight were all with Gramps anyway. But we all help each other raise each other's kids. When I was in the Marines or on the road with the teams I was on, the Malones raised my kid. When Jai was doing twenty-four-hour stints as a resident or during finals in med school, Malones raised Josie. And now that our schedules are more manageable, we help raise my cousins' kids. That's how it works for us. That's what we do."

Cella reached across the desk and patted Van Holtz's hand. "So as you can see . . . I'm totally qualified to handle a Bo Novikov."

"Yeah . . ." Van Holtz admitted, gazing at her, "I'm really starting to see that."

Crush looked at his watch again. Then he checked his phone. He had several text messages from a possible dealer he'd been hoping to use as a CI. Of course, now that was all dead in the water. A reminder that made Crush begin to feel angry again about being pulled out of the work he loved so much. All because of that vicious sow, Baissier. To think, after all these years, she still hated him. Then again, he really hated her.

Deciding it was time to get to his seat, he filed the messages and—

"Hey, Crush. Crush!"

He bit back a sigh, regretting he'd told the hybrid his nickname because now she wouldn't stop using it, and prepared himself to tell the sweetest girl he'd ever met he had to go.

"I'd like you to meet my fiancé," she said, skipping up to him. "Bo Novikov."

Crush's head snapped up and he looked directly—well, almost because the man was four inches taller—into the eyes of the meanest player ever in shifter sports history and Lou Crushek's personal hero.

Then Crush stared—and he kept staring.

CHAPTER FIVE

Cella tracked her father down in the busy hallway, the meeting place for teammates and their family or guests before the game began.

"Hey, Daddy." Decked out for the game except for her stick, skates, and helmet, Cella reached up and hugged her father.

"Hey, kid." He hugged her, tight. "How are you feelin'?"

Cella leaned back and gazed up at her father. "I'm fine."

"Good, good. I know it's hard, but your focus has to be on the game. Remember that."

"I know, Dad. My focus is always on the game."

"Yeah, sure. Of course." He patted her shoulder and gave her what she could only term a brave smile. Then he hugged her again. "You know I love you, right? We all love you."

What the *fuck* was going on? "Daddy, I know."

"Good, good."

Pulling away from her father and wondering when, exactly, he'd lost his mind, Cella asked, "You all set in the suite?"

"Sure. Guys are all here, too. They're rootin' for ya." The "guys" were some of the best shifter players from the East Coast teams' past. Her father's friends now. Every few months or so during the season, they'd all come in to watch a game, bullshit about the past, and drink. There was always lots of drinking.

Maybe her father had already put away a few Guinnesses, but Cella didn't think so. He was just acting . . . weird.

"Have a good game, baby." He kissed her forehead.

"Thanks, Daddy."

Her father gave her one more brave smile before walking away.

Realizing she couldn't worry about the craziness of her family right now, Cella turned and took a quick look over the crowd to make sure she wasn't missing anyone—like an investor—whose ass she could be kissing.

Cella had no moral issues with that sort of thing. It was important sometimes to keep the team getting all the cool extras. And what was a little hand-shaking, fake smiling, happy-go-lucky bullshit spreading if it meant getting those extra soft and fluffy towels in the locker rooms or first-class trips to Hawaii or Rio?

Since there didn't seem to be anyone tonight who needed a little Cella-attention, she decided to head back to the locker room, but then she caught sight of him.

"Malone."

Cella barely bit back her roar and glared at Smith standing behind her. "Stop sneaking up on me, hillbilly."

"Be more alert, Yankee."

"So everything set?"

"Yep. MacDermot pulled a surveillance team together to work the taxidermist. She said to give 'em a couple of days. What were you just staring at?"

"That bear from earlier. MacDermot's new partner. The cute one. He's here."

Smith followed Cella's gaze. "Hair's shorter."

"It's known as a haircut. Basic grooming, Smith. You should look into it."

The She-wolf grinned. "Always so sweet on me, ain'tcha, Malone?"

Cella grabbed Smith's arm. "Come on."

"Where?"

"I wanna go torture the bear some more."

Smith shook her off. "Can't you do that on your own?"

"Would it kill you to be a girl for just five minutes?"

"What's my pussy gotta do with anything?"

"Oh, come on!" She glanced back at the bear. "It'll be fun."

Cella reached for Smith, but she found nothing but air. And when she turned to look for her, the She-wolf was long gone.

"How does the bitch *do* that?"

Crush cleared his throat and tried again to speak in actual sentences. "Um . . . it's nice to meet you, Mr. Novikov." Holy shit. Holy shit! He was talking to Bo Novikov. *The* Bo Novikov. There was only one player greater than Bo Novikov and he no longer played. But Crush had been following Novikov's career for years and had been like a little kid when he'd found out Novikov had been picked up by the New York Carnivores. Now Crush didn't have to worry about paying for those away trips just to get a chance to see Novikov play more than a couple of times a year.

And now . . . now Crush was standing in front of the man. *Talking.* To *him.*

Holy shit! *Holy shit!*

"Call him Bo!" Blayne cheered. "Right, honey?"

"I don't care," the hybrid sighed.

"What's wrong?" Blayne asked. "And what happened to your face?" When he didn't answer, she accused, "You've been fighting with Ric again, haven't you?"

"And there you go taking his side. You never even ask what happened."

"Did it involve a list?"

Novikov crossed his arms over his chest. "Can I go now?"

"No!" the wolfdog snapped. "You're going to learn to be nice to your fans if it's the last thing I make you do. Now be nice to Crush. He's a polar, too."

"I'm only half polar," Novikov reminded her.

"What you are is a mother—"

"Is he supposed to be nice to fans?" Crush, ever the detective, had to ask, barely realizing he was cutting into Blayne's sentence.

Blayne blinked. "Huh?"

"Well, isn't he known for *not* being nice to his fans? So is it fair of us as fans to ask him to be something he's not?" Crush thought on that a moment before deciding, "No. It's not fair."

Looking kind of smug, Bo Novikov gazed down at Blayne.

"You can just get that look off your face, Bo Novikov!" Then Blayne stomped her foot and pointed at Crush. "And you're not helping me, Crush! And after I got you such a nice haircut!"

"I didn't know my hair was contingent on the approving or disapproving of your appropriate fan theory treatment."

"I don't even know what that means."

"In Blayneland," Novikov explained, "everyone helps everyone and there is respect and love throughout the universe."

"Really?" Crush asked honestly. "Are there faeries and horses with wings in that universe, too?"

"Yes," Novikov replied flatly. "There are."

"You guys!" Blayne whined, sounding just like a cranky six-year-old.

Crush began to laugh, but it faded when Gwen returned to his side with another player. "Lou Crushek, this is my fiancé, Lock MacRyrie."

The grizzly held his hand out and when Crush did nothing but gape at him, he went ahead and shook Crush's hand, smiling a little.

"It's nice to meet you, Detective."

"You're the Tank," Crush finally said.

MacRyrie blinked. "Sorry?"

"That's what everyone calls you. The Tank."

The grizzly looked surprised. "I have a nickname?"

"You have a *cool* nickname," Blayne corrected, her annoyance from mere seconds ago completely gone. "The coolest!"

"It fits," Novikov noted, which got him everyone's attention. "What?"

"Was that a compliment?" MacRyrie asked.

With an eye roll and a sigh, "If it must be to make you feel better."

Again Crush started to laugh, but the sound—and happiness—died in his throat as she—*she!*—suddenly appeared in front of Crush. Grinning.

Why was she here? Why? And why could he not shake this feline? Was this how antelopes felt when a cat ran them down? And why was she here ruining what should be one of the greatest nights of his goddamn life?

That was it. That was *it*! Never again would he ever have another Jell-O shot. In fact, no more liquor. Ever. Because clearly Crush would never be allowed to live down that one goddamn night—and he blamed the goddamn Jell-O shots!

Letting out a breath, Crush snarled, "*You.*"

"Baby!" she cried out just before she attacked him, wrapping her arms around his waist. "Oh, baby, I've missed you!"

"I am not your baby." He tried to pull her arms off him. "Away, female!"

"Aren't you glad to see me?"

"No."

Still wrapped around him like a spider monkey, the feline rested her chin on his chest and asked the small group, "Have you guys met the new man in my life?"

Blayne's eyes grew wide, her smile huge, and Crush immediately knew he had to stop this.

"I am *not* the new . . . would you get off!"

"He's shy," the female felt the need to explain.

"I am not shy. You're insane." He finally pried her arms off his body and pushed her back. "Now stop harassing . . ." Crush studied her, his heart dropping. "Why . . . why are you dressed like that?"

She had on a Carnivore jersey, shoulder pads under that, hockey pants, socks, and shin pads.

"Why do you *think* I'm dressed like this?"

"Because hell has come to earth?"

She laughed and Novikov said, "You're such a fan, figured you'd know Bare Knuckles Ma—"

"No!" And the grizzly and the hybrid male snarled a little at his outburst, both pulling their females back from the hysterical polar. "No, no, no, no!"

The feline's grin was wide and happy. "Come on, baby, don't be like that."

"No! You cannot be Bare Knuckles Malone. You *cannot* be. *You*"—and he pointed at her with an accusing finger— "cannot be the daughter of the greatest player ever. And you cannot be the most feared enforcer in the league right now. *You? No!*"

"I'm sensing I should be insulted by that tone." The feline grinned. "But I'm not! Because I have such a giving and loving nature and you are just so cute. We will have such adorable cubs. And since I'm never home, my little girl"— she raised her hand barely to her waist to illustrate her child's height—"can raise them."

"I am not cute and I'm not having kids with you!"

"You guys, you guys." Blayne slipped between the pair. "There's no reason to be angry."

"I'm not angry." Flinging her arms out and turning in a circle like a little girl, the feline exclaimed, "*I'm in love!*"

"That's it." Crush stepped away. "I'm leaving."

"You can't run from our love!"

Crush had almost reached the elevators when Blayne leaped in front of him. "Don't go, Crush."

"I can't stay. The game's about to start, I need to get to my seat . . . I can't stay." He reached around Blayne, punching the elevator button. When he leaned back, he realized that the wolfdog was staring up at him. And the more she stared, the sadder she looked.

"What? What's wrong?"

Then she looked mad. He assumed she was mad at him, but when she grabbed his hand and walked back over to the others, it was the feline who received Blayne's wrath.

"Why are you being mean?" Blayne demanded.

"I'm not being—"

"Bullshit! I know when a feline's being mean, and you're being mean. I don't like it."

"Now ask me if I care if you—owww! You bitch!"

Blayne had dropped Crush's hand to latch on to the feline's hair, digging her fingers in and twisting.

"Get off me!"

"Excuse us," Blayne said before she stormed off down the hallway, dragging the feline with her.

Crush watched the pair disappear around a corner; then he looked at Novikov. He knew the man had the same expression Crush did, and they both started off at the same time to follow, but Gwen grabbed their arms. "Don't get in the middle."

"Yeah, but—"

"You're not listening to me. Do not get in the middle of this. Trust me."

"It's really not that big a deal," Crush felt the need to explain. "She drives me nuts, but Blayne didn't have to get so upset about it."

"Blayne felt she did, so you might as well not get in the middle." Gwen glanced at him. "Rough couple of days, Crush? Maybe a rough couple of years?"

Crush, feeling uncomfortable, asked, "What are you talking about?"

"Whatever Blayne Thorpe saw, she's worried about you."

"Worried about me? Why? I mean, life is what it is."

"Ooooh." Gwen cringed. "Yeah, if Blayne asks you a similar question, I wouldn't give that response."

"Do *not* give Blayne that response," Novikov agreed. "Otherwise, she'll make me adopt you."

"That would be kind of weird cause I'm older than you."

"Is that really the only reason you can come up with of why that would be weird?"

Blayne stalked around the corner, the feline following behind, eyes rolling, feet dragging. Stopping between Crush and Gwen, Blayne waited for Malone to reach them, her foot tapping.

Once the feline stood in front of them, she said, "Now what was it you wanted me to say again?"

Blayne went for Malone's throat, but Novikov caught her first, yanking the swinging, spitting, and screeching wolfdog away.

"Is there anyone," Crush asked, "that you *don't* irritate?"

The feline looked him over, and grinned. "Come on."

She grabbed his hand, but Crush immediately yanked it back. "I'm not going anywhere with you. I'm going to my seat and forget I ever met you and then I'll decide whether to sue the makers of delicious Jell-O products or just the MacDermots for using Jell-O in a clearly despicable way."

"You really are cute, you know?" And for once it didn't sound like the feline was mocking. "My suggestion is to go after MacDermot and Llewellyn. The Jell-O people are probably a huge conglomerate that will have you tied up in court for years. And I need you to come with me because I'd prefer not to end up on the wrong side of Blayne Thorpe."

"You already seem to be on the wrong side of Blayne."

"If I was really on the wrong side of Blayne, I'd be in little consumable pieces for the hyena population. You wouldn't want that, would you?"

"Morally . . . I guess not."

"Morally, huh?"

"Should I get a dictionary so you can look up the meaning?"

Laughing, the feline grabbed his hand and started walking. "According to Blayne," who was watching them walk by, panting hard, fangs out, "I owe you for being so mean to you. You apparently have a broken heart that needs to be mended." She glanced back at him. "Just break up with your girlfriend or something?"

"No."

"Well, she thinks you're wounded and my tormenting you is beneath me."

"So you two just met then?"

"I like how your sense of humor comes out when it's to make fun of me."

"You need to pick up the step, Malone," Novikov yelled after her. "We've got a game to get to."

"Yeah, yeah, yeah."

After a few minutes of following along, Crush asked, "So where are we going anyway?"

"You'll see."

"If you're just going to find another way to publicly embarrass me, can we do it at another time? Like *after* the game?"

"I don't waste my time embarrassing anyone when I've got a game about to start."

"And why is that?"

"Because embarrassing others is a pastime and pastimes are for *after* the game. Like video games or going out to clubs."

"Can you be more cat?"

"Not even if I tried."

She took him down a small set of stairs to a door manned by a couple of very large security guards. "Hey, guys."

"Hey, Cella," one said while opening the door for her.

"He's with me. This is . . ." She stopped, looked at him. "What's your name?"

"You're *just* asking me that?"

"Yes."

"MacDermot didn't tell you?"

"She did but"—she shrugged—"it slipped my mind."

Knowing that if he tried to make a run for it, she'd just hunt him down, Crush decided to just get this insanity over with. "Name's Lou Crushek."

"I thought Blayne called you Crush."

"My *friends* call me Crush, and since you're not—"

"Crush it is then." She yanked him inside the big room with the giant windows overlooking the rink and dragged him until they reached the plush leather seats.

"You'll watch the game from here."

Crush took a quick look around. When the Sports Center first opened years ago, Crush had taken what Conway still called "a sports geek tour of the place." So he knew this room, although he and the other tourists had only been allowed a very quick walkthrough. "But . . . but this is the—"

"Owner's box. Right. And you can sit here. Right by my daddy."

Crush gawked down at the older tiger male sitting in one of the seats, an open Guinness in his hand. Crush gawked, but he couldn't speak. No words would come out. So, like an idiot, he just stood there. Gawking.

"Daddy," Malone said. "This is Lou Crushek, aka Crush. He's my new boyfriend." The man blinked in surprise and then grinned. "Crush, honey, this is my daddy, Nice Guy Malone."

Crush shook his head at the hand held out to him. "I think I . . . I need to . . ."

Surprisingly soft hands brushed hair off his face. "Oh, baby, you've gone all white. Which is kind of amazing considering you're a polar."

"He better sit down."

Father and daughter shoved Crush into a seat.

"What's wrong with him?" Nice Guy asked.

"He's a fan, Daddy. I think he's overwhelmed at meeting you."

"Good kid," Nice Guy said before glancing at his daughter and asking, "And he's single, right?"

"*Daddy*."

"Just making sure. Look, you go before you hear about it from Novikov. I'll take care of the kid."

"Thanks, Daddy." She winked at Crush. "And I'll see you later, handsome."

And that was about the time that Crush completely freaked out.

Cella was at the door pulling it open when a big hand slammed against it and shoved it back, yanking her forward a bit since she still had her hand on the knob.

"You can't leave me."

Startled by the desperation she heard in that voice, she turned around and looked up at the cop. "Of course, I can."

"No. You *can't* leave me."

"Look at you, already attached. But I play with the Genghis Khan of time management. I have to go." She pulled at the door again and again it was slammed.

"What are you doing?" she asked, getting exasperated.

"You can't leave me."

"You keep saying that."

"Because it's true. I'll just go with you."

"I can't take you to the locker room until after the game."

"No, but I can go to the seat I paid for."

"The seat in the nosebleed section? That's where Blayne said you were headed. Why would you want to go there?"

"Because I can't stay here," he whispered.

"Why not?" she whispered back.

He leaned in closer, and still in a whisper, "Because that's Nice Guy Malone."

"I know," she again whispered back. "I recognize him from all my birthday parties and when I find him inappropriately fondling my mother. Not seeing the problem. Just talk to him."

"Talk? Talk to him? To Nice Guy Malone?"

Good God, the man was having a panic attack.

"What am *I* supposed to say to Nice Guy Malone? I mean he's . . . *he's Nice Guy Malone.*"

And that's when she understood. Kind of like if she'd had the chance to sit and chat with John L. Sullivan, one of the last known heavyweight bare-knuckle champions. She'd probably be having a full-on panic attack if she'd met him—partly because the man had died in 1918, but also because he was her hero.

And her father was the hero of this uptight cop that Blayne Thorpe suddenly felt so protective of, which did nothing but make him even cuter than he already was simply because he had excellent taste.

"You have to take me out of here," the polar begged.

"No."

"Why do you hate me?"

"I don't hate you. I just want to make sure you don't regret this night for the rest of your life by walking away. Besides, my dad's a total talker. Mr. Storyteller. All Malone males are. So you won't have to say a word." She went up on her toes and kissed his cheek. "Now balls up and go talk to your lifelong hero."

Cella shoved and her father was there to grab the polar's arm. "Come on, kid. I'll introduce you to everybody."

"Introduce me?" And she heard his voice crack a little.

"Way cute." Cella chuckled and headed out, ready to have some fun on the ice.

CHAPTER SIX

"Would you like a menu, sir?"

Crush shook his head, and wondered how he could get out of this. "No."

"Go on," Nice Guy pushed.

"We have a lovely peppered, ringed seal sandwich with spicy hot mustard. It's a favorite among our polar clientele."

And wow, but did that sound good. But no. No. He couldn't. This was getting completely out of hand!

"He'll take it," Nice Guy volunteered for him. "And some of those sweet potato fries, too." The waiter nodded and walked off. "You might as well enjoy this, kid."

"I have no idea how I got here. This can't end well."

Nice Guy studied him for a few moments, then said, "You're a cop, aren't you?"

Stunned, Crush stared at his hero. It was usually the last thing anyone ever accused Crush of being. Meth dealer, mass murderer, biker, but no one ever said, "You're a cop, aren't you?" It was why Crush was so good at his job. He could infiltrate any lowlife, underworld association he wanted simply because he looked as if for ten bucks and a pack of smokes, he'd cut someone's throat.

Of course, that used to insult him, but not anymore.

"Uh . . . well . . ."

Nice Guy patted his arm. "It's all right, kid. You don't need to admit anything. I just know cops when I see 'em."

"No one else ever guesses it right."

The tiger shrugged. "I was always 'Nice Guy' Malone, but I wasn't always 'Nice Guy' Malone."

Crush frowned while Nice Guy's teammates laughed around them.

"What," Crush asked, "does that mean?"

Cella, now with her skates on and stick and helmet in hand, made her way to the long, covered hallway that would lead out onto the ice. But when she was still a corner-turn away, a small wolfdog sped out in front of her, blocking her path.

Not wanting to fight, Cella immediately held her hands up. "I made it up to him! I made it up to him!"

"Huh?" Blayne shook her head. "Oh, whatever. I'm not talking about that."

"Oh." Cella lowered her hands. "Then what's up?"

"I need your help."

"After you just busted my balls?"

"*Those are two separate issues!*" Blayne bellowed.

Cella's eyes narrowed. "Blayne . . . did you have sugar today?"

She lowered her gaze. "Maybe."

"And on that note . . ."

Cella tried to go around her, but Blayne skated in front of her. She had on her quad skates for derby practice and the tiniest shorts known to man or God. Thankfully, the little wolfdog looked *good* in those shorts.

"I need your help," she said.

"With what?"

"My wedding. Gwen's wedding. It's all gone to shit!"

"You knew Novikov was difficult."

"He's not the problem. Gwen's mother. Lock's mother. They're the problem."

"How are they a problem for *you*?"

Her lips briefly pressed into a thin line. "Apparently, I'm like a daughter to them," she said flatly.

"Oh. Well, have fun with that."

"Cella, I need your help."

"With what?"

"Your mom."

Of course. Every bride wanted Barb Malone as their wedding planner, but that just wasn't possible. "My mom is booked for the next three years. I think she even turned down one of the Kennedys." Cella glanced off. "Or maybe it was just a close relative of the Kennedys. Either way—"

"So you're saying no?"

"I'm saying no."

"*Fine!*" Blayne and her sugar high bellowed.

Cella watched her skate off, waiting until she was about ten feet away before she softly said, "Unless . . ."

Wild dog ears honed in on that and Blayne stopped. "Unless?"

Cella faced her, shrugged. "Maybe if you could help me with Novikov and the way he treats the team . . ."

Blayne clenched her fists. "We made a promise to each other that I would never involve myself in his hockey career and he would never call derby a 'chick sport.' "

"Oh. All right. Well"—Cella turned around, headed toward the team—"good luck to ya!"

With a speed that Cella always marveled at, Blayne shot in front of her. Damn shame the girl couldn't ice-skate very well, because, wow.

"Fine. I'll do it. *If* you get your mother to take on my wedding and Gwen's."

"Why not make your lives easier and just have one joint wedding? Novikov won't care and MacRyrie will learn to put up with him for one day if it makes Gwen happy."

"My God . . . that's brilliant!"

"I know." Cella pointed at herself. "Because that's what I do. I solve problems. Now move your skinny ass."

As Cella walked away, Blayne yelled from behind her, "I love you, Cella!"

"Shut up."

Cella got in line with the other players, waiting for their team and names to be announced.

"Thanks for joining us," Novikov muttered.

"Oh, shut up." She stepped in next to Van Holtz. "Hey."

"Hey."

Cella noticed how the wolf stared placidly across the room.

"Feel better?" she asked him.

"Mhmm."

"Dee-Ann stop by?" The wolf grinned and Cella said, "Then I'm glad I stopped by before then."

"So am I."

Cella chuckled until she heard someone whistling and whispering, "Hey . . . you. Hey," at her. She looked around at her own teammates, then over at the waiting Alabama Slammers. A young wolf grinned at her, winked.

MacRyrie snorted next to her. "He must be new."

The opposing team was called out and the wolf made sure to stare at her until he hit the ice.

"Cella," and she could hear the warning in Van Holtz's voice. His "captain" voice, she called it. It was different from his "owner" voice and his "goalie" voice.

She shrugged. "I didn't do anything."

"Just make sure you don't."

"I'm only here to play the game."

Traditional bagpipe music began playing over the loud-speaker—it was New York, after all—and the announcer called out the Carnivores, each first-string player announced individually and skating out onto the ice, spotlights directly on them.

Cella patiently waited her turn, glancing back and winking at Jai, who stood with her med team. Her best friend grinned and gave her a thumbs-up.

Then she gave her the finger.

Yep. Best friend *ever!*

Cella heard it. "Number 29, Marcella 'Bare Knuckles' Malone!"

Grinning, she skated out onto the ice, raising her free hand to wave at the crowd. She heard a lot of female cheers, which made sense since she had a lot of female predator fans. But it was when the announcer called out Novikov's name that the crowd lost its collective mind. Cella didn't blame them, though. He might be an obsessive-compulsive borderline sociopath, but damn if the man wasn't the best hockey player she'd ever known . . . next to her dad, of course. At least . . . that's what she told her dad.

"Then for about three years," Nice Guy continued, "I was a leg breaker for a couple of bookies who worked for the O'Malley boys. I was really good at it, too."

The O'Malley boys? Crush closed his eyes. *Good God.* "And how old were you when you—"

"Thirteen."

"Thir . . . thirteen?"

"Tigers don't have growth spurts like you guys. I was always big. Always looked way older than I was. And when I was working for bookies, I thought about robbing banks. But that's a federal crime and I decided not to bother. Ya know?"

"Um . . . uh . . . uh-huh." Crush closed his eyes again. "You just broke legs, right? You've never actually . . . uh . . . um . . ."

"Killed someone? Nah. Of course not." Nice Guy glanced at the ceiling. "Wait, on the ice . . . ?"

And Crush gritted his teeth.

"No, no. That guy survived. Soooo . . . no. All clear there."

All Crush could do was shrug. "Okay."

Cella slammed her body into the wolf who'd winked at her, making sure to ram her elbow under his helmet and into his throat. He fell to his knees and she dropped her gloves, slapped his helmet off, and proceeded to pummel his face raw before her teammates managed to drag her away from him.

With a snarl from the ref, she hit the box for a two-minute penalty.

Pulling out her fang guard, she glanced over at the black bear sitting next to her.

"Hi, Bert."

"Hey, Cella."

"How's the wife?"

"Good. Good. Your daughter?"

"Great. Turning eighteen this weekend."

Bert winced. "Uh-oh. I wish you luck."

"Yep." Cella spit out blood, and wiped blood off her knuckles. "You coming to the Ice Party this year?" she asked.

"Probably not. You know me. Not much of a partier." Bert nodded. "Okay. I'm back in. See ya, Cella."

"See ya, Bert."

Cella spit out more blood, removed her helmet, and shook out her hair. She was seriously considering getting her hair cut. Maybe a mani-pedi, too. Oooh! Maybe she could drag Lady Dour of the Clan Dour, aka Meghan, to go with her. Honestly, was *all* that studying necessary? And constant thinking? The girl needed to relax! She was a Malone, wasn't she? And the Malones knew how to relax. It was time her daughter got on the train with the rest of them.

So yeah. Haircuts and mani-pedis, hopefully with a mother-daughter discount. And the kid would just have to suck it up.

Her time in the box up, Cella stood, pulled on her helmet, popped her fang guard back in, and hit the ice.

And the first thing she did was slam her body into that same Alabama wolf, drop her gloves, and pummel his face. . . .

"So," Crush felt the need to ask, "what made you give up your . . . uh . . . leg-breaking ways? Hockey?"

Nice Guy chuckled. "Nah. Hockey just made me a better leg breaker. Playing hockey was something that I did naturally. Like breathing. And most of what I did was to get money for equipment. So, no. It's not why. It was Barb." When Crush frowned, "My wife. Cella's mother. We'd known each other since grade school, but unlike the Malones, Barb's father became rich and moved the family uptown. Then my high school was playing football against Trinity Parochial, and I locked on her as soon as I saw her again. But she wouldn't have anything to do with me."

"Because you were breaking people's legs at thirteen?"

"No, that didn't bother her. Besides. They weren't people. They were degenerate gamblers. But I did beat up her kid brother for his lunch money. That kind of pissed her off."

"Yeah. I can see a girl holding that against you."

"Didn't stop me from trying, though. Malones, we don't back away from a challenge. Gifts for her. Flowers, candy. A cool car for me . . . stolen, of course."

"I didn't need to know that."

"The latest clothes. Everything I figured a girl would want. Then she finally said it. 'You're a lowlife and I wouldn't date you if you were the last tiger on the planet.' " He tapped his chest. "That one hurt. Right here. So I figured if I was gonna get her, I had to stop breaking legs, stealing cars, throwing degenerate gamblers off rooftops—"

"Again . . . that I didn't need to know."

"That's when I realized hockey wasn't just that thing I

did, but a way I could get legit. Get on the right team, become the best player—I could get a girl like her."

"And you can get your equipment legally."

"Didn't really care about that."

"Of course, you didn't."

"Before I knew it, I was considered the best in the league and I had the She-tiger of my dreams."

"Except for the extreme illegal activity during your important developmental years—that was a surprisingly sweet story."

"Mhmm." Nice Guy suddenly looked him over, eyes narrowing. "What do you know about my daughter?"

"Apparently nothing," he muttered, but when Nice Guy tensed, Crush quickly added, "I knew about Bare Knuckles Malone." Who didn't? She had one of the worst reputations in the league next to The Marauder and was one of the first female enforcers for a pro-team who wasn't a She-bear. "But I didn't know the woman I was talking to was Bare Knuckles. Her face is impossible to see from my usual seats and any time they show her on the big screen, she's wearing a helmet."

"Yeah. She does that for safety reasons." What safety reasons? But before Crush could get into it, Nice Guy asked, "And how long have you two been dating?"

"Dating?"

"She said you were her boyfriend."

"Uh . . ."

Gold eyes narrowed. "You're not just using my little girl, are you?"

"No. No, no. It's just—"

"Just what?" And that came from "Mac Truck" Lewis, a wolf and one-time goalie who used to play with Nice Guy. It suddenly occurred to Crush that every man here was not only friends with Nice Guy, but like a father to Nice Guy's daughter. That was the beauty of hockey, it transcended breed or species, because it was all about whether a player could skate backward while keeping an eye out for a little black puck.

These men were like Bare Knuckles Malone's godfathers. And he was the nonplaying idiot they thought was dating her. Hell, they thought he was her boyfriend. A status he'd rather chew rocks than be cursed with. But he wasn't about to say that to a bunch of his heroes who adored her.

Besides, he hadn't felt this unsafe since he was alone in the middle of a three a.m. Hells Angels beach party.

"It's just . . ." Crush cleared his throat and scrambled for a satisfactory lie. "I'm not sure I'm worthy of her. I worry about that."

The men relaxed, smiled, and Nice Guy patted Crush's shoulder. It felt like he was being beaten with a baseball bat.

"Don't worry about that. My girl has good instincts. Just like her mother." When Crush only stared at him. "Hey, I haven't broken a guy's leg for money—and hockey doesn't count—since I was sixteen. See? She knew I had potential."

Chapter Seven

One of the Slammers cut across the ice, heading right for Novikov. Cella shoved past the winger in her way and went after him, but she didn't think she'd reach him in time.

"Reed!" she called out. "Move!"

As a canine, the hillbilly took orders pretty well, and shot in front of the player, blocking him from getting near Novikov.

She reached her teammate and blocked another player, ramming him into the glass by using her legs to launch her body at the guy. They both hit the glass and then dropped to the ice. She was ready to pull off her gloves and take the guy on since he was calling her all sorts of things she found insulting, but the crowd roared, signaling a successful goal, and the end buzzer went off.

Cella got to her feet and skated away from the other player, but kept her eyes on him as she did.

"Bitch," the maned wolf sneered.

"Loser," Cella shot back, laughing as one of her teammates picked her up around the waist and carried her off the ice before she started another all-team brawl.

She kind of had a reputation for doing that.

Once off the ice, her teammate—Bert!—let her go, shaking his head and chuckling.

They all marched back to their respective locker rooms and Cella slapped hands and laughed with her female teammates before jumping in the shower and washing off all the blood from the game. When she headed back to her locker, she found Jai waiting for her.

Cella grabbed a dry towel. "Hey. What's up?"

"How's your knee?" Jai asked.

"Fine."

"Are you lying to me?"

"No. It's fine. See?" She pointed to her weak left knee before going back to towel-drying her hair. Thankfully, the swelling hadn't started yet, although it would swell. It always did after a game.

"Put some ice on it anyway."

"Yeah, yeah, yeah."

"Don't yeah, yeah, yeah me. Just do as I tell you." Jai checked her clipboard. "I gotta go. I've got some artery repair to deal with. I swear"—she shook her head and held her clipboard to her chest—"Novikov is so mean. Got a guy bleeding out in surgery."

Cella stood up straight, flipping her hair off her face. "Then maybe you should . . . you know . . . take care of him?"

Jai rolled her eyes. "He's just a coyote."

"Jai!" God, the mountain lions . . . such bigots when it came to the canines, especially the coyotes and wolves.

"I'm going, I'm going. Had to check on you first, right?"

"Cella!" someone called out. "Your dad is outside. Along with some polar bear. Said they're waiting for you."

"Tell them I'll be out in a bit."

"Polar bear?" Jai asked, still letting that coyote bleed out in her surgery.

"Yeah. He's that guy I woke up naked with at MacDermot's house."

The other females stopped dressing and focused on Cella.

"I didn't fuck him," Cella added. Then she grinned. "At least not yet."

"Oh, that's classy," Jai chastised.

"Man. Bleeding. Needs surgery."

Jai sighed. "Well, if you're going to get pushy about it . . ."

Cella shook her head and grabbed her cell phone from inside her locker. She speed-dialed her daughter's number and waited for the brat to answer.

"Hi, Ma."

"Hey, baby. You all right?" She made sure to check in on Meghan after every game. Although, she didn't know why she bothered. The kid always seemed so put out.

"I'm fine." Then Cella mouthed along with her daughter's next word, "Studying."

Of course, she was. "Well, I shouldn't be too late tonight."

"And that affects me how?"

"Could you at least *pretend* to care if I come home? Would it kill you?"

"It's not that I don't care. I'm just at the college library with Josie. It's open late. Uncle Tommy's picking us up when we're done and then Josie and I are spending the night at Aunt Kathleen's."

"Why?"

"Babysitting some cousins. Now, did you kill anyone tonight or did you allow them all to make it out alive?"

"No, smart-ass. I didn't kill anyone." With the phone caught between her raised shoulder and ear, Cella pulled on a pair of panties and then a pair of grey sweatpants.

"Then just your usual mayhem?"

"Can't disappoint the fans." She reached for a bra. "Hey, I was thinking—"

"No."

"You didn't let me finish."

"Okay. Finish."

"I thought we could go and get a mani-pedi and our hair—"

"No."

"Again, you didn't let me finish and why not?"

"I've got too much to do."

"You're seventeen, not forty working for a Fortune 500 company. Get over yourself." Cella tugged her bra until it fit perfectly, then said, "I don't know where you got this haughty, superior, 'I'm better than everyone' attitude you've draped yourself in but . . ." Cella's words faded away when she realized that her female teammates were hysterically laughing at her.

"You don't know?" one sow bellowed over all the laughter. "How could you not know?"

"Anything else, Ma, or can I leave you to the comedy stylings of your teammates?" Smug *and* ungrateful. That was the kid Cella had been cursed with.

"I'll talk to you in the morning."

"Love you."

"Love you, too." Cella disconnected the call and roared at her teammates, but that only made them laugh harder.

"So when are you coming to the Island to meet the rest of the family?"

Crush froze. He wanted to scream, "Never!" But he knew that would be a bad idea. They were now in the hallway outside the locker rooms and it was packed with family and friends of the Carnivores and word seemed to have already spread that he was, somehow, the boyfriend of Bare Knuckles. A player he considered kind of reprehensible since she seemed to fight more than skate.

"Uhhhh . . . that's up to your daughter?"

"Well, make it soon." Nice Guy gave a small shrug. "Trust me on this."

Not sure what he was talking about and, to be honest, not really caring, Crush said, "Sure. Will do." It was the same answer he gave his bosses when he didn't know what they were talking about and didn't care.

The Marauder came out of the locker room, his well-known and vicious scowl leading the way. With that expression on his face, you'd think the team had lost. But they hadn't. Although, they had barely won.

Still, there seemed to be one thing that could make the Marauder smile no matter what, and she was skating toward him on those skates with four wheels, bruises on her face and drops of blood on her tank top.

Blayne skated her way through the crowd and threw herself into his arms. Novikov lifted her up, hugging her close.

"You were the best!" Blayne cheered. Crush noticed that the wolfdog seemed to cheer a lot. Was she a cheerleader in high school?

"Did you even see the game?" Novikov asked, his smile still there.

"What does that have to do with anything? You're always the best." She hugged the behemoth again and then she spotted Crush. "Hi, Crush!"

Although Crush wasn't much of a smiler, he couldn't help himself around her. She was just so damn cheerful. "Hiya, Blayne."

She smiled, peeking over at Nice Guy, and observed, "I see Malone made it up to you."

"Yeah, she did."

Blayne leaned in a bit, her arms still around the Marauder, and whispered loudly enough to be heard ten miles away, "You look so good with your haircut! Isn't Gwenie the best?"

"Yes, she is." He motioned to her bruised face. "Fist-fight?"

"Nope. Derby training."

"Looks tough."

Novikov snorted. "Chicks in shorts. It's terrifying."

"Shut. Up." Blayne looked back at Crush and asked with all sincerity, "And why didn't you tell me you're Cella's boyfriend?"

Even though Crush wasn't and he was definitely freaked

out that the rumor had already spread past the hockey players and, it seemed, throughout the Sports Center, the bear in Crush still had to ask, "Why?"

"Why what?"

"Why would I tell you that?"

"Because we're friends!"

"We are?"

"Ya are now," Novikov muttered.

"Of course, we are. I like you."

"You don't even know me."

"Please," Novikov suddenly cut in, "don't use bear-logic on her. It's completely ineffectual and brings on tears when she gets frustrated. Just accept she likes you and go about your day."

"Is that what you do?"

"As her father says, 'There are always bigger battles ahead.' "

"You know," Blayne snapped, "I am right here listening to both of you."

Malone walked out of the women's locker room. She wore grey sweatpants and a white T-shirt, her hair and body freshly washed, all her wounds and bruises tended. Crush watched Malone go up on her toes and look over the crowd. When she spotted them, she came over.

"Hey."

"You did great, baby." Her father hugged her.

"Thanks, Daddy. You going out now?"

"Just for a few drinks with the boys. Gotta get home to your mom. What about you two?" He smiled. "Big plans?"

"You bet." She kissed her father on the cheek. "See you later."

Nice Guy Malone held his hand out and Crush shook it. "It was really nice meeting you, Lou."

"You, too, sir."

"Call me Butch." With a wink at his daughter, Mr. Malone walked off.

Cella kept smiling until her father was in the elevators and gone. Then she faced Crush and said, "So what do you wanna do tonight?"

"Uh—"

"Cella!"

Malone looked over her shoulder and smiled at the tiger male who came to her side. He wasn't nearly as big as Butch. Crush was guessing he wasn't Siberian, either.

"Hey. What are you doing here?"

"I was a block up meeting with a client."

"Lou Crushek," she said, "this is Brian Carpenter. My daughter's father."

Startled, but having trained years not to show it, Crush nodded. "Nice to meet you."

"You, too."

"And before you ask, Bri, I'm not discussing wedding plans with you."

"Fine. Bachelorette party then."

"I'm definitely not discussing that with you."

"No strippers, Cella."

"Oh, come on!"

"No. Strippers. I mean it. Are we clear?"

"You really just came over here to tell me that?"

"Why else would I come over here? To watch my daughter's mother get the shit beaten out of her? I can see that during family get-togethers. Now say it with me . . . no strippers. Male or female."

"Fine. Whatever."

The tiger smiled. "Thanks, beautiful." He kissed her cheek and gave her a quick hug. "Gotta go."

"And don't forget about tomorrow. We gotta come to an agreement about what we're going to get baby girl for her birthday so they can deliver it by Sunday."

"I thought we already decided."

"We did not decide."

"Maybe *I* already decided."

"Really? You wanna go that route with me? Really?"

"You're being difficult."

"I'm always difficult. That's what you love about me."

"Yeah. Right."

He walked off and Malone faced Crush. "So, about tonight—"

"I'm going home."

"Oh." And she had the nerve to look surprised. "Okay. Well . . . I hope you had a good time."

That Crush couldn't lie about. "I had a great time. Thank you."

"You're very welcome. I hope I get to see you around some time."

"Yeah. Sure."

Crush walked away from her, heading toward the elevators, and home.

"Man, does that guy run hot and cold." She faced Novikov and Blayne. "At the very least you'd think he'd want to sleep with *the* 'Bare Knuckles' Malone."

Shaking her head and throwing her hands up in the air, Blayne let out a big, overdramatic sigh.

"What's that for?"

Unable to speak—which was amazing for Blayne—she motioned to Novikov.

"What?" Cella pushed.

"You're really surprised he left?" Novikov asked.

"Yeah. I wore these sweats on purpose—they make my ass look great. I have a beautiful smile—as always. And we had a great game."

"We had an okay game," Novikov felt the need to correct. Cella balled her fingers into fists and he waved the correction away. "Forget I said anything."

"I will. So explain to me what I did wrong with Mr. Uptight."

Blayne lunged forward, forefinger jabbing dangerously, but Novikov pulled her back and held her with one hand.

"I'll run it down for you. You introduced that tiger as your daughter's father."

"Bri is her father."

"You discussed your gift-giving plans."

"It's Meghan's eighteenth on Sunday and we're planning to give her a car, but we have to figure out which one. Something sporty or something reliable? I'm thinking sporty."

"Right. You also briefly talked about wedding plans and a bachelorette party."

"My mom is the planner for Bri's wedding here and I'm maid of honor in the States so I'm handling that bachelorette party for Rivka. I still don't see the problem."

"That's because you're looking at each thing individually when you should be stepping back and taking in the whole discussion. Then pretend for five seconds that you're a normal person rather than, ya know, *you,* and think about how a normal person would see that whole thing without having any context whatso—"

"Oh, my God!"

Novikov nodded. "Exactly."

Crush neared the front door of the Sports Center, the full-humans instinctively moving out of his way, when the feline suddenly cut in front of him. She slapped her hand against his chest, stopping him from going any farther.

"It's not my wedding."

Crush frowned. "Pardon?"

She took a breath—she must have run all the way up—and repeated, "It's not my wedding. He's father to my child, but he's not marrying me. He's marrying someone else completely."

"And will he get custody?"

"Custody of who?"

"The child that can barely reach the stove, but you leave alone for hours?"

"Barely reach the . . . You mean Meghan?" She laughed. "Meghan's seventeen."

"Uh-huh."

"Seriously, I was joking. You have heard of jokes, right?"

"Thought jokes were supposed to be funny."

"It helps if one has a sense of humor." She patted his chest. "But with some work and care, I'm sure I can give you one."

"No thanks."

Startled, she took a step back. "You're not going to give me a chance to prove I'm a wonderful person?"

"You already think you're a wonderful person. What do you need me for?"

She dropped her hands to her hips, squinting up at him. "What?"

"I'm trying to figure out if you're just a dick or if you're really an uptight, overthinking good guy?"

"How about I make the decision for you."

Crush stepped around her and walked out, determined to get away from this *insane* feline. And, as the door closed behind him, Crush heard her bark, "Well I guess it's just you being a dick then, huh?"

CHAPTER EIGHT

Cella woke up swinging, but her wrists were quickly caught and held and a strong voice snapped, "Ma!"

Cella opened her eyes, immediately relaxed. "Hey, baby. Was I sleep-punching again?"

"No." Meghan released her.

"What time is it?"

"Three a.m."

"Really?" Then Cella grinned and threw her arms wide, wrapping them around her daughter. "Baby, it's your birthday!"

Meghan hugged her back, but sighed. "Yeah. Great birthday."

"What's wrong?" Cella leaned back. "You and Josie have a fight?"

"No. I got my . . . ya know."

"Your period? Would you just say it? You're going to be a doctor."

"I'd prefer to say my menstruation started, but then you'd get bitchy about that."

"That just sounds snobby."

"Anyway, I was wondering if you could take me to the

twenty-four-hour drugstore on Jericho Turnpike? I'm out of supplies."

"Your cousins don't have anything you can use?"

"I'm sure they do . . . they also have brothers that I'd rather not sit around with on my birthday discussing this."

Cella shuddered, remembering life with her own cousins at that age. Nothing was sacred or secret.

Throwing off the covers, Cella got out of bed. "Come on."

After changing out of her shorts and tank top and into a pair of sweatpants and a T-shirt, she grabbed a set of SUV keys and they went out onto the street that the Malone family had taken over long before little Meghan was born. It was a street that Nassau police steered clear of. So did any local car thieves or home invaders. Every once in a while, those who didn't know the area well enough or thought they were too smart to get caught came here looking to steal or just cause problems.

Yeah . . . that never ended well.

Cella pulled away from the curb, and headed to the pharmacy. Her daughter, yawning, rested her head against the window.

"You know, baby, you can always take one of the cars yourself if you need to go somewhere."

"Fine!" her daughter suddenly exploded. "I'm sorry I woke you up! And I'm sorry I'm bothering you to help me out! Next time I won't!"

Cella hit the brakes, stopping the car at the end of their street. She let the silence percolate for a bit before she asked, "Something amiss, my love?"

Well, she hadn't meant to do that. "No, no. Of course not," Meghan lied, hoping her mother would let it go.

Then again, her mother didn't let anything go. That was what made Cella Malone a great hockey player and killer cat.

But, at the very least, she started driving again.

"Look, Meg, I know you don't like deep, meaningful conversations, but you can't yell at me and not tell me what's going on. What I'm doing wrong."

"You're not doing anything wrong. I'm just under a lot of stress right now."

"The last thing you should have, kid, is stress."

"There's just a lot going on, okay? I've got school, Daddy's wedding, or weddings. I've never actually left the country before and now I'm going all the way to flippin' Israel."

"It's gorgeous there. You'll love it. And you'll have all of KZS watching your ass while you're there. You couldn't be more safe if I vacuum-sealed you in a puncture-resistant bag, which I've thought about."

"I'm not worried about my safety, Ma."

"You should always be worried about your safety anytime you leave the . . . front yard."

Meg's eyes crossed and she stared out the window.

"Is this about college?"

Meghan cringed, not ready for this conversation. She might never be ready.

"I don't know what you're worried about. You're going to do great at Boston U."

"Uh-huh."

"You're smart, you're gorgeous—because you've got my genes—and you'll have the Boston Malones watching out for you."

"Uh-huh."

"If you want, we can go up there and spend time with the family one of these upcoming weekends. Go check out the campus, look around . . ."

Get her off the subject! Get her off the subject!

"It's not school. It's . . . it's . . ."

"It's what?"

"It's . . . you."

"Me?"

"And the aunts."

Her mother sighed and Meg could hear the frustration in her voice. "What did Deirdre say to you?"

"Ma."

"That old bitch is really getting on my last goddamn nerve."

"Ma! This is what I'm talking about." And she wasn't making this part up. "All you do is fight with the aunts. Especially Deirdre."

"Because she's evil."

"She's not evil. She's blood." Meg turned in the seat and looked at her mother. "What is it about Aunt Deirdre that bothers you?"

"Bothers *me*? That woman hates me, and she's been trying to turn you against me since your birth. The placenta hadn't even come out yet when she started in."

"Ma."

"Don't 'Ma' me."

"You know what I want for my birthday?" Meghan snapped. "For you not to fight with Deirdre."

"Why don't you just ask for the sun?"

"See? That's what I'm talking about." She crossed her arms over her chest. "That'll be my birthday all day today. Getting between you and Deirdre."

"No one asks you to get between us."

"I can't have you fighting an old woman!"

"Don't let her age fool you. She-tigers who manage to live that long are naturally mean and those disfigured knuckles of hers are not from an accident but brawls that she usually started."

"Like you?"

"I don't start brawls, baby, I finish them."

Fed up with the conversation, Meg blew out a breath and focused her gaze straight ahead. The silence lasted until they pulled into the parking lot and that's when her mother said,

"You don't want me to fight with Deirdre? I won't fight with Deirdre. *I* won't fight with her."

"What does that mean?"

"It means that no matter how hard she pushes, I will not let her goad me into a fight."

"Ma, you're not physically capable of doing that."

"I can do *anything*."

"Gliding around on ice while beating up guys ten times your size—*this* is what you can physically manage. *Not* fighting with your elderly aunt? Not so much."

"But I will. For you. Not only that, I'm not going to fight with Deirdre until after you leave for the second wedding."

"*Ma.*"

"I've made up my mind."

"But why would you do that?"

"Because I love you. And no matter what that old bitch told you, I did not desert you."

Startled, Meg looked at her mother. "I know."

"Do you?"

"Of course, I do. It's not like you ran off to Times Square to be a hooker. You joined the Marines. Besides, there's no way to desert a Malone cub when you've got ten thousand aunts, uncles, and cousins in North America, Hawaii, and Puerto Rico alone."

"Don't forget Alaska."

"Ma, Alaska *is* part of North America."

"Whatever."

When Meg's eyes crossed, her mother laughed and took Meg's hand in her own. Cella's were covered in scars, old and new, some from hockey, some from her work as a "contractor," and some from just being the East Coast Bare Knuckle Champion five years running.

"I want you to have the best birthday you can possibly have with your personality—"

"Thanks."

"—and if that means putting up with that vicious old

woman and her annoying machinations, I'll do it. Because I love you and I want you to be fucking happy."

"Uh . . ."

"Now let's go into this pharmacy and get you some goddamn tampons. My treat!"

Meg watched her mother get out of the SUV, slamming the door behind her.

"I'm so never bored with this family," she sighed, pushing the door open and following her mother into the store.

CHAPTER NINE

After a few more hours of sleep and a hearty birthday breakfast with Meg that Meg cooked, Cella was on her fifth lap of her Sunday-afternoon run around the neighborhood when she finally admitted that something was definitely going on, and it had nothing to do with the preparations for Meg's birthday party that evening. Cella noticed it when every time she passed one of her relatives' house or RV, someone greeted her, asked her how she was doing, whether she wanted some coffee, or if she needed a chat. Malones didn't chat. They gossiped, but that's what they called it. Gossip.

Instead of asking one of her uncles, great-aunts, or cousins what the fuck was going on, though, she ran back to her parents' house. But she knew that was a mistake as soon as she walked into the kitchen. Again, her father, brothers, and aunts were all clustered around the table, but now her mother, lips in a tight, unhappy line, was involved. All of them whispering to each other, and it looked like arguing.

"Oh!" her Aunt Maureen said, way too brightly. "Look who's back!"

Panting, sweat dripping onto the floor, Cella stared at her

family. They stared back and then smiled. All of them smiled. At her. Even her Aunt Deirdre.

That's when Cella went up to her room and a much-needed shower.

She was just stepping out, reaching for a towel when she heard the knock at the door.

"Yeah?" she said, cautious. But when Jai peeked around the open door, Cella let out a breath. "Thank God it's you."

"What's wrong?"

Cella motioned for Jai to close the door. "I think they're plotting my death."

Jai laughed, then stopped. "Oh. You're not kidding."

"They're acting weird. They're up to something. Malones just don't smile at ya . . . unless it involves a con or a two-by-four to the back of the head."

"Yeah." Jai nibbled her bottom lip. "Or they care about you and your happiness?"

"They're Malones. They don't give a shit about my happiness."

"That's where you're wrong. They seem to love you more than you realize."

Cella's eyes narrowed. "Why are you saying that? What's going on?"

"It's about the upcoming family wedding."

"Whose wedding? Shannon's? Sinead's? Annie's? Emma's? Ella's?

"No."

"Johnny's? Jackie's? Conor's? Jamie's?"

"My God, please stop. I'm talking about Bri's wedding."

"Bri's not family."

"Just your daughter's father."

"That don't make him family. Just makes him a breeder."

Jai smiled. "I love hanging around you. You guys never fail to entertain me."

"Spit it out, Davis. What's going on?"

"There's concern. About the effect Bri and Rivka's wedding is having on you."

"Me? What about me?" The wedding had been in the planning stages for what felt like an eternity, and although Meghan might have some concerns about the event, why would the family care one way or the other? And, especially, why would they suddenly be worried about Cella?

"The family's concerned that you're devastated about all this. The engagement. The wedding."

Cella blinked. "No, I'm not."

"That you're hiding your pain behind a façade."

"A façade of what?"

"General good humor and bravado."

"I always have good humor. And I am full of bravado."

"That's very true."

"Besides. How upset can I be? I'm the maid of honor."

"Uh-huh."

"My mother is the wedding planner for the wedding here and I asked her to do it. They have another planner for the ceremony in Israel, which Meghan is invited to."

"Uh-huh."

"And the only reason the rest of the Malones aren't invited is because of, well . . . ya know . . . the thing."

"Right. The thing."

"Which was not my fault but my cousin's and he's returned almost all the artwork, including the Monet, to Israel."

"I'm well aware."

"And not only that, but when Bri told me he was marrying Rivka, I said, 'Yeah. Great. And you may want to send your support check before you leave on your honeymoon.' "

"I'm sure you did."

"Then why would any of them be concerned?"

"I think they're under some delusion that you care."

"I care about my kid. I didn't eat her at birth or anything.

Care about you. My parents. Josie, of course. Tolerate my brothers."

Jai nodded. "I agree with all of that."

Turning back to the mirror, Cella said, "My God, my family's so insane. It's no big deal. After the wedding this will all blow over."

"Well . . ."

Cella again faced her friend. "Well, what?"

Jai bit her lip again before announcing, "They're talking matchmaker."

Cella stumbled back against the sink. "No!"

Jai raised her hands. "Now don't panic."

"Don't panic? Are you insane?" Cella bet this was her Aunt Deirdre's idea. Her mother always said that Deirdre could convince most Malones that John F. Kennedy was a Protestant. And while Kathleen ran the New York Malone females, it was Deirdre who was the equivalent of her enforcer. Only she was way meaner than Cella could ever dream of being on the ice.

Jai reached over and patted Cella's hand. "Don't worry. Your father says it's not necessary—"

"Well, at least he's being reasonable."

"—because you already have a boyfriend."

"Boyfriend? What boy . . ." Cella gasped. "Oh, no."

"Do you know who he's talking about?"

"God. The bear. The polar bear from Friday night." She'd told Jai about what had happened with the bear on their drive home from the game. "Christ, I thought Dad knew he wasn't my boyfriend."

"Apparently he doesn't know that. And it sounds as if he likes the guy. 'He's a fine, slightly tongue-tied boy,' according to him. Which is perfect because maybe you can use the bear to get your aunts off your back for a little while."

"What are you talking about?"

"Your mom told my mom that if you've got a boyfriend already, your aunts will back off the matchmaker thing. The problem is Deirdre's convinced them you don't have a boyfriend. That Butch was mistaken."

"But he was! I was kidding when I said he was my boyfriend."

"Your father seemed to have missed that."

"How could he miss that?"

"It doesn't matter. But maybe if you use your Malone charm, you can get the guy to help out."

"Help out with what?"

"Pretend to be your boyfriend for a couple of days. Give him tickets to the next game or something. I'm sure he'd help for that since you say he's a fan."

Cella wasn't so sure. "You don't understand. That bear barely tolerated me and he thinks I'm a bad mother."

"Why does he think . . . ?" Jai rolled her eyes. "Did you do that thing again? Where you pretend Meghan can barely tie her shoes, but you've left her alone to fend for herself?"

Cella shrugged. "You had to be there. It was funny at the time."

"Funny or not, you've got a problem. You could probably get one of the other players to have your back or someone from KZS to pretend to be your boyfriend, but your father already met the bear. Although, I'm surprised he's okay with a bear. I thought the Malones would be all, 'he must be tiger.' "

"Only if I hadn't already had the kid. My aunts are happy because I've been a good little Malone female and given them a girl to carry on family tradition. Which only leaves me wide open for anything the aunts may dredge up. But I'm betting this is Deirdre. She's trying to start a fight with me."

"She always starts fights with you."

"Yeah, but . . ."

"Yeah, but what?"

Cella let a breath out, her neck getting tight. "But I promised Meghan I wouldn't fight with Deirdre until after the wedding."

Jai let out a loud laugh until she realized Cella wasn't joining her. Then she stopped. "Oh . . . you're serious."

"It's a long story involving sleep-punching, tampons, and an early-morning drive to the pharmacy. I don't want to get into it."

"I don't think I want you to get into it."

"That old bitch. I bet she knows. I bet she *knows* I promised Meg I wouldn't fight with her."

"Now you're being paranoid."

"I'm not. She knows I'll never agree to a matchmaker, which will set off a whole chain of events and then she can make me look bad in front of my kid."

Instead of debating that, Jai asked, "So what are you going to do?"

"I'll just talk to the family. Calmly. Rationally. I'll make it clear these old-school rituals no longer apply in modern society. I'll make it clear how ridiculous this all is."

"You mean you're going to act like an adult?"

"Yes. I'm a thirty-six-year-old adult and I can act like one."

Determined, Cella finished drying off and changed into a pair of sweats, black T-shirt, and sneakers. With Jai by her side, she returned to the kitchen. And again as she walked in, her family stopped whatever conversation they were having and stared at her.

"Where's the kid?" Cella asked.

"At the mall with Josie, using the gift cards she got for her birthday."

Perfect, but before Cella could continue, Aunt Kathleen asked, "Do you remember your cousin Pete? Lives in Atlantic City?"

"Cousin?" Jai softly asked.

"Fourth cousin, twice removed," Cella elaborated. "Yeah, I remember him. Why?"

"I still say—" Barb began, but Kathleen held up a finger, silencing Cella's mother. Much to Barb's annoyance.

"Stay out of this, Barbara Feeney."

"It's Malone now, even though you keep forgetting that."

And this was why Cella was convinced her mother deeply loved her dad. Because being a strong-willed female and marrying into this family? It better be love.

"He's got an RV dealership," Aunt Maureen explained around Barb and Kathleen's bickering. "Maybe we could all go down and visit him. Wouldn't that be nice?"

Cella and Jai glanced at each other, and Cella asked, "Go down there?"

"Sure. We can play the slots, maybe a little blackjack, and you can spend some time with Pete and the rest of the family."

"Aren't most of the AC Malones under federal indictment?" Butch asked, looking more annoyed by the conversation as every second passed.

"The feds don't have nothin'," Deirdre snipped, glowering at her brother.

"And do you really see Pete leaving his business and moving here?" Barb asked.

"A good girl would move there."

"If being a good girl's an actual requirement, doesn't that rule out all the Malone females?" Barb shot back.

"I don't see what the problem is," Deirdre said. "She's always wanted to leave. Being that she's too good for the family. So here's her chance."

"Do you really think I'd leave my kid?" Cella asked.

"You left her the first time," Deirdre tossed back. "And the second. And I think there was a third."

"Bitch!" Cella roared. She and Deirdre went for each other at the same time, her father and the aunts holding Deirdre back while Jai shoved Cella with her entire body toward the door.

"We'll be back," Jai called out over the yelling. She grabbed a set of keys for one of the family SUVs and continued to push Cella out the door and into the backyard.

"You should let me kick her ass for that last shot!"

"You promised," Jai reminded her before catching hold of Cella's arm and dragging her toward the car. "Besides, you cannot beat up an old woman."

"In the seventies that old woman was the Malone Bare Knuckles champ."

"Right. Which is also why you can't afford to be beaten up by her, either. Your fragile Malone ego would never get over that."

They stopped by a dark blue SUV. "She's just going to keep at me, Jai. She has nothing to lose because she didn't promise anything. But if I fight with her, I end up breaking my word, which a Malone never does . . . to one of our own, I'm not talking the general populace, of course."

"I know, hon."

"So what am I supposed to do?" Cella demanded.

"You're going to get on the phone and track down that bear. I'll drive."

"Okay," Cella said, when Jai pulled to a stop in front of a nice little house in Queens. "This is the address MacDermot gave me."

"It's cute."

"Whatever."

Jai put her hand on her friend's shoulder. "It'll be okay, Cella. I promise."

"She's just trying to get between me and my kid."

"And so far she's failed."

"Has she?"

"Hey, listen to me, Meghan loves you. She will always love you. And nothing Deirdre does will ever change that."

"If you believe that, why are you here with me?"

"Because I'm your wacky sidekick?"

"The wacky sidekick with advanced medical degrees who can repair arteries and heart valves?"

"You say tomato . . ." When Cella groaned and began to rub her temples, Jai reminded her, "You know this could be a lot worse."

"They're trying to match-make me with a cousin, Jai."

"Not a close cousin."

"That's not the point!"

Realizing she wouldn't calm Cella down with words, Jai pointed at the bear sitting in a chair on the front porch. "Is that him?"

"Yeah. That's him."

"He doesn't look that cranky." Cella had told Jai the bear was cranky. But he seemed rather pleased with himself sitting there. And he was handsome. A big boy with white hair and black eyes, a Rangers baseball hat sitting on his head.

"Well, he *is* cranky. So wish me luck."

Jai killed the engine and looked at her. "You want me to go with you?"

"Why else would you be here?"

"My knowledge of the Queens area?"

"Look, I've got one shot at this. So I'm asking you as a friend . . . don't let me blow it."

"Yeah, but are you going to be okay lying to your dad . . . ?"

"No, I hate doing that." Jai had no doubt that Cella adored her father and vice versa. Like Jai and her father, Cella was Butch's protégée and pride and joy. He loved his sons, but it was his daughter who could do no wrong.

"But," Cella went on, "once the kid's on her way to Israel with her dad, I can have it out with Deirdre, and I can tell Dad the truth. Trust me, it'll be easier to wrangle this difficult bear than it will be to get the family off this matchmaker thing now that they're all onboard."

Jai realized her friend was right. "All right. Let's go. Just remember . . . cool and calm." Two words most Malones didn't know. "You need this guy's help, so don't let him goad you into one of your 'moments.' "

Cella nodded. "I'll do my best."

That was all Jai could ask for.

They stepped out of the family's SUV and walked to the house, stopping at the bottom of the stairs.

"Hi," Cella said and gave a little wave.

The bear's head slowly turned, his black-eyed gaze focusing on them. With a lazy smile, he said, "Hi."

And that's when Jai saw Cella's entire body tighten—and not in a good way.

Cella's eyes narrowed. "How are you?" she asked, walking up one of the steps and resting her hand on the railing.

"I'm doing great. And you?"

"Good."

He took a deep breath like he was just enjoying the fresh Queens air this Sunday morning, his gaze looking around before he moved back to her. "So what can I do for you?"

When Cella didn't answer, Jai moved a little closer. "We need a favor."

"A little favor or a big favor?"

"Well . . ."

He swung long legs off the banister and rested his elbows on his knees. "Why don't you both come closer and tell me what you need? I'd be more than happy to help you out."

Jai took another step, but Cella swung out her free arm and placed it against the other rail, preventing Jai from going anywhere. She waited a second for her friend to get the message. Then Cella walked up the steps herself, stopping at the top.

"You seem in a better mood today," she observed.

He gave a little laugh. "I know. I know. I can be a dick sometimes. I try not to be, but I can't help myself. I just get so . . . uptight." He looked Cella over from head to toe and back again. "Maybe I just need something to relax me."

Before Cella could respond to that little bit of not-too-subtle innuendo, the bear's cell phone went off.

He growled a little, looked at the caller ID, and grimaced. "I gotta take this. Be right back."

He walked to the front door, but looked back at her before going in. "Don't go anywhere." With a wink, he stepped into the house and closed the door.

"Why are you so tense?" Jai asked her, following her up the steps until she reached the porch.

"I don't know."

"Well, stop it. You're going to put him off. I thought you wanted his help."

"I do but . . ."

"But . . . what?"

Cella shook her head. "I don't know. He's just acting weird."

"In what way?"

Cella almost laughed. That was so Jai. She loved to talk shit out. To analyze. Without any of the Malones realizing it at first, it was good to have the Davises as part of their family. They were the rational to the Malones' irrational.

"Look, the guy I met the last couple of times was a total uptight fussy-jeans. He looked like a mass murderer but underneath the scowl and barely tolerant nature was this . . . this . . . Boy Scout."

"And this guy?"

"Smiles too much and seems like the kind of Boy Scout who would help an old lady across the street so that he could chuck her back and let her get hit by a truck."

"Why don't you just say you don't know how to deal with a nice guy?"

"I know I don't know how to deal with a nice guy. That's why I've been torturing the man every time I've seen him. But I don't feel like torturing him at the moment. I feel like shooting him in the head."

"Do you ever have small emotions, Cella? Little ones? That don't involve either sex or death?"

"I'm a tiger. I'm either fucking or killing something. I can't be all sitting up in a tree, lounging like *you* people."

"Mountain lions don't just sit in trees and lounge. We're looking for our next meal."

"Hey."

Cella looked over at the far end of the porch. The bear, now without his Rangers hat and his hair combed off his face, stood on the outside of the banister, watching her and Jai.

"What are you doing?" Cella asked him.

"Enjoying the beauty of the day. And you?"

Cella glanced back at Jai and her friend gave a small shake of her head. She didn't like this anymore, either.

"Where's your hat?" Cella asked.

"My hat?"

"Yeah. The one you were wearing two minutes ago? *That* hat?"

"Oh. My hat. Yeah, uhhhh . . ."

The front door opened and the bear—you know, the one that had just come from around the house—walked out, offensive Rangers hat back in place, so that there were now *two* bears. Two exact copies.

"So . . . where were . . ." The second bear stopped, glanced over at the other end of the porch and the lookalike bear standing there. When he looked back at Cella and Jai, he grinned and said, "I can explain this—"

"What's going on?" another, more cranky voice, said from behind her.

Cella looked over her shoulder and she felt nothing but relief at seeing that searing scowl, those ancient jeans, and a goddamn *Islanders* hat on his head. The Rangers? Really? At least her bear understood loyalty.

"I said"—the bear she'd woken up naked with stepped closer, a bag of groceries in his hand—"what the hell's going on?"

"Can't we just come visit our brother?"

"Not and live to tell about it. No."

"Can you believe the way he treats us?" the one with the Rangers cap asked Cella. "Born just a few minutes apart and he never has any time for us. Isn't that unfair?"

"You never mentioned all that," Cella observed, "when you were pretending to *be* him."

Crush threw his bag of groceries down, his scowl turning worse, his big body vibrating. "*You're still doing that?*" he bellowed.

Cella laughed and walked up the stairs. She could feel Jai's hand swipe past her T-shirt, just missing her, as she made a wild grab to stop her.

"You guys," Cella teased. "Did you do that to a lot of girls? Pretending to be each other?"

"We were kids," the one with the hat explained, still grinning. "We didn't know any better."

"Well you know what?" Cella asked, stepping close to him. "I'm an adult. And I still don't know any better."

Then Cella punched the smug bastard in the face.

Crush only had a split second to laugh before Chazz was over the banister, landing on the porch. Crush shot up the stairs, ready to beat his brothers to death before he let either one hurt Malone. But Chazz grabbed a bleeding, roaring Gray and yanked him back.

"Dude," Chazz said, eyes wide, "I know her."

"What?"

"I know her. She plays on the Carnivores. That's . . . that's Bare Knuckles Malone." They both gazed at the She-tiger. "You were just hit in the face by fuckin' Cella Malone!"

Crush's eyes crossed. His brothers were such idiots. And how did Chazz know Malone on sight? Probably oozed his way into the team locker room, the bastard.

Chazz desperately searched the pockets of his jeans and

Windbreaker jacket until he pulled out a marker. "Could you sign my arm?" He held the marker out to her.

"My chest. Can you sign my chest?" Blood pouring down his face, Gray grinned at Chazz. "I can't wait for Marcie to see this."

"Marcie?"

"His wife," Crush explained to Malone. "Gray didn't mention her?"

Malone pointed an accusing finger at his brothers. "You were hitting on me while your *wife* was sitting at home, waiting for you to come back?"

Crush doubted all that.

"What she doesn't know . . ."

Malone pulled her fist back again, but Chazz held up his hands. "Wait, wait. Hit me."

Crush blinked. "You *want* her to hit you?"

"She's *Bare Knuckles Malone,* dude!"

Crush leaned forward and said next to Malone's ear, "Please tell me I wasn't this bad with your dad."

"You were, but you were really adorable about it. This is just annoying."

"Wait a minute." Gray stood straight, swiping blood from his nose. "What is *she* doing here with"—his brother eyed him with contempt—"*you*?"

"I'm his girlfriend," Malone said.

Crush sighed. "Are we here again?"

"Don't start."

"You?" Gray and Chazz said together. "*You*?"

"You're dating Marcella Malone?" And Chazz didn't bother to hide his disgust. "How is that even possible?"

"What the fuck is that supposed to mean?"

"We thought you were still a virgin."

Crush went to hit Gray, but Malone stepped in front of him, managing to hold him back without doing much of anything.

Wanting his brothers to go, Crush asked, "Don't you have

wives and children to get home to? I'd hate to think you're only making *me* miserable today."

Gray smirked. "Aren't you going to ask why we're here?"

"I know why you're here and you can tell her no."

"We all know she doesn't take no for an answer."

"That, and the eventual liver damage she's well on her way to experiencing, is not my fuckin' problem. Now get out."

Chazz threw up his hands and started to walk around them, but Gray snatched the marker from him and asked Malone, "Do you think I can still get your—"

Malone slapped the marker from Gray's hand. His brother jerked back and Crush caught the feline's arms before she could start slapping the crap out of him in front of the whole neighborhood.

Laughing, Gray followed Chazz. Crush watched until his brothers got in their truck and drove off. Then he went back down the porch stairs, picked up his groceries, and headed into his house—closing the door behind him.

CHAPTER TEN

Cella followed Crush, but stopped when the door closed in her face.

Gasping, "Oh, no, he did not!"

"Cella—" Jai began, but Cella didn't want to hear it.

The bear hadn't locked the door, so Cella threw it open and marched inside.

"What are you mad at me for?" she demanded, following the bear into his tidy kitchen.

Placing his bag of groceries on the table, the bear said, "I didn't say I was mad at you. Just don't want you in my house."

"Well . . ." Cella stopped talking. What had she just seen? She spun on her heel and walked back through, meeting up with Jai in the middle of the bear's living room.

Together the friends studied the area, gazes moving around until Jai observed, "I've never in my life seen so much hockey stuff in one place that wasn't a museum or your father's closet."

Jai wasn't kidding, either. There were framed and signed jerseys from what Cella assumed were the bear's favorite players, including her dad; someone's signed skates; a glass case with signed pucks; and framed signed sticks, crossed, on his wall.

"It seems," Jai went on, "that he favors the Islanders, Philly Flyers, and the Carnivores."

"I knew he was a fan, but . . . wow."

"At least he didn't ask you to punch him in the face."

"It seems he's a fan of my team, not of me. According to him, I fight too much."

"You do fight too much," he called from the kitchen.

Cella's right eye twitched, but Jai caught her arm, held her in place. "Cella . . . remember. Calm. Rational. You need him."

Cella went back to the kitchen, Jai behind her. The bear was unpacking his grocery bag. Cella folded her arms across her chest, and asked, "So why don't you want me in your house?"

"Because I can just look at you and tell that you're trouble."

"*I'm* trouble? It wasn't my brothers softly threatening me with some unknown 'she.' And you gonna tell me about that?"

"What would make you think I'd tell you anything at all?"

Cella opened her mouth to say something rude, but Jai cut her off.

"Calm down. Let's discuss this."

Cella rolled her eyes. "Discuss this? Really?"

"I have two words for you, Malone," Jai reminded her, "matchmaker and cousin."

Realizing she was right, Cella pulled out a chair and dropped into it.

The bear eyed them both. "Matchmaker?"

Jai shrugged. "Like I said, we need a favor."

"What kind of favor? Does it involve money? Gambling debts?"

Annoyed—again!—Cella slammed her hands on the table

and went to stand, but Jai shoved her back down by pushing on her head. "Sit!"

"I'm not a dog!"

"Do as I say." Jai faced the bear again. "I know you two have a history but we, *I*, have a big favor to ask."

"Let me guess. This involves her father and him thinking I'm her boyfriend?"

"Well—"

"I told you that was going to be a problem," he told Cella. "You don't listen, do you?"

"Look—"

"She doesn't," Jai quickly cut in. "She's a determined, unreasonable female, and she desperately needs your help."

"Jai!"

"Quiet, difficult female!"

Cella and Jai scowled at each other until, at the same moment, they both burst out laughing. Cella was not surprised when she heard the bear sigh.

While the two females found reasons to laugh, Crush finished putting away his groceries and put down food for Lola. That was around the time the laughter stopped.

"You have a dog?"

"I'm fostering for a friend." He whistled and Lola came out of the hiding place she always went to whenever his idiot brothers broke into his home. It used to be his apartment, now it was his house.

Lola trotted into the kitchen, but commenced to barking as soon as she saw Malone and her friend.

The two women looked at him and he shrugged. "She's not a cat-friendly dog."

"You foster this dog?"

He didn't know why Malone sounded so disbelieving. Bears had pet dogs all the time.

"Yeah. You have a problem with that?"

Lola continued to bark, so Crush said, "Cut it." She did and trotted over to him, turning and sitting down on his foot while facing the two felines.

Malone and the other woman exchanged another glance and Malone said, "This is your dog."

"She's a foster. That's all."

"Uh-huh. How long have you fostered her?"

"Three years."

The felines began laughing again and Lola snarled at them. That was his girl.

"What?" he asked.

"She's your dog. *Your* dog. No one fosters a dog for three years."

"It's hard to place her."

"A purebred English bulldog?" the woman with Malone kindly asked. Unlike the She-tiger, this woman had basic manners.

"I don't have papers or anything and she's been fixed."

"No one has shown interest in it?"

" 'It' is a *her*," he snapped at Malone. "And there have been a few interested people but they weren't the right family for her."

"For three years?"

"Why are you here?" he barked, fed up with this line of questioning.

"I need a boyfriend or my aunts are bringing in a matchmaker so they can possibly hook me up with a distant relative."

With a snort, Crush picked up Lola and put her in front of her food bowl.

"What's that mean?" Malone asked.

"It means you're insane. I thought you just acted crazy for the crowd. But no"—he faced Malone, briefly studied her pretty face—"you're really crazy."

"Crazy's relative," the woman with Malone remarked. When Crush only stared at her, she smiled and added, "I should introduce myself. I'm Jai Davis."

Crush tipped his head to the side and studied her. "Jai Davis? Head of the medical team for the Carnivores?"

"You know the head of our medical team?"

He shrugged at Malone's question. "They mention her at the beginning of every game."

"Wow," Malone said, eyes wide. "You really *are* a fan."

"Why are you here?" he barked again, annoyed with having strangers in his house. "In my space?"

"I'll tell ya what ya can do with your space—"

"Cella."

Hearing her friend's voice, Malone took a deep breath and said, "I need a favor."

"From me?"

"Yes. From you."

Crush sized the feline up before answering, "No."

"No? What do you mean no?"

"I mean no."

"But I haven't even told you what it is yet."

"I know. But I don't deal with crazy in my private life."

Malone crossed her arms in front of her chest, gold eyes locked on him until she snapped at her friend, "And you can stop laughing."

Her hand over her mouth, Dr. Davis choked and mumbled, "Excuse me," before quickly walking out of the kitchen.

"Thank you very much, cop, for embarrassing me!"

Crush gawked down at the feline, mouth open.

"What are you looking at me like that for?"

"*I* embarrassed *you*? Is that what you just said to me?"

"Your point?"

"You've been embarrassing me since I met you. It's like your goal or something."

"My goal is to get you to loosen up. You're so uptight."

"Why do you care if I'm uptight or not?"

"Because I'm a caring and giving person."

Imitating her stance, Crush crossed his arms over his chest and stared down at her.

Finally, after a couple of minutes, she finally admitted, "All right, fine. In truth, I just like how your face gets all red when I embarrass you."

"Honesty. How nice of you to finally use some."

"If it makes you feel any better, I only torment those I actually like."

"Why would that bit of information make me feel better? That's like saying 'I only set fire to the ones I love.' "

"It's nothing like that. I just think you take yourself too seriously. Although, after meeting your brothers, I can see why you're more tense than most polar bears."

"Tenser."

"What?"

"It's not 'more tense,' it's 'tenser.' "

"Really? You're correcting my grammar?"

Frustrated again—because she was kind of right—Crush snapped, "It's not like I invited you over here to abuse you about your grammar. You came over uninvited."

"Because I need your help."

"In some wacky scheme?"

"Of course it's not wacky. I just need you to pretend to be my boyfriend so my aunts don't bring in a matchmaker in the hopes of getting me married off to my cousin."

As the feline stated her purpose in coming to his house, Dr. Davis walked back into the kitchen. But she took one look at Crush's flabbergasted expression, covered her mouth, turned, and ran out again, her laughter floating in from his dining room.

"You really think that's a reasonable request, don't you?" the bear asked her.

"Define reasonable."

"Not crazy?"

"What do you mean by crazy?"

The bear rubbed his eyes with both hands and Cella marveled at the size of them. Although the way his biceps bulged kind of pulled her away from his hands.

"Why are you staring at me like that?"

Realizing he was now watching her, Cella answered honestly, "You're kinda hot."

"Is this your way of seducing me into doing what you want?"

"No, I only seduce for fucking. But for you to pretend to be my boyfriend, I was going to offer access to the owners' box for the rest of the season. But in this particular instance, I was actually doing neither. Simply noting your hotness."

"Okay. But you are willing to bribe me into being your boyfriend. Something a cop always loves to hear."

"It's not like I'm trying to bribe you into doing something illegal. *That* would be wrong."

Jai stood in the doorway again, but after a moment of wide-eyed staring, she shook her head and said, "I'll wait in the dining room for you, Cella, because I . . . I . . . I just can't." She burst out laughing and again walked away.

"How do you get rational, well-respected people involved in your insanity? I mean is it something you taught yourself to do or is it part of your sociopathic nature?"

"First off, I'm not a sociopath. I looked closely at that checklist and I'm in the clear."

"Checklist? You mean the Robert D. Hare Psychopathy Checklist?"

"I don't know. It was online."

"But being a sociopath was such a concern for you that you felt the need to check it out online?"

"Once, but I'm in the clear. So you gonna help me or not?"

He leaned in and said, "Not."

"So you're just going to make me *have* to beat up an old woman?"

Startled, the bear stood tall again. "When did beating up old people come into play? How is that an option?"

"I didn't say that was an option. She's just going to make me do it."

"You're blaming the potential victim of your elder abuse?"

"First off—"

"Again with the first off?"

"—she's only 'elder' in the strictest sense."

"You mean by actually being old?"

"And second, I'm the one being abused."

"And you get there how?"

"Because she's the one who's going to challenge me to a bare-knuckle brawl when I refuse to marry my cousin just so she can ruin my relationship with my kid."

"So if anyone comes up to you and says, 'I challenge you to a brawl,' you just have to do it? Is that how this works?"

"No. Of course not." Jeez. Where did the bear get his crazy ideas? "But if my aunt *officially* challenges me to a brawl, I have to say yes or lose respect among the Malones."

The bear placed the palms of his hands against his eyes and again rubbed them. "Why?" he finally asked.

"Because that's how Malones settle things."

"But that's not normal."

"Define normal."

"Not *you*!" He dropped his hands, black eyes scowling. "Your world of brawling with old people is not normal. Verifying from the psychopath checklist that you're not a psychopath is not normal. Coming to my house on a random Sunday to bribe me to be your boyfriend is not normal!"

"You wouldn't be my boyfriend, just my *pretend* boyfriend."

Roaring, the bear suddenly picked Cella up, tossing her over his shoulder.

"Hey! What the hell?"

Ignoring her, he stalked through his house until he went out on his porch and down his steps. There, on his lawn, is where he dumped her.

Crush walked back into his house and slammed the front door, locking it. Then he stalked back to his kitchen and stood there for a moment to get his raging annoyance under control before he walked back into his dining room.

Dr. Davis still sat at his dining room table, all calm and controlled. He could see the mountain lion side of her, watchful but not panicked.

He sat down across from her. "I'm sorry about—"

"No apologies, please. We did come here uninvited."

"I just don't know how to . . . she's just so . . . my life is usually so . . ."

"I get it. Your life is quiet and normal and Cella is anything but."

"Actually, up until about two weeks ago, my life was kind of a nightmare. Until my recent transfer, I was undercover. Every day that I woke up, I didn't know if I'd see the end of it. Would they realize I'd tapped their phones? Did they have a cousin that maybe I'd previously arrested? Would they find out I had photographed them dealing? But all that seems less of a challenge compared to her."

"So in other words when you come home you like peace and quiet?"

"I don't know. I will say that I'd like to come home and *not* see someone beating up on the elderly."

The doctor laughed, gold eyes bright. "I understand that, which is what Cella wants, too. She'd really rather not get into it with her aunt. But Deirdre doesn't make it easy on her or anyone."

"This is going to sound really wrong but . . ."

"Why am I friends with her?"

"You two couldn't be more different. Unless I'm missing something."

"You're not missing anything. We're both felines, but when she shifts she's four hundred pounds and nearly nine feet long from nose to tail. I'm one hundred and fifty pounds and not even seven feet. She's loud, I'm skulky. She loves to attack from behind. I'm known to pounce from overhead."

"But you're friends."

"Because I know that no matter what happens, Cella Malone always has my back. Always."

"And you think I'm being a prick."

"No! Not at all. I mean, from the outside looking in to the world of Malones . . . complete and utter craziness."

"But . . . ?"

"But think of it this way. You get a couple of free dinners, your brothers could—accidentally, of course—see you hanging around Cella Malone and maybe the Marauder since she's the *only* one on the team who can tolerate being around that man. You'll get a chance to spend time with Butch Malone, and he does like you."

"He does? Really?" Then Crush realized what a complete geeky loser he sounded like and lowered his voice several octaves to say, "Oh. Yeah. That's nice."

Dr. Davis smiled, but didn't openly make fun of him. "And what's most important to me—you can help make a girl's life a little bit easier for the next four weeks or so."

"The five-year-old?"

"I promise you Meghan is eighteen as of two-oh-three this morning. She's an amazing girl who wants to be a doctor and always feels the need to smooth things over between her mother and the Malone aunts. I can assure you the aunts do not make it easy."

"They give Malone a hard time?"

"Not always, but one in particular . . . Cella's tried, very hard, to find her own way in life. But her Aunt Deirdre fears her effect on Meghan."

"But Meghan is Malone's daughter."

"Exactly. Of course, Meghan's kind of my daughter, too. And my daughter, Josie, is kind of Cella's."

"And so you always have Malone's back?"

"Always. If you want, you can think of it this way: You do this and you're helping *me* out. Because if Cella gets into it with her aunt, she'll come to me to complain, and I'll be up all night listening to her rant. And then what if I'm not a hundred percent with my job? On the day that the Marauder is playing? Gasp!"

"That's extortion, Dr. Davis." Crush laughed.

Her smile . . . gorgeous. "You're absolutely right. But think about it. You'll be helping out your favorite team, keeping them safe."

"Low, Dr. Davis. That's very low."

"Due to my smaller size, I have to be able to fight a little dirtier than the bigger cats."

"Dirtier and a lot smarter."

"We have no choice when the Pride lions are running around calling us house cats."

Crush blew out a breath. "Something tells me this might be the stupidest thing I'll ever agree to do."

"Really, Detective Crushek? Because something tells me . . . this will be the best thing that's happened to you in a very long time."

Cella sat in the SUV, waiting for Jai to come out. That big, bastard bear was probably asking *her* out. All that class and education compared to Cella's complete lack of both.

She briefly wondered if she could get away with just lying to her aunts until after the wedding. It would probably work with all of her aunts *but* Deirdre.

A knock at the driver's window made Cella jump a little, but finding Crush standing outside her car door just confused her. She rolled down the window. "Hi."

"Hi." When he stood there, not speaking, she tentatively asked, "Is there something you need?"

"A promise. Two, actually."

"Pretend we never met?"

He smiled and she had to admit—he had a really handsome smile. "No. I just need to know that when we're done with your crazy scheme, the world will think you broke up with me."

"To protect *my* fine reputation?"

"You mean your reputation as a brawler and homicidal maniac? Yeah . . . not really my concern."

"Oh."

"But I don't want Nice Guy Malone thinking I broke his daughter's heart. Can you promise me that?"

"I can definitely promise you that. And the second?"

"That if you ever see me reaching for a Jell-O shot again, you'll take me out like you did that goalie in last month's game against the Utah Sinners."

Laughing and cringing at the same time—she really took that goalie *out*—Cella nodded. "If it gets you to help me . . . you've got it."

"Then I'm in."

Unable to help herself, Cella asked, "So you'll be my pretend boyfriend?"

"Yes."

"Will we have pretend sex? What about pretend children?" She pressed her hands to her chest and happily sighed, "How about a pretend dog?"

"Leave Lola out of this and don't freak me out." He stood tall—really, *really* tall. "So when do we start this?"

Cella grimaced and admitted, "Tonight."

"Tonight?"

The passenger door opened up and Jai slipped into the seat as Cella explained to Crush, "Kid's birthday dinner. Please?"

He looked off, blew out a breath, then finally nodded.

"Yeah, all right. I'll follow you. Just let me take Lola to my next-door neighbor's and then I'll be ready to go. Oh, unless I need to dress up?"

"The only parties Malones dress up for are wakes and weddings."

"I don't think I'd consider a wake an actual party."

"It depends on who died."

He shook his head, refusing to respond to that. "Let me take care of Lola before I change my mind about all this."

"You can bring Lola if you want," Cella offered, feeling pretty impressed with herself for doing so.

Crushek stopped, looked at her. "You want me to bring my fifty-pound dog—"

"Thought it was a foster?"

"—to a predator-only birthday party?"

Cella blinked. "Well, when you put it like that . . ."

With another sigh, the bear headed back to his house and dog.

"He had a point about bringing the dog," Jai murmured, finally closing her door.

Cella shrugged. "Yeah, I kind of realized that once I said it. But by then the words were already out of my mouth. . . ."

CHAPTER ELEVEN

Cella and Jai had returned to the house with the bear following behind in his own truck. As soon as they'd walked in, her aunts descended on him. But they'd barely gotten out their prying, annoying questions before Nice Guy came to the rescue, pulling Crush away and out back to meet with the rest of the uncles, male cousins, and her father's old hockey buddies.

And that had been four hours ago. She hadn't been able to speak to him except to ask if he needed salt for his steak and did he want more potato salad. He seemed to be doing okay, although it was really hard to tell. The man so rarely smiled and around her dad he just looked sort of . . . terrified. Terrified he'd end up making a fool of himself in front of his hero players. Poor thing.

But Cella kept her eye on him, just in case he looked particularly miserable. As she peeked in on him through the kitchen window, he still didn't look too bad, so she went back to washing the dishes.

"Okay," her mother said from behind her, putting more plates in the sink. "I take it back."

"Take what back?"

"That bears have no purpose on this planet other than to annoy me. That Mr. Crushek is very cute."

Cella chuckled. "You are such a bigot, Ma."

"Of course, I'm not. I just think cats are better than everyone else. Doesn't make me a bigot. It makes me a realist." She kissed Cella's cheek. "You holding up all right?" she whispered.

"Yeah. But she's pushing me."

Deirdre had been in rare form the entire evening. Lots of jokes at Cella's expense, always under the guise of "just kidding" or "Isn't she adorable when she's fucking up?" But Cella knew better. The woman wanted to make her look bad in front of Crushek, and in front of Meghan. And any other time, Cella would go toe-to-toe with the witch, but not this time. Instead, Cella sucked it up, smiled, and found reasons to walk away. For the first time at any family party, Cella spent more time in the kitchen helping with food and doing the dishes than she did outside with her uncles, father, and godfathers.

Kathleen walked in through the sliding door, more dishes in her hands. "I'll get one of your cousins to take over here," she promised, placing the plates in the sink. "Go spend more time with your girl."

"Did Bri leave yet?"

"No. He was giving that bear the third degree for a while, but now he's avoiding your brothers."

"I told them to lay off Bri."

"They don't know how. But Pauline's taking care of it."

"Great. Thanks."

Kathleen stood on the other side of Cella. "He seems like a very nice boy."

"Bri?"

"No, idiot. The bear. I have to admit, I was a little put off when he first walked in. I haven't seen a scowl like that since my grandfather died. But he's very sweet."

"He is."

"And he doesn't know what to do with you."

"Who does?"

Kathleen relaxed against the counter, her arms crossed over her chest. "He doesn't have any family except those brothers, eh?"

"Nope."

"Heard you already punched one."

"He was pretending to be him. It was rude."

"Don't worry. I think he liked when you did that anyway." Kathleen patted her shoulder and whispered in Cella's ear, "That's the kind of man you want, Cella Malone."

"Any more ice?" one of her brothers yelled from the yard.

Cella rinsed soap off her hands and dried them. "In the outside freezer. I'll get it."

"Hurry up," another cousin told her. "We're putting out the cake."

"Yeah, yeah. I'll be right there."

Cella went out the side entrance to the open garage door and to one of the two big freezers. She was reaching for a bag of premade ice when the cold air around her shifted and she caught a scent. Cella lifted her head, took another sniff.

She went to the standing safe she kept at the far end of the garage, punched in the combination, and pulled open the heavy steel door. She took out a .45 and quickly added the silencer. A sound behind her had her spinning around, weapon raised, both hands clasped around the grip. But when she saw Crush, she lowered it.

He came close, whispered in her ear, "Bears, about a block away. No one I recognize. Are they Group?"

"Trust me, everyone in the Group knows not to come to my street uninvited. And there are no bears in a ten-mile radius of any Malone property."

Crushek shook his head. "Then I don't like it."

Making sure the silencer was on tight, Cella said, "Let's go check it out before my family gets involved."

She motioned to the other side of the street and he followed her out of the garage. Crushek had had a holstered gun clipped to the back of his jeans when he'd gotten in his car, but she hadn't had a problem with that. Being armed was just smart planning now that he was playing in her side of the pool. Besides, every Malone eighteen or older knew how to use a rifle. When questioned, they said it was because they went on hunting trips. But Malones didn't hunt. Not like that anyway. Yet they always had rifles in their homes. That was just the way of things.

Moving down the street, Crushek raised his hand and, with two fingers, signaled for her to go around the other side of the cars and SUVs that lined both sides of her block.

They could see a black Range Rover parked at the head of the block and it wasn't one of the Malone vehicles. Again, she raised her weapon, as did Crushek, but as they got close, Cella saw her Uncle Ennis come out of his house. He'd left the party a few minutes earlier to round up some of his homemade wine. And behind him were six of his sons, Cella's cousins.

Cella reached out and grabbed Crush's arm, pulling him back. When he looked at her, she shook her head. He scowled in question, not understanding. But these were interlopers on Malone territory and they would be handled by the Malone men.

Uncle Ennis's gold eyes locked on her and with a tilt of his head he motioned to the Range Rover. Cella shook her head. They weren't friends of hers or Crushek's.

He nodded and motioned to his sons. They disappeared off the porch and into the dark, melding into the snow and ice-covered trees and buildings. Moving silently, quickly—and with baseball bats. They didn't shift for this sort of thing. They never had.

Ennis's oldest, Derek, smashed the passenger side window and his younger brother, Bobby, took care of the driver's side. Ennis's youngest, who wasn't even twenty yet, leaped onto the roof, unleashed his claws, and tore at the metal, ripping it open. A couple more of her cousins destroyed the windshield while Derek and Bobby dragged out the front seat occupants and their younger brothers pulled out the ones in the backseat. They were all bears. Big, dangerous, but stupid. Stupid to come here.

Bobby slammed the head of the one he'd pulled from the driver's seat onto the hood of the vehicle, making sure to press it into the shattered windshield glass. And there he held him while his brothers battered the other occupants with baseball bats and two-by-fours. They also kicked and stomped until the outsiders were nothing but bloody messes that were still breathing. Then, while the bears were shoved back into their vehicle, Bobby leaned in and whispered something to the driver. When he was done, he yanked the bear up and shoved him into the driver's seat.

Cella's cousins stood back and watched the Range Rover drive off; then a couple of them gathered up the blood-covered weapons and went about getting rid of them.

Removing the silencer from her weapon, Cella said to Crushek, "Come on. They're about to bring out the cake."

"Happy Birthday" was sung, the cake was cut, and a barely used Jeep with a bright green ribbon around it was given. All in all, a good night, and yet no one mentioned the fact that four men had been severely beaten. Everyone knew, but no one seemed to have an issue with it. It was just sort of . . . accepted. Apparently, that's what anyone who came on this street uninvited could expect.

And yet Crush couldn't get all "By the Book" Crushek on the Malones about it because he knew those bears didn't just happen to be in the wrong place at the wrong time. Why they were here, however, he still didn't know. Had they come for him? Planning to pick him up once he'd left Cella's house? Maybe. Or had BPC—and those bears were definitely BPC—locked on Malone's family for some reason? Crush didn't know. What he did know, however, was that he didn't like it, which was why he didn't care that all of those attacking tiger males had moved like one, well-trained unit, proving they'd done this many times before; he didn't care that Malone had a most likely unregistered .45 in her garage—although that silencer was a little worrying, but she'd probably got that from the She-wolf. What he did care about was that those bears were in Cella's neighborhood. With her and Dr. Davis's daughters and all those cubs. Kids being around, the elderly, these were little things that didn't mean shit to BPC, or more specifically, Peg Baissier.

Now he sat on the front porch steps of Butch Malone's house and watched the street. He couldn't help himself. He felt like he'd brought BPC here.

"Detective?"

Crushek looked up into Meghan's gold-and-green eyes. "Off to drive the new car?"

She snorted. "Not my idea." She glanced back at the cousins waiting for her. "Figure we'll go get a shake or something to shut them up."

"Hope you had a good birthday."

She was quiet for a moment and he realized she was thinking about what he'd said before she finally replied, "Yes. I did."

Wow, mother and daughter couldn't be less alike. He saw that now. He also understood what Malone had been talking about. He didn't like to say it, didn't like to think it. But her Aunt Deirdre was a bitch. She saw Malone as a threat. She'd probably spent years trying to make her feel unimportant. When that didn't work, she'd tried to make the rest of the family feel that way about Malone instead.

But from what Crush could tell . . . that hadn't worked, either.

"I'm here! I'm here!" Josie Davis came running around the corner and over to the car.

"Here." Meghan threw the keys at her friend. "She likes to drive more than I do," she explained when Crush only stared at her.

"Just like your mother."

"Me?"

"Yeah. She never does anything anyone would expect of her, either."

Her head dropped, but he saw the smile, the bit of pride.

"It was really nice meeting you, Detective," she said.

"You, too."

She started to walk away, but she stopped, glanced back at him, and whispered, "And thank you. Seriously."

Wondering if she knew about the war between her mother and great-aunt, Crush just watched her head over to the Jeep, her cousins yelling for Meghan to "get a move on!"

"I swear," Malone said, dropping down next to him on the stoop. "She's really my kid."

"Believe it or not, I can tell."

"You really came through for me tonight. Thank you."

"I have to say, Malone, it was really hard. To spend *hours* with Nice Guy Malone, Destruction Anderson, and six-time V.I.P. winner Please End It Ferguson was really, *really* hard on me and I'm not sure I can ever forgive you."

Her smile wide, "Destruction promised you a jersey, didn't he?"

"*Yesss.*"

She laughed, bumping his arm with her shoulder. "I have to say you made the night for these guys. You know, it's not like they'll ever be in the Hockey Hall of Fame with all the full-human players; you're not going to find videos of them or their pics and trophies memorialized in Madison Square Garden. But it's fans like you that make it all worth it."

"I tried not to be geeky about it. I made sure not to ask any of them to punch me in the face."

"That's probably a good idea 'cause they probably would have hit you."

"Oh."

"So are you busy next Saturday?"

Crush leaned in and whispered in case any of her aunts were around, "Is that the wedding?" Dr. Davis had mentioned he'd be needed for a wedding. God, the things he did to protect his favorite team.

"No," she whispered back, "that's at the end of the month. I'm talking about the Ice Party next Saturday."

"Ice Party?"

"Yeah," she said, her voice back to normal. "Ice Party. You've been, right?"

"No."

Her mouth dropped open. "How can you be a polar and not have gone to the annual Ice Party?"

"Luck?"

"Well, you can come with me."

"I agreed to a birthday party and a wedding."

"Those are requirements to prevent me from beating up the old woman."

"Stop saying that."

"But the Ice Party will be a blast. You gotta come."

"No thanks. Islanders game." He looked at his watch. "I better go. First real day of work tomorrow."

"Good luck and be careful. I honestly don't think those bears were here for me or mine."

And he knew she was probably right.

Cella watched the bear head toward his truck. Tommy came out of the house and stood behind her.

"You want me to follow him?"

"Just make sure he gets home okay. I'm not sure who those guys were that Ennis and the boys dealt with."

"No problem."

"Bring Kevin or Liam with you."

Her brother nodded and walked off, and Cella went back into the house to help her family finish the cleanup.

But before she returned to the backyard, she pulled out her phone and speed-dialed a number.

"Yeah?"

"Smith. It's Malone. We may have a bigger problem than we realized with BCP."

CHAPTER TWELVE

Knowing she had a busy day ahead, Cella woke up early. She took a quick shower and dressed. Once done, she pulled up the leg of her sweatpants so she could tape up her knee, deciding not to think too much about how it already hurt when she hadn't even worked out yet.

She was just finishing when her daughter walked in. There was a knock first, but barely. It was more like one fluid movement. Kind of a knock-open thing.

"Morning, baby."

"What's going on?" Meghan asked, closing the door behind her.

"Be specific. You know I hate vagueness."

"Fine. So you want me to believe you're actually dating that bear?"

"I am for the time being," Cella muttered, pulling down her pants leg.

"I don't see what the big deal is, Ma. Cousin Petey has an RV dealership."

Cella's head snapped up, her hands curling into fists.

After a moment of mutual staring, Meghan laughed. "I'm only kidding."

Letting out a breath, Cella fell back on the bed. "Do not do that to me!"

"Sorry. Didn't mean to give you a heart attack so early in the day."

"Just don't get caught up in this craziness."

"I don't mind the craziness."

"How can you not?"

"If it bothers you so much, Ma, how come you get caught up in it?"

"I'm trapped by circumstance, baby. You're not."

"And poor Detective Crushek?"

"He's . . . being a very good guy."

"He *is* a good guy. So be nice to him."

"Why do you say it like that?"

"Because he's a thoughtful, calm, well-spoken nice guy—that's not really your type."

"Maybe I'm going a different way this time."

Meghan laughed. "Yeah. Right, Ma."

Cella stood, took a couple of steps to make sure she'd taped her knee up right, then went to her dresser and picked up her brush. She could see her daughter in the mirror, standing by the door, her hand on the doorknob.

"Now what's wrong?" Cella asked, facing Meg.

"Have you told him about what you do?"

"No problem there. He's a huge fan. Not of me, but at least of your grandfather."

"No. Not hockey." Hand still on the door, she turned her body toward her mother. "Your other job. Does he know about that?"

"He's a cop, baby. It shouldn't be a problem."

"Shouldn't be and aren't are two different things, Ma. He's like proper town sheriff and you're covert ops. He may not be okay with that."

"That's not my problem. I just wish you didn't have such an issue with what I do."

"I just worry about you. But then I remember . . . you're the best, right?"

"Yeah," Cella answered honestly. "I am."

Crush sat at his new desk, at his new job, at his new precinct. And he was bored. Really, really bored.

Was this to be his life? Sitting around? Waiting. Even MacDermot hadn't come in yet. Apparently she had flexible hours. *Must be nice.*

It seemed their being partners wasn't a done deal yet. It was—get this—"up to MacDermot."

Up to MacDermot? She got to make the decision whether they'd be partners? And yet she hadn't?

Crush didn't know whether to be disgusted or hurt. Just two more years until he hit his twenty years . . . would he make it? He didn't know anymore. A month ago, he would have thought he'd make it to his thirty years before even *thinking* about retirement. At least. But now. Sitting here?

"Hey!"

Crush looked up. MacDermot stood across from him. Smiling. Holding coffee. Having worked with MacDermot in the past, he didn't remember her being much of a cheery person before noon. *Someone got laid this morning.*

"Here." She placed a large Starbucks coffee on his desk. "Your hair looks good. Now . . . you busy?"

He looked around to emphasize he was just sitting here, then looked back at MacDermot. He didn't say anything. The beauty of MacDermot? Apparently he didn't have to say anything.

"Then come on." She walked off and Crush sighed, picked up his coffee, and followed.

Cella put on her practice clothes and headed out to the rink. If any of the rookies showed up for the coaching she'd offered, she figured she could work with them for a couple of hours, then get in her own practice before heading out to meet her mom in Midtown for her first meeting with Blayne and her whole gang of wedding trouble. Getting Cella's mom hadn't been as hard as Cella had feared once she told Barb it was the fiancée of the very wealthy Novikov who needed her help, then her mom was all over it. Still, with the involvement of a grizzly sow and an O'Neill She-lion, Cella felt she should at least go for the initial meeting. But, first, practice.

But when Cella walked out onto the ice, she stopped, her mouth dropping open a little. She'd expected the rookies, and even then only one or two. Most of the guys had day jobs, getting their extra training in when they showed up for practice during the week. But all the rookies were there, and the second string. About twelve guys in all.

Reed skated over to her. "There might be more tomorrow."

"More?"

He shrugged. "I only told a couple of guys, but the information spread pretty fast. Sorry."

"No, no. It's okay. I'm just surprised."

"You shouldn't be." Skating backward, he winked at her. "Well, tell us what to do, Coach."

Figuring she could still meet her mom, but that her own training would have to wait, Cella motioned the rest of the guys over.

"Let's go. We've got a lot of work to do."

Dez MacDermot knocked on the door again.

Okay, so maybe working regularly with Lou Crushek wasn't the best idea for her. Gentry had been pushing it since Dez's last two partners had transferred back to their old units. According to the first one, Jerry the fox, the reason he'd left was, "MacDermot is fuckin' crazy. I wouldn't work with her again if you put a gun to my head." Seemed a little bit of an extreme reaction to one bad incident involving a rocket launcher. Everybody got out alive, didn't they? So what, exactly, was the problem? And she'd always felt she'd work best with the canines, yet they didn't follow orders the way well-trained dogs did.

Then there was Joanie the cheetah, whom Dez left alone with Cella and Dee-Ann in an interrogation room while she went to get a soda. Gone from the room ten minutes, tops. But by the time she got back, Cella had the cheetah pinned to the floor, basically throttling her with those always-bruised fists, while Dee-Ann was going through Joanie's purse for no other reason than, "Just curious what a cat keeps in a purse."

Needless to say, Joanie ran back to her old precinct.

So Gentry had once again brought up Crushek. "He's a bear. You've worked with him before. He's a bear. Smith and Malone can't just pin him to the ground, nor does he carry a purse because he's a bear. . . ."

And it had sounded very reasonable to Dez. Hey. She was flexible. After living with a man who sported a mane and a constant sense of entitlement, Dez felt certain she'd do great with a bear. Based on what she'd seen on Animal Planet documentaries, they were real easy to get along with as long as you didn't leave food lying around and didn't startle any females with cubs.

Now, however, Dez was starting to think she'd been wrong about all that. Or, at the very least, she shouldn't have assumed that grizzlies and polars were just different-colored versions of each other. Because, man, was Crushek a cranky asshole!

"Are we just going to keep standing here and knocking?" he suddenly demanded, making Dez grit her teeth. It was the trick she'd learned in the Marines so that she didn't pull her gun on people who irritated the shit out of her. "We have a warrant," he needlessly reminded her.

"Yes," she replied, trying not hiss like Cella sometimes did. "But maybe you haven't realized where we are—"

"You mean Staten Island?"

"Yes," she said again. "A street in Staten Island populated completely by bears."

"Is that why you brought me? Figure I could make things easier for you with the bears?"

"That is not why I brought you along, but can you just let me handle it?"

"Whatever."

Deciding to get away from him, Dez said, "You stay here. I'll go around the back."

"Fine."

Dez waited until she'd pulled open the back gate before rolling her eyes to the sky. Who knew one flippin' bear could be so damn difficult? God, how did Conway manage to put up with Crushek for so long?

She walked to the back door and banged on it with her gloved fist. While she waited a moment, she readjusted her Kevlar vest. Honestly, they didn't even try to make these things for women with tits bigger than a B-cup, something Dez hadn't been since she was thirteen.

The door opened a bit, a woman peeking around it, eyes squinting at Dez. "Yeah?"

"Mrs. Martin?"

"Yeah?"

"Detective Dez MacDermot. We have a warrant to search your house."

"This ain't a good time right now."

"Warrant, ma'am. Doesn't need to be a good time for you. Just open the door or it'll be torn off its hinges."

"By you?"

"Not me, because I would just set it *on fire*."

The woman sniffed and pulled the door open, standing to

her full height. God, she was at least six-four. Definitely a She-bear.

"Is it just you?" the woman asked.

"Why do you ask?"

"Just curious if I'm going to have a bunch of ham-handed cops tromping through my house."

Dez peered at the woman for several seconds. Moving slowly, she placed her hand on the gun in her holster and took several steps back and to the side. "Please step out of the house, Mrs. Martin."

"Why?"

With her right, Dez gripped her weapon; with her left, she dropped the warrant paperwork. "Because I told you to get your ass out here."

Grinning, the sow took a step out of her house. "Or what, full-human?"

Using her right hand, Dez raised her gun, pointing it at the sow's head.

"You better be a very good shot, Detective."

"I'm one of the best. But I wouldn't waste the bullets."

Dez pulled the trigger on the bear mace she held in her left hand, hitting the sow in her sensitive nose. Screaming and cursing, the sow covered her face. Dez shoved her gun back in its holster and pulled out her baton. She flicked her wrist, the baton extending to its full length, and swung at the sow's knees. Something cracked and the sow dropped, still screaming, definitely still cursing.

Dez was reaching for her titanium cuffs when she heard the roar. Mace raised, she spun toward the male grizzly running at her from the other side of the house. She wanted him to be closer before she hit the trigger, but he didn't even get ten feet within range before the boar went flying, shoved off his feet by Crushek.

"Go to your gun!" he barked.

She dropped the mace and again reached for her weapon. A Smith & Wesson .44 Magnum with custom grip that took her six months to qualify on. She'd just started to turn, hearing the heavy footsteps running up behind her, when Crushek wrapped his hand around her head and yanked her behind him. She heard shots ring out. Other than Crushek taking a couple of stumbling steps back, he was silent.

The footsteps were now moving away from them and Dez went around Crushek. "Are you okay?"

The polar jerked his shoulder. "Just hit the vest. Come on." He started off.

"I need to cuff her."

Crushek raised his hand and slapped the grizzly sow's back between her shoulder blades. She'd been trying to get to her feet, but she went back down, out cold.

Shrugging, Dez ran after Crushek as he stalked across the Martins' yard. He walked to the detached garage, stopping at the wood door. He lifted his arms chest height, palms out, and rammed them forward. The door snapped off its hinges, careening inside, and Crushek went in after it.

Both hands on her weapon, Dez followed the bear inside. The big garage door was open and the inside was empty except for a piece-of-shit Chevy.

"We follow?" she asked about the bear they could see running off down the street.

Crushek didn't answer. He simply lifted his head and sniffed the air. Following his nose, he moved to the car. Sniffed around it. With a little snarl, he gripped the car under the front grille, raised it, and flipped it up and off, knocking it out of the garage.

Trying really hard not to be impressed, Dez walked over. The pair of them stared down at the metal door built into the floor. Crushek reached down, gripped the ring, and tugged. Twice.

He motioned Dez away with a jerk of his head and stood right next to the door. He sort of jumped forward and down, big hands ramming into that metal door, power coming from those shoulders and arms. Mouth dropping open, Dez took another quick look around to make sure they were still alone, then watched the polar hammering away at that solid metal door, over and over until it bent and buckled under him. Off the hinges, the door fell into the open hole and Crush stared into the darkness.

He lifted his gaze to hers and Dez now jerked her head. "Go."

Crushek jumped down while Dez stayed put, her gun still up, finger on the trigger. A few minutes later, Crushek came back up, a little canister in his hand.

"What's that?"

He shrugged, lifting the top. Sniffed it and frowned. Then he stuck the tip of his pinky into the contents and brought it to his mouth. He tasted it, dark eyes rising to meet hers.

"Well?" she asked.

"Honey."

Dez couldn't help gasping, annoyed. "They tried to kill us for honey?"

Crushek grinned, something she wasn't sure she remembered ever seeing before. "Honey infused with *cocaine*."

"Dude . . . that's so many levels of wrong."

Then they laughed and Dez suddenly felt that maybe they could make this work, after all.

CHAPTER THIRTEEN

After a great session with everyone who'd shown up, Cella had been forced to take another shower. No way did she want to hear her mother complain about Cella "stinking like a damn male." Now, back in her sweatpants, T-shirt, sneakers, and a hoodie sweatshirt, Cella jogged up the stairs and out the main front doors, ignoring all the full-human males checking her out. Men who could never handle her.

"Cella!"

She smiled and ran toward the waiting cab. She got in and slammed the door. "Van Holtz Steak House on Fifth," she told the cabbie before settling in next to her mother. "I see you have your power suit on."

It was a black suit that made her mother's gold eyes pop and gave her that air of total control. A control the woman always seemed to have—except when it came to her husband's family.

"So what's the skinny minny?"

Cella chuckled, marveling at how the woman was able to refresh her lipstick in a wildly moving taxi. "I'm glad you wore your suit. You're going to need it. Although, you may have wanted to add a little body armor."

"My sweetest girl, you still don't have faith in your dear old ma?"

"I always have faith, Ma. But I know the players in this and you're in for a battle, I think."

"We'll see. I'm just here to help."

Cella looked at the coat her mother had on. "Aren't you hot in that?"

"I'm melting, but it is snowing, sweetie. Don't want to confuse the prey." Her mother's nickname for full-humans.

"Stop calling them that."

Barb dropped her lipstick into her giant purse and relaxed back into the seat, eyeing her daughter.

"What?"

"You and that very handsome, but decidedly lumbering *bear*? Do you expect *me* to buy that lie, Cella Malone?"

"What did you expect me to do? Let her marry me off to my *cousin*?"

"Or you could stand up to the old bitches and tell them to leave you the fuck alone."

"Ma."

"What? You let them walk all over you yesterday when you're usually the one to beat them down."

Remembering what the bear had said to her the night before, Cella replied, "I'm trying not to beat up old women."

"I don't mean physically, you idiot. You just never let them push you around. But yesterday . . . you ran off and came back with that cop."

"I'm just trying to keep the peace."

"And the bear?"

"The bear just happened to be in the right place at the right time. Would you rather it had been a wolf?"

Barb shuddered. "It's bad enough you spend time around that pit bull."

Cella chuckled, shook her head. "That pit bull has my back. God, you're as bad as Meg about Dee."

"She has crazy eyes."

"Why don't you just tell me the problem with the Smiths? Because that's your issue, isn't it? Any other wolf is tolerable, but not the Smiths?"

"Do you know anyone who likes the Smiths?"

"Do you know anyone who likes the Malones?"

"We're cats. We're naturally adored and very low maintenance. Dogs need all that care, training, and long walks, or you have to call in that Dog Whisperer guy for help."

Cella laughed out loud, her mother joining her.

The cab stopped and Barb paid the driver while Cella got out. She waited at the corner for her mother. Once Barb stood in front of her, Cella asked, "You're sure you're ready for this?"

"This is what I do, baby."

With a nod, Cella took her mother's arm and they walked into the restaurant.

The hostess smiled at them even while sizing up Cella's casual outfit. The Van Holtz chain was one of those snooty restaurants that the Malones didn't really go to unless, of course, it was a very special occasion or someone else was paying. Mostly because, by nature, the Malones were hagglers and the Van Holtzes really weren't. But, it was one of the best shifter-run restaurants around. They had a wild boar with mushroom sauce that was to die for.

"Hi. We're here to meet with Thorpe and—"

"Ah, yes." The hostess began to laugh before grabbing a couple of menus. "Right this way." And she walked off . . . still laughing.

After frowning at each other, mother and daughter followed the hostess through the restaurant and down to a row of private rooms. She stopped at a set of double doors and opened them. Luckily, she was a fellow shifter, a wolf, which allowed her to step back before she got hit with someone's purse. The hundred-dollar Chanel knockoff slammed into the opposite wall and landed on the floor. It was gold-colored. A She-lion's purse. Some Prides could afford the real thing, some couldn't, and some weren't willing to pay for the real thing. That was the O'Neills.

With a sweep of her arm, the hostess invited Cella and Barb in.

Cella picked up the big gold purse and handed it to her mother. "Good luck to ya," she said, then went the other way, looking for a lunch that didn't involve wedding plans or arguing She-predators.

Crush dragged the She-bear out of the back of their van and into the precinct elevator with MacDermot.

"Shut up!" MacDermot snarled, and he didn't blame her. The sow had not stopped roaring and complaining for the last hour. She was probably just coming down from whatever high she'd been on, but Crush, and he was sure Mac-Dermot, didn't care.

"You fuckin' bitch," the sow screamed-slurred. "You fuckin' bitch whore!"

The elevator stopped at the fifth floor, where the sow would be booked and put in a titanium cell. At the very least, they'd be done with her.

"What about her sons?" Crush asked when they arrived at booking, where another sow was manning the desk. "I say we go back out and track them down."

"I'm up for that."

"You stay away from my boys! Stay away from my boys!"

"*Shut upppp!*" MacDermot yelled, making Crush chuckle. The woman had no patience for screamers. She never did.

Crush's phone went off as two uniforms took the sow from him. "Hey," he told MacDermot. "We got a text from Gentry. She wants us back upstairs."

"Okay." MacDermot finished the paperwork the sergeant at the desk needed to book the sow.

MacDermot had just pushed the clipboard across the

desk when the sergeant snapped at the uniformed officers, "Don't uncuff her here—"

But it was too late. The sow spun around, free of her bonds. Facing MacDermot, she swung her big fist and sent the full-human flying out of the room.

Shocked, everyone stood there staring, even the sow. Then, just as Crush was about to panic, thinking about what he could possibly tell MacDermot's husband at the funeral that would explain this, a bellowed, "*You fucking cunt whore!*" from the hallway reminded Lou Crushek that Bronx girls didn't go down easy.

Cella ended up eating her lunch in the restaurant kitchen with Ric Van Holtz. It never hurt to suck up to the boss and get a duo of wild boar and impala with that damn mushroom sauce in the bargain.

"So how's it going with the rookies?" he asked before picking up the giant burger sitting in front of him for his own lunch.

"Not bad. And not one fight this morning."

"No bleachers thrown then?" Van Holtz bit into the burger, his eyes closing. He groaned. After swallowing, he pointed at the burger. "Amazing," he whispered. Then more loudly snapped, "I thought I said I wanted this well done?"

A young wolf, his arms and hands wet and covered in bubbles, stuck his head in from the other room. "You said medium rare."

"No. I said well done. Get it right next time."

"Okay, okay. I'm sorry. Jeez."

The kid disappeared back to his regular job and Van Holtz went back to his burger.

"My cousin Stein," Van Holtz explained, like that told her why he was being such a ballbuster.

"You're ridiculous," Cella told him. "I *heard* you say medium rare."

"Ssssh." Van Holtz looked at that doorway. "I have a strategy, Miss Malone."

"The 'I'm a douche' strategy?"

"You break them down first so you can build them back up."

"And when does that building begin?"

"Whenever I say it does."

Cella laughed. "You're worse than my dad. Of his four children, I'm the only one who could handle his idea of training."

"And look at you now."

"The reality is I had it easier than the boys because I was daddy's little princess."

Van Holtz frowned. "You? Really?"

"What d'ya gotta say it like that for?" She pointed at herself. "Don't I look like a fuckin' princess to you?"

"In what world," Smith's voice said from behind Cella, "are you a princess?"

Damn Smith, sneaking up on her again. How did she do that? "In the same world that Smiths are considered upstanding and law-abiding citizens rather than backwoods crazies."

"Sassy talker."

"Psychopath."

Smith walked over to Van Holtz's side, pressing up against him. "You in here chattin' up my man, Malone?"

"Well, it's about time he had a woman with some curves."

"Don't most just call that back fat?"

"No brawling," Van Holtz quickly warned them when Cella pulled her fist back and Smith went for that damn bowie knife she kept holstered to the back of her jeans.

Once it seemed that he'd diverted any fights in his precious kitchen, Van Holtz asked Smith, "You want something to eat?"

"Later maybe."

"Where have you been?" Cella asked, cutting another piece of meat. "I called you earlier."

"Yeah, sorry. I was checking in with the people MacDermot put on surveillance detail for us."

"They get anything?"

"Nope. But I did pull some favors and get video footage from stores in a one-block radius of the taxidermist. Printed a few pics." Smith pulled out a manila envelope and took out several photographs. "Anybody look familiar to you?"

Handing his half-eaten burger to his mate—the man never took Smith's "I'll eat later" seriously—Van Holtz looked through the photos, sliding each one across the table to Cella when he was done. After several moments, he retrieved one of the photos he'd passed to Cella, studying it a little more. "This man . . . Do we know him?"

"I don't." Having finished Van Holtz's burger, Smith was now working on his plate of fries. "But before I came here, I showed these pics to the surveillance team. They pointed him out, too. Said he met with the taxidermist, but never in his store. Always met him a block away. I told them if he comes back, to put someone on him."

"We should touch base with MacDermot, too." Cella pushed her empty plate away. "She'll want in on this if it turns out to be something."

"I called Gentry," Smith said. "She'll send MacDermot to meet us at the office later. Although, I do wonder why we never go to your office, Malone."

"Do we need to get something done?" Cella demanded. "Because that won't happen if we're at the KZS office. It's like twenty of me instead of just one."

"And just one of you is terrifying enough."

"Cella!" her mother called from somewhere in the restaurant.

"In here, Ma!"

"Is there a Malone that don't yell?" Smith asked.

"Is there a Smith that don't lick its ass?"

"Don't be jealous of those who got the talent and dexterity."

"You'd be amazed at my dexterity."

"Malone, are you sweet on me? And here in front of my mate and everything."

Cella's eyes crossed and she turned in time to see her mother strut her way into the kitchen.

"I assume, Ma, from your sexy walk that all went well?"

"Why do these people question me? When it comes to weddings"—she held her hand out—"by this claw, I rule."

"She," Smith muttered, "is so your momma."

Trying not to laugh, Cella said, "Ma, you remember Dee-Ann."

"I do?"

Cella scratched her head and tried harder not to laugh. "You've met her four, five, maybe ten times."

"Huh."

"But you do remember Ric Van—"

"Of course, I do!" Because vast wealth always managed to jog her mother's feline memory. "Good to meet you again, Mr. Van Holtz," she said, shaking his hand.

"Ric, Mrs. Malone. Call me Ric."

She gave her best "think of me whenever you're shopping for a wedding planner" smile, then turned back to Cella. "Was the double wedding your idea?"

"Anything to reduce the pain potential."

"Double wedding?" Van Holtz asked. "Blayne and Gwen together?"

Knowing exactly where this was going, Cella held up her hand and quickly rattled off, "You'd have to go to Novikov's wedding anyway 'cause of Blayne and he'd be at Gwen and Lock's wedding, also because of Blayne. This way the torture is all condensed to one day, so shut up and stop complaining."

Van Holtz snarled a little, but didn't bother to argue.

Barb kissed Cella's cheek. "Just like your ma. Now," she went on, "can we head home together?"

"Can't. Gotta work tonight."

"You'll be careful?"

"I'm always careful. I can't risk this pretty face, can I?"

Smith snorted while Barb dug into her bag and pulled out one of her cards, handing it to Van Holtz. "In case you're ever ready to settle down with a nice, *respectable* She-wolf of your own." Then she gave Smith another once-over before leaving without another word.

"Charmin'," Smith said, both she and Cella laughing.

"I can't even be mad at her," Cella admitted. "She's just so ridiculous sometimes."

"Other than beatin' the shit out of you on a regular basis—"

"You wish!"

"—I don't think I've ever done anything to her."

"That doesn't matter. Apparently, there's a Smith-Malone history that no one will talk about in my family."

"Really? Need to ask my daddy about that."

"Does your father actually speak, Smith? Words, I mean. Not just barks and howls at the moon."

Smith shrugged. "When he's of a mind . . ."

Whatever the hell that meant.

Chapter Fourteen

Michael Patrick Callahan tried to shift again, but whatever they'd shot him up with wouldn't let him shift back to human. It kept him lion. Kept him prey.

Panting, he stood behind a tree, watching and listening for the hunters. Their problem was that Mikey had overheard them. He knew that whatever they'd forced into his system would wear off and he'd be able to shift back to human again. But they didn't want that. Having a dead human body on their land was probably a bigger pain in the ass to manage than having a dead lion. And once Mikey knew that, once he knew the effect of this drug wouldn't last for several days or weeks, his goal became clear.

Avoidance.

The mistake a lot of people made was to believe true predators ran around challenging everyone, going claw-to-claw with anyone or anything that crossed their path. They didn't. From the proudest lion male to the lowliest, pain-in-the-ass hyena, a long-living predator always knew when to run and when to stand his or her ground.

And men with high-powered weapons fitted with silencers? You ran. Especially when Mikey didn't have access to his thumbs at the moment.

So for nearly four hours, he'd been running around this property. A property he didn't know anything about. He had no idea where he was. The last thing Mikey remembered was sitting in the back of a limo with a hot piece of ass he'd met at a club and receiving a phenomenal blow job. The next . . . it was late morning, he was a cat, and he was in a cage.

His mom and sisters had always warned him not to trust full-human women, but this time he'd let his hormones take over and now here he was. Hiding, running . . . and praying.

But Mikey was grateful for one thing. The Callahans. His family. They were lions, but not like any other Pride out there. In fact, other lions didn't even consider Callahans a Pride but a roving band of "gypsies," and that was fine. Because most lion males knew they were completely on their own should something happen; the Pride females would rarely bother to track down a lost male unless it was a much loved son. That wasn't the Callahans. Family was family to them and Mikey had no doubt his family would search for him—and God help those who'd taken him.

Yet that was something to think about later. Right now he needed to get out.

Mikey tensed. He could smell the full-humans nearing. Hear their footsteps as they tried to tiptoe through the trees.

He saw one. The clothes were expensive. That gun even more so.

Mikey tried to shift again. His body rippled. Soon. He'd be able to shift soon. But he'd run out of time.

The hunter swung toward him, weapon raised. Mikey charged past him, making sure to hit the man's body with his paw as he did. Ribs snapped, caving in on impact, the man falling backward, and Mikey kept going. He finally neared the tall, brick wall that surrounded this place. The full-humans that were hunting him were beginning to panic now that they realized he'd be able to shift to human any second now. It would be easy for him to get past the doors once he had thumbs, but at the moment Mikey still had to knock those doors down. Unfortunately, the few doors he'd found were solid, impenetrable steel.

That wall, Mikey was sure, had been built to keep his kind in. He could smell the other breeds that had run and died here. Had others made it out? If they had, were they killed later? Mikey knew that once he got out of here, just running back to his family would only put them in danger. He'd have to do something else, but he could worry about that later.

Mikey heard men yelling orders, could hear running. It was the men who guarded this place. They didn't hunt, not like the others. They simply prevented the shifters from getting out. Some had extremely powerful weapons and tranq guns. Knowing he'd have to work fast, Mikey moved behind the hedges and tried again. For several brief, wonderful seconds, his right claw turned into a hand. Mikey stopped, took a breath, tried again. Several guards in white, to blend with the snow-covered grounds, came into view. They hunted in threes now; this was no longer a casual, fun thing for rich friends. They had to stop him.

What about when I get past that gate?

He couldn't worry about that now. One terrifying situation at a time.

Snow and ice cracked beneath boots, the men drawing near.

Mikey waited until they were close and he charged again. They heard him, all three turning and firing at the same time. Shots hit, tearing into his shoulders, but missing major arteries. Mikey kept coming, ramming into two at once, his four hundred and thirty pounds crushing them.

More screams rang out as Mikey turned and swung his claw, ripping across the third man's face. Then Mikey took his chance and shifted to human.

It took two tries, but it worked. He snatched the keys from the man closest to him and ran to the thick steel door built into the wall. He put the key in, turned the lock. Alarms sounded. Loud and powerful, an electronic voice announcing which door had been opened. Mikey ignored all that and shifted back to lion before racing out of the gate and onto the sidewalk.

Men were coming at him from behind and from both sides once he was out, so he charged straight forward, deciding to shift back to human once he was in the middle of the street because he knew that a naked, bleeding man would be much less terrifying to the general population than a bleeding lion. But as he ran across the asphalt, his body readying to change to his human form, something big and heavy plowed into him, lifting his entire body into the air. He spun up and back, feeling like he was flying, before he came spinning down to earth.

Mikey knew even before he landed that now he was completely screwed.

Sophie DiMarco hit the brakes on the stolen $140,000 Maserati, but it didn't help. She still collided and shoved forward that . . . that thing that had been hit by the delivery truck in front of her, sending it up and over and down until it landed right in her path.

And what exactly was that thing anyway?

Knowing she couldn't get out of the car and go look, Sophie shifted the Maserati into reverse, ready to make a run for it. But before she could floor it, the thing she'd hit stood. And it was . . . human. Big, blond, and golden, he looked around, dazed eyes trying to focus. Although being hit by the car she was driving should have killed him, he was still walking. Even more surprising when she saw the bullet holes riddling his body. Then she saw them. Men dressed alike, in white boots, white winter coats, and white fur hats. She'd guess they were guards or military or something.

She only had a split second to do something and Sophie, being almost naturally kind of difficult, did the most insane thing she could. She leaned over and pushed open the passenger door.

"Get in!" she screamed. "Now!"

The man looked at her, eyes blinking. Then he was running, his hand pressed to the side she'd rammed into.

"Hurry!"

The men weren't coming after them. They were raising their weapons and aiming. They were going to shoot them down on the street.

"Close the door," she ordered. "And hold on."

Sophie placed her right hand on the seat next to her and looked over her shoulder, hitting the gas. The perfectly engineered vehicle shot off, the sound of gunfire ringing from behind and ruining a perfectly good payday for her!

She tore down the street and turned at the first corner. She changed gears and spun the car around. More men were coming from behind big hedges that blocked the high brick wall behind it.

"In front of you," the man said.

She looked and saw a car driving straight for her. She recognized the fur hats of at least two guards sitting in the front seat.

"Shit." She hit the button to automatically lower the window and shifted gears once more, putting the Maserati back into reverse. "Hold on."

The car headed backward again. Guards ran into the street, under some delusion that she'd stop. She couldn't. At this point she was in too deep. And she'd prefer not to do time for stealing this car.

She pulled the .45 out of her holster and aimed out the window, shooting at the car still coming at her. She hit the other car's windshield, blood spurted, and the car swerved. Sophie brought her arm back, dropped the gun, and changed hands on the wheel. She shifted and spun the car, moving forward, other cars falling in behind her.

Tearing down the busy streets, she cut across boulevards, and used other cars as shields.

"No cops," she muttered, surprised she hadn't heard even one siren yet.

"There won't be cops until you clear . . . whatever town we're in," he told her.

Sophie smiled a little. "Good."

She kept moving, pushing, using every trick she'd ever learned or taught herself. Cars came at her from different directions, from alleys, behind other cars. She didn't let any of them stop her because she knew none of them could really keep up with her.

But there was one who kept trying. She knew she had to shake that one off if she hoped to get out of this. She went down an alley and around a truck parked outside a deli. She tore outside the other end of the alley and spun the wheel hard. She went a few feet up and hit another alley. She went halfway down that one and stopped behind a shoe store.

Sophie still had the window rolled down, so she listened and watched in the side mirror. Cars sped by, heading down the street. She only had a few minutes before they'd come back and do a street-by-street search.

"I'm bleeding all over your nice seats."

Yeah. He was, but how was that her problem?

With one more look at him, she opened the door and stepped out, abandoning the car. Such a shame, too. That car would have brought in some nice money.

Mikey wasn't surprised she bailed. Even though she had a set of keys, he could tell that she wasn't the owner of this car. Trying to get it out of wherever they were with a bleeding man sitting beside her was going to be impossible.

Honestly, Mikey was just glad he didn't have to worry about risking her life, too.

He did, however, briefly toy with the idea of getting in the driver's seat and driving out of here. She'd left the key in the ignition. But all he could do was stare at those keys, watching them sway.

He heard a car pull in and Mikey thought, *Here we go.*

His door opened and the girl leaned in. "Come on. I haven't got all day." She took his arm and pulled it over her shoulder, helping Mikey from the car.

She was strong, but definitely full-human. Together, they made it to a really nice late-model BMW with dark-tinted windows. She put him in the back, laying him out across the seat, and went to the driver's side. Within seconds, she had them back on the road.

"You know this town," Mikey said, lifting his hand to look at all the blood on it.

"I know every town."

Right. In case she had to make a run for it.

"I need you to take me into the City." Realizing he might not actually be in New York, he added, "Manhattan."

"Give me the address." She glanced back at him, smiled. "And don't worry. I'll get you home."

Except he wasn't going home. But that was okay. He just knew he wasn't going to die *there,* wherever "there" might have been. And at the moment, that meant everything to him.

CHAPTER FIFTEEN

"Look at me."

MacDermot lifted her head, one eye managing to open, the other swollen shut.

"What do you think?" she asked. "Think makeup will cover it?"

"Although I've always found lion males inherently stupid, I'm pretty sure that even Mace Llewellyn's gonna notice this."

"I was afraid of that."

Crush tipped her head back a bit with one hand and carefully placed the ice pack on the swollen side of her face with the other.

"Ow," she complained.

"You should have decked the bitch when you had the chance," he reminded her.

"Gentry hates when I do that."

Crush took her hand and placed it over the pack so she could hold it in place herself. Once he had her set, he sat down in the chair next to hers. "Why are we here?"

"Evil taxidermist."

"And how do we know he's evil?"

"Lots of reasons, but most important is the Smith sixth

sense in play. Any time Dee-Ann Smith says, 'Somethin' ain't right,' something is usually not right."

"This is my life now? Really? Listening to hillbilly She-wolves and their hillbilly gut reactions?"

"Her hillbilly gut reactions have saved my ass more than once. Suck it up."

"And Martin's sons?"

"Those idiots aren't going anywhere without their mother. We'll get them."

Before Crush could argue that point, the front doors to the Group offices opened and the hillbilly with the sensitive gut walked in. And right behind her was Ulrich Van Holtz. It was strange enough that the Carnivore goalie, known as The Gentleman, was also the owner and captain of the same team. That was normally unheard of. But the fact that Van Holtz was also in charge of the Manhattan division of the Group pretty much blew Crush's mind.

Then again, the Group's offices had completely confused him in general. He'd kind of expected either a back alley or, at the very least, a cold, sterile federal or state type office. Instead, the Group's office reminded Crush of those high-end advertising agencies with comfortable leather seats and fancy art on the brightly colored walls. Although, he could tell that was just the front of the building, the first place one saw. Watching staffers having to punch in codes to get into the next level reminded him this was nothing like an advertising agency.

"Sorry we're late," Van Holtz said when he walked into the reception area, but he stopped, eyes blinking wide as he gazed down at MacDermot.

"Desiree! What happened?"

"I'm okay. Really." She pulled the ice pack down. "You don't think this will freak Mace out too much, do you?"

Smith stepped past Van Holtz and studied the full-human's face for a moment. "Well . . . it was nice working with you."

MacDermot cringed, then immediately regretted making that face and quickly returned the ice pack to her face.

"He'll just have to understand," MacDermot muttered. "He'll have to get over it. I'm not giving up my job over one incident."

"A good number of those words . . . not in a cat's vocabulary, darlin'." Smith patted her shoulder. "I got something that can help with that swelling, though," the She-wolf offered, but MacDermot immediately pushed herself into Crush's side.

"You keep your wacky Southern voodoo away from me."

"Tennessee Smiths don't do voodoo, Desiree. We leave that to our Louisiana kin. Besides, it'll help."

"I don't care what you tell me it does, forget it, Dee. No way."

Smith looked them over and said, "Not sure you should be cuddling up to the bear that way, Desiree. Don't think Malone will like it much."

Crush looked around. "Wait . . . what?"

"I'm not cuddling up to anybody. I'm just avoiding you and your witchcraft. And why the hell would Cella care who I cuddle up with?"

"Heard they're together now. Ain't that right, bear?"

"It's not . . . it's just . . . it's kind of . . ." God! He'd known this was just going to be wacky! He hated wacky!

The She-wolf leaned down to see his face. "What's the matter, son? Cat got your tongue . . . and other parts?" she finished on a whisper.

Crush glared at the female, wondering how disgusted he'd be with himself if he slapped around a She-wolf for no other reason than she was getting on his nerves. But then he sensed something flying at him. He raised his arms to protect himself, but a feline landed in his lap, big grin on her face.

"Hi!"

Crush scowled at Malone. "You. You're making my life a misery!"

"What kind of reaction is that? How can you be my pretend boyfriend if you're going to be a dick all the time?"

"So you *are* Cella's boyfriend?" MacDermot asked.

"No. I am not."

"Pretend boyfriend," Malone corrected. "He's my *pretend* boyfriend."

"And what is that exactly?"

"It is what it sounds like."

" 'It is what it sounds like?' " MacDermot repeated back at her. "You mean ridiculous?"

"You know, I don't need the tone."

As frustrated as Crush, MacDermot lowered the ice pack to her lap and snapped, "You need something all right. Therapy . . . a real boyfriend. Something."

Malone's eyes grew wide at the sight of MacDermot's face. "God, Dez! What happened to your face?"

"An angry and high on cocaine-infused honey sow decked me."

Malone and the two wolves leaned in to get a closer look.

"You were hit in the face by a sow?" Malone asked. "Are you sure?"

"Of course, I'm sure. I know what came swinging at me and it was definitely her fist."

"But by a sow? I mean honestly, sweetie, you'd be better off getting hit by a building."

"And she was high?" Smith shook her head. "Damn, girl."

"It's really not that big a deal."

"Well, what did the doctor say?" Malone asked, showing real concern for once for someone other than herself. It was a nice change.

"I didn't go to the doctor."

Malone punched Crush's shoulder and . . . *ow.* "You didn't take her to the doctor?"

"I didn't need to go to the doctor," MacDermot cut in, getting defensive.

"You were unconscious and you didn't go to the doctor?"

"I wasn't unconscious. I didn't even black out."

Malone and the She-wolf blinked in surprise. "Wow," they both said together.

"Okay," MacDermot sighed. "Now you guys are just making fun of me."

"No, we're not. You were hit by a She-bear."

"And you're full-human."

"So?"

"Look, look at this." Malone pulled her cell phone out of her sweatpants pocket.

"Don't show her that," Smith nearly begged, her gaze moving up to the ceiling.

"Look what happened to this guy who had a run-in with a not-high, black bear sow . . . which is way smaller than a grizzly, and the grizzly who did this to you *was* startled."

MacDermot took one look at the picture, squealed, and quickly slapped the phone out of Malone's hand. "*What the fuck are you showing me that for?*"

Crush was kind of wondering the same thing.

He also wondered if all that bear talk had conjured up its own set of problems when the perky fox admin said from the front desk, "Mr. Van Holtz? There are two grizzlies outside. They're asking me to buzz them in."

"They're not ours?"

"No, sir."

MacDermot walked around to the other side of the admin's desk and looked at the fox's computer screen. With her one open eye, MacDermot studied whoever was at the front door. "Nope. They're not ours."

Van Holtz nodded. "Let them in, Charlene."

"Yes, sir."

He pointed at Malone and Smith. "And you two, don't start anything."

"Even if they deserve it?"

"Dee-Ann . . ."

The two grizzlies walked through the door, the taller one smiling at Van Holtz.

"Mr. Van Holtz?"

"Yes."

"Hello. I'm . . ." The grizzly caught sight of Crush, his words trailing off. Their gazes locked and clashed, and the grizzly's lip curled. He recognized Crush and not merely as a fellow bear.

Cella didn't know what she expected, but it wasn't for Crushek to suddenly stand up, place Cella on her feet, and then snarl at the grizzlies, "What? You got something to say?"

Suddenly all those proper bear manners went out the window and the grizzlies were moving toward the polar, and Crush was moving around Van Holtz, going head-to-head with these two assholes. But before any of that could happen, Smith stepped between them all, facing the grizzlies, one side of her mouth lifting into a slight and rather scary smile.

The grizzlies stopped, refusing to go any closer, not surprising considering Smith's past history with BPC.

"Why don't you gentlemen sit," Charlene, the admin, said, running over and offering chairs near the door, her smile wide. "Mr. Van Holtz has a meeting scheduled right now, but he'll be back as soon as he's done. Okay?" Without waiting for an answer, she offered, "Would you gentlemen like something to drink? Coffee, tea, or some honey?"

Smith sucked her tongue against her teeth. "That Charlene," she teasingly complained about the admin, "always ruinin' my fun."

Chapter Sixteen

They all headed toward Van Holtz's office, the BPC grizzlies left behind to seethe. As they came around the corner, Cella realized that Crush wasn't with them. She stopped and retraced her steps, finding the bear standing outside the game room where many of the Group's rescued hybrid teens hung out. He stood there, staring in and she stood next to him.

"You okay?" she asked when he didn't say anything. "What was the deal with those bears?"

"That was nothing." Crush pointed at the window and quickly changed the subject, which made her think whatever had happened between him and the grizzlies was not "nothing."

"Why are there kids here?" he asked.

It was his tone that made her concerned, but she still didn't know if that tone was due strictly to the BPC reps or not.

"Smith found them on the streets," Cella explained. "She brought them in."

"Why didn't she turn them over to CPS?"

"Child Services had most of them and lost them. All

these kids are runners. Dee-Ann"—she kind of hoped using the She-wolf's first name would loosen him up a bit—"was just trying to help out by bringing them in."

"Helping them or helping the Group? Are you people training them as agents?"

He sounded so accusatory, Cella felt her hackles go up.

"*I'm* not training them to do anything. At all. This is Dee's deal, not mine. I'm not even in the Group."

The bear faced her. "What do you mean you're not in the Group?"

"I mean I'm not in the Group."

"Then what the hell are you doing here?"

"Can't I just come to see you?" When his expression grew impossibly darker, she quickly said, "I'm kidding. I swear I'm kidding. I'm just here to represent KZS as per Van Holtz's request. So don't worry, I'm not stalking you if that's—"

"Wait," he cut in. "You're KZS?"

"Yeah. I didn't tell you that? I could have sworn I told you that."

"No. You never told me that."

"Oh." She shrugged. "Oops."

"Oops? That's all you can say?"

"What do you want me to say?"

"Nothing." He walked around her and headed off down the hall.

Cella followed Crush, catching up to him as he stood in the hallway trying to figure out the way to Van Holtz's office.

"Okay, what's the problem, Crushek?"

"You're in KZS."

"Yes. I just said that."

"So you're basically a well-trained assassin who can handle herself in any situation."

"There's no basically about it." When his eyes narrowed, she explained, "Look, you're either one of four things at KZS: management, administrative, clean-up, contractor. I'm a contractor." A good one, too, known for her long-distance taps.

But Cella could tell by the look on the bear's face that he was absolutely horrified about what she did, about who she was, and she felt really insulted by that!

"Oh, whatever." She brushed past him and headed to Van Holtz's office, the bear right behind her. She opened the door and stepped in, dropping into a seat on the far side of the room—away from all judgmental bears.

"Everything all right?" Van Holtz asked, his gaze moving back and forth between Cella and the bear.

When the pair did nothing more than nod, he went ahead and got started.

Crush was impressed with how things were run between the three organizations. They worked together, concentrated on each other's strengths rather than what they couldn't do, and helped to keep each group honest.

So Crush wasn't really surprised that BPC wasn't a part of this meeting. Peg Baissier, with her title of "Chief Technical Advisor" had been running BPC since 1762 . . . at least that's how it felt to Crush. And she was a sow who liked her control. She definitely didn't believe in sharing it. And to share anything with any other species besides bear she considered treachery. She didn't announce that last part to the tri-state bear populace she and her people were supposed to be protecting because lots of bears worked for lots of different people. But Crush knew for a fact that's what she believed.

He also knew she was an evil bitch, which was why he stayed away from her.

Yet Crush wasn't really thinking about Peg Baissier as he listened to, and approved of, what was being said around him. Instead, he found his gaze straying constantly over to Malone. She pretended to ignore him, but he knew he'd pissed her off. But he couldn't help it. He'd thought she was just some dingbat hockey player, not part of KZS. If she was KZS that meant she was trained in nearly every form of hand-to-hand combat, most weapons, and foreign languages and cultures. She would be well traveled and highly intelligent. And Crush knew this because KZS was the one organization that Baissier kept her distance from. She'd take them on if necessary, but it was never her favorite plan.

And yet, this woman, this *feline*, who said she was a KZS "contractor"—read "killer"—also said she needed Crush to be her "pretend boyfriend" because she couldn't seem to control her own elderly aunts that she might have to beat up?

Huh? What?

"Detective Crushek?"

Crush looked up, realizing that everyone was staring at him. "Yes?"

Van Holtz handed him a picture. "Do you know him?"

He took the picture, glanced at it, nodded. "Yep. I know him. You know him, too, MacDermot."

"I do?" MacDermot took the picture, glanced at it, and handed it back to Van Holtz. "Oh, yeah. Wow. He looks kind of different. Real cleaned up." She nodded. "Yeah. We know him."

The room fell silent until Malone barked, "And?"

"And what?"

Malone began to say something else, but the She-wolf placed her hand against her shoulder and Van Holtz asked, "And who is he?"

"Oh. Frankie Whitlan. Frankie the Rat. Frankie the Snitch. Frankie the Talker."

"Big Dick Frankie," Crush tossed in.

"Oh, my God," Malone said to Smith. "Now there are two of them."

Van Holtz raised his hand to calm the two females and said to Crush, "Detective, perhaps you can tell us something about this man. I assume he was some kind of informant."

"He was a scumbag."

"And a lot of cops used him. Some got their gold shields because of Frankie."

"So," Malone asked, "he's a scumbag because he ratted on his criminal friends?"

"No. He's a scumbag because he played both sides of the fence."

"Crushek's right. There were rumors that he only ratted out the guys in his way. Don't let his nicknames fool you. Frankie Whitlan was a murdering motherfucker. He ran a massive drug ring and I think gun running—"

"But he started in gambling. Was a leg breaker for bookies in the Bronx."

"Then ten years ago . . . gone."

"We figured either he'd been hit and dumped or—"

"Federal protection. The timing was interesting because we were trying to take him down for the murder of a stock market analyst and his entire family, including three kids. The rumor was he'd done it himself, which was rare because he usually had someone else do his killing for him."

"But if he's in federal protection, why is he back?" Smith asked. "Seems kind of stupid."

"Hard to leave the life. Lot of those mob guys find their way back to their old neighborhoods just because they miss their favorite pizza place."

"Yeah, but why is he hanging out with the taxidermist Smith found?" Malone asked. "He was missing his favorite taxidermist?"

Van Holtz nodded. "She has a point."

"Let me see what I can find out," Crush offered. "Some guys I know."

"Some guys you know . . . what?" Malone pushed.

"Some guys I know. Don't harass me."

"*Harass*—"

"All right then," Van Holtz cut in. "I think that's enough

for tonight. I'm sure Desiree would like to go home and take some much needed migraine meds."

"I appreciate that." MacDermot stood. "Because the worst part? I feel like I have to blow my nose. I can't express to you how that's the last thing I ever want to do."

"Come on, darlin'." Smith put her arm around MacDermot. "Let me get you home."

They all filed out into the hallway, Malone silently following Smith and MacDermot.

"I guess this is a little strange for you, isn't it, Detective?" Van Holtz asked as they walked back to the front office.

"Just new. I don't like change."

"I understand that. It was strange for Dez in the beginning, too."

He watched as MacDermot stopped in front of that big glass window Crush had looked through earlier, the one with all the kids behind it, and waved. After a few moments, a hybrid girl came out the door. She was a bear hybrid, probably mixed with canine. Nearly six-four, she had a very young face, but way more scars on her arms and neck than anyone that age should have.

Eyes wide, she gazed down at poor MacDermot's face. "What happened?"

"Nothing I can't handle," MacDermot teased. "Apparently, I'm tough like that." Laughing, the pair hugged, then the girl hugged Smith and finally Malone.

"How's it been going?" MacDermot asked the girl.

"Eh." Not exactly a ringing endorsement.

Finally, Crush knew he had to find out more about what was going on here. It was driving him nuts. "Who are these kids?" he asked Van Holtz, his voice low.

Crush thought there might be some backpedaling or bullshit. There wasn't.

"Hybrids," Van Holtz immediately replied. "They didn't have homes and it's hard for them to mainstream into full-human society, so we take them in. That's Hannah," he said, glancing at the bear hybrid. "She's been with us for a bit now." He leaned in, lowered his voice even more. "Dee-Ann and Blayne rescued her from a dogfighting ring."

Horrified the girl had been used that way, Crush still had to ask, "Did you recruit her?"

Van Holtz shook his head. "After what she and some of these other kids have been through? No. Although, they have the option to join us when they're twenty-one. But not before then. We're just giving them a place to crash, an education, and some options. Everyone deserves options."

"But shouldn't you be helping them mainstream?"

"Well—"

A good-sized shaggy-haired dog ran out into the hallway, spun in circles for several seconds, and shot off.

"That was Abby."

"Does she always run around as—"

"Yes. She also begs for food, scratches at the door to be let in or out, and snaps at flies, which is always entertaining. But we're working on her."

"Hey," Smith reminded them. "We left them BPC bears sittin' up front. Not sure we want little Abby around them."

Hannah sighed. Deeply. "I better go get her."

"If Abby gets on your nerves, Hannah, why do you watch out for her?" Van Holtz asked with a small smile.

"One word," she replied. "Blayne."

"Can't handle the sobbing?"

"Can you?"

The girl had a point. Crush knew he couldn't handle it.

Hannah started off, but Abby suddenly returned. Sliding into the middle of the hallway, she barked and barked, then ran back the way she'd come.

Knowing a panicked bark when he heard one, Crush didn't think twice before going after the girl and everyone else. But the naked, blood-covered male lion in the middle of the reception area did take him by surprise, though.

Cella stopped when she saw the naked, blood-covered male stretched out on the floor. Her gaze went to Charlene. "What the hell?

"He's been shot," Charlene told them. "A couple of times."

"Charlene," Van Holtz ordered, "call Dr. Hayes. He's probably on the medical floor."

Crouching on one side of the lion's body, with Smith on the other, Cella reached over and pushed his still-growing mane out of his face. "Oh, shit."

"You know him?" Smith asked.

"Mikey Callahan. His ma's gonna lose her mind."

Gold eyes opened and looked into Cella's face. "Cella."

"Baby boy, what happened?"

"Bad day."

"He's with KZS?" Smith asked.

"No. I'll explain later."

"He's been hunted," one of the grizzlies said.

Cella glanced up. She'd forgotten all about the BPC grizzlies. "How do you know that?"

He crouched beside her, pointed at Mikey's bicep. "Here you can see he was given a drug to keep him lion. Look at his neck. He was chained while human, then forced to shift."

"Forced?"

"While KZS and the Group have been going after pissant hybrid dogfights, the bears have been focusing on the real hunters going after real shifters. Their methods have improved."

"Not liking your tone, son," Smith warned. She had a real warm spot for the hybrids, although she'd never admit having a warm spot for anyone.

"Don't you?" He stood up, towering over Smith. "Well, that's not really the problem right now. Is it?"

"And what is the problem?"

The grizzly pointed across the room into a far corner. "She is."

As one, they all looked at the full-human girl standing in the corner. She was Italian American, Cella would guess. Pretty and young, wearing an old leather jacket with some bloodstains on one side and driving gloves. And, at the moment, just realizing she was in serious trouble.

Mikey's grip tightened on Cella's hand and she looked at him.

"She brought me here. She saved my life. You know what that means to us, Cella."

Mikey Callahan, like Cella, was another Traveller, although the Callahan Pride had lasted a little longer before they'd been asked to go their own way and leave Ireland. Loyalty was all to the Callahans, like it was to the Malones. If the girl had saved his life—and why would he lie when he was bleeding out onto the Group office floor?—then she had to be protected.

But before Cella could move, MacDermot stepped in front of the girl, her face swollen, but the Bronx attitude firmly in place.

"If I were you," MacDermot said to the tall grizzly, "I'd just walk away."

"I know you feel like you have some power here, full-human. But you don't. Just breeding one of us, doesn't make you one of us."

Charlene kneeled on the floor and placed Mikey's head in her lap. The fox was small compared to the rest of them, but she had a .45 holstered to the back of her skirt and when the fox nodded at her, Cella knew she'd watch out for him.

Standing, Cella and Smith slowly made their way around the room, closing in on the two grizzlies.

"I think you better go," MacDermot pushed.

"We'll go, but we're taking her with us. Since we can't trust you to do what needs to be done with her."

"You're not taking her anywhere."

He reached for MacDermot, his hand grabbing her jacket, but MacDermot already had her hand on her gun. Still, none of them actually expected little Abby to jump between the bear and MacDermot, barking and baring her teeth, biting at his wrist so he'd release MacDermot.

"Shit," Smith snarled, her bowie knife out, she and Cella moving fast. But before either could reach him, the bear casually kicked Abby out of the way. He knocked her into the chairs. The girl gave a surprised yelp.

They were all so focused on Abby that they didn't see Hannah until she rammed into the tall grizzly, knocking the bigger bear into the door. Smith went to help, but Cella caught her arm, holding her in place as Hannah battered the second bear with her forearm, hitting him across the chest and then up into his jaw.

Abby shifted to human and grabbed the bigger bear by his hair. She dragged him away from the door, ignoring his surprised roar of pain, and MacDermot leaped forward to help the pup, ramming her foot into the bear's knee.

The full-human girl, seeing her chance, charged out, barreling through the doors and into the freezing cold outside.

Smith looked down at Cella's hand and then at her. "Reason you did that?"

"Figured the girls could handle themselves."

The two bears got back to their feet and Abby shifted back to canine, running and hiding behind Cella. Poor thing, she never knew whether she should be escaping or fighting. Hannah, though, now blocked the door, giving the full-human girl more time to get away.

MacDermot placed her hand on the kid's forearm and tugged until Hannah moved to her side.

"I think you need to go," MacDermot said again to the grizzlies.

"Or what?"

She shrugged. "I'll let a naked girl beat you up again. Because *that* was funny."

One of the bears snarled, aggressively stepping into MacDermot, but then Crushek was there. He got between his partner and those bears, his hands slapping against the bigger grizzly's head and digging his claws into his face, the pair roaring at each other. Windows and furniture rattled; Group members poured into the room, guns raised. But they weren't needed because Crush yanked the big grizzly close, nearly tearing the other bear's face off in the process. "My partner said it was time for you to go." He pushed the bear into the second grizzly, sending both of them careening out the door, and roared, "*So go! Go run home to Mommy!*"

The grizzlies fled and Crushek stood between the two sets of doors, his back to them, chest heaving, hands now covered in grizzly blood.

The front office was completely silent, everyone staring. Which was when Smith leaned in and whispered to Cella, "You may want to take it down a notch, darlin'—your nipples are hard."

Cella brought her fist up, her knuckles colliding with Smith's nose, then she returned to Mikey Callahan's side.

CHAPTER SEVENTEEN

Crush sat at his kitchen table, chin resting on his raised fist, and stared across the room. He'd crossed a line. Not with his boss or even his own moral code. No, he knew he'd crossed a line with Peg Baissier. She'd always hated him, which seemed only fair since she was the one woman Crush openly admitted detesting. But Baissier was very protective of the BPC "brand." And what had happened to her "boys" tonight was not something she'd let go. Crush knew Baissier well enough to know that she'd never let this insult slide. Not her.

Yet she would never come at him directly. That was too easy. No, she'd find another way to get to him. Or, as she'd put it more than twenty years ago, she'd find a way to "make you hurt." Since he knew she wasn't one for idle threats, he felt pretty sure she'd make good on that promise. Especially now.

Still, Crush wasn't worried about himself too much. Not that he wanted to suffer or anything, but it was what it was. Yet there were others who had now crossed her, too. Mac-Dermot. Van Holtz, Smith, Malone. Even those two hybrid girls. They'd all unknowingly crossed a line with Baissier.

Crush had warned Van Holtz and Gentry, who'd shown up at the Group offices an hour after everything went down. They understood, and when he and MacDermot had left, they'd been meeting with Smith and Malone, and Van Holtz had promised to ensure the girls would be protected.

But Crush couldn't shake the feeling that . . .

He heard the knock at the front of his house, and Lola raised her head from the kitchen floor. She snarled and Crush stood, removing his .45 from its holster and heading to the door. But one sniff had him lowering his weapon and pulling the door open.

"It's you."

"Is that any way to talk to your pretend girlfriend?"

Rolling his eyes, the adrenaline practically pouring out of his body, Crush said, "You are *such* a strange feline."

"Tell me something I don't know." She lifted her hands. "You going to let me in or what?"

"It's late, Malone. And I'm just not in the mood to—"

"Great. Thanks." She pushed past him and walked into his house. Gritting his teeth, he followed her into his kitchen.

As soon as Malone stepped in, Lola barked at her, running around Malone and sitting down at Crush's feet. Still barking.

Crush reached down and picked up the fifty-pound dog. "I know, girl. I know. No one wants these nasty cats in their home. Worse than rats."

"I can't believe you buy into that canine-media propaganda."

"For someone so anti-dog, seems you're kind of close to them."

"Well, Smith and Van Holtz aren't like those *other* dogs. You know, they don't talk like 'em or strut like 'em. They're different."

"I'm becoming completely uncomfortable with the direction of this conversation," he said, ignoring her laughter.

Crush kissed Lola's head and walked into the kitchen, going right to the cabinet where he kept all her treats and taking out an extra-large bully stick.

"Here." He placed Lola on the floor with her treat. "I think you deserve this, baby-girl."

"Why don't you just accept that she's your dog?" Malone asked, dropping into one of the chairs around the kitchen table.

"She's a foster. One day I'll find her a nice family with kids."

"Why can't she just stay here with you?"

"No one for her to play with." Crush opened the refrigerator, glanced in, then closed the door again.

"You're restless," she observed.

"It's been an . . . interesting day."

"More like average for us."

"Great. Wonderful to hear. And good to know that I have more to look forward to. Next, I guess Gentry will ask me to . . ."

"Kill someone?"

Crush shoved his hands into the front pockets of his jeans and hunched his shoulders.

"Doubtful," she said. "Usually MacDermot's department is busy just cleaning up my mess and Smith's. And Smith and I sure are messy."

"Are you saying I'll have to clean up corpses?"

"Oh, God, no. We have specialists for that sort of thing. I just mean that you'll probably spend a lot of time keeping me and Smith out of prison."

"That's what I'm reduced to? Keeping you and your wolf friend out of prison?"

"Trust me. There will be more to it than that. In some ways our world is much more difficult than the full-humans'."

"I understand their world. It's easy. Dangerous, but easy."

Malone threw her legs up on the kitchen table like she owned the joint, crossing them at the ankles.

"So you want to tell me what's going on?"

"What do you mean?"

"Well, let's see. First off, you went after your two replicas—as I like to call your brothers—as if they were covered in whale blubber. And then those two grizzlies at the office—"

"They kicked a child, threatened my partner, and went after that full-human girl. What was I supposed to do? Just stand there?"

"First off—"

"Again with the first off?"

Malone scowled at him and Crush raised his hands, knowing he was snapping. "Sorry."

"First off, what happened at the meeting—totally righteous. But you challenged them *before* the meeting, too."

"So there's no 'second off'? You have all these first offs, but no second offs?"

Malone folded her hands over her stomach.

"What?"

"Are you going to keep playing this game to avoid telling me what's going on? Or are you just going to talk to me?"

"About what? Because something tells me you already know."

"That Baissier was your foster mother? That she had you quietly outed as a cop? Yeah. I know. But I still want to hear it from you."

Crush crossed his arms over his chest. He didn't think much about the fact that Malone knew all those details about his life. She was KZS, so it wasn't surprising. Instead, he did kind of wonder what it would be like to discuss this with someone other than himself or the dog. Usually he kept personal stuff . . . well . . . personal.

But the crazy woman before him had little room to judge when it came to personal drama, so perhaps talking to her would be better than nothing.

"In the eyes of the law, Baissier is a foster mother. But what she was really doing was recruiting. She only took in bears under the age of twelve. I was five by the time I held my first gun. A little .38. Could fight with knives by the time I was ten, and could tell you a whole lot of different ways to kill people by the time I was thirteen."

"That's why you asked about Hannah and the others."

"I knew if Van Holtz was recruiting kids, we'd have a problem."

"He's not. I promise. That is not happening. Smith—Dee-Ann—travels around. She's found the majority of these hybrid pups and cubs living on the streets. She brings them in, gives them food and a place to sleep. If they stay, Van Holtz makes sure they either go to school or get tutoring and Blayne helps with teaching them how to handle being two or more things at once."

"I get everybody else, but what's the deal with Abby?"

"Dee-Ann found Abby in an alley, eating out of a trash can. She's been with the Group for a while and she shifts only when she feels like it. And I can assure you no one has tried to recruit her to do anything except get her to use the ladies' room rather than going out back to pee . . . because we all find that really weird."

"You find *that* weird?"

"Yeah. Don't you?"

Ignoring her question, Crush said, "And Van Holtz said Hannah was rescued from dogfights?"

"She was. I was surprised they didn't just put her down."

"They didn't pick her up at the pound, Malone."

"No, but she's been through a lot. More than most could ever hope to handle. You just don't snap back from that."

"But do you really think being around people like Smith and you is good for her?"

"Good for her? I've been nothing but nice to that girl."

"I'm not talking about how nice you've been. I'm talking about the influence on a damaged young woman by hanging around a KZS killer and some backwoods hillbilly hit-wolf."

"I'm a contractor!"

"I don't care."

"And it's not like Smith and I sit around, telling tales to Hannah about who we've taken out over the years. All we've ever tried to be for that girl is a support system."

"Not everyone's made out for this life, Malone."

"I absolutely know that. My Meghan's not. Neither is Josie. They're both going to be doctors. And Hannah can be anything she wants. I know for a fact that Mace Llewellyn offered to pay for her and Abby to go to any school they like, anywhere in the world. And maybe she will. Maybe she'll go to college. Become an engineer. A scientist. A very strong forward," she finished on a mumble.

"A strong . . ." Disgusted, he took a step back from the heartless feline. "Oh, Malone!"

"*What?* We're talking opportunities here. That's all. Besides . . . did you see how she handled those grizzlies?"

"You're recruiting!"

"For hockey!" Then she calmly added, "God's game."

"You really call hockey God's game?"

"All Malones call it God's game. Because it *is*."

The bear blew out a breath. "I think I'll let this go now."

"I would." Because Cella had her mind made up.

"So how's the lion male?" he asked.

"Better. Docs took care of him and once he's ready, the Group will move him to a safe house. And my uncles have already gone to the Callahans to let them know."

"Your uncles? Why not KZS?"

"The Malones are closer to the Callahans than KZS will ever be. We understand them and we can get on their territory without being shot at."

"I always thought tigers and lions didn't get along."

"We don't. But even you can tell we're not your typical tigers. And the Callahans aren't your typical lions. You won't be seeing them trading their males around like used cars. That's not their way."

Studying her, he guessed, "I have a lot to learn about your family, don't I?"

"You could say that. But not tonight. I'm not up for that."

"Fair enough. But maybe you can tell me what happened to the lion?"

"That grizzly was an asshole, but he was right. Mikey had been hunted. Unfortunately, he has no idea where he was, but he said he was like in some kind of animal reserve. A local one. And since the bears scared off that girl who helped him, I don't know when we'll be able to track the place down."

Crush stepped closer, his hands still in his pockets. "I know why MacDermot and I let her go, but why did you?"

"For lots of reasons, but mostly because Mikey asked me to. She saved his life and that deserves our loyalty."

"You're not worried she'll say something?"

"To who? I mean who'd believe her? Not anyone who could really hurt us."

"You have a point. Besides, she can't talk even if she wants to."

"And why's that?"

Crushek grinned. "She's a car thief. A really good one. Only takes high end. Has specific clients."

"You know her."

"I know a couple of dealers who've hired her for special requests. She's also a driver. She's been involved in a few heists, but being a car thief is her true love. She's been doing it full-time since she was sixteen."

"You know her," Cella repeated. "But you won't ever tell anyone who she is . . . will you?"

The bear shrugged, smiled. "I can't risk the information getting back to BPC. Plus, she protected one of our kind—for that she deserves our loyalty. Right?"

Okay, so the bear was judgmental, uptight, and so straitlaced it made her laugh, but he was smart, brave, and wicked fast. And loyal to a car thief he didn't really know.

"You want this girl safe," Cella suggested, "we need to bring Baissier down, and we need to do it now."

"What makes you think we can do that? I've known that woman for a very long time, Malone. You can't take her down just because your friend wants to protect some girl."

"I know. I'm not saying it'll be easy, but I think Whitlan's the key."

"Why do you think that?"

"Do you really think Baissier's after some taxidermist? She was watching that taxidermist for a reason. Smith and I think that reason is Whitlan."

"So? What if he is the reason?"

She shrugged. "Maybe Baissier's working with him."

He snorted. "Peg Baissier? Working with a full-human? On anything? What are you? High?"

"It's a possibility."

"It's also a possibility that a lion male might be shy and retiring, but that's not happening, either."

"I'm telling you she's up to something."

"She's *always* up to something. That doesn't mean she's doing something we can use against her."

"You don't know that."

Crush studied Cella. "What if she is up to something?" he finally asked. "What does KZS care? Or is the real problem here Baissier's power among the bears?"

Cella picked at dried blood on the sleeve of her sweatshirt. "Knowing that woman as well as you do, Crushek, can you really say you feel comfortable with her having that much control over an army of grizzlies and polars? Considering how much she hates every other species?"

He didn't answer and Cella looked up, not surprised by the frown on his face.

Cella nodded. "Yeah. That's pretty much how the rest of us feel, too."

"I understand, but thinking for a second that she'd involve herself with a scumbag like Whitlan . . ."

"According to you, he played the NYPD, the FBI, and the *Mob*. You really don't believe he could do the same with her? Someone so arrogant she thinks she's untouchable?"

"She is untouchable."

"Not if we get something on her. Not if *you* get something on her. And you start with Whitlan. That *is* what cops do, isn't it? Look into shit? Investigate?"

"I usually like to have this little thing they call *evidence*."

"Look, Smith's gut—"

"If I have to hear about that She-wolf's internal organs one more time . . ."

"Check it out. Please." When he only scratched his head and blew out a breath, Cella asked, "What? What is it?"

"I have a history with Baissier and it's not exactly a big secret. At least, not among the bears. They might think I'm just trying to ruin her life."

"You're not?"

"No." And she loved how appalled he looked at the mere suggestion that he might do something for revenge. So earnest this guy. "I just want her to stay away from me and I'll stay away from her."

Cella smirked. "You just tossed her boys out the fuckin' door of the Group offices. Do you really think she's going to stay away from you now?"

"How she handles her own shit is up to her. I'm talking about me. I mean, can't the Group handle looking into this?"

"The Group?" Cella laughed. "You know how the Group handles really high-level shit like this? They give it to Dee-Ann and she starts killing people with her bowie knife . . . that her own father gave her when she was ten. Trust me when I say, you do not want Dee-Ann Smith getting anywhere near Whitlan or Baissier."

The bear briefly closed his eyes. "What about KZS?"

"KZS is made up of cats. In general, we're a lazy species.

So we don't do what you'd call actual"—she made air quotes with her fingers—" 'investigations.' "

"Then what do you do?"

"Someone says, 'I'm thinking they're a problem' . . . and then they send one of us in to eliminate the problem."

Scowling, the bear demanded, "You do that for *every* situation? Even nonlethal ones?"

"Oh, God, no! Of course not. If you just irritate us, then we just come to your house and pee all over everything." She shrugged. "Sometimes shit in your shoes." When the bear only stared at her with his mouth open, Cella quickly added, "Not me, though. *I've* never done that. Not ever. Because it's . . . it's . . ." She thought a moment. "It's '*morally*' wrong." She smiled, proud of herself for remembering the phrase.

"Did you just air quote morally?"

Not sure how to answer that, she said, "Just for clarity?" Probably would have sounded more believable without making it a question, but God, the bear had so many damn rules! How was she supposed to keep track of so many damn rules?

"I don't think I want to hear any more," he said.

"Well, I'm gonna go anyway." Cella tapped the table with her fingertips. "A girl never wants to wear out her welcome. Besides, I just wanted to check on you. It's the least I can do for my—"

"Pretend boyfriend?" He shook his head. "Explain to me why you can't handle your aunts when you're a KZS agent?"

"Contractor."

"What?"

"I'm a contractor. They call, I go in. Otherwise, I play hockey, I argue with my kid, I sleep."

"They call, you go in, and do . . . what? Exactly?"

"Anything up to a thousand yards away."

He stared at her, briefly confused. But then his eyes grew wide and he asked, "You can take out a target at—"

"Thousand yards away. Yeah. Can't you?"

"No."

"Yeah. I'm good. I get the feeling they want to promote me, though. That's why they've been having me work with Smith and MacDermot. But I don't want anything getting between me and the Carnivores, ya know? Hockey is always my priority, right under my kid and the family. Eliminating high-level targets is, like, number four or five on my list of things to do."

"I don't know what to say to that."

"Fair enough. And as far as my aunts go, you're the one who said it was wrong to beat up the elderly so—"

Crush's eyes crossed. "You were leaving, right?"

She laughed, stood. "So you'll look into Whitlan?"

"It's not like I have any other options, now does it?"

"Not if you want it handled all legal and shit. But, hey, no matter what, you're really helping me out with my family and I appreciate it. Thanks."

"Yeah. You're welcome."

She winked at him and headed out, but she stopped in the kitchen doorway.

"Something wrong?" the bear asked her and she heard real concern in his voice.

Crush watched the She-tiger stand in his kitchen doorway. When she faced him, he didn't know what she was thinking. She sized him up, her gaze moving from his feet to his face. Walking back into the kitchen, she grabbed one of the chairs and pulled it over until it was in front of him. Then she stood on it, bringing them eye to eye. Actually, she was already six feet tall, so she kind of stood over him now.

"Yes?" he asked.

"You sound suspicious."

"You make me suspicious."

"I make everyone suspicious." She wrapped her arms around his neck.

"Are you really going to kiss me now?" he felt the need to ask. "After everything that's happened these last few hours?"

"Yep."

"Why?"

"I could give you lots of reasons—"

"Give me two."

"—but it's mostly because I want to."

"Oh . . . that's a good reason."

Cella laughed and leaned in. Crush watched her, curious what she'd do.

He'd never been with a feline before. He usually stuck to full-humans or other bears. And considering the issues he had with this one female, he wasn't sure why he was letting her kiss him now. Must be the curiosity thing. The true bane of his existence. It helped him as a cop, but had been known to completely fuck up his personal life. Then again, it could be that he needed to stop hooking up with women who had so much to hide. They never seemed that way on the surface, but once he dug a little . . . well, that was always a mistake. And unlike some of the guys he knew on the force, he didn't go in looking for something, didn't start digging trying to find proof that the woman he was currently with was nothing but a liar or married or had a boyfriend or was a certified psychotic. Yet even without trying, these were the things he often found out and that often led to tears and anger and lots of screaming—none of which was from him. Crush was never quite sure how someone else's criminal history hidden behind several layers of false names and Social Security numbers was his fault, but there you go.

Yet, as the feline pressed her face into his neck and sniffed, he had a feeling he wouldn't have to dig anything up. Cella Malone was so direct it had a tendency to be off-putting. She seemed to have no qualms about discussing her work with KZS, easily admitting that, "Yeah, sure, I kill people for a living." She was blunt and annoying and rude and insisted on involving him in the most ridiculous bullshit.

But when her nose rubbed against his neck and brushed against his ear, he kind of didn't care about all that. Who would? What she was doing felt so good that at the moment, nothing mattered.

Malone's forehead brushed against his chin, then his cheek, and yet she still hadn't kissed him. Not yet.

"You always keep your eyes open?" she asked softly.

"I like to see what's coming at me."

"Oh, very nice." She studied him. "You going to put your arms around me?" Crush still had his arms crossed over his chest.

"I'm comfortable."

"Such a sexy, uptight hard-ass." She rubbed her nose against his and despite his best intentions, Crush couldn't help but smile.

"There you go. Now you don't look nearly as fierce."

"I figured you'd like fierce."

"I do, but I'm helping you out for future females. You don't want to scare them off, do you?"

"I'm told my non-expression is more terrifying."

"Because we have no idea what you'll do. Sniff and move on or start tearing off limbs."

"That's lovely. Thank you."

"Uh-oh. The scowl's back. Better distract you before I end up torn limb from limb."

"If you're that worried—"

She kissed him, cutting off the rest of his words.

It wasn't a nice kiss, either. Oh, it was amazing, and he never knew anyone could have such soft lips, but it wasn't "nice." In fact, he didn't know a woman could make a simple kiss so wonderfully raunchy and dirty. Crush secretly liked dirty. And he got the feeling Malone liked dirty, too, but that she didn't keep it a secret.

She invaded his mouth with her tongue, fingers digging deep into the back of his neck and head, kind of holding him there. Crush's entire body loosened, his arms falling away from his chest and to his sides, then reaching around her waist and pulling her off the chair. The chair ended up between them, so Crush kicked it out of the way. Keeping a solid grip on her, he returned her kiss. But he wanted more.

Without thought to anything but the demands of his body, Crush pushed her up against his refrigerator, his body pinning hers there. He let his hands slip from around her waist and travel up until they could grip her breasts, fingers squeezing while his thumbs circled her nipples through her shirt and bra. Her entire body shook and then her hands were pressed against his chest, pushing him back.

"What?" He heard the growl in his voice, and was kind of appalled by it.

"Jesus, Mary, and Joseph!" Malone shoved and he released her, watching her drop to the floor.

She panted, gold eyes watching him close. Gold eyes that were accusing him. "You didn't tell me you were a powder keg about to go off."

"What the hell does that mean?"

She stepped away from the fridge, but she never took her eyes off him.

"You kissed me," Crush quickly argued, feeling the need to defend himself.

"I know," she shot back.

"Then why are you looking at me like—?"

She pointed an accusing finger. "Don't play coy with me!"

"What?"

"You and I both know what's going on here and I see now that I'll need more time than just some quickie on your kitchen table. I'll need a whole night to work with"—she moved her hands around in the air as if rubbing his entire body—"all this."

Crush scratched his head. "I'm so confused right now."

"That's 'cause you're not paying attention." She shook her head. "I gotta go."

"Why?" And his own question caught him by surprise.

"The kid's expecting me home tonight, otherwise I'd totally stay. But I'm trying the whole good mom thing."

"Yeah. Good luck with that."

"I don't like the tone and do not snarl at me."

She took a step, stopped, walked back to him, and placed her hand against his crotch.

Crush jerked at the feel of her stroking his cock through the thick denim of his jeans. Of course, the way those fingers were working him, he might as well be naked.

"Goddamn," she murmured, then again shook her head and snatched her hand away. "*See what you're doing?*"

"What *I'm* doing? How is this my fault?"

"It is your fault. You and your big cock! Dammit!"

"You're insane."

"Certifiable." She wagged a finger. "But you're not getting out of this now. Better put some time aside, because when I nail you, I'm going to need *all* night."

Her cold gold eyes scowled down at his crotch again and, after what felt like forever, she stamped her foot, spun away from him, and stormed out, slamming his front door behind her.

Crush looked over at the dog gazing up at him from under the table. Where it was safe.

"I don't understand how this is my fault," he told Lola, which got him a vicious bark.

"You don't have to be mean about it."

When Cella got back home, she walked in through the front door, passing the living room where her family was enjoying pie and TV. When they saw her, they all cheered, "Cella!"

Annoyed, she snapped, "Oh, shut up!"

Cutting through the kitchen, Cella headed into the backyard. She stopped by the table where Meghan and Josie sat doing schoolwork and glared down at her daughter.

"I hope you appreciate what a good mom I'm being," Cella told her.

"You mean at the moment? Ow!" Meghan lifted her leg and rubbed her shin, which was probably where Josie had kicked her under the table.

"You're a wonderful mom, Aunt C.," Josie said, ignoring Meghan's brutal glare. "And Mom's inside."

Taking the hint, Cella headed to the Davises' house. When she walked in, Jai's mother took one look at her face and pointed in the direction of the office that mother and daughter shared.

Cella marched through to the office, dropping into a free chair across from Jai's desk.

"And hello to you, too," Jai said "Is something wrong?"

"That man is hung like a donkey."

"Oooookay."

"I will need all night to work that shit. And I *will* work it."

Jai sat back in her chair and her eyes briefly closed. Oh, and there was a sigh.

"Explain to me why you can't just say 'he's really cute, I think I like him, I can't wait to get to know him better'? Why can't you say that?"

"Because I'm freaking out."

"Freaking out about what?"

"I like my pretend boyfriend. Which is just weird."

"Honey, calling a man your pretend *anything* is weird."

Cella chuckled. "I like calling him that. It annoys him." Cella threw her hands up. "You see? I enjoy annoying him."

"Sweetie." Jai leaned over, took Cella's hand. "You enjoy annoying everyone."

Cella thought on that a moment and finally admitted, "You might have a point."

CHAPTER EIGHTEEN

Crush woke up the next morning and decided that he wasn't going to sit around waiting for Baissier to come at him—or, even worse, fantasizing about a long-legged and heartless feline with an amazing tight ass and right hook. Instead, he was going to do his job and find out why Whitlan was really back in town. And then, he'd take him down. If it turned out Crush could nail Baissier in the process . . . well, that would just be a bonus, now wouldn't it?

So, just before noon, Crush walked into a Yonkers bar. As soon as he opened the door, with the early afternoon sun behind him, those already drinking or "working" looked up to see who was coming in. But as Crush's shadow grew on the floor and he stepped farther in, they all quickly turned away except the bartender.

"Hey, man." The bartender laughed. "Dude . . . what happened to your hair?"

Cella looked at her vibrating phone again, before quickly sending the call to her voice mail.

"What are you doing?" Rivka asked.

"Avoiding someone." To be specific, Cella was avoiding

Blayne. As the Group's hybrid kids got older, Cella and Blayne had been eyeing some of them for their respective teams. Although Blayne could give two shits about the males, she wanted Cella to leave the females to her for her precious roller derby team. But after watching Hannah handle herself in that fight with the grizzlies yesterday, Cella knew she wanted the bear hybrid to try out for the Carnivores. Which meant that she would be forced to listen to Blayne Thorpe whine about it.

Before putting her phone back in her pocket, she checked the time.

"Do you have to go?"

"Not yet, but I promised I'd meet some of the guys for training today. But don't worry, I have time. Your bachelorette party is more important than anything right now."

"I don't care about a bachelorette party."

"Of course, you don't. You're in love, blah, blah, blah. But your friends *do* care and that's all that matters." Cella wasn't lying when she'd told Jai that she adored Rivka. She really did. How could she not? A fellow She-tiger, Rivka always looked so cute and girly with her curly black hair that it was hard to believe she was one of KZS's Cleaners. Born and raised in Israel, she'd been recruited by KZS when she was twenty and they'd moved her to the States. With minimal equipment, she could dispose of a battalion of bodies in less than six hours. She was also loyal, dependable, and took great care of Cella's kid. In the end, that was all that mattered to Cella: Were you someone worthy of being around Meghan? The fact that Bri actually loved her, too, was the least of Cella's concerns.

Returning to her checklist, Cella said, "I'm thinking open bar."

Rivka put her nearly empty cereal bowl on the side table. "Are you insane? Do you have any idea how much these feline bitches can drink when it's on someone else's tab?"

After debating an open bar, crafting a reasonable guest list and making wardrobe decisions, Cella had just moved on to dinner options when the front door to Rivka and Bri's extremely high-priced penthouse opened and a voice from the hallway called out, "Where's my pussy at?"

The two females looked at each other, then back at the living room archway. A few seconds later, Bri came sauntering through with a large deli bag smelling delightfully of fresh pastry and coffee.

He stopped in the archway and stared. "Oh. Cella. You're here."

Tilting her head to the side, Cella asked, "Do I count as your pussy, too?"

He scowled. "No, you do *not*." Bri walked farther into the room. "And what are you doing here"—he pointed at Cella and Rivka—"canoodling?"

Cella tried to see it from Bri's point of view. Both females were on the couch, Cella's back against the armrest and her legs over Rivka's legs with Rivka toying with Cella's shoelaces. Okay. The visual might be easy to misinterpret by regular full-humans, but a feline should . . . oh, forget it. Bri was still a guy and to him nothing was more frightening than having the mother of his child good friends with his fiancée. And considering how much Cella enjoyed messing with Bri's mind, she could understand his concern.

"Don't get paranoid. You always seem to forget, baby's daddy—"

"Stop calling me that."

"—that as cats we're naturally affectionate when we actually like someone. I *like* Rivka, but that doesn't mean I want to bone her." She looked at Rivka. "Do you want to bone me, sweetie?"

"Doesn't everybody?"

And *that's* why Cella loved Rivka. How could anyone think Cella had a problem with Rivka marrying Bri? She had a great sense of humor and actually made the man much less uptight accountant guy.

"Do not freak me out before my wedding," the male warned. "Just do not freak me out."

"Speaking of which, do you know what's going on with our kid?"

"What do you mean?"

"She's acting really stressed out. Especially anytime I mention school to her."

Putting the coffee cups on the table, Bri dismissed Cella's concern with a wave of his hand. "She's probably just worried about her decision to stay on Long Island with the family and go to Hofstra. A decision I'm sure you're not making easy on her."

Cella stared at the tiger standing in front of her until she finally managed to grind out, "What do you mean her decision to go to Hofstra?"

"Oh." Bri looked at his fiancée, then back at Cella. "Meghan, uh . . . didn't mention that to you?"

Crush knocked on the door in the back of the bar and it slowly opened. The man protecting the door looked him over, then asked, "Let him in?"

"Of course."

Crush walked into the room. He could tell from the general funk that an all-night poker game had been going on. But as soon as he stepped in, most of the players picked up their winnings and headed out the door into the alley behind the bar.

Dave "Charming" Lepke smiled at Crush. "Come on in."

Crush walked in, making sure to check the dark corners and behind the door before moving across the room to stand in front of the well-known gambler turned bookie. In his late sixties, with a full head of white hair, Charming still had the imposing build and attitude of a man who used to break guys' arms for being late paying back their gambling debts.

"I was hoping to buy in," Crush told him, holding up a wad of money. "But everybody ran away."

"You should be used to that."

"I never really get used to it."

"Your money's no good here and you know it."

"I know. And yet I'm here. Don't you wonder why?"

Charming studied him for a bit before he motioned his man out. Looking at Crush and back at his boss, the bodyguard asked, "You sure?"

"I'm sure."

With a warning glare at Crush, he walked out, the door closing behind him.

"How could you not tell me?" Cella yelled at her daughter's father while pacing in front of him. "How long have you been keeping this from me?"

"Calm down."

Cella stepped into him and gritted out between clenched teeth, "*Tell me to calm down again.*"

"That's it." Rivka pushed her arms between the two, forcing them apart. "Bri, why don't you put the food in the kitchen?"

He walked out and Rivka faced Cella.

"Why didn't she tell me?" Cella asked.

"Because she wants to stay. She wants to stay with the Malones."

And Cella asked with all honesty, "But why?"

Rivka started laughing, her hand covering her mouth.

"Oh, shut up."

"Cella, she's not trying to hurt you."

"No. She just hates me."

Rivka put her hands on her hips. "You just leap, don't you? From the tallest building of stupidity."

Cella shrugged. "It's a skill."

"So," Crush asked, "should I expect any visits from your associates?"

"Not from mine. They're terrified of you, kid. And you being a cop doesn't change that." Charming lifted his chin. "What'd ya come here for?"

"I had questions."

"About?"

"Frankie Whitlan. Heard he's back."

Charming laughed. "Is back? Frankie Whitlan's *been* back. For years. I wouldn't say right under everybody's nose, but he hasn't exactly been hiding, either. But he is protected."

"By who?"

"Everybody. Feds. Your people. Everybody he's ever worked with, he's got dirt on. Not your typical bullshit, guy-cheating-on-his-wife dirt, either, but put-you-under-the-jail dirt. He goes down, a lot of people go down with him."

"Then why hasn't anyone taken him out?"

"Because he makes a lot of people a lot of money. And Whitlan's smart. Very smart." Charming leaned forward, resting his arms on the table. "And I'll give you this, because I'm such a great guy, and because I'll never hear from you again after today . . . Whitlan has an office on Staten Island."

"An office? What does he need an office for?"

"Outwardly, he's gone legit. Has rich friends, lives a rich life. But he hasn't changed. You want to find him, start there." Charming tapped the table. "But be careful. The man likes to kill."

"What do you mean?"

"Well, people I've heard of, not me, of course, or those I know personally, but others . . . they kill because they have to. Because someone's stealing their money, damaging their merchandise"—Charming eyed him—"or is just a *rat*. But Whitlan kills because he likes to. Heard a story a few years back that he used to round up his friends, hire a couple of hookers for the night, go to some desolate part of Jersey or upstate, and then send the hookers out."

"Out to do what?"

"To run. He and his friends would hunt them down. First it was just about fucking them, then he started killing them. Had to stop, though, when the ones running the girls got a little fed up at losing perfectly good merchandise every week."

The door opened and Charming's man walked into the room. "They're here."

"You better go," Charming told Crush. "And good luck, kid."

"Did you know?" Cella demanded of Jai, one skate tapping against the floor of Jai's Sports Center office.

"Did I know what?"

"That my Meghan was going to goddamn Hofstra?"

Jai leaned back in her ten grand, ergonomically perfected chair, arms crossing over her insubstantial chest. "What's wrong with Hofstra? *My* daughter's going there."

"We're not talking about her or you. We're talking about *me*."

"I thought we were talking about Meghan."

"Yeah. Her, too."

"No. I didn't know she was planning to attend Hofstra in the fall."

"But you're not surprised, either, are you?"

"No. The girls want to stay together. Why not let them?"

"But if she stays, she'll be trapped here. Forever."

"Okay." Jai sat forward, placing her arms on the desk. "Let's analyze that statement, shall we?"

"Let's not."

"You can only be trapped somewhere if you're not allowed to leave. But if you *want* to stay, then I don't see how you can be trapped. And Meghan wants to stay. Also, *you* left, so how trapped can she be?"

"And you saw how hard it was for me to make that happen."

"I know. Terribly hard." Jai placed the tips of her fingers against her chin. "Let's see if I can remember how it all went down. Ahhh, yes. You walked into your parents' kitchen, said, 'I joined the Marines. Did anyone feed the baby?' And walked out. Other than your mother's quiet sobbing, I don't remember much about you being caged for such a decision."

"Some days, you know . . . I just really fucking hate you."

"Do yourself a favor, Cella. Let your daughter make her own decisions, so you don't lose her to your aunts. Because, let's face it, that's what really has you worried."

"It—" Cella began, but a knock at the office door cut her off.

"Come in."

When Cella saw Blayne walk in, she rolled her eyes and walked out. She was in no mood for a fight over Hannah.

"You can't avoid me forever, heifer!" Blayne yelled from the safety of Jai's office.

Cella spun around and yelled back, "Get in my way, Thorpe, and I'll claw your entire face off!"

Feeling her point had been made, Cella faced forward but stopped short when she found Reed standing there.

"Are you done tormenting the wolfdog?" he asked.

"At the moment."

"Then can we get started? Everybody's waiting for you."

"Everybody?"

"They've multiplied since the last time."

"No pressure though."

"You can stop acting like a victim, feline. I just watched you happily threaten the sweetest being on the planet."

"It wasn't happily." When he only stared at her, she insisted, "It wasn't! Just necessary."

"You going to be all right?" MacDermot asked as she finished the last of her fries. They sat in the booth at the back of the diner near the Sports Center, her Yankees cap pulled low to hide her swollen face. Of course, it didn't hide much of anything and everyone kept looking at *him* like he was the one who'd actually hit her. Although their reaction told him a lot about full-human society.

"I'm fine."

"You seem fine, which I find a little weird." She finished

her soda. "Gentry still wants to put a security detail on your house."

"Why?"

"I think she cares if you die."

"Why?"

"And we're done." She slipped out of the booth, reaching back to grab her jacket.

"What did I say?"

"Nothing. You're just kind of weirding me out. I don't know how you just accept all this."

"What am I supposed to do? Cry?"

"Don't irritate me, Crushek. I've had enough of males whose reactions I don't understand."

Crush smirked. "When you got home, did Llewellyn roar a lot in disapproval over your dangerous life as NYPD that led to your face looking like that or did he just lick your bruises?"

"Both. But what really freaked me out was . . ."

"You really liked the licking?"

She shrugged. "It was comforting."

"Don't worry. We all like the licking."

"Yeah, whatever." She pulled the hood of her parka over her head since it was another day of close to zero temps outside. "We'll talk tomorrow."

After MacDermot left, Crush sat at the table a little while longer. He knew he should feel *something* about all this, but he just . . . didn't. What did that say about him as a person?

Deciding to pay the tab and go before he thought too long about that particular question, Crush pulled out his wallet and took out a couple of bills. He was just throwing them on the table when he realized that the other side of the booth was no longer empty.

He looked up, blinked, then looked around, convinced someone was playing a joke on him.

"Um . . ." He shook his head, confused about what he should say to the man sitting across from him. "Do . . . do you need something, Mr. Novikov?"

"Peace. And. Quiet." Bo Novikov looked up from the menu he was studying. "If I have to listen to one more rookie whine about me shoving the Zamboni at him when he wouldn't get out of my way, I'm going to go off. And you can call me Bo or just Novikov. Calling me Mr. Novikov makes me feel like your dad."

"But then wouldn't you be Mr. Crushek? Or I'd be Mr. Novikov?"

The pair stared at each other until Novikov said, "That was a really bear moment."

"Yeah. It really was. Sorry." Unable not to ask the question, though . . . "So you shoved a Zamboni at your teammate?" Crush had no idea how much those things weighed, but they were motor vehicles designed to keep the ice on a rink smooth. And since there were few motorized work vehicles that were light, he'd guess there was much poundage involved.

"He annoyed me."

"Okay."

"I didn't think it was a big deal, but then your girlfriend told Blayne."

"My . . . my what?"

"Malone. Your girlfriend, right?"

"She's not—"

"She always goes for the jugular, that female. She's lucky she's a good player."

"Or you'd throw a Zamboni at her?"

"Nah. Wouldn't be right. She's a woman. I was raised better than that." There was silence for several moments while Novikov finished looking over the menu and placed it on the table. "I did, however, toss her out a five-story window once into a Dumpster, but she's feline. She cleared the Dumpster and totally landed on her feet. So you wanna stay and have lunch with me or what?"

CHAPTER NINETEEN

After spending the week chasing down drug-dealing bears and tips on Whitlan, Crush was grateful when the weekend came and he had a whole Saturday to sit at home with Lola, relax, and watch the Islanders game. It was still early and he had no intention of getting up for several more hours, when he heard the purring. No. That wasn't right. He didn't hear purring. He felt it. All over his body. And wow! That was kind of amazing. So amazing, he woke up. Unfortunately, as soon as he woke up the wonderful spell was broken and he was forced to face the reality that his house had been broken into—again.

"Why are you here, Malone?" he asked, even as he reached for her.

"We had a date."

"No, we didn't."

"Ice Party. You're supposed to come with me as my date."

"But I specifically told you no."

"That was before you kissed me."

"You kissed *me*. Besides, Islanders game today."

"You're saying *I* am less important than the Islanders?"

"Yes."

She stroked a finger across his chin. "I think you're lying," she purred. "I think you're absolutely fascinated with me and you're dying to go to the party."

"Look, I'm sure there are a lot of guys out there who haven't gotten to know you who would be really glad to— oh, God, please stop doing that."

She was licking and grazing her teeth against his jaw, making Crush's toes curl, his hands clench. But he had to fight it.

But she'd started purring again, her hands sliding up his arms, gripping his shoulders, and her hips rocking back and forth against him. They weren't even naked! She was fully dressed and Crush had on his sweatpants. And yet he felt like he might come at any second.

Deciding he needed control, he grabbed Malone's arms and rolled her onto her back. But, Crush quickly realized that only made things worse. Because now he had her right where he really wanted her. On her back, his cock between her legs.

Pinning her to the bed, both of them panting and gaping at each other, Crush was moments from pawing off her clothes with his claws. And the way her fingers tightened on his shoulders and her legs wrapped around his waist, he got the feeling she really wouldn't mind.

But before Crush could do anything, a male voice from downstairs bellowed, "Celly! Let's go!"

"Who's that?"

"My brother. He drove me here."

"Your brother is in my house and you're . . ."

"Rubbin' up on ya? Yeah."

"And I could totally hear it!"

Malone cringed and yelled, "Shut up, Tommy!" She let out a breath, looked back at Crush. "I didn't bring him in. I swear. He just—"

"Broke in? Like you?"

"That's one way of putting it."

Crush released the feline and rolled away from her. "Out."

"Okay, fine." She sat up. "Don't come. But my Aunt Deirdre swung at me earlier today."

Confused, Crush lifted his hands. He felt like he was praying for guidance. "Why is your elderly aunt swinging at you?"

"Because I'm not afraid to tell her that her soda bread sucks."

"It totally sucks," Tommy agreed from the first floor.

Ignoring the male cat, Crush asked, "Still, it seems a little overly aggressive. Are you sure she doesn't have dementia of some kind?"

"No. She just doesn't like me."

"*I'm* not sure I like you."

The feline slowly got to her knees in front of him and slipped one arm around his neck.

"Do not kiss me," he told her. But she did it anyway. And before Crush could stop himself, he had his arms around her and her body pulled close to his. They nearly had each other's pants off when her idiot brother yelled, "Are you two at it again?"

Malone pulled away first and quickly got off the bed.

"You want to come with us?"

"I haven't showered or anything and I need to take care of Lola and—" Crush frowned. "What are you doing?"

"Pouting. Until I get what I want."

"Dude! Just tell her you'll meet us there," Tommy yelled.

"Yeah, but—"

"Dude!"

"All right!" he roared back, and the male tiger laughed at him. "I'll meet you there."

"Promise? Because I know you. You won't break a promise. So promise me."

"Fine. I promise. I'll be there."

"I'll text you the coordinates so you can find it."

"Can't you just give me—?"

"We're trying to keep out the riffraff so we have it in the middle of nowhere. You'll need coordinates." She stretched across the bed and kissed him again. "I'll see you there."

Crush fell back on the bed and again wondered what he'd gotten himself into with this crazy feline.

Cella got in the SUV with her brothers. "Okay. Let's go."

"Where's the bear?" Liam asked.

"He'll meet us there."

"So he's dumping you already?"

Cella let out a breath. "No. He's not dumping me."

"Because I think you should go for the RV dealer in A.C."

"He's a cousin, you idiot!"

"What is the deal with you and all these rules?"

Cella made a fist and turned, but Tommy, who was in the driver's seat, caught her hand. "Would you two cut it out? I'm not going to have all this fuckin' arguing all the way to the party! Now everybody face forward and be quiet!"

All the siblings faced forward and were quiet—for about five minutes. Then they argued all the way to the party.

Crush followed the directions his GPS gave him based on the coordinates provided by Malone. He ended up in Macon River County. One of the vacation places that only shifters knew about. There were quite a few of these, but Crush had heard a lot about Macon River because it was very bear-friendly. Some places were bear-friendly, some places bear-only, and some places simply didn't like to have bears around at all. Of course, that was usually anyplace with a lot of wolves, coyotes, or mountain lions. Other cats and wild dogs had more tolerance, but didn't get too close to bears, either. And wherever there were bears, there were foxes some-where—stealing shit.

When Crush finally hit the end of the directions, he

parked his truck beside a bunch of other trucks, SUVs, vans, and Hummers. Vehicles big enough for all sorts of bears.

He stepped out and looked around. Beautiful country that no rational human beings would be wandering around with close to zero degree temperatures and hard-packed snow and ice on the ground and covering the trees. Although for Crush, it was kind of pleasant.

He started walking, hearing music off in the distance. He didn't know what he expected with it so cold out. Maybe the Malones would have a little barbeque. Seemed weird in the middle of an East Coast winter . . .

Crush stopped at the top of the rise, gazing out over the area beneath.

During Crush's time in undercover, he'd gone to more than a few outdoor raves. How could he not? The best drug dealers always showed up to those things. Either to sell or party, but they were there. But those raves clearly had nothing on *this*.

The first thing Crush could see was the giant dance floor packed with partially dressed shifters. Polar bears, Arctic foxes and wolves, Siberian tigers, snow leopards. Grizzlies and black bears, too, probably from Kamchatka, tough Russian country. Dressed in shorts, T-shirts, fur bikinis, flip-flops, they writhed on the dance floor to what sounded like Caribbean tech music.

A musk oxen—where the hell did they find a musk oxen?—ran behind Crush, two tigers and a leopard chasing him down. Farther down in the trees, Crush could see two polars fighting over a seal. When he looked down and to his left, he could see an ice lake through the trees and a rough hockey game going on.

And when he looked right next to him, Crush could see an Eskimo. Okay. Not really an Eskimo, but Blayne Thorpe dressed in the biggest, warmest parka zipped so high he couldn't see her mouth, the hood pulled down so low over her forehead, he could barely see her sunglass-covered eyes.

Big mittens on her hands, big ski boots on her feet. Honestly, he only recognized her because of her scent.

"Hi, Blayne."

She said something, but he couldn't really understand it through the layers of parka.

"Huh?"

She unzipped a bit of the parka so that he could now see her mouth. "I said, 'Hi, Crush!' "

He laughed. "How are you, sweetie?"

"Okay. Cold."

"Hon . . . why are you here?"

"I'm marrying a man more Arctic bear than African lion. I figure I better get used to it. It's not bad, though. They have a really big hot tent."

"Hot tent?"

"Yep. All the more African-based shifters are there. I try not to see it as segregation, though."

"I'm sure it's done strictly for health reasons."

"Can I ask you a question, Crush?"

"Sure."

"Do you like Bo?"

"Uh . . ."

"I don't mean in a weird way. I'm not talking about hockey and I don't mean sexually."

"Oh, that's good . . . 'cause . . . yeah."

"I just mean in general."

"Well . . ."

"For instance, do you find him rude or overbearing or obsessively psychotic?"

"No."

"Okay. That's good. Um . . . do you ever want to stab him in the face or set him on fire or go back in time and destroy the origin of his bloodline?"

"No."

And there in her big parka, Blayne did a little shimmy. "I knew it! I knew he could have friends!"

"I don't know if we're actually friends, though."

"Sha-sha-sha. Don't ruin this for me."

"Okay."

"Now come on." She took his hand with her mitten-covered one and together they headed down toward the party.

"Is this your first Ice Party?" she asked as they walked.

"Yeah."

"Me, too. I'm having a blast!"

"Even though you're dressed like you're on a National Geographic expedition?"

"Hot tent!" she reminded him.

They walked to the edge of the dance floor and that's where Blayne stopped. She looked up at him and then out at the dancing bodies. Crush followed her line of sight. It took a second, but then he saw what Blayne was trying to show him. Malone.

In denim cutoff shorts, black motorcycle boots, and what he could only assume was a white-fur bikini top, Cella danced between two males. She held a Guinness in her left hand, leaving her right hand free to fist-pump at the most appropriate times, usually when one of her cousins yelled out, "Malones, call back!" And all the Malones yelled in return, "Maaaaalonnnnnnes!" Followed, of course, by what Crush had always termed the "Long Island Fist-Pump."

Blowing out a breath, enjoying how he could see it in the air, Crush looked at the wolfdog still holding his hand. "Really?" he asked her.

Blayne laughed. "What did you expect? She's a Long Island girl."

"I guess."

"And you've gotta admit, she looks fierce as hell in that outfit."

Yeah. Crush did have to admit that.

"And I have to admit," Blayne went on, "although freezing to death, I'm really enjoying the party side of the snow-loving." She turned toward him, still holding his hand. "You're staying, aren't you?"

"Why do you ask?"

"Because something about you tells me that you're the duck-out-the-first-time-you-get-the-chance guy. Unless you're about to arrest someone." She blinked, thought a moment, then asked, "Are you here to arr—"

"No, Blayne. I'm not here to arrest anyone."

"Cool! Want me to get Cella for you?"

"Sure. Okay."

"No problem." She finally released the grip she had on him, put both her hands to her mouth and screamed out, "*Cella!*"

And yes, that was something he could have done himself, but why quibble?

Malone turned, saw them, and ran over. When she was about ten feet from Crush, she launched herself at him, hitting him hard, her legs wrapping around his waist, her arms around his neck. "Hi!"

"H—"

She didn't let him finish, her mouth pressing against his, arms tightening around his neck. And for those few seconds Crush forgot about everyone else.

When she finally pulled her mouth away, Crush still had his eyes closed.

"I'm glad you came."

Wait. He had? When?

"I was afraid you were going to bail on me."

Oh! Came as in attend. Got it. He was there. He was okay. He could handle this. Her. Whatever.

"I promised."

"You did." Still wrapped around him, she leaned back a bit and gave him a once-over. "You're kind of overdressed."

"I see that now."

* * *

Cella took Crush on a tour. She loved this yearly party and was excited to be able to share something with him that she was pretty sure he'd enjoy. She got the feeling that Mac-Dermot's party from a couple of weeks ago was probably the first time in a long time that he'd gone to a party that had nothing to do with his job. He had to learn to relax. Guys like him ended up with heart conditions and high blood pressure. She didn't want that for Crush and would do what she could to make sure he learned what relaxing was all about.

"There's a couple of hockey games going on. Pro players over there and just-like-to-get-drunk-and-fuck-around-on-the-ice over there. There's equipment to borrow if you didn't bring your own. There's ice holes over there with fresh-water seals. I'm told they're just like ring seals."

"Baikal seals. Someone went all the way to Russia to get those?"

"Not when they can just go to the Maine seal farms. Have you been to *any* bear-only towns?"

"No."

"So much to show you."

"A lot more, I hope."

And the way he looked at her when he said that . . .

Cella shook her head. "Cut it out."

"What?"

"Being so damn cute. More to see." She pulled him over to the other side of the dance floor. "Picnic tables are here. Malones already grabbed eight of them, so you should be able to find someplace to sit." She pointed at an outside barbeque grill. "That's where you can get polar bear stuff. Seal, walrus, I think they have whale this year. Beluga or something."

"Hi, Detective Crushek."

Cella pulled Crush around to see her daughter and Josie walking up to them, a batch of the young cousins behind them.

"Hi, Meghan. Josie. It's good to see you guys again."

"We're glad you came," Meghan said. "But please don't let my mother's outfit bother you. It's for shock value only at this point."

"Thank you very much, but I look fabulous in this outfit. Don't I look fabulous in this outfit, Crushek?"

"I can't express to you how many ways I'm *not* getting between a mother and daughter."

Meghan's smile was bright and wide. "Smart man."

"Thank you."

"What are you two up to now?" Cella asked.

"Josie wants to flirt with the Callahans."

"All right, but no separating and don't let any of them abscond with her." She pointed at Josie. "I promised your mom and grandmother we'd keep you safe since they didn't want to come. So don't do anything that will get me in trouble."

"I promise, Aunt C."

"Good. Now go."

The girls walked off and Cella turned back to Crush. "What?" she asked when she saw him staring at her.

"Abscond with her?"

"Yeah. Callahans used to take mountain lions for brides."

"Hundreds of years ago, right?"

"Uh . . . last one was two years ago. Some chick from Arizona."

"And the filing of kidnapping charges . . . ?"

"Kidnapping charges? Why would they do that?"

"Because that's what it is?"

"I guess."

"You guess?"

"Look, why file kidnapping charges when you can haggle for some new RVs and . . . wait. Where are you going?"

Cella caught up with the bear. "What's wrong?"

"Nothing. I guess I should have realized sooner your whole family are gypsies."

"Sssshhh," Cella whispered. She took a desperate look

around to make sure he hadn't been heard. "Look, Crushek, we don't use that word."

"Why?"

"We just don't," she insisted. "It's bigoted and you do not want to get on the wrong side of the Malones. Plus, we've got the Callahans here, the Ryans—"

"But there's absconding. You're worried your friend's daughter will be absconded."

"The Malones aren't leaving little Josie on her own. No matter how cute a Callahan boy is."

"Okay."

"You can call us Travellers."

"Are you Travellers?"

She shrugged. "We were."

"What does that mean?"

"It's a long story. Come on. I'm not done showing you around. And remember . . ."

"Right. No bigotry. Just . . . absconding."

With a short laugh, Cella took Crush's hand again and led him over to the big tent set up in the field. They'd had to up the size this year. "This used to be just for human mates, but the last couple of years we've been getting a lot more of the hot breeds."

Cella walked into the tent, Crush behind her. With their own dance floor and their own barbeque pit, the other cats, wolves, bears, etc., lounged around in their heavy sweaters and ski pants with their thermals under that. Many of them still had on their jackets, but they all seemed to be having a good time.

Crush grunted and Cella looked up at him. "What?"

"Are those African wild dogs?"

Cella sighed, looking over at the dance floor. It was filled to capacity with completely sober wild dogs, howling, barking, and dancing to whatever eighties crap they were forcing the rest of the tent attendees to listen to.

"Yeah. I don't really know why they're here. I can't believe any cats invited them. They're not close to bears, and wolves can barely tolerate them."

"I've discovered that if there's a good party somewhere, wild dogs will find it and take over."

"It used to be just one pack from out on the Island. Now there's like seven packs who've attended the last two years. I will say, my mom thinks it's great. The wild dogs love to get married and my mom networks at these things."

"Smart lady."

A hard fist rammed into Cella's back.

"Hey."

Yep. Hard and unyielding. "Why are you here?" Cella asked Dee-Ann.

"It's my day off. My mate says, 'Let's go out. Dress warmly.' Next thing I know, I'm trapped in the middle of nowhere New Jersey with cats, bears, wild dogs, and Blayne."

"You know Blayne loves you."

"Shut up." Smith nodded at Crush. "How y'all doin'?"

"We're fine," Crush replied.

"You two are a 'we' now?"

"She was only talking to you," Cella explained.

"Okay." He studied Cella. "What?"

She motioned behind him and Cella watched Crush look over his shoulder and jump. Not that she blamed him; Novikov stood right behind him—breathing.

"Oh . . . hi."

"Hi."

Crush glanced at Cella and Smith, then back at Novikov. "Do you want something?"

"You ever play football?"

"American or Australian rules?"

"For this discussion, American."

"Yeah. I have."

Novikov thought a moment. "Have you played Australian rules football?"

"No."

"Fair enough."

At that point, Cella and Smith locked gazes, watching each other to see who would start laughing first.

"So you wanna play football now? American football?"

"Okay. But I thought you'd be playing hockey with the guys outside."

"That was my plan, but apparently my hockey skills are too frightening for some loser lion."

The lion male sauntered up to Novikov and Smith's eyes crossed, Cella covering her mouth to stop from laughing out loud.

"Why don't," Mitch O'Neill Shaw sneered, "you just admit that you fear my football skills? Just say it, Bro!"

"If you call me 'bro' again, I'm biting off your face."

Crushek stared at Mitch for several seconds until he finally pointed his finger at him and said way louder than seemed necessary, "I sold you crack cocaine once."

And everyone in that tent froze, slowly turning to look at the two males talking to each other.

Mitch, mate to Smith's wolf cousin, Sissy Mae, scowled at Cella's bear, making her wish she'd kept her gun on her. Then he snapped his fingers, scowl disappearing, and crowed, "And I sold you meth!"

"Hey," both idiots, er, males said, laughing.

"I thought you were dead," Crushek volunteered.

"They tried. Put a bounty on my head, shot me, forced me to recover in motherfuckin' Tennessee." Mitch glanced at Smith, his laughter dying off. "No offense, Dee-Ann."

"Whatever," the She-wolf grumbled.

"Anyway, eventually my mother got involved and . . . well, you can imagine how it went from there. How about you?"

"Moved to the Brooklyn division."

"Hey. That's a nice deal."

"Yeah. I guess. Had to cut my hair, though."

"Are you two girls done?" Novikov snapped.

"Wait a minute," Mitch complained. "You're not playing for Novikov, are you?"

"He asked me first."

"Bro, come on! Cops working together."

"Can't. It's a moral thing."

"Are you still going on about being moral?"

"It's a lifestyle choice."

"Are we doing this or what?" Novikov growled.

Crush faced her. "Are you cool with that?"

Startled, Cella looked around for who he could be talking to. When she didn't find anyone, she replied, "Huh?"

"You invited me and I don't want to desert you."

"Awwwwwwwww," Cella heard from behind her.

She looked over her shoulder to find a small pack of She-dogs standing there, watching. One of them, the black one married to Smith's cousin Smitty, gestured at Crush and mouthed, *He is soooo sweet.* Then she added, *Marry him.*

While Cella debated if she could snap the little dog's neck before Smith got in the way, another voice yelled for her from outside the tent.

Deciding the She-dog wouldn't be much of a challenge for her, Cella walked across the tent and looked outside.

"Marly Callahan," she called back. "What can I do ya for, lass?"

"A friendly challenge," Marly offered. "You and me . . . in the ring."

Malones and Callahans cheered and bets were yelled to family bookies.

"Wait a minute," Smith quietly cut in. "Callahan? Didn't we just save her brother?"

"Exactly. Now she's honoring me with a proper fight."

"All right."

Crush tapped her shoulder. "Should I assume I'm not deserting you?"

"Yeah, yeah. Go on." She waved him away. "I'll see you after your game."

"Yeah, well . . . good luck."

"You, too."

Once he was gone, Smith asked, "So which one of you is falling faster?"

"Shut the fuck up. And you're my cutman."

Smith shrugged, reaching for the bowie knife she had holstered to her jeans. Cella caught her hand, growling as she scowled at her. "I mean, if I need you to do that, you idiot."

"Malone, look at you sweet-talkin' me."

"All right," Novikov finally admitted. "Maybe I underestimated him."

"I'd heard he was good enough to play pro."

"How does that help me?"

"It actually doesn't." Crush looked over at the other team. "It also doesn't help that your teammates hate you so much, they're playing for the Shaw brothers. Even MacRyrie . . . he's going after you like you're covered in honey."

"Thank you."

"You're welcome."

"It wouldn't be bad if we had a better team."

"They are trying. Loyal fans."

They both looked over at the panting, exhausted wild dog males who'd volunteered to play. When they saw Novikov staring at them, they smiled and waved—still panting.

"At least we have our own cheerleaders," Crush offered.

"Yeah. Blayne and the Wild Dog-ettes."

"I must say, your woman has a *lot* of energy."

"She's had eight Shirley Temples. At this point, she's just out of control." Novikov sighed. "I hate losing."

"Me, too."

"You have any ideas?"

"Nope."

"Mr. Crushek?"

Crush smiled down at Meghan and Josie. "Aren't you watching your mom fight?"

"No. No, thanks. Really rather not."

Crush and Novikov laughed.

"Understood," Crush said.

"I see you guys are losing," Meghan observed—or stated the obvious, whichever.

"Yes, we are."

"Is it true those are O'Neill lions?" Josie asked.

"The one doing the moonwalk . . . that's Mitch O'Neill. His half brother, the one doing the rump shaker, is Brendon Shaw."

"An O'Neill is an O'Neill, Mr. Crushek."

"Not sure what that means."

"That's all right." Meghan smiled. "Can you hold them off for a couple of minutes?"

"Sure."

The two girls walked off and Novikov asked, "That's really Malone's daughter, huh?"

"You never met her before?"

"I have . . . but I never really believed it."

"Why not? They look alike."

"And that's about it."

"Hi, Gramps."

Meghan grinned up at her grandfather. The great Butch Malone.

"Hello, my love," he said with a warm smile. "Having a good time?"

"I'm having a great time."

"What about you, young Josie?"

"I always have a good time at the Ice Party, Uncle B."

"Good. Good. Still can't watch your ma fight, though, huh?"

"I'd rather not. If she's not getting pummeled, she's pummeling." Unfortunately, while walking over, Meghan had managed to get there just as Marly Callahan landed a right cross to her mother's jaw, sending the woman who'd given birth to Meghan flipping back and almost out of the ring, the ropes the only things that managed to keep her in.

"It's a mutual pummeling right now," her grandfather assured her. As if that helped somehow.

"Great," Meghan lied.

Butch leaned down a bit. "So what do you think of your ma's new beau?"

"We like him." They really did, she and Josie. There was something about him. Something just . . . honest. Her mother needed that in her life. More than she realized.

"Good. I think she likes him, too," her grandfather confirmed.

"We know she does. Too bad he's busy getting his ass kicked in football by an O'Neill."

Every male Malone turned away from the fight, focusing on Meghan and Josie, just as the girls knew they would.

"That bear is losing to an O'Neill?"

"So's Mr. Novikov."

"What the hell . . . ?" Uncle Tommy glanced at his father. "What's going on?"

"It's just the two of them, really. The wild dogs are the only other teammates they have, and they're kind of . . . tiny."

"What about MacRyrie, Van Holtz—"

"All the Carnivores are playing with the O'Neills," Josie said. Since she did "sad" well, Meg let her run with that.

"Betraying bastards," her grandfather growled, all of Meghan's uncles and male cousins agreeing.

"What do you want us to do, Da?" Liam asked.

"What do ya think?"

When Marly Callahan went down for a third straight time, Cella was declared the winner, her Aunt Kathleen raising Cella's arm in the air.

"Nicely done, girl," the older Malone praised her.

"Thanks."

While everyone went to get or pay their gambling money, Cella stumbled over to Marly's side, holding out her bloody hand. A big grin on her battered face, the She-lion grasped Cella's hand and let her haul her to her feet. Arms around each other's shoulders, they pressed their foreheads together and Marly whispered, "You took care of my brother, Malone. There's a debt."

"Don't worry about that now. He's safe, that's all that matters."

"Ma!"

The two women looked down at Cella's daughter and Josie.

"Your girl sure is a beauty, Malone."

"She is."

"And so is her mountain lion friend."

"You keep your brothers' grubby paws off my girls. Both of 'em."

"But we've got some lovely RVs to trade," Marly teased.

"Ma," Meghan pushed.

"What is it?"

"Football. Remember?"

"Did Novikov start a fight with the guys?"

"Not exactly . . ."

A bottle of Gatorade was held up in front of his face and Crush took it, smiled. "Thank you."

"You're welcome."

He cringed, unable to stop himself. "Malone, your face."

"Yeah, but you should see what I did to Callahan."

"I'm standing right here," the She-lion complained, handing Novikov a separate bottle of the sports drink. "I can hear you."

"What's going on?"

"The wild dogs were running out of steam, so your brothers and cousins offered to play."

"Uh-huh. Except you guys"—Cella motioned to Crush, Novikov, and the other hockey players who'd been playing with Mitch O'Neill—"are all standing here, with the ball. And those guys"—she motioned to the field where a battle between lion and tiger males was taking place—"are in their cat form and mauling each other."

"I must admit, the game seemed to go off the track right after that first play."

"Especially when the rest of the O'Neill males showed up."

"Gwenie invited her uncles," Blayne chirped in, her entire body bouncing around in kind of a mix of 90s-style dancing and just a hyperactive fit. "Apparently, the O'Neills hate the Malones. I had no idea!"

Cella studied Blayne. "Have you been drinking Shirley Temples again?"

"I don't have to tell you anything!" Blayne yelled before she backflipped away from them.

"Should you go after her?" Crush asked Novikov.

"No. She's heading right for that tree over there and—bam! Down she goes. She'll be out for a bit." He shrugged, focusing back on the fight. "I'll scrape her up later."

"You having a good time?" Malone asked him.

"Yeah. I'm having a great time."

"Good."

He cringed. "But I can't ignore this anymore." He took the towel he had hanging around his neck and wiped the blood off Cella's face, moving carefully so as not to hurt her any more than she had been.

Of course, he had to grip her chin a little tighter to keep her from starting another fight when the wild dog females all sighed out, "Awwwwww" behind them.

MacRyrie tapped his shoulder. "Uh . . . Crushek?"

"Yeah?"

"Do you have brothers?"

Crush looked at Malone, then released her and faced the grizzly. "Why do you ask?"

MacRyrie pointed behind them and they all turned. Chazz and Gray stood there in T-shirts and loose dolphin shorts that no men their size should ever wear. In the distance, Crush could see his brothers' wives and cubs at a picnic table, but if they knew what his brothers were up to, they didn't seem to notice or care.

The three of them scowled at each other, none of them speaking. Then Gray and Chazz looked at Cella and back at him, Gray raising his arms in what Crush felt was a clear challenge and . . . well . . . what did anyone expect?

Clothes went flying, Crush's jeans hitting Cella in the face, and then three polar bears were in the middle of a brawl right there. Since cats fought all the time, the Malone-O'Neill battle going on behind them was quickly forgotten as everyone focused on the vicious bear scrimmage.

"So, he's not close to his family then?" one of the wild dog females guessed.

"There's only the three of them and no, they're not close."

Marly rested her elbow on Cella's shoulder. "Anyone a little bothered that it's those two against poor Crushek?"

Cella was more than a little bothered, but who would get between three polar bears during a fight? But just as she had the thought, Novikov and MacRyrie ran past her, both in their shifted form. A few seconds after that, the rest of the first-string players followed.

"Does Novikov have tusks?" Marly asked.

"They're not *tusks*," Blayne yelled while slowly dragging herself to her feet. "They're fangs. Like the mighty saber-toothed cat of yore."

Marly scratched her head. "Yore?"

Chapter Twenty

"He's doing it wrong," Van Holtz noted.

The entire table looked over at the polar bear working the in-tent barbeque.

"He's going to make everything dry."

Novikov sighed. "Guess you're going over there to show him how it's done."

Crush, still feeling where Chazz had slammed his head into a tree, quietly stated, "I wouldn't."

Now they were all looking at him. Crush still couldn't believe these guys had backed him up in his fight against Chazz and Gray. And, man, had those idiots been jealous because he'd had the goddamn Carnivores on his side. It had been *great*!

"You know him?" MacRyrie asked about the polar working the barbeque.

"He was DEA before he retired. Now he lives in Staten Island and is a butcher. His name is Billows, but they call him Wishbone."

"Why?"

"The story I heard from other shifters in NYPD is that there was a case involving some crack house in Staten Island. There was a little firefight and one of the guys made a run for it. Wishbone caught him and during the struggle, the guy stabbed Wishbone in the leg, which just pissed him off because he has a real short temper. So they say he had the guy by his legs, told his partner to 'make a wish.' Then he . . ."

Unable to find the right words, Crush illustrated by yanking his hands apart and all the men exclaimed simultaneously, "Ohhhh!"

"Anyway," Crush went on, "I've been to his butcher shop a few times since he caters to polars and, I think, lions, and he's still known in his neighborhood for being kind of short on temper. So if I were you . . . I'd let him make his dry meat."

They all silently agreed to let the butcher keep making his dry meat while they went back to their conversation.

Eventually, they went to get something to eat. Crush gawked at the array of things to choose from, smiling up at Wishbone when the former cop turned around.

"Crushek."

"Hey, Wish. How's it all going? How are the kids?"

"Pretty good. And you. Heard you moved to the Brooklyn House."

"I did."

The polar glanced around, stepped closer. "Watch your back, Crushek."

"From other cops?"

"No."

Crush's eyes crossed. "Right."

"Bears who work for her"—and he knew who Wishbone meant when he said "her"—"going around asking questions about you."

"Anything specific?"

"Just digging. Probably trying to discredit you. Don't know how far she'll go, though. I don't know what you did to piss her off, but . . ." He picked up a tray of whale fat slabs. "Just be careful, man."

"Thanks, Wish."

Suddenly not hungry, Crush stood there staring at the table. When the answers to his problems didn't miraculously appear amid the deer steak and zebra burgers, Crush started to walk away.

"Have you tried the bison dogs?" Van Holtz asked. How long he'd been standing there, Crush didn't know.

"I haven't."

"They're good. Different. Add a little Dijon mustard and relish."

Deciding to follow the wolf's suggestion, Crush filled up his plate and found an empty table. He dropped into a seat and Van Holtz sat down next to him. In silence, they ate until the table began to fill up with Cella's aunts. They mostly ignored the two males, eating their own food, and talking shit about some of the other party attendees.

When Crush was nearly done, Cella's Aunt Karen leaned over and asked Kathleen, "No one thinks it's strange that them two are friends?"

The entire table looked over at Cella and Dee-Ann Smith, both of them laughing.

"It is surprising," Kathleen admitted. "Considering the past."

Crush wiped his mouth with a napkin. "You mean when Cella was in the Marines?"

Kathleen and her sisters laughed. "God, no. I'm talking long before that. When we hexed them."

Crush looked at Van Holtz. They both frowned at each other before Crush asked, "You hexed the Smiths?"

"Not me personally. Our ancestors. But the Smiths deserved it. They were eating us."

The bison was sticking in his throat, but Crush was a cop. There were just some things he simply couldn't walk away from.

"Wolves were eating tigers?"

"They weren't wolves then. They were cannibals."

Van Holtz leaned around Crush to see Kathleen. "Excuse me?"

"You didn't know that? You're living with one of them."

"She's not a cannibal."

"And I don't raise horses. But my ancestors used to."

"I'm still unclear—"

Kathleen cut Crush off. "Some time in the sixteen or seventeen hundreds, I forget which, the Malones were once again forced out of Ireland."

"Once again?"

She fluttered her hands. "Anyway, they were traveling through England and there was this area they were warned not to go through, but they went anyway because, ya know . . . tigers. Figured they could handle anything, but what they didn't know was that the Smiths were lying in wait."

"Lying in wait to . . . eat you?"

"And rob. That's what they did. Most of the Malones got away, but the Smiths actually caught a few."

"And ate them?"

"Among other things. The matriarch of the Malones at the time, she got really pissed and she said if they were going to be as low as dogs, they should *be* dogs. Then they hexed them."

Crush finished off his hot dog and, after chewing thoughtfully, finally said, "I'm not sure turning violent, vicious, cannibal killers into actual predators was the best idea your ancestors had."

"In their defense, though, at the time there was a lot of wolf hunting in England, so they probably thought the Smiths would be destroyed, but who knew the inbreeding cannibals had their own witches? A spell here, a spell there, and they were able to shift back and forth just like us. From what I understand, my relatives were sorely disappointed by all this."

"You mean because now the Smiths didn't have to track down any weapons . . . because they had *become* weapons?"

"Yeah," Kathleen sighed. "They clearly hadn't thought long term." She patted Crush's leg. "But we all have stories like that, right? Mr. Van Holtz here is descended from German barbarians."

"It's true," Van Holtz admitted. "We're the real reason Julius Caesar charged back across the Rhine and burned the bridge his troops had built before we could cross it."

"What about you, dear?" Kathleen asked Crush.

"Well, my parents died when I was really young, but when I was older I managed to get a little information about my great-great-great-grandfather, who liked polar bears and used to sit around thinking about how much he'd like to be a polar bear. Then one day he woke up and he was a polar bear." Crush thought about that a minute and added, "In retrospect, not nearly as interesting as barbarians fighting Julius Caesar."

"No. But not a story you have to hide, either."

"She's got a point." Van Holtz blew out a breath. "It's not like I've heard any of the Smiths running around talking about their cannibal days."

"Exactly." Kathleen patted Crush's leg again. "I'm sure your ancestor was a very nice man."

"He was kind of a cop. You know, for his time. Well . . ." Crush thought back, remembering what he'd found out. "Kind of a cop slash executioner. He had a real thing for injustice—"

"There you go!"

"—and witches. Used to burn them at the stake unless he drowned them or piled rocks on them first."

"Oh."

The group went silent until Crush finally stated, "Still liking the barbarians against Roman forces story better."

"Yeah," they all agreed.

The sun went down, the snow began to steadily fall, and nearly everybody was out on the dance floor dancing to Mungo

Jerry's "In the Summertime." The hotties, of course, had on what some would call ski gear, but even they couldn't stay in the hot tent. It had been a great party.

She knew that Crush was having a good time, too, dancing with her, a little blood still in his hair from his earlier seal hunt with Novikov. He didn't even seem to mind that she could only currently look at him through one eye since the other one was swollen shut from the fistfight. Smith offered to "cut you like in the *Rocky* movies," but as Cella told the She-wolf when she'd offered, she'd rather wait until the swelling went down on its own.

A slower Motown classic came on and Cella immediately went into Crush's arms, the two grinning at each other while swaying to the music. Like most bears, the man had some nice rhythm considering his size.

"You and the girls need a lift home?" he asked.

"No. I'm going back with the girls, and some of my cousins. We'll be making brownies at Jai's place and talking boys all night. But thanks for the offer."

"No problem."

"Glad you came to the party?" she asked.

"Very."

"You coming back next year?"

He gazed down at her. "Maybe."

She chuckled. "Oooh, 'maybe.' That's promising."

He laughed, his arms tightening around her waist. Cella rested her head against his chest. And that's when she knew— she was in trouble. Deep, deep trouble.

Chapter Twenty-one

Tuesday morning, Ric Van Holtz dragged himself out of bed and made his way to his kitchen to get the coffee started. He ground the beans, pulled down a coffee mug, and waited while his fourteen-cup coffeemaker did its work.

And when that hand slipped across his naked hip, he didn't jump . . . anymore. It took some getting used to, living with the sneakiest of wolves, but Ric wouldn't change it for the world. Eyes still closed, he turned his head and soft lips pressed against his.

"Glad you're home," he murmured, nuzzling the She-wolf who pressed her long body next to his. "What's going on?"

"The bear's information was right. Found Whitlan's office. And he's in it."

Ric opened his eyes, and nodded. "Take it down. Tonight. Bring him in alive, Dee-Ann."

She grinned, kissed his neck. "You've got it."

Crush's phone woke him that morning from the most erotic dream he'd had in a while, involving a She-tiger in hockey pants, and he wasn't happy about it.

He swiped the cell phone off his nightstand. "What?"

"It's MacDermot."

"What?"

"Meet me at the office at six."

Crush glared over at his bedside clock. "It's six-thirty."

"No. I meant six tonight."

"Why?"

"Group and KZS are taking down Whitlan. Tonight."

"Wait. They found him? How did they even know—"

"God, you're like my kid. Asking ten thousand questions."

"I'm a bear. That's what we do. And this is our case."

"Flexibility is key for this job, Crushek. Get used to it. Besides, I've just accepted the fact that Dee-Ann Smith has contacts you and I just ain't got. And if she wants to find you—she'll find you. Now, I'll see you at six."

"But—"

"If it makes you feel better, your girlfriend will be there."

"My—"

"Also heard you're a hell of a kisser."

Crush sat up. "*What?*"

Cella packed up her duffel bag, throwing in a few extra clips for good measure, and zipped it up. She looked around, made sure she had everything. She did, and what she didn't have, KZS would provide.

Pulling on a light denim jacket, she picked up her bag and rushed down the stairs, through the kitchen, waving at her mother and father, then around the side of the house. Meghan and Josie were already heading to the Jeep, schoolbooks in hand, discussing something in whispers.

"I'm working tonight, babe," Cella called out. "I'll see you tomorrow."

Cella tossed her bag into one of her brothers' cars. She didn't know which one.

"That's fine. I'm babysitting Deena's kids tonight. But can we talk tomorrow, Ma?"

Cella, about to get into her car, stopped and looked over at her daughter. "Talk? Oh, you mean about you heading to Hofstra in the fall? Sure . . . we can talk about that."

Josie, an apple in her hand, stared first at Meghan, then at Cella.

When her daughter didn't say anything, Cella got in her car, pulled out of the driveway, and headed in to work.

MacDermot was standing outside the office waiting for him. She had two big cups of coffee and a pastry bag. When he got close she demanded to know, "Why are you looking at me like that?"

"Malone told you about . . ."

MacDermot laughed. "She didn't have to. Everybody told me how cuddly you two were at that freezing party."

"Ice Party."

"Whatever. Although really, *you* should have told me."

"Why the hell would I tell you?"

"We're partners."

"We're partners, MacDermot, not girlfriends. We're not going to sit around talking about dates or our periods or your husband's problems with roaring at his neighbors."

MacDermot sighed. "We got another noise citation last week. I keep trying to convince them it's the dogs, but no one seems to believe me."

Crush snatched one of the coffees away from her. "Can we just get this over with?"

She held up the pastry bag. "I brought treats."

"What kind?"

"Honey buns and—"

Really mad now, Crush barked, "Do I look like a grizzly to you? Do you see a hump? Or an 'I'm stupider than you might think' look on my face? Huh? I thought we already discussed this."

MacDermot's top lip curled the tiniest bit. "Am I going to have to shoot you? Because I will shoot you."

Crush snarled and turned away from her.

"What about cinnamon?"

"What about it?"

"I also got cinnamon twists because *I* like the honey buns. I've made it my business that the only predator whose diet I worry about is the one who fucks me regularly. And last I looked this morning—that wasn't you. *Now do you want the goddamn cinnamon twist or not?*"

Crush turned back around, eyed MacDermot. "You always this cranky?"

"Only when I have to deal with more than one predator a day." She held out the bag. "And you better eat this now. The ones inside do not share."

He took the bag. "I'm top of the food chain, MacDermot . . . *no one* takes my cinnamon twists."

"Great. First I have to deal with Captain Ego at home and now Commander Boar Rage at work."

She turned and headed into the office. "Come on."

Crush followed her, stepping into the first-floor elevator. But instead of pushing the button for their office floor, she pushed the one for the basement. Crush hadn't had a chance to fully explore the place yet, so he had no real idea what was on this floor.

They stepped out and walked down a long hallway, finally stopping at a room. MacDermot kicked the steel door with her foot and after a few seconds a She-leopard opened it.

"You're late, MacDermot."

"You gonna start with me now? Because I have no problem shooting every one of youse."

She pushed past the female and walked inside. The She-leopard winked at him, her smile telling him she enjoyed fucking with MacDermot. Damn cats and their damn emotional torture.

Crush walked into the room and immediately stopped, his gaze looking over everything.

"Your gear's here," MacDermot said, pointing at a locker.

"What is this?" Crush asked, slowly walking up to her, his eyes still locked on what he was seeing.

"What's what?"

"This, MacDermot. All of this."

"What? You mean the rocket launcher? That's a just in case, really."

Crush stared at her. "A just in case?"

"You never know. Hurry up. We'll take one of the vans and go check in with the others."

"You mean the Group?"

"And KZS." MacDermot pointed at the other shifters in the room. There were about twelve. He knew some of them, had never seen the others, and they represented many breeds. Knowing MacDermot, Crush would bet that most of them were military trained. "This is our team. The best of the best, as far as I'm concerned. You and me, we take lead."

"You and I."

"That's what I said."

"No . . ." Crush shook his head. "Forget it."

"Right. You and me take lead, NYPD is there as backup for the Group and KZS."

"Who are their team leads?" a black bear asked while he pulled his vest over his incredibly wide chest.

"Malone and Smith."

When the rest of the team members nodded their heads, seeming to approve, Crush could tell that Malone had already earned a good reputation with the others.

"You guys get the vans and meet us at the Group offices."

"You're going now, MacDermot?"

"You know they're always late. As it is, I'm guessing it's going to be a long night."

Crush felt the need to ask, "So while we're backing up Group and KZS, what are they doing?"

"No idea."

"Don't you care?"

"Not particularly." MacDermot shrugged. "They do most of the wet work."

When the rest of the team nodded in agreement as if that made things all better, Crush replied, "I can't express to you how much that one sentence freaks me the fuck out."

MacDermot grinned, patting his bicep since she couldn't reach his shoulder without getting on a stepladder, "You'll get used to it. Now let's go get your girlfriend."

"She's not my—"

"Who's his girlfriend?" the She-leopard asked.

"Malone."

And when all the females replied, "Awwww," Crush sighed and briefly thought about retiring and opening up a little bar on a Barbados beach somewhere.

Cella ducked the fist to her face and swung her own left, slamming it into Smith's jaw. She danced back on her toes, and smiled at Smith. Cella loved fighting Smith. She was one of the few who could actually take a punch to the face without all that sobbing and pleas for mercy.

Cella hated that.

Smith came back up, swinging at her again. Cella ducked, but she got a knee to the face and then Smith kicked her right out of the ring—again.

She slid face-first into a big pair of feet while the crowd that had been growing steadily since she and Smith stepped into the ring cheered and roared.

"What the hell are you doing?"

Hey. She knew that voice. "Daddy?"

Big hands reached down and picked her up off the floor. "Now you're freaking me out."

Cella shook her head, trying to clear her vision. She saw coal-black eyes staring at her. She knew those eyes! From somewhere.

"Hey . . . you."

"You don't know my name, do you?"

"I will . . . as soon as that ringing stops in my ears. But I will say you're very cute."

"Hey, Malone," Smith called from the ring. "Don't you remember? That's your boyfriend."

"Pretend boyfriend. He's a perfect pretend boyfriend . . . I think."

"I don't understand," MacDermot cut in. "Why are you two beating the hell out of each other when you know we're going to work tonight? The team will be here soon."

"Don't yell at me, cop." Cella wrapped her arms around the bear's waist and rested her head against his chest. "Don't make me get my boyfriend to beat you up."

"You're bleeding all over my shirt."

"It's black."

"Yeah, but now it'll be sticky."

Now that the bell Smith had rung had finally stopped ringing, Cella looked up at, uh . . . Crushek! That was his name! "Yeah," she shot back, "sticky with my love."

Both MacDermot and Smith laughed and, after sighing, the bear wrapped his arm around her waist and lifted her off the floor.

"Hey!"

"Come on."

"Come on where?"

"To get you cleaned up."

He walked off with her, stopping by one of the Group members, a fellow polar, to ask, "Bathroom?"

The polar grunted and jerked his head. Seemed it was enough, though, because Crushek found the co-ed locker room. He placed her on the long sink and pushed her hair off her face to look at her bruises and cuts.

"So is that how you guys communicate with each other? Grunting?"

" 'You guys'?"

"Bears. He grunted and you seemed to know exactly where to go."

"Why waste words when a nod in the right direction is all that's needed? God, you heal fast."

"Hhhmh. It's a Malone thing."

Crushek wet a paper towel and began to remove the blood from her face. He had such a nice touch, too. Considering the size of those hands, she always expected him to be much more fumblelike about it.

"So do you always fight your team members?" he asked.

"No. But I always fight Smith. She's gotta jaw like granite. I figure if I can survive a fight with her, I can survive a fight with damn near anybody."

"Yes. That's what you want to base your friendships on. Whether your buddies can take a hit to the face."

"What about Jai?"

"Jai?"

"The one you keep calling Dr. Davis. All serious and shit about it, too."

"It's called respect."

"You're just a suck up because she's the team doc."

"Can you blame me? She's actually helped the victims of you and the Marauder. She should get a medal."

"Don't call them victims, just the opposing team. No use giving them special titles like victims. And," she went on, "I wouldn't have to hurt anyone if they didn't go after Novikov. I'm only protecting him. That's my job, in case you don't remember."

His eyes narrowed. "Wait a minute. You hit Dr. Davis?"

"Of course not. That's the point. I have a healthy range of friends. Some I can punch in the face and some I'd never, ever consider it. Well, actually, I have considered it with Jai because she can be a snobby bitch, but I'd never do it. She'd crumple like a house of cards and then I'd feel bad."

"That's big of you."

"I am all heart." Cella laughed and reached for Crushek's T-shirt, pulling him closer so that he rested right between her legs.

"I am still thinking about our last kiss, which is huge for me because I find most beings downright forgettable."

"Isn't that a cat thing?"

"Yeah. But once we lock on ya, it's hell getting rid of us."

He gazed down at her. "I thought I was just your pretend boyfriend."

"But I think a pretend boyfriend should come with benefits."

"Shouldn't they come with *pretend* benefits?"

"No. Real benefits for pretend boyfriends. That's my motto." Cella studied him for a moment and said, "Want to know how you, as my pretend boyfriend . . . can help me out?"

"Pretend help you out?"

"Uh-uh. The real thing." She slid off the counter. "Come on. I need you to watch my back."

He scowled, his gaze locked on her mouth. "Is that some sexual talk I'm unfamiliar with?"

"No. I need you to keep an eye out for Blayne," she whispered.

"Uh-huh. And why would I need to do that?"

"Because I asked you to. God, what kind of pretend boyfriend are you?"

"A confused and fictitious one?"

"Yeah, yeah." She grabbed his hand. "Come on."

Crush had no idea what to do with this woman. He wasn't sure if she went out of her way to confuse him or if she was just confusing in general. Either of these scenarios was possible with her.

But still, he was curious to see what she was up to and what she felt the need to hide from Blayne Thorpe, a woman who seemed to love everybody and have absolutely no secrets. He really hoped it wasn't anything involving life or death. He'd hate to have to choose sides.

Malone eased the locker room door open and peeked out, looking first one way, then the other. Once she seemed satisfied, she tugged and led him into the hallway. She moved quickly. Crush just needed to lengthen his stride a bit to keep up with her as she went down to the game room that was, as always, filled with hybrid kids.

Malone took another quick look around and then dragged him into the room, closing the door behind them. "Keep a lookout for Blayne."

"But she can see right through the big window."

"Just do what I ask. If you see her, let me know."

"You should stop involving Blayne in whatever you're doing. You're upsetting the Marauder's equilibrium."

"I don't even know what that means." She stopped, faced him. "How do you know that?"

"No reason."

"You're lying. What are you hiding from me?"

"Nothing." When she kept scowling at him with those gold eyes, he finally admitted, "We just had lunch . . . couple of times."

"Awwwww. You've made a friend!"

Annoyed, Crush snapped, "Don't we have something we're *supposed* to be doing? Like . . . our jobs?"

"Do you have any idea how long it takes for shifters to get their shit together so we can head out? Trust me, we have time. Besides, this is for my job. The one you care the most about now that you have a friend. . . ."

"Shut up. I have to put on my body armor."

She made a sound that seemed distinctly . . .

"Did you just purr at me?"

"Yeah." And she kind of growled that. "Body armor over

all those muscles . . . what kind of response do you expect
from a girl?"

"Not purring, but, uh, thanks?"

She winked and walked farther into the room, Crush behind her. The kids stopped what they were doing to watch
them, some of them recognizing Crush. Not who he was
specifically, though. He could just hear them whispering to a
friend close-by, "Cop."

Then a few left the room while some others just kept
watching.

Like Malone had said, street kids. Who'd already been
through a lot, he guessed. Just like Hannah had.

Fascinated, he didn't even realize they'd stopped walking
until Cella said, "Hey, Hannah."

Hannah looked up from her book, brown eyes growing
wide when she saw Cella and Crush.

"Oh. Cella. Hi."

"How's it going?"

She shrugged massive shoulders. "Fine."

"So, kid." Malone released Crush's hand and stepped
closer. "You busy week after next?"

"Busy?"

"Uh-huh. Busy. As in you have something to do?"

"I never have anything to do." She held up a book. "I usually just read."

"Reading. Right. Reading is good for you. I love reading." And when Crush snorted, he got quite the glare. "Magazines," she amended. "I enjoy reading magazines." Another
scowl at him, then she said to the girl, "But you know what's
really fun? Hanging out with me for a few hours at the
Sports Center."

"Why do you want her to hang out with you at the—ow!
Do you mind? I actually need that femur!"

"Okay," Hannah said. "I'll ask. Why do you want me to
hang out at the Sports Center?"

"Well, you see, the Carnivores and the minor team for

New York are having tryouts and I thought you'd like to come and—"

"*Aaaah-haaa!*"

Crush was so startled by the scream coming from behind him that he spun around and roared.

Accusing finger pointing, Blayne Thorpe stormed her way over to them. Where had she been hiding? He didn't really know. And how long had she been hiding? No clue.

"I didn't know I'd have to deal with such betrayal!"

"Jesus, Mary, and Joseph!" Malone shot back. "You with the drama! And you knew I was going to ask her. You knew!"

"But I didn't think you would! The travesty! Well, you just keep your grubby cat paws off Hannah."

"I will do no such thing. And my paws are *not* grubby, canine."

"You can't just walk in here and—"

"I can and I will. I'm giving her the opportunity of a lifetime and I'm not letting you and your girl power sensibilities get in my way."

Blayne gasped. "How dare you!"

"Cut the shit, Thorpe."

"You know what? You don't want to mess with me, Malone."

"Why? What are you going to do? Sob me to death?"

While the two idiots argued, they didn't notice that Hannah was desperately looking for a way out of the room, but the females had her backed into a corner. She looked incredibly uncomfortable and Crush got that. Some bears just didn't like a lot of yelling and drama around them.

Desperate brown eyes sought his, long fingers curling into fists. Not wanting her to snap and possibly bite little Blayne's head off in the process—she was the closest—Crush grabbed both feline and canine around the waist and took them back out into the hallway. By the time he put them down, the two *grown* women were slapping at each other like, well . . . like regular suburban girls. Seemed odd since neither of them were regular anything.

"Stop it," he ordered, using his best cop voice.

"She started it. Sneaky cat!"

"Dumb canine!"

"That is *enough*! I mean it." Crush stood between the two women, but he faced Malone. "What are you doing?"

"I want Hannah to try out for the Carnivores and Little Miss Mood Swing wants her to try out for derby."

"Derby, I'll have you know, has a long and proud tradition."

"Of tiny shorts and makeup use."

The two went for each other again and Crush pushed them apart. "Here's a suggestion . . . why don't you let Hannah decide?"

They both stopped, gazed up at him. "Why?" they asked.

Disgusted, Crush walked back into the game room and over to Hannah. Her eyes were on the pages of her book, but Crush knew she wasn't reading. Not with her right leg bouncing and her cheeks a bright red.

"Hey."

She cleared her throat. "Hey."

"Do you remember me?"

"You're Cella's boyfriend."

"I'm not—" He stopped, and calmed down. "Right. And you took on those two grizzlies the other day."

"That big one hurt Abby, and that full-human girl, she didn't do anything. She was just helping."

"I know. You absolutely did the right thing. Not that you care, but I was impressed."

She peeked up at him through long, dark lashes. "Really?"

"Yeah. Unfortunately for you, though, you also impressed the two nutbags I took out of here."

She frowned. "Huh?"

"Let me just ask you a question, Hannah, and you give me a straight and honest answer. Extremely honest."

"There is no 'extremely' honest. There's honest. Or there's dishonest."

Yep. She was his kind of girl. If Crush had ever had a sister, he'd guess she'd have the same kind of argument.

"You're right."

"So what do you want to ask me?"

"Do you want a shot at playing hockey or do you want a shot at playing derby?"

Frowning, she answered, "I don't think I'd be very good at either."

"Only you would know that but, I'm afraid, if you want either of these two off your back anytime soon, you're going to have to fall on your face to prove it."

She briefly closed her eyes. "Yeah. I was afraid it was getting to that point. Blayne's been circling me for months like a stray circling an injured rat in an alley. And then Cella . . . I just wasn't exactly sure why."

"Do you even like hockey or derby?"

"Hockey's okay. I don't know much about derby, but I've seen the shorts. I'm not comfortable with those shorts, Mr. Crushek."

"You can call me Crush. Besides . . . I'm guessing I wouldn't look good in those shorts, either. Although I've been told I have nice calves."

That made her smile and Crush asked, "Can I make a suggestion?"

Hannah studied him a moment, then nodded her head. "Okay."

"If you tolerate hockey, then go to the Carnivore tryout. Get it done and over with and chances are neither will bother you again."

"You clearly don't know Blayne."

That made him laugh a little. "I don't know her well, no, but I'm sure sobbing will be involved. But that could work for you, too. Seem all broken up about your humiliation at hockey and maybe cry a little, I'm guessing she'll totally back off. I won't promise, however, that she won't try to find something else to obsess over. I haven't known her two weeks and I already sense that she obsesses over a lot."

"You'd be amazed."

"But you'll definitely get Malone off your back."

"I just don't . . ."

"Don't what?"

"Don't want to embarrass myself in front of Cella. I mean . . . she's Bare Knuckles Malone. *The* Bare Knuckles Malone."

Realizing he was talking to a fan, Crush grinned. "Kid, until you've spent two hours with your childhood hero—Malone's father—and listened to him go on and on about his participation in every illegal activity short of first-degree murder and sexual assault . . . you really don't know what embarrassment is."

She laughed and Crush was immediately charmed. He could tell she was a very sweet kid, no matter what she'd been through. It wasn't easy to keep that part of yourself when you've been through hell, though. No. Not easy at all.

"That really happened?" she asked.

"It really happened. And as you mentioned, I'm a cop. I was torn between whether I should annoyingly discuss every goal he'd ever made or arrest him for anything that hadn't passed the statute of limitations."

"What did you do?"

A little ashamed, Crush shrugged. "I annoyed."

Cella waited in the hallway with Blayne, the pair glaring at each other until Blayne said, "I thought we were friends."

"We are very good friends," Cella snarled back. "In fact, I like you a lot, you little bitch. But you get between me and a potential player and I'll twist your little head around until you can look at your spine."

Instead of firing a threat right back, Blayne said, "Gwenie can do that."

"Gwenie can do what?"

"Turn her head so she can look at her spine."

Horrified, "Really?"

"Yeah."

"What is she? A house cat?"

"Nope. She's just Gwenie." Blayne grinned. "And I adore your mother!"

"She's good, isn't she?"

"So good!" Blayne scowled again. "But you're not taking Hannah from me."

"Like hell I'm not."

The game room door opened and Crushek walked out.

"Well?" both females asked as soon as he closed the door.

With a smirk, he pointed at Cella.

"Ha!" Cella crowed, then danced around a stomping, snarling Blayne.

"I hate both of you!"

"Why do you hate me?" Crushek demanded. "I was just trying to help."

"Oh, shut up!"

Cella clapped her hands together. "Eat that, canine!"

"I'll never forgive either of you!" Blayne howled before turning and running down the hall. Then she spun back around and returned.

As she passed, Cella sweetly asked, "Wrong way, honey?"

"Shut up, Betrayer!"

The wolfdog disappeared around a corner and Crush shook his head. "Is there anywhere you go that you don't bring pain and destruction?"

"As a matter of fact . . ." Cella gasped, remembering that people were waiting for them. "That's right! We've gotta get to work."

She ran back to the locker room to change, but she could hear the bear behind her bark, "That statement does not give me confidence, feline."

CHAPTER TWENTY-TWO

"MacDermot!"

MacDermot sat up. "I'm awake. I'm awake."

She was now, but she hadn't been for the last hour. Not that Crush blamed her. This was boring. And it wasn't that he hadn't done surveillance before. He had. A lot. But he'd always known what he was looking for. Instead, their entire team was sitting around doing nothing, while the Group and KZS teams were doing . . . something. Any time Crush asked, no one could give him an answer. Something that really bugged the shit out of him. What exactly was his role here? The role of NYPD? Was this his life now? Sitting around, waiting for someone else to get done doing . . . whatever?

Maybe I should start updating my résumé.

"Any more coffee?" MacDermot asked him.

"Here." Crush handed her his large thermos. "There's a little left."

"Thanks." Yawning, MacDermot poured herself a cup. After a sip—and a shudder—she asked, "What are you doing?"

"Getting these files together to pass off to Conway."

"You're going to miss undercover, huh?"

"Yeah."

"There still might be an opportunity to do it for our division."

"Yeah. Right. Hard to go undercover with shifters, Mac-Dermot. They can smell what you are." He heard her snort and Crush looked up to find MacDermot laughing. "What's so funny?"

"If you told me ten years ago someone would say to me in all seriousness 'shifters can smell what you are' . . ."

Crush had to smile. "I guess it is weird for you. Going from your life to this one."

"Weird but entertaining. How many girls from my old neighborhood can say that they walked into their house two days ago to find a four-hundred-pound lion asleep in the middle of their living room with their son sleeping on top of him?"

"And the dogs?"

"Out cold, curled up next to him. He said later they'd ambushed him."

"You know, lion males annoy the living shit out of me, but Llewellyn . . . a hell of a lot better than your first husband. I don't know what you were thinking that first go-round."

"Yeah. Me, neither. But sometimes . . ." She smiled, shrugged. "Sometimes a girl gets a second chance."

"Believe it or not, I think you're one of the few people who actually deserves one."

"Thanks, Crushek."

"Well . . . we're partners now so, you know, you can, um . . ."

"I can call you Crush?"

"Yeah. If ya want."

She pursed her lips. "Does Malone get to call you Crush?"

He rolled his eyes. "Don't start."

"Do you call her Cella or Maaarcella?" she crooned.

"Seriously? Are we going to start this now?"

"It's not like we've got anything better to do stuck in the back of this van."

"So we're girlfriends now? Is that's what's going on here?"

"I'm almost sad you cut your hair, otherwise I could have given you ponytails."

"*This* will not be the course of our relationship."

"You and your fancy Queens talk."

Crush decided not to let the woman get to him and asked, "So . . . how long are we just going to sit here? Doing nothin'."

"We're not just doin' nothin'. We're getting paid overtime to do nothin'."

"We didn't work all day. How are we now paid overtime?"

"You ask too many questions."

"MacDermot—"

"Zip it."

"Yeah, but—"

"Zip it."

"Fine, but my whole career is not going to be . . ." Crush stopped talking and moved his gaze to the roof of the van.

"What?" MacDermot asked him.

Crush didn't have a chance to answer her, though, reaching over and yanking her to the floor, dropping down next to her as something big and heavy slammed into the van, crumpling the roof on top of them.

When he was sure he hadn't been crushed to death, he asked, "Are you all right?"

"Yeah. Yeah."

The back doors were yanked open by one of their team.

"Are you two okay?" the wolf asked.

"Yeah." MacDermot quickly low crawled out of the van, Crush following her.

Once outside, he stood and looked at the roof of the van. "It's a body. Why is there a body on the roof of our van?"

The entire NYPD team looked up at the building, their

gazes moving until they could see the edge of the building's roof. Then they were dashing away, trying to avoid the next falling body.

"MacDermot?" he growled, not enjoying having bodies flung at him.

"Fuck!" The full-human gave an overall shake. "Crush, Jenny. With me. The rest of you watch the exits. No one comes in or out. And make sure no one sends any fuckin' air support."

She looked at Crush. "You ready for this?"

"No."

"Good. Let's go."

Cella was thrown back, her body slamming into the brick wall, seconds before some bear was slamming his quite sizable fists into her face and chest.

When they'd gone into the building—Cella's team and Smith's—they thought they'd only be dealing with full-humans. But as they'd moved from floor to floor, doing a sweep, they'd found nothing but empty offices—not even furniture or phones—and the ever-increasing scent of bears. That, however, hadn't stopped them. They just figured they'd have to negotiate with the bears to get to Whitlan.

Yet when they'd hit the roof, those BPC bears had come after them like they were covered in honey or threatening their cubs. The question for Cella, however, was *why* had the BPC bears come after them? No one had challenged them. Both teams had immediately lowered their weapons when they saw there was no Whitlan, and no one had spoken a threatening word. And still, BPC opened fire.

Now an enormous fist was swinging at her again. Cella caught the bear's arm by the wrist with one hand, holding it. She swung her other fist, hitting the bear in the face. He stumbled, stunned. Still holding his arm, Cella brought her foot down, ramming it into his knee. She heard it crack and the bear crumpled.

She gripped his head with both her hands and twisted, snapping his neck. She stepped over his body, but another bear was coming for her. He never got near her, though. A bowie knife rammed into the thick muscle between his shoulder blades. He screamed, chest arching out.

Smith yanked out the blade and swung around in front of him, slicing his throat. The bear dropped to his knees, hands around his throat. Cella kicked him in the chest, not worrying he'd get back up. Smith had a thing about making sure she hit at least one artery, if not two, when she used her blade.

Smith jerked her head. "Behind you."

Cella moved to the side and caught hold of one of the arms reaching for her. She yanked him closer, kicked him in the face, then twisted his big arm, but unfortunately not enough to break any bone. The bear grunted in pain and grabbed Cella by the hair with his free hand, yanking her around and holding her in place so he could head-butt her. Considering the size of the bastard's head, Cella nearly blacked out, her knees buckling. But she couldn't drop to the floor because the bear still held her by her hair, which was starting to feel like it was being pulled out by the roots. Since she had no intention of getting a receding hairline before she was forty like her Uncle Harry, Cella kicked him, battering the bear's chest. She could hear ribs breaking, but the bear didn't seem to let it bother him. Instead, he reached for the .45 he had tucked into the back of his jeans. Cella, unfortunately, had lost her gun in the earlier stages of the fight. Desperate, she unleashed her claws, ready to start tearing flesh from skin, but a series of booming bangs distracted her and the bear, both looking at the thick steel rooftop door that had been closed by several bodies barricading it.

The grizzly's lip curled and he snarled out, "Polar."

Cella knew then it was Crush, even before the steel door buckled and was ripped off its hinges. It flew across the roof, colliding with several bears and grazing one of Cella's team-mates.

Crush walked out onto the roof, several of the NYPD shifter team following behind him, each armed. His head turned and he scowled when he saw Cella dangling by her hair.

He roared and the grizzly holding her roared back while aiming that goddamn .45.

Ripping at the grizzly's arm with her claws, Cella screamed out, "Gun!"

Crush pulled his weapon so quickly, Cella barely saw it. And he shot three times. Twice to the chest and once to the head. The grizzly's body jerked, his arm dropping enough that Cella's knees hit the ground hard. She grunted as the pain in her left weaker knee ripped through her while the grizzly fell back, tipping over like a diseased tree. Cella went with him, untangling his fingers from her hair once they hit the ground. Once loose, she rolled over the bear, using him as a shield until she could pry his gun from his hand. She waited until whoever was firing at her stopped, then rolled up and onto one knee. Out of habit, it was her left knee, and she forced herself to ignore the pain. She quickly raised the weapon she held and did what she did best right after bare-knuckle brawling and hockey. She killed the enemy. One shot to each head, taking out the bear fighting Smith first because she knew that the She-wolf would imme-diately back her up and keep any grizzlies off her.

As always, Cella was fast and efficient, not one to waste bullets. She could only do this better if she was on another building with her rifle. Yeah. She was that good a shot.

Smith finished off a few grizzlies with her blade and was coming toward her when her gaze moved behind Cella.

Knowing someone was behind her, Cella spun, her wea-pon still raised. Smith moved up beside her, both of them about to open fire, but someone else shot first and the grizzly jerked forward. He fell to his knees, then dropped, MacDermot walking up behind him with her own .45.

"You two all right?" she asked, ever the cop even while she unloaded a few more rounds in that bear because he twitched a bit.

"Yeah," both Cella and Smith answered.

Smith reached down and helped up Cella, scowling when Cella refused to put any weight on her left leg "Say a word to Van Holtz about my leg . . ." Cella warned the She-wolf under her breath.

"What the fuck happened?" MacDermot demanded.

Smith shrugged. "Went bad."

MacDermot gawked at them. "You really don't think that's going to be enough of an answer, do you?"

"What else is there to say?"

While the pair bickered, Cella scanned the roof until she saw Crushek. Limping, she moved toward him, stepping over the bodies and around teammates that were busy calling in for a cleaning crew.

Cella stood beside Crushek, watching as he turned over one of the bodies. He scowled down at it.

"What's wrong?"

"These are all Baissier's men. They're all BPC."

Cella sighed. "Yeah . . . I know."

Chapter Twenty-three

They returned to the precinct, including the KZS and Group members. Clean clothes were retrieved for those who had blood on them, and calls were made to appropriate management personnel. No one panicked, but clearly everyone was worried. Crush didn't know why, though. Baissier's idea of retaliation was never to come straight at anyone. That wasn't how she played the game. So hit men sent to exact revenge in the middle of the night? Not going to happen.

While Crush was helping the wounded team members remove their weapons and equipment, Gentry arrived. She walked through, asking questions, confidently nodding, until she reached him; then she caught hold of his arm and pulled him from the room.

"What the hell happened?" she asked. Once they were in the hallway she no longer looked so confident.

"According to Smith, 'went bad.' "

"What the hell does that mean?"

"It means BPC was already there when KZS and Group entered the building."

"They have Whitlan?"

"No. He was already gone. But as soon as BPC saw them, they started shooting."

"Unprovoked?"

"One could have been startled into it, but the others . . ."

"The bodies?"

"KZS cleanup team. I didn't know bodies could be disposed of so quickly."

"Just be glad it was KZS and not Smith. She has hyenas on retainer." Gentry folded her arms over her chest. "So . . . what are you thinking?"

"They'd only start firing at us on orders from Baissier."

"Over one full-human?"

"I'm thinking Whitlan has enough on Baissier to take her down and keep her down."

"She still has a lot of support."

"Some say not as much as she used to. Her ego has made her a liability. Her viciousness a threat. But no bear's going to order her out without hard proof."

"To be honest, Crushek, I'm more worried about you."

"Me?"

"You're the one person who knows the most about her and yet has absolutely no loyalty to her. And you've got a good, solid rep among bears. If *you* find information about her and Whitlan—she won't be able to talk her way out of that."

Gentry may be right, but still . . . "She won't come at me head-on. At least not the way anyone else would."

"You're not worried at all?"

"I'm not stupid, Chief. Just numb."

"So there's no point in telling you to be careful is there?"

"Only because I'm always careful."

She nodded, and headed back to the room with the teams. "Keep your phone on. I'm sure there will be meetings tomorrow. I may need you to attend."

Crush followed her into the room, but he stopped in the doorway, taking a quick scan. He walked over to Smith's side. "Where's Malone?"

She looked around, then shook her head. "Don't know. She was just here."

Cella sat on the bench down the street from the police department's building and rubbed her knee. It had swollen up to the size of a softball and the pain was something she didn't even want to think about. She knew she could have stayed inside, but when dealing with this much pain, she let instinct take over. And being wounded around a bunch of predators was just not something she was willing to do.

So, instead, she sat on this bench and waited for the pain to pass. It had to pass, right? It had to.

Cella closed her eyes and again wondered how much longer she could keep this up. She had a game coming and practices before that. She knew that icing her knee would definitely help, but would it swell up like this again?

She could ask Jai for help, but she knew that would go badly since her friend would push for surgery again. Knee replacement, which meant Cella's career would be over. So going home tonight? No way. Hotel. She needed a hotel.

Taking a deep breath, she tried to stand, but immediately sat back down hard, a small squeal of pain going out over the cold night air.

"Are you all right?" a male voice asked. A kind male voice. But all Cella knew was that a stranger was near her while she was wounded and the beast inside her took over, her roar ripping through the night, her claws unleashing. She was up on her good leg, her arms swinging out to tear the man in front of her apart. To destroy the threat. But an arm wrapped around her, yanking her back.

"Sorry," she heard another voice say. "Sorry. She went off her meds. I'm getting her back to the hospital."

"You sure you don't need some help? Maybe I should call nine-one-one."

"No, I've got her. But thanks."

Cella felt the threat move away, leaving her alone with the bear. Why she didn't see him as a threat, too, she didn't know.

"I'll take you home."

"No," she told Crush, pushing on his arms until he carefully lowered her to the ground. "No. I can't go home. Not like this."

"You talking about your knee? Or your face?"

She winced. "That bad?"

"Your face isn't that bad, but Meghan will notice. And your knee . . ."

Cella shook her head. She couldn't let Jai see her knee and she definitely couldn't let her kid see her face. It was one thing when Cella got a few bruises during a good ol' family bare-knuckle fight or during a hockey game. But Meg always freaked out when she saw her mother's face and knew she'd been working.

"Can you take me to your place?" she asked him. "Please."

"It's probably not safe there."

"I dare somebody to come at both of us tonight."

"Okay."

Crush went to her and started to put his arms around her.

"I can walk, Crushek."

"Bullshit. And you've got a game coming up. I can't risk the Marauder's enforcer, now can I?"

"It's always about *him*, isn't it?"

"Pretty much. Now come on. I'm tired and hungry."

He slipped his arms behind her back and under her legs, carefully lifting her so he didn't do much to her left leg.

"Thanks," Cella said before he could get moving.

"For what? Isn't this what pretend boyfriends do?"

Laughing, she put her head on his shoulder. "Excellent point."

CHAPTER TWENTY-FOUR

Crush pulled into his driveway and turned off the engine. He reached for the door, but stopped and warned, "Do not move until I come get you."

"I wasn't."

He smirked at her. "Liar."

"All right. Fine. I'll wait."

God, the woman was impatient, but considering how much pain Crush was guessing she was in, she wasn't much of a complainer.

Walking around to the passenger side of his truck, Crush pulled open the door and lifted Cella out. She wrapped her arms around his neck and smiled. "Thanks for this. And for earlier."

"No problem. You hungry?" He kicked the truck door closed and headed to his porch.

"I could eat."

"Hope spaghetti's okay. I only really know how to make spaghetti. And whale blubber, but I figured you'd rather the spaghetti instead."

She chuckled. "Spaghetti's fine. Although it's called pasta now."

"I'm old school. It's called spaghetti."

Still holding Cella in his arms, Crush managed to unlock his metal screen door. He held it open with his foot and juggled his keys until he found the one for the front door, unlocking it and stepping inside.

Crush walked through his house until he reached the kitchen. He placed Cella on top of his kitchen table, then flicked the light on. "Let's get you some ice for that knee."

"Okay."

Crush went to his freezer, where he kept his seal and walrus blubber, and grabbed a couple of ice packs. He turned to walk back over, but stopped. And stared.

"Where, exactly, are your pants?" he asked.

She pointed at a spot over her shoulder. "Over there somewhere."

"And you took them off because . . ."

"Gotta take care of the knee, right? Ice through black denim probably not very effective."

"Uh-huh."

"So are you going to bring me that ice pack or should I come over there and get it?"

Crush walked back across the room until he stood in front of her. "I should get you a dishrag or something. You shouldn't put this right against your skin."

"Oh, come on. You know I can handle . . ." She stopped talking, looked him over. "You're right. Give me your T-shirt."

"Why?"

"You want to put a *dirty* dishrag on me?"

"As opposed to my *dirty* T-shirt? There's blood and gunpowder on this thing."

The feline held her hand out. "Gimme."

"I have clean ones in the laundry room."

"But I want the one you're wearing." She gave him another once-over. "And I want it now."

* * *

Okay, so her knee was throbbing and she had a headache from getting hit in the face by the big fist and head of a bear. But he was just so cute! And, what was that word? Gallant? Carrying her inside and offering to make her "spaghetti."

Cute. Cute. Cute.

"Fine. Since you're so adamant."

"I am that."

He placed the ice pack on the table and took off his light jacket, tossing it over one of the chairs. Cella dropped her hands behind her, her palms flat against the wood table, propping her up.

"You sure I can't just get you—"

"Waiting."

With a long sigh, Crush reached back with both arms and gathered up his shirt, pulling it over his head and off. And honestly, watching all those muscles flex—and God, there were *so* many muscles—really did make a girl forget all sorts of aches and pains.

Crush tucked the ice pack inside the shirt and then carefully placed it on Cella's knee. She winced and, since he was staring at her face, he started to pull back.

"It's not that bad," she assured him. "It's sore but I'll live."

Nodding, he settled the ice pack on her. "How is that?"

"Fine."

He took a step back. "I guess you have your father's knees."

Cella scowled. "Big and hairy?"

He blinked in surprise and quickly shook his head. "No. No. I mean, he had the same problem with his right knee. You both skate the same way because of it . . . just different knees."

Cella rubbed her nose. "Wow. You really *are* a fan."

"Don't make fun of me."

"I'm not. I'm just fascinated by how hyperaware you are about stuff."

"Those who can skate, do. Those who can't, obsessively watch and either praise or criticize."

"Which do you do?"

"Depends on how good you are."

"That's right. I'm not as good as my dad."

"I never said that. I just think you fight more than you skate."

"I'm the enforcer. I'm supposed to fight."

"Bullshit. You're supposed to protect your team."

Laughing, Cella explained, "I do protect my team. By fighting."

"Everything is a bare-knuckle brawl to you, isn't it?"

"No. But it should be. Imagine the shit that could be worked out with a good and proper fight. That's how we handle it. Business deal goes bad, a bare-knuckle fight fixes it."

"How does it *fix* the problem?"

"It just does. Think about it. Politicians can only get their long-winded and boring bills through Congress if they're willing to raise their fists." She brought up her fists, snarled a little. The bear shook his head, but he smiled.

"I guess you're all about anarchy then."

"No way. Malones have lots of rules and everyone abides by them or they get their asses kicked."

Since the bear was laughing and smiling—not a scowl in sight—Cella wrapped both arms around his neck.

"What are you doing?"

"Getting cuddle-y," she answered honestly.

"Your knee is severely swollen, your lip split, you have a black eye, and I think your nose is broken."

"Oh. Right." She released him long enough to pop her nose back, eyes crossing from the pain. Shaking that off, she put her arms around his neck again and smiled. "All fixed."

Crush laughed, then cut it off by clearing his throat. "You are—"

"Amazing? Dynamic? Enthralling?"

"I was going to say nuts. Crazy. Loony tunes."

"You say tomato, I say whatever. Now come here and kiss me."

Again, Crush had *no* idea what to do with this woman. He knew what he'd *like* to do with her, but he was having a hard time getting past the fact that she'd gotten her bell rung by violent bears. She was bruised, battered, and swollen. Not only that, she'd killed. A lot. Shouldn't she be somewhere trying to emotionally recover from all that? Or off licking her wounds? Shouldn't he be getting her tea and making her listen to something soothing and Irish? Like Enya?

But he couldn't shake the feeling that if he even suggested such a thing, he'd end up looking like her. Besides, he'd be lying if he said he didn't find her kind of hot right now. Was that weird? That was weird, wasn't it? For the first time, he regretted that he'd spent most of his time with full-humans. He had no idea how to handle a true She-predator. An apparently horny She-predator.

The scent of her lust made him dizzy and he didn't even bother to try to stop her when she began to tug him down for that kiss. Even worse, he wasn't sure he could control his own reactions. He wanted to slam her against the table and take her hard. But then he saw her black eye and he knew he couldn't do that. Or, at the very least, he shouldn't do that. He shouldn't. Right?

"Are you going to kiss me," she asked when their faces were inches apart, "or just keep staring at me like I might break apart at any second?"

"What if you do?"

"What if I do what?"

"Break apart? You've already been bear-handled once tonight."

She was silent for a long moment. "Are you telling me you're worried about giving it to me too rough?"

"Yeah. A little. You drive me crazy, Malone. I'm thinking all my gentlemanly ways might hit the skids."

Her smile was small, pretty. "God," she whispered, "now I've gotta fuck you. You're making me all squirmy."

"I'm not trying to—"

"Too late. You did."

She leaned in, took his mouth with her own. And it was like she was draining all common sense right out of him. He could barely breathe. Knew he could no longer think. Especially when he realized she was actually squirming. Something about knowing he was making her wet made him even crazier. He wasn't used to feeling crazy, feeling like he had no control.

He knew he had one chance to pull away, to tell her to stop this and when she felt better, they could consider doing this sort of thing properly. He had one chance—and he let it fly right by.

As soon as his arms wrapped around her waist, Cella knew she had him. The way he was gripping the back of her T-shirt, hands twisting in the material. God, and his mouth. When he kissed a girl, he really kissed her. Standing a little taller, making Cella come up with him, his mouth desperately moving against hers, his tongue exploring.

She'd had good kisses before, but never like this one.

And even better was how he felt under her hands. All that hard but smooth skin, bunched-up muscles playing under her fingers.

Yeah, if he really thought she was willing to wait until she was all healed and one hundred percent, he was nuts. Besides, what could she say? She was always horny after a tough night fighting guys who started attacking her for no apparent reason.

Cella moved her hands down to Crush's waist and pulled him between her legs.

"Wait," he said, taking his mouth away from hers.

"What?"

"Your leg. I don't want to hurt it."

He had a point, but she had to ask, "Because of me or because I've got a game coming up?"

He gave a small shrug, his eyes downcast like a little kid's. "Can't it be both?"

Too much in lust to feel the need to be angry with the big idiot, she stretched out her good leg and hooked her foot through one of the slats of the kitchen chair. She pulled it closer.

"Sit," she ordered him.

He tugged the chair closer and sat down. She was, in a word, overjoyed, to see the hard-on the bear was struggling with. Although she was usually a big fan of foreplay, they could do that later. She had one need at the moment and she, like most felines, demanded instant gratification.

Cella grabbed her backpack and unzipped it. "Get your pants off."

"Uh . . . okay."

While the bear got off his pants and thankfully without her telling him, his boxers, Cella dug deep into her bag until she found the strip of condoms Jai always made sure to shove in any and all bags Cella had.

"It's not that I don't trust you," Jai would say when Cella would find the condoms at the most inopportune times, "it's just that I'm making sure there are no surprises. We're both too old for surprises."

Cella yanked one off and tossed it to the bear. "Put it on."

"You sure are bossy."

"Yes. I am." She wiggled off her panties, maneuvering them around the ice pack, and tossing them in her bag. By then the bear had the condom on.

She motioned with her hands. "Move a little to the left. A little more. Good. Stay there."

Using her arms, Cella pushed herself off the table and

onto the bear's lap. She smiled when she landed. "Now put me on your cock and let's get to work."

And that was around the time Crush started laughing.

"I'm serious!"

"I know you are. That's what makes it so damn funny."

"Look, you wanted to protect my precious game legs. This does the trick. I'm all about making things happen."

"You are such a Marine."

"I know. Or would you rather I was all lost and confused, the heat of the moment making me an irrational mess?"

"No. That seems to be my job this time around."

"I really make you crazy, huh?"

"Yeah. You really do."

"Then stop making me wait. Because we both know I'm one of the few women who can really handle you."

"You think so?"

"I know so. You know it, too. At least your body does. Your cock keeps getting harder the longer we sit here. It's actually pointing at the ceiling. I'd climb up on it myself but, you know . . . game coming up."

"Shut up."

Snorting, Cella took his hands and placed them on her waist. "All ya gotta do is pick me up and put me down on it. Trust me when I say, the rest of it will work itself out."

Crush knew, deep down, that getting this involved with Cella Malone was a one-way ticket to crazyville. His nice, quiet, extremely dangerous life would be turned on its head as soon as he had this woman's pussy on his cock. His quiet nights at home—when he wasn't being a cop and risking his life—would be over. There would be no quiet anything with Malone in his life. Was she worth the trouble?

He wasn't sure, but then she leaned in, sniffed his neck, and gently scraped a fang across his jugular. The last of Crush's restraint snapped, his hands tightening around her waist. He lifted her up, pulled her in closer, and while staring into her eyes, slammed her down hard on his cock, at the same time bringing up his hips.

The feline roared, her head dropping back, her arms wrapping around his neck. She held on tight, breathing in deep and taking a moment before she looked at him.

Panting hard, they watched each other.

"Well," she sighed, "that does feel good."

Crush couldn't even answer her. He was too wound up. Too hard. God, the things he wanted to do to this woman. It was taking every ounce of strength he had to —

"I'm a lot tougher than my pretty eyes and perfect bone structure might lead you to believe, Crushek. I can handle whatever you got for me."

Unable to form words—at least coherent ones—Crush leaned closer, breathing in her scent. He growled, low, his fangs easing from his gums, his hands sliding up her sides, then her arms.

Crush moved forward, his hands tightening around hers, his body pushing her back until he had the top half of her pressed down to the table. Did he mention he loved how flexible she was? Because she didn't seem to mind at all how he had her.

And he had her right where he wanted her.

He had her arms pinned above her head with his own, his head pressed against her chest. The low growl he unleashed rumbled through him and straight into her while he slowly rubbed his face against her T-shirt–covered breasts. And the entire time, she still sat in his lap, on his cock, completely filled and ready to burst.

Cella realized she was having trouble catching her breath, her body beginning to shake. It felt really good to have him so close to her, inside her.

But he wasn't moving. Why wasn't he moving?

Taking both her wrists in one hand, Crush used the other to push up her shirt and then his teeth to rip her bra in half. Her back arched and he took that for the invite it was, wrapping his mouth around her breast, his tongue teasing the nipple. And, uh, what were his lips doing? Because they were doing something *amazing*. And ridiculously intense. So intense, she tried to move away, but his grip on her wrists only tightened.

She knew what he was doing, the tricky bastard. With every twist and tug and tease of her breast, her pussy tightened around his cock like a vise. His growling grew harsher, louder, and the vibration of it against her flesh had her nearly out of her mind. She panted, she mewled, she might have hissed a few times. Then she was coming. Coming so very hard that she cried out.

The bear lifted his head to gaze at her with those black eyes.

"You all right?" And she wondered if he realized he was still growling at her.

Unable to answer since she was still panting, Cella nodded.

"Good." Remaining inside her, Crush slowly stood, releasing her arms so that he could carefully lift her legs and drape them over his forearms. " 'Cause I'm not really done yet."

Grinning, Cella lifted her arms over her head again and gripped the edge of the table. "Glad to hear it."

It was too much. *She* was too much. The way she watched him with those bright gold eyes. She was challenging him. Wasn't she always, though? And he no longer minded. He was really getting to like it. To like her. Difficult, crazy woman that she was.

Still careful of her leg, Crush stepped close to the table while pulling her out just a bit. She gripped his table so hard, her knuckles turned white. Her demanding gaze never left his face. He knew what she was telling him, without saying a word: "Fuck me as hard as you want. We both know I can take it."

So that's exactly what Crush did.

He fucked her hard, gripping her legs tight, his gaze locked with hers. Until her pussy contracted around him again. Her neck arched, her legs shaking in his arms, her panting turning into harsh cries. She was coming again and so was he. Coming so hard, he couldn't see straight, could barely stand. He could only feel and wow . . . did he feel *great*!

Crush erupted inside her, his breath leaving him in a long rush, his legs nearly buckling. He slammed his elbows against the table to stop from falling and took a moment to get his breath back.

After several long minutes, Cella sighed into the silence, "Holy shit! You're the best pretend boyfriend *ever*."

Chapter Twenty-five

A fresh ice pack was placed on her knee and Cella opened her eyes, smiling up at the bear standing over her.

After pulling up his pants, he'd carried her up to his room and laid her down on his bed, covering her with a blanket. Then he was gone and Cella was too tired and sated to really give a shit. She might have dozed, but not for long.

"The swelling's down," he told her, adjusting the ice pack.

"It usually doesn't last too long. Although, last night I thought it would last forever."

"It must be a nightmare after every game."

"It is. But what can I do?"

"They can't fix it?"

"Sure. If I want a full knee replacement."

"The way we heal, would that really be a problem?"

"No. As long as I never want to play pro hockey again."

"Right. Rule number twenty-three A." Geez, he knew all the pro shifter hockey rules by code, including the one that said any replacements or additions to a shifter's body meant automatic dismissal from the league.

Cella chuckled. "*Super* fan."

"Sorry. I didn't mean to let my geekiness flow."

"It's all right. You can't help yourself." Awkward silence descended after that, so Cella said, "I'm cold."

"Oh." He jumped up. "I'll get you another blanket."

"Why would I need a blanket at all when I have a polar bear?"

He frowned, confused. "Huh?"

She gestured to the bed and demanded, "Cuddling."

"Oh. Oh, right." He shrugged. "Didn't want to crowd."

"Did I bare a fang? Claw at major arteries? Roar and roar and roar until you run screaming from the room?"

"Not that I noticed."

"Then you're not crowding. She-predators always let you know when you're crowding. Didn't date many of us in your past, huh?"

"I've dated a few."

"A few? After you were eighteen?"

"What does my age have to do with—"

She crossed her arms over her chest. "Why am I still waiting?"

Crush started to get on the bed and Cella growled. "What are you doing?"

"What now?"

"You're dressed."

"Just my jeans."

"I want *naked* cuddling."

"Are you always this demanding?"

"Feline," she reminded him, making sure to sound as haughty as possible. Not really hard.

"What if I don't feel like being naked?"

"Naked!" she roared. He quickly looked down and she bit the inside of her cheek so she wouldn't start laughing, too.

"Fine. Naked it is." He stripped off his boots and jeans and crawled in beside her.

"Happy now?" he asked, wrapping his arms around her waist.

"I'm always happy when I get what I want." She snuggled in closer, keeping her leg bent so her ice pack stayed put.

"How are you feeling?" Crush asked her, his big hand rubbing up and down her side.

"Much better." She lifted her face. "How do I look?"

"Beautiful. And you know it."

"Doesn't mean I don't like to hear it. Bruises, cuts gone?"

Big fingers brushed her cheeks. "Not yet, but I doubt Meg will see much of anything by tomorrow."

"Good. The kid gets so worked up when she sees real damage."

"The way you play? She must see that all the time."

"She's a smart kid. She knows when it's from hockey or training with Smith or dealing with a family issue, and when it's from a situation that could have had her sobbing at my graveside."

"She hates what you do."

"Yeah. She does. But KZS is here to protect our own. And as long as there's been a KZS, there's been a Malone part of it. Usually more than one. Although, it was easier when all I did was take out stuff from a distance."

"You don't anymore?"

"No. I mean I still do, but like I told you, they want to move me up the ranks, and in order to do that, I have to have more fieldwork than just eliminations. Honestly, anyone with a good eye and a steady hand can take out a target a thousand yards away at nearly a hundred stories high with adjustments made for heavy winds and inclement weather."

The bear leaned back a bit, and gazed at her. "Not really."

Crush knew he was in deep. Deeper than he'd meant to ever be, but what could he do? Bears ran on emotion. If you startled them, they killed. If they felt trapped, they killed. If they were hungry . . .

And those bears that were human most of the time were no different. When he'd busted through that roof door, all he saw was Cella on her knees and a gun aimed at her head. After that, there was no negotiating for him. No ordering anyone to put down their weapons. Instead, he'd just roared and started shooting. To protect her and to protect his team.

And instead of coming home and thinking about that, as bears liked to do—think, analyze, debate—he came home and fucked a feline. A feline who continued to refer to him as her "pretend boyfriend." Like that was normal.

Then again, nothing about this woman was normal. Not even for a shifter was she normal. Because she was a Malone and that meant she was different from all the other tigers out there in the world.

"What's wrong? You're scowling at me like I decked your dog. . . ." Cella looked around. "Where is your dog?"

"At Mrs. Hanson's. My next-door neighbor. She babysits Lola when I'm out."

"You have a babysitter for the dog?"

"She gets lonely."

"Your. Dog. Just face it already."

"Let it go."

"So why are you scowling?"

"Just wondering . . . we've had sex. Am I still your pretend boyfriend?"

"Why? Are you pretend breaking up with me?"

Crush blew out a breath. "Forget I asked." He gazed at her. "Tell me something about yourself."

"Like what?"

"Anything." Then he added, "Anything that doesn't involve your family. Just you."

"Oh. Wow. Okay. Uh . . ." He watched her struggle with that simple request. "Um." Finally, after what felt like a really long time, she said, "I don't like beetles."

"The band?"

"No. The insect."

"You don't like beetles?"

"Yeah."

"Okay."

"I think they're gross."

"What about spiders?"

"Don't mind spiders. They deal with ants and flies."

"I'm sure beetles serve a purpose."

"Don't care."

"Okay."

"Now you're judging?"

"I'm not judging. You don't like beetles. That's okay. I don't like lizards."

"What's wrong with lizards?"

"You're going to judge me about lizards but I can't judge you about beetles?"

"When you ask me a lot of personal questions . . ."

"I asked you one."

"Why?"

"What do you mean why?"

"Why ask me a personal question? Why do you care?"

Annoyed that she was clearly annoyed, Crush sat up until his back rested against the headboard, and he pulled her onto his lap, replacing the ice pack on her knee, then wrapping his hands around her waist. "I ask you questions because I give a shit. Because despite my best intentions to not get emotionally involved, I like you."

"Why didn't you want to get emotionally involved?"

"Because you're crazy."

"Oh. You've got a point." She looked off and said, "I really like Australia."

"Okay."

"I went once. For vacation, not a job. Hung out with the dingoes."

"Full dingoes or—"

"Shifter dingoes." She nodded. "They were fun."

She pressed both her hands to his chest, fingers stroking. "Maybe we can go out sometime."

"What do you mean go out?"

"You know . . . out." She unleashed her claws, kneading his chest. "Like a date out."

Crush closed his eyes, his entire body tightening. Lips pressed against his throat, fangs grazed the tendons.

"Is that a yes?"

"Huh?"

"All that groaning you're doing, I was wondering if that was a 'yes, let's have an eventual date.' "

"That depends."

"On what?"

He gripped her shoulders and rolled until she was flat on her back and he was between her legs. The damn ice pack long forgotten.

"Am I going as your date or your pretend date?"

She brought her hands up, dug her claws into his scalp, scratching him right at the base of his neck—which felt fucking awesome!

"Real date," she promised. "But still pretend boyfriend."

Crush grinned. The feline would always be difficult, wouldn't she?

"I can live with that."

"Good. Now where's the rest of those condoms?"

CHAPTER TWENTY-SIX

Cella turned over, burrowing closer to Crushek, the sun coming in through the windows annoying her. But the bear tensed beneath her and when he moved, so did she. Both of them pulled their weapons at the same time, hers from under her pillow, aiming it at the foot of the bed.

Cella blinked at the man standing quietly at the end of the bed. "Mario?"

"Morning, Miss Malone."

She nodded. "Right." She pressed her hand to Crush's forearm so that he'd lower his weapon. "I've gotta go. I'm being called in."

"Are you going to be okay?"

"I'll be fine." She kissed him. "I'll call you later."

"Okay."

She tossed off the covers, but heard the bear growl. She motioned Mario away with a jerk of her head.

"Jealous already?" she asked after the driver left, teasing just a little.

But Crush's answer was deadly serious. "Yes."

She laughed, kissed him again. "Later."

"Yeah. Be careful."

* * *

Crush watched from his window as the Town Car pulled away from the front of his house and turned the corner at the end of his street. After that, he went back to bed to get some actual sleep, loving that Cella's scent was still all over his sheets and him.

But then, an hour later, a new scent filled his room. A scent he didn't much like that had him reaching for his .45. He had his hand around the holster when Chazz brought his fist down on Crush's hand.

Crush roared in pain and anger and, naked, charged his brother, tackling him to the floor. He had him pinned when Gray grabbed him from behind. Crush brought his elbow back, ramming Gray in the throat and his fist in Chazz's mouth again. Then he stood, grabbing both his brothers around their necks and lifting them to their feet. He slammed their heads together, knocking them out, and dropped them.

"Now, now."

Crush looked up at the six grizzlies coming through his doorway, one of them the big one from that day in the Group offices. "Is that any way for brothers to act?"

Cella walked into the Queens office building that housed the KZS offices. And as soon as she stepped inside, her boss latched on to her arm and dragged her toward the elevators.

"What the fuck happened?" Nina Bugliosi demanded. As usual, the lynx was demurely dressed in a bright green, mini-skirted power suit with a strand of black pearls around her neck and matching earrings.

"They shot at us first."

"Are you sure? You sure Smith didn't do something?"

"What, we're blaming her now for everything?"

"Canines can't be trusted."

"You get slapped around by one coyote in grade school and *allll* canines can't be trusted?"

"The bitch sucker punched me and that's not the point."

"We're not blaming Smith or the Group for something they didn't do. It was the bears."

The lynx looked Cella over before tartly replying, "I thought you were all about the bears."

"Huh?"

"You and the bears. Heard you were fucking one."

"Amazing how that's not your business."

The elevator doors opened, but before Cella could walk out, her boss shut the doors and hit the "Stop" button.

"What are you doing?" Cella snapped, thinking about how close her nose had come to getting cut off.

"You're not going to tell me about who you're fucking?"

"It's private."

"Since when, Malone?"

"Since I said so. Besides, aren't we in the middle of a crisis? Aren't you supposed to be handling *that*?"

"I'm your boss, Malone. You *have* to tell me."

"Or we could shift right here and four-hundred-pound me can slap around one-hundred-pound you." Because that was something Cella could get away with. Breaking her boss's nose while human . . . well, that would get her written up.

"Fine," Nina snapped. "Be that way."

Nina released Cella from the temporary hostage situation, but they'd only taken two steps away from the elevator when they were both dragged back inside by Nina's She-lion boss, Gemma Cosworth. Or, as the rest of the "ghetto cats" liked to call her, Her Ladyship the Duchess Cosworth. Because she, like all lions it seemed, thought all other cats were beneath her.

"Well," the older feline snarled at Cella, "you've fucked this up royally, sewer cat."

Cella raised her hands, palms up. "How is this all my fault?"

"It is until I decide it's not. And if I find out you snuck up behind even *one* of those bears . . ."

"There was no sneaking. We walked out on the roof. Smith said, 'Hey, y'all,' and they opened fire on us."

"Where are we going?" Nina asked, glancing at her watch. "I have a lunch date this afternoon." When Cosworth only stared at her, the much-smaller woman quickly added, "Which I, of course, will cancel."

Crush walked into the Manhattan annex office of BPC and threw his still unconscious brothers to the floor. He knew she'd be here. Knew this was where she'd come during a time of crisis, when the organization was under threat. And she'd leave her little "soldiers" to man the main Brooklyn offices. Or, as Crush liked to call them, her "meat puppets."

"You wanted to see me?" he asked of the polar sow sitting at the desk.

She looked at the bears on the floor, then up at Crush. "I sent six other—"

"They're in the Dumpster outside my favorite coffee place." He shrugged. "You know me and coffee."

"Yes. I remember." She gave a little laugh. "Did you kill them?"

"Didn't have to."

"Well, you certainly haven't changed."

"And I don't plan to start now."

"Still," she gestured to one of the chairs in front of her desk, "sit. Tell me how things have been going. How have you been doing?"

Crush dropped into the chair across from Peg Baissier. "I've been just fine. And you?"

Thirty-four years. It had been thirty-four years since Baissier had taken in Crush and his two brothers. And, in the beginning, he'd fallen in line just like all the others before him. It wasn't hard. So young and yet learning to fight like in the martial arts movies. But when Crush had turned twelve, he'd found out what Baissier had gone out of her way not to tell them. That his parents had worked for her. Had died carrying out her orders. It wasn't that they were soldiers that bothered him; it was that Baissier hadn't told him. She'd hidden it like so many other things she'd hidden. And Crush, curious bear that he was, had looked into it. After school, instead of heading home for more training, he'd become friends with wolves, coyotes, foxes. He'd learned to break and enter, to hot-wire cars, to snoop, to steal. Then, once he had the skills down, he'd put them to use not breaking the law but finding out what his parents had done and how they'd died. By the time he was sixteen, he knew more than he'd ever wanted to know about his parents, about Baissier, about all of it. But he finally knew the truth.

At the time, Baissier had no idea. Instead, she thought he was just being a hardheaded kid. She made it plain she didn't like him, always calling him "the contrary one." Or "Mr. Difficult," because he questioned everything and refused to play along—with anything. If, in the middle of August, she said it was hot outside, Crush went out in a fur jacket. If she said it was nighttime, he wore sunglasses. He mostly did it to piss her off, but he also did it to ensure that he never became what she wanted him to be. Another meat puppet to carry out her orders.

"What do you want?" he asked, already fed up at seeing her face.

"There was a big mess last night, eh? Glad to see you're okay, though."

"I'm not in the mood to play this game with you. What do you want?"

"Just wondered why you attacked my people."

"They attacked us first."

"Attacked you? Or attacked those cats and the politically correct Group?"

"This is bullshit. Why don't you just tell me the truth?"

"And what truth is that?"

"What you want with Whitlan."

"Who says I want—"

"I like how you didn't ask who he is. Just went into your denials." Gray began to wake up and without even looking away from Baissier, Crush slammed his fist in his brother's head, knocking him out again. "You haven't fuckin' changed a bit. Have you, *Mom*? That is what you told us all to call you, right? Mom?"

"You always were an ungrateful little fuck."

"And don't forget disloyal." Crush stood. "Send all the meat puppets you want. Come after me all you want. But if you worked with Whitlan on anything, for any reason, I will nail you to the cross."

"It's always a pleasure to see you again, Lou."

"Yeah," he said, walking out, "fuck you, too."

Holding an ice pack to his head, Chazz settled down across from his foster mother. He'd be honest here . . . he didn't really know what was going on. But he knew Peg could get rather . . . fixed on things. And right now she was fixed on his brother. It didn't help that the idiot couldn't play along, for just a bit. He always had to be such a hard-ass.

"Now what?"

Peg Baissier sat back in her chair, her hands steepled under her chin. "I'll tell the families the boys died in the line of duty."

"And Lou?" Peg slowly raised her gaze and Chazz shook his head. "Can't we just let it go? He can't hurt us."

"You know I would never hurt your brother." Right. Of course, she wouldn't. Still . . .

"Is it true?"

"Is what true?"

"That you blew his cover?"

"From what I understand, that was an accident and had nothing to do with me. And those who slipped up were reprimanded."

"Uh-huh."

"Chazz, honey, I would never hurt your brother. He's a pain in the ass, but he's still my foster son. That means something to me."

"Okay. But don't hurt his dog, either."

"Oh, my God! I would never hurt his dog." She shook her head. "Honestly, stop listening to Lou's craziness. I wouldn't hurt his dog, I'm not going to hurt him. But I do *not* want this thing to snowball, either. This is how wars start, and we can't afford that right now. Understand?"

"Don't worry. We'll handle it."

"Excellent." Peg focused on her computer screen and Chazz stood, reaching down to grab his unconscious brother's arm. "Come on, idiot. Let's get you an ice pack."

Thirty minutes after the last Crushek was dragged from her office, one of Peg's trusted men walked into her office, closing the door behind him. The black bear sat down and waited until she spoke.

"We need that boy distracted until we find that mother-fucker Whitlan and take him out." They had to take him out. They had to. Peg raised a finger. "But Crushek is to remain unhurt." Peg knew there'd be no coming back from that among their own.

"Distracted or devastated? Because he's made some interesting friends lately."

"I don't really give a shit, I just want him out of my way." She simply couldn't afford to have that boy find Whitlan first. Anyone else, especially one of those dogs or cats, she could easily dismiss as more evidence the other species were out to get her and the rest of the bear community. But among the bears, whether he knew it or not, Lou Crushek was known as an honest cop and bear. If he came out against her, especially after all these years without saying a word one way or the other . . .

No, they had to find a way to keep Crushek busy until she finished this.

Peg flicked her hand, dismissing her employee. "Make it happen. Let me know when it's done."

CHAPTER TWENTY-SEVEN

Crush sat at his desk and Dez, sitting at her desk with her legs up, lifted her sunglasses long enough to take a look at his face. "You didn't look like that last night, did you?"

"Don't you remember?"

"I'm running on two hours of sleep. I don't remember shit." She pointed at a Starbucks coffee cup on the desk.

"That mine?" he asked.

"You think I'd be fuckin' pointing at it if it wasn't for you?" she snapped back.

"Are you going to be like this every fuckin' morning?"

"Yeah. As a matter of fact I am going to be like this every fuckin' morning."

"Hey!" Gentry snapped, standing beside their desks. "What did I say?"

Dez seemed to mull that over for a few seconds before replying, "Don't annoy you?"

"And what are you doing? You're annoying me, that's what you're doing." She motioned at the elevator. "Let's go."

"Where?"

She glared down at Crush. "You're going wherever the fuck I tell you to go."

Crush looked down at Gentry's feet. "Did you know you're wearing bunny slippers?"

Dez leaned over and again lifted her sunglasses. "And they're blue."

"Goddammit." Their boss stormed back into her office to change out of her adorable and less-than-threatening bunny slippers and into some proper shit-stompers.

"My question," Crush whispered to Dez, "how did she find bunny slippers in her size?"

"I heard that, you white-haired bastard!"

And when Crush and Dez started laughing, Gentry's mood did *not* improve.

The front door to the penthouse opened and Van Holtz, looking exhausted but still extremely handsome, motioned them in.

"Thank you for coming. Chief Gentry should be here in a few minutes."

Cella kind of expected him to take them to his living room considering the formality of this meeting, but Van Holtz walked right past it and into his kitchen. Like always. At the large table sat Dee-Ann Smith with her feet up on the chair next to her and a Led Zeppelin trucker cap on her head. Walking up to her, Cella remarked, "Where's your banjo?"

"Stuck up your—"

"Dee-Ann," Van Holtz warned from his stove. "Be nice."

"The feline started it."

Yanking the chair out from under Smith's feet, Cella sat down and smiled at her.

Smith's eyes narrowed. "Why are you smiling at me?"

"Because it annoys you when I do?"

She shrugged. "That actually makes sense."

"Please," Van Holtz sweetly suggested. "Sit. Breakfast will be ready in a few minutes."

When Nina and Cosworth only forced fake smiles and still did not sit, Smith snarled out, "He said sit down."

"*Dee-Ann.*"

Cella scratched her nose to keep from laughing, then said

to her bosses, "He makes the most amazing waffles you'll ever have."

When Cosworth sat, Nina had to grudgingly go along.

So there they all sat or cooked. Three cats and two dogs. Cella didn't think it could get any more awkward. But after a few minutes, the doorbell rang again and Van Holtz walked out to answer it.

That's when Smith suddenly turned to Cella and said, "You smell like bear."

Without even looking at her, Cella slammed her fist into Smith's face, knocking the She-wolf out of her chair and onto the floor. Then, while Smith got back in her seat and popped her jaw back into place, Cella tried not to shake out her hand. *That girl's face . . . like granite!*

Crush and the others followed Van Holtz into his commercial-quality sparkling kitchen. Already seated at the table were Cella, representatives from KZS, and Smith, who was busy moving her jaw around.

He immediately looked at Cella and she gave a small smile and a shrug. But an instant later she frowned and her hand reached up to her own face, her forefinger pointing at her eye. He knew she was silently asking about his black eye and swollen cheek, but what could he say at the moment? So he shook his head and pulled out a seat, dropping into it.

"Thank you all for coming this morning," Van Holtz said, standing at the head of the table. "I know things took a difficult turn last night, but I wanted to touch base and have a frank discussion regarding how we should move forward on this issue."

The room full of shifters and one full-human stared at Van Holtz for a solid minute before they all looked at Smith. She shrugged and muttered, "Let's talk now before we get in a big fight with a bunch of bears."

"Ohhh," they all said.

* * *

While Van Holtz created one of his brilliant breakfasts and chatted with management, and MacDermot showed Smith the latest cell phone pictures of her adorable son, Cella and Crush wandered into Van Holtz's living room.

"What happened to your face?" she asked.

He sighed. "Long story."

"Then you better start talking so you don't have to finish it over our breakfast."

"It's no big deal."

Cella crossed her arms over her chest. "I'm still waiting." When he still didn't answer, she guessed, "Your brothers did this to you, didn't they?"

"No." He cleared his throat. "It was six grizzlies."

"Were they alive when you dumped them?"

"Yes. Think I should tell the others?"

"I do."

He smirked. "Wait. How'd ya know I dumped them?"

"You don't like trash in your house. Especially with Lola there."

"Admit it. You like Lola."

"Don't I have enough dogs in my life at the moment?"

"If you say so." Crush gave a small jerk of his head. "Come here."

"Why?"

"Because I told you to."

"Oooh." She stepped closer to him. "I like it when you're all demanding and bossy. Maybe you can handcuff me later."

"You ladies all say that, but then when I go for it—you all panic."

"Such a lack of faith."

"Now get your ass up here and kiss me."

Cella went up on her toes and Crush came down a bit until their lips touched. She realized she kind of melted into that kiss, her body resting against his, her hands reaching up and gripping his biceps. Big arms slipped around her waist, pulling her in close. They kissed and clung to each other in Van Holtz's living room until they both realized that they were no longer alone. Pulling away, they looked over at the archway. Smith and MacDermot stood there, both eating bacon, both watching them.

It was the bacon that, for some reason, made it all . . . weird.

The She-lion, Cosworth, pushed back from the table and stood up, glaring down at Crush.

"Your foster mother is Peg Baissier?"

Crush, after tearing off the fat and handing the meat of the bacon to Malone, said, "Yeah."

"And you didn't tell us this before because . . ."

Now chewing said bacon fat, "Because I haven't lived with the woman in more than twenty years?"

"I don't care if you haven't lived with her for five thousand years."

Crush frowned. "But then we'd be dead and most likely not having this conversation. Unless, of course, we were time travelers."

Smith chuckled. "I do love me some bear logic."

"What I'm trying to say," Cosworth growled while cutting a lethal glare at Smith, "is that perhaps you're actually working for Baissier."

"That's a possibility. Although the firing back and hitting the target might make me not so welcome at the annual Christmas party. Plus . . . Baissier hates me."

"But your brothers work for her."

"So?"

"And you're all triplets."

"So?"

Cella placed her elbow on the table and her chin on her raised fist.

"Isn't there a bond or something between triplets?" Cosworth demanded.

"Oh! You mean like when one of my brothers burns his hand and the other two feel it?"

"Yeah!"

"No. That doesn't happen."

Cella and Smith snorted, both quickly looking away while Cosworth's golden feline eyes narrowed.

"Calmly," Gentry warned, tapping her forefinger on the table. "You don't want me breaking out in a five-hundred-pound, seven-foot panic."

"All I'm asking," and he could almost hear that Cosworth wanted to add something like "troglodyte" in there somewhere but was too afraid of Gentry, "is whether you can be trusted?"

"I don't know if you can ask me that."

"Why not?"

"Because I'm sure even a sociopath would think they can be trusted. Or if I'm delusional, I wouldn't *know* I was delusional and I may think I can be trusted when in fact, I can't, because I'm delusional."

"You're delusional?"

"No." Crush pointed at her, thoroughly enjoying their discourse. "But if I *were* delusional, I wouldn't *know* that I was delusional." He grinned, believing his point made. "Because I would *be* delusional."

Crush, proud of himself, sat back. A good thing since if he hadn't, he would have had that She-lion's claws around his throat, her spit-filled roar splattering his face. Thankfully, Cella and the little lynx grabbed their boss and dragged her out of the kitchen.

"We'll be right back!" Cella said, yanking the struggling female out with her.

Crush looked around at the sow, wolves, and full-human staring at him. "I thought I made some very valid points."

The She-wolf shrugged. "Sounded like it to me."

MacDermot nodded. "I thought so, too. And can I just

say . . . I love that you're my partner now. Because you are actually more annoying than I am. And I'm *annoying*." She grinned. "And the best part? You're not even trying to be!"

"And he's the one you're fucking?" Cosworth demanded, pacing back and forth outside Van Holtz's front door.

"You've gotta admit he's cute."

Nina nodded. "Very cute. I love polar bear eyes. All black and mysterious."

Cosworth faced them, hands in their faces, snarling. But before she could light into them, her cell phone—thankfully—went off. She glanced at it. "It's Löwe."

Cella's boss's boss's boss. *Heh.*

"Why don't you deal with that and we'll finish up here," Nina suggested in her best innocent voice. It was why she was management and wasn't even thirty-five yet.

Cosworth was debating that when her unanswered phone went off again. Gritting her teeth, she ordered, "Whatever you do, rein this shit in. Understand?"

"Absolutely," Nina promised.

They waited until Cosworth was on the elevator and the doors had closed, then Nina looked at her. Cella expected a little bit of a strategy discussion, but instead her boss said, "Your boyfriend is *so* cute."

"He's not my boyfriend. He's my *pretend* boyfriend."

"Why?"

"It annoys him."

Nina, heading back to the penthouse, shook her head. "You are such a feline, Malone."

Once the cats were back, thankfully without the cranky She-lion, Crush handed over a plate of fat-reduced bacon to Malone. She smiled, winked at him, and began eating.

"What is with you and the fat?" Nina asked him.

"Polar bears mostly eat fat rather than actual meat," Dez offered. When everyone stared, "I was watching Animal Planet last night."

"Anyway," the little lynx said, crossing her eyes, "I don't care what I just told Cosworth to keep the She-lion roaring to a minimum. We need to put a stop to Baissier and we need to do it now. She is out of control."

"I agree." Van Holtz shook his head. "But we can't kill her."

"And why is that again?" Dez asked.

"Because we can't prove she's done anything wrong and she still has enough clout to at least get the benefit of the doubt. And trust me when I say we don't want to go head-to-head with bears."

Crush pushed his half-eaten plate of bacon fat away. "I'm telling you, though, she wouldn't go after Whitlan unless he had something on her. Something besides his word. Because she could discredit him on that shit in two seconds."

"Then how do we deal with this?" Cella asked.

The She-wolf raised those cold, dog eyes. "Leave it to me."

Van Holtz looked at his mate. "Dee-Ann . . ."

"If he's alive, I'll find him. That's what I do. Besides, I got this far."

"Be careful," Crush warned her. "Baissier hates wolves."

"Darlin', I'm always careful."

"What about you, Crushek?" Gentry asked.

"What about me?"

"She attacked you in your home. You can't go back."

"Ever? I just bought that house."

Gentry sighed, looking at Van Holtz.

"I think what Chief Gentry means is you should go some-place safe *for the time being*. I can arrange something until we sort this all out."

"Yeah . . . great."

"What about Malone?" the She-wolf asked.

"What about me?"

"You and the bear are fuckin'."

"Aw, baby, now don't be jealous. You're just a little too butch for me."

"I think," Crush cut in before the two She-predators could get into it, "she means that Baissier probably already knows about us, which means she might come at me through you. Or even your family."

Cella and the lynx looked at each other and started giggling.

"Oh," Cella said when no one joined in. "You're serious."

"It's best to take precautions," Van Holtz suggested.

Crush pushed away from the table and stood, taking Cella's hand. "Could you excuse us for a minute?"

He walked out, Cella with him, stopping when they reached the living room again.

"Baissier's desperate," he reminded Cella.

"I know she is."

"Well, I don't want you or your family to get caught in the middle of that."

"Don't worry about my family. The Malones can take care of their own."

"What about Meghan? Josie?"

"Archangel Gabriel couldn't touch them, much less some overwrought bear." She reached up, pressing her palm to the side of his face. "But to ensure their safety, I'll crash somewhere else. The family will protect Meg and Josie. I can take care of myself."

"You'll crash with me."

"At a Motel Hell off the turnpike? I'd rather live in an alley."

"I think," Smith said from the archway, "we can do a tad better than that so as not to hurt your feline sensibilities, Malone."

"You'd better, Smith. You do know how I like my comforts."

CHAPTER TWENTY-EIGHT

"It's got a stocked refrigerator and a full bar, none of that mini shit in the suites. Also room service. Y'all need anything, you just let me know." The She-wolf grinned. "Just ask for Sissy."

Crush looked around at the Kingston Arms suite Dee-Ann Smith had gotten them into. The Kingston Arms hotel chain was an extremely high-end establishment that usually only the wealthiest full-humans and shifters could afford to stay at. He was sure that Baissier had probably stayed at a few, but he doubted she'd hand over money for one of these suites. It was really hard to justify ten grand a night on one's expense report.

Cella scanned the living room they stood in and nodded. "This is nice."

Nice? She thought this was just nice? God, what was she doing with him? Even with his pay increase working for Gentry's division, he'd never be able to afford a place like this. And he wasn't sure if he really wanted to be able to. With that kind of money came all sorts of high-level problems.

"Oh," the She-wolf said, "I'm sure this ain't as fancy as a

Malone RV or camper, but I'm sure y'all will somehow manage to make do."

Sneering, the She-wolf walked out, the door slamming behind her.

"Is there *anyone* you don't manage to irritate?"

"She's a Smith wolf."

"So?"

"I was put on this planet to irritate Smith wolves."

He shook his head, feeling exhausted after the last couple of days. "Just be glad she didn't eat you," he sighed.

"Um . . . what?"

Cella's phone rang and she quickly answered it.

"Hello?"

"Hey, Ma."

"Hey, baby. Are you all right?"

"Yeah. Everyone's fine. Now tell me what's going on."

Cella liked hearing the strength in her daughter's voice. Yeah, she'd only turned eighteen, but she was already growing into her fangs. Becoming what Cella's Great-Gram would call, "a proper little She-bitch."

As an adult Malone female, Meg should no longer need protecting, but Cella wasn't taking any chances. Not with her two girls and Jai. "Unsecure line, baby, but you can get specifics from Kathleen. Just understand, you, Josie and the rest of the cousins, Jai, too, don't leave that street unless you've got your uncles with you. Do I make myself clear?"

"Yes." And, unlike Cella, her daughter would be smart. The kid wouldn't be wandering off, looking for trouble. "Are you all right, Ma?"

"Me? I'm fine."

"Grams told Deirdre you were with Detective Crushek. She sort of sang it to her."

Cella grinned. God, her mother could be trifling. "Yeah.

That's where I am. Just for a little while, though. Until this gets straightened out. Okay?"

"Sure. And good for you."

Cella got on the sofa, her feet on the cushions, her ass on the back of the couch. "Good for me? Why?"

"Because you never get any time away. You're either playing hockey, being a cat killer—"

"Stop calling me that."

"—or arguing with the aunts. Now you don't have to worry about running home to be here for me in the morning or feeling guilty when you can't. You can enjoy spending time with Detective Crushek."

"Are you saying that because you like him?"

"I'm saying that because I think he's good for you. You need someone . . . centered."

"I'm centered."

"*Ma.*"

"I can be when I try." Cella plucked at a loose string on her jeans. "But you do know, right? You know that you are and always will be my priority. You know that, don't you, baby?"

"I know that and have never doubted it. Ever. Nothing Deirdre says or does will ever change that. But I also know the rules that you live by, Ma. That we all live by." There was a long pause. "And I don't mind them. I don't mind those rules. I don't mind my life. I don't mind babysitting the cubs or helping out the aunts when I need to. I've never minded."

"Yeah. I see that now."

"But I'm sorry I lied to you. I just didn't know how to tell . . ."

"Yeah. I know. I'm sorry, too. It seems I'm a Malone female, after all. I didn't even ask you what you wanted. Just assumed I knew best."

"You only want me happy. That's why I had trouble telling you I wasn't going to Boston U. I didn't want to hurt you."

"Don't worry about that now. We'll work it out when I get

back. But maybe you and Josie can still get a room on campus? Stay with the family on the weekends to do laundry and get some of Kathleen's stew. At least for freshman year. I just want you to understand that not everyone's an outsider." She glanced over at Crush staring out the window, lost in his own thoughts. "There can be a place in your life for a lot of different people."

"Actually . . . I was thinking that, too. Daddy already said he'd pay for me to live on campus with Josie."

"Look at you. Always ten steps ahead with the planning."

Meg laughed. "And who do you think I learned that from? Now, I gotta go and maybe you can have lunch with Detective Crushek." Cella rolled her eyes and chuckled. Her daughter was just *so* obvious. "Talk to you later, Ma?"

"I'll call you later tonight," Cella promised her. "This will be over soon, baby."

"I know, Ma. I know you'll take care of it."

Meg disconnected the call and Cella tossed her phone to the couch, looking over at the hulking male across the room. She hadn't seen him this tense since she'd first met him. And she knew exactly what was bothering him, too.

"It's not your fault, Crushek."

If she hadn't said his name, Crush would have thought Cella was still talking to her daughter. Hands shoved into the front pockets of his jeans, he turned. But instead of her still being across the room, abusing the expensive furniture with her boots, she was standing right behind him.

"Huh?" was all he could manage.

"You heard me."

"You're separated from your daughter—"

"According to her I needed to get away."

"—your family—"

"They're the reason I need to get away."

"—your job—"

"I'm a contractor, I have flexible hours."

"It's my fault."

"It's that bitch's fault. You can't help it she's a narcissistic mess."

"Yeah, but—"

The She-tiger growled and walked away. "I don't want to talk about that sow anymore!" she announced, arms thrown wide.

"Okay, okay. We don't have to talk about . . . about . . ." Her sweatshirt flipped past his head, followed by her right sneaker, then her left. That one bounced off his forehead. "Uhhh . . . Malone?"

"Uh-huh?"

"What are you doing?"

"Getting naked so you can fuck me." She faced him, arms going behind her back to unhook her bra. "My knee's feeling better."

"Well, the swelling's down."

"Yeah." She slipped off the bra, held it out with two fingers. "So we can do one of my favorite positions."

"Malone, we have to discuss—"

"Where are we going to fuck? How about this huge couch we've got?" She took a quick look around. "This must be a bear suite."

"Malone—"

"Or"—she tapped her chin, slowly turning—"you can take me facedown on that dining room table. It's really smooth looking, so my tits won't get chafed."

"Um . . ."

"There's even a kitchen table in there. It looks sturdy."

"Stop it, Malone."

"Stop what?"

"You know what. And you can stop smirking, ya goddamn tease."

She placed her hands on her hips. "Would you prefer I grin broadly?"

"It would be a little more honest since you know exactly what you're doing to me."

"Not exactly." Now she did grin broadly. "But I do have a general idea." She walked toward him. "Would you really rather sit around this gorgeous hotel room that we're not paying for, blaming yourself for something not your fault, and being miserable?" She pressed her hand to his chest and stroked it. "Or would you rather spend the rest of the day fucking me stupid?"

He sighed, big and loud. "I don't know."

"You don't know? You don't know what?"

"There's a lot of things we should be doing. I mean, can't this wait?"

Her hands dropped back to her hips, but now there was definitely some attitude. "Can it wait? I'm standing here naked—"

"Not completely."

"—and you'd rather do some *things* rather than be with me?"

"It's nothing personal. There's just a lot going on."

Her mouth dropped open, her feline sensibilities insulted. "Fine! You go do what you need to do."

He watched her swipe up her clothes before she stormed away, adorable ass moving side to side. If she'd been in her animal form, he'd bet her tail would be twitching up a storm. Enjoying himself, Crush let her get as far as the hotel room door. . . .

Disgusted she'd bothered to give this bear the time of day and determined she'd never make that stupid mistake again, Cella snatched open the room door, only to have it shut again by big, clumsy bear hands!

"Do you mind?" she sniped, yanking the door open again.

"Yeah," he said calmly, almost bored. "I do mind." He slammed the door shut again.

"Well that's too goddamn bad." She pulled on the door, but he leaned his shoulder against it, arms wrapped around his chest, black-eyed gaze staring across the room. Then he sighed again, still sounding bored!

"Move!"

"I need you to calm down, ma'am."

Ma'am? Did he just call me ma'am? "I don't want to calm down. I want to leave."

"Sorry, Ma'am." *Again with the ma'am?* "I can't allow that."

"You can't . . . are you kidding me?"

"Ma'am"—he took her arm and pulled her away from the door—"why don't you just go sit down until you're calm, okay?"

"Get your hands off me!"

"Ma'am—"

"*And stop calling me 'ma'am'!*"

"Yeah," he said, pulling her around so that he stood behind her and had both her arms in his grasp. "I'm going to have to call this in."

"Call . . . what?"

"I tried to cut you a break, but you're way out of control." And then she felt it, against her wrists. Heard that distinctive sound.

Cold titanium cuffs.

"You're handcuffing me?"

"It's for your own safety, ma'am." He made her walk forward until she hit the sofa, held her cuffed arms with one hand while pressing between her shoulder blades with the other until she was bent over, her ass hiked up by the seatback.

"You're arresting me?"

"You didn't give me much choice, ma'am. Now if you'll just remain calm . . ."

Cella bit her lip, having to fight not to laugh.

He crouched behind her, strong fingers sliding up the back of her calf.

"Shouldn't a female officer be frisking me?" she asked, making sure to sound as haughty as possible.

"Don't have time to wait for that, ma'am. I have to think of others' safety first."

"But I'm mostly naked . . . what exactly do you think I'm hiding?"

"You'd be amazed what people can hide on their persons, ma'am."

Cella's eyes closed, the feel of the bear's fingers slowly dragging up her inner thigh driving her wild.

"Especially women, ma'am." His fingers brushed against her panties. "Women can smuggle all sorts of things around with them that could put everyone at risk." He pressed his fingers right up against her pussy. "Mhmm. Yeah. Unfortunately, ma'am, we'll have to get rid of these panties to ensure a proper pat-down. It's for your own safety and mine," he murmured, big fingers slowly dragging down her panties until he had them at her ankles. "Step out of them."

Cella lifted one foot, then the other.

He leaned forward, the panties in his hand. "Now again, for your safety and mine, I'm going to have to . . . go a little deeper. If you cause me any problems over that . . ." He swung the panties by his forefinger. "I'll have to gag you. Understand?"

Cella, already panting, could only nod.

"That's good." He dropped her underwear right in front of her so that she was forced to look at it, get the blatant threat of it. God, what a deliciously dirty bear she had to play with.

"Spread your legs, ma'am. Farther. Good." He brought his body over the top of hers, trapping her between him and the couch. He pressed his mouth against her ear. "Just relax, ma'am. This will go much easier if you relax."

Cella closed her eyes, her body tensing when she felt his

finger slip inside her. "Relax," he coaxed. "The sooner you relax, ma'am, the quicker I can get this done. But you've gotta relax."

He stroked in and out with his finger, pulled back, then pressed inside with two. She let out a low moan and he warned, "Quiet, ma'am. Any complaints and you know what I'll have to do."

Those two big fingers took up an amazing amount of room and Cella bit down on her lip to stop herself from groaning again . . . or growling . . . or purring.

"I can't help but think you must be hiding something, ma'am. You're so wet here. And what, ma'am, is *this*?" He pressed down on a spot inside her that Cella had always thought she was the only one who knew of, and she almost came off the couch. Only his body managed to keep her in place.

"I need you to calm down, ma'am."

Cella's body began to shake, her knees weakening.

"What is this?" he asked, fingers pressing, stroking. "Can you tell me, ma'am? It's better you come clean now rather than let me find out later. I can help you now."

She shook her head, unable to find any words with her body unraveling.

"I don't think you're listening to me, ma'am." He sighed, shook his head. "That's a real shame."

Cella didn't know what he was saying, what was going on. She only knew what she felt and what she felt was that monumental orgasm ripping through her, so strong, she nearly threw the three-hundred-pound bear off her.

But like the good cop he was, he never lost his grip, never lost control.

Doing her best to bite down on the couch cushion, Cella groaned and writhed through that orgasm until everything went quiet.

Crushek stood up, one hand still gripping her by the cuffs, the other gently sweeping down her back.

Then he said, "I see you don't take direction real well, ma'am."

Uh-oh.

Crush worked hard to control his breathing, to keep going without just fucking the perfect woman with the perfect ass because he had absolutely no self-control.

When he thought he was ready, he stepped back, his hand still holding the cuffs, the other on her shoulder to help lift her up.

"Over here," he ordered, walking Cella around the big couch until they reached the already lit fireplace. "On your knees, ma'am."

He saw her head turn slightly, like she was about to look back at him, but she stopped, and instead slowly went down on her knees. He grabbed a pillow from the couch and dropped it in front of her. "Put your face down there and get your ass in the air." When she hesitated, "Now, ma'am."

Cella licked her lips—making him absolutely crazy!—and bent down, resting her cheek against the pillow and moving around until she could easily get her ass higher up. Her hands were still cuffed behind her back and he wondered which of them was more turned on by that.

Crush unzipped his jeans, making sure to do it in front of her and to do it slow. Then, taking his time, he walked around behind her and dropped to his knees.

"I'm sure you understand why it has to be this way, ma'am."

He heard Cella chuckle. "For your safety and mine?"

"Exactly. And do you know *why* I'm doing this?"

"No."

"Because you lied to me." He reached over to the jacket she'd worn into the room and picked it up off the couch. He dug into the pockets until he found the smuggled items.

"You don't think I saw what happened between you and that She-wolf?"

"Those aren't mine," she quickly lied, her surprised laughter nearly slipping out. "She must have slipped them into my pocket."

"Don't make it worse by lying to me, ma'am." Crush finally located what he was looking for and pulled out the strip of condoms that Smith had laughingly handed Cella after the feline had asked for them.

"This is contraband," Crush said, holding it up. "I can't ignore this."

"Can't you just let me go?"

"No, ma'am. I really can't." And he meant that more than he could have realized. "I can't let you go. I definitely can't let *this* go."

"What are you going to do?"

"You've been very bad. Punishment seems the only correct response."

Deciding to keep his clothes on, Crush lowered his jeans and boxers just enough to get his cock out. He took a moment to slip on one of the condoms before he completely forgot and was balls-deep inside Cella Malone.

He moved closer in, pressing his thighs against the back of her legs so that she could feel the denim against her bare flesh, knew that he was taking her while fully dressed. Holding his cock, he rubbed it against her pussy, smiling when he saw that she was even wetter than she had been when he'd made her come.

Her body tensed and she suddenly announced, "I think I'll need to put up a fight."

"I see you're not going to make this easy, are you, ma'am?"

"Not if I can help it."

Crush reached forward and slipped his hand into her hair, his fingers gripping the silky strands until she knew he held her. Then he tightened his grip a little more until she gasped. He pressed his cock against her.

"Feel free to scream, ma'am. No one will stop me. I am the law."

Then Crush shoved his cock home and he doubted he'd ever want to leave again.

Cella didn't know which was driving her wilder. The flat, "I've been a uniform cop for twenty years" voice, the fact that he still had on his clothes, that he understood exactly what she wanted with her only giving him hints—or the feel of his big cock taking current residency inside her pussy?

Fuck it! It was all driving her wild.

So wild she could barely see straight, her hands wiggling in those cuffs, her body writhing beneath his. Especially when she realized he hadn't moved. He'd entered her, but now he was just . . . there. Waiting. Letting her feel every amazing inch of him.

Unable to wait any longer, Cella squeezed her muscles, grinning when she heard him gasp and the muttered curse. Then his hands moved to her waist, holding her steady as he took her hard.

Yet even as he plowed into her, her wrists bound, taking what he wanted from her, Cella realized that she'd never felt safer before. More cared for.

And it was when she understood that, knew the truth of it, that she suddenly came without warning. Considering it was her second orgasm in a short amount of time, she usually needed what she liked to call a little clit love. But here she was, exploding all over the man, her body shaking and nearly twisting out of his hands. Then he was coming right behind her, the hands on her hips turning to claws, digging into her flesh but stopping before any real damage could be done.

While Cella tried to get her breath back, the bear removed the cuffs, his hands rubbing her wrists. He stretched out on the floor and Cella collapsed on top of him. They lay in silence for long minutes until Cella admitted, "You have the biggest cock . . ."

Crush laughed, his hand slipping into her hair, massaging her scalp. "Why, thank you."

"Just felt I should share that."

"I have to admit, Cella, I don't think I'll ever get tired of your after-sex pronouncements."

CHAPTER TWENTY-NINE

Cella crawled over the bear, landing on his chest and bouncing up and down until he woke up.

"Must you do that?"

"Yes." She laughed, kissed his neck. "I have to get to the Sports Center."

"No," Crush whined, reaching for her. "Stay with me here."

Cella batted off his hands. "Do you really want me to tell the Marauder that I didn't show up for a game because I was busy having sex with you?"

"He's all about personal responsibility. He'll blame you, not me."

"You bastard." She pinched his nose and covered his mouth until she felt she'd gotten her message across.

"Now," she said once she'd released him and he could breathe, "are you coming to the game tonight?"

"Of course, I am. It's my team. And the Marauder's playing."

She covered his nose and mouth again, not letting him push her off until she was sure she'd really gotten her message across. "Are you coming to the game tonight?" she asked again.

"How could I ever dream of missing you play?"

"See? That wasn't so hard, now was it?"

She kissed him and scrambled off before he could grab her and pull her back. "Do you need tickets or anything?"

"Nope. I'm meeting Conway at the Sports Center."

"But you are coming to the locker room after, right?"

"Can I bring Conway and totally show off that I'm gettin' it on with Bare Knuckles Malone?"

"What kind of pretend girlfriend would I be if I didn't let you do that?"

"So we're still going for the pretend, eh?"

"Yep. I'll see you after the game."

He grumbled something and turned over.

Cella stopped outside the bedroom to find Lola standing there. She'd had Tommy pick up the dog and bring it, her, whatever, to the hotel room. And Crush had been so happy when he'd seen her that Cella just knew she'd have to really face the fact that the man had a dog and that dog, no matter how unattractive, would always be around.

Cella stepped aside and gestured to the bed. "Well, go on. Since I'm not there."

Lola ran past her, but the poor thing couldn't leap up on the bear-sized king with those short legs. So Cella, her lip curled in disgust, slipped her hand under that chubby ass and hoisted her onto the bed.

Then, without even a thank-you, the dog ran and cuddled up next to Cella's bear, burrowing against his chest.

Wishing she could do that herself, Cella forced herself to leave and head down to the lobby. Mario the driver waited right outside, smiling when he saw her approach.

"Hello, Miss Malone."

"Hi, Mario."

She handed over her equipment bags to Mario and settled into the backseat. She'd just started to relax when her cell phone went off. She dug it out of her backpack and looked at the text message.

GOOD LUCK TONIGHT, SEXY.

Grinning, Cella texted back:

I BETTER SEE YOU LATER. YOU KNOW HOW I AM AFTER A
GAME. HEH.

"Yep," Cella told Mario. "Best pretend boyfriend ever."

"Oh, come on, Miss Malone," Mario playfully shot back. "Pretend boyfriend, my butt. Everybody at KZS knows you're dating that bear."

"It's not official or anything," she argued.

"Lame."

"Shut up, Mario."

They reached the Sports Center pretty quickly considering it was nearly rush hour, and Mario parked right by the front doors.

Once Cella had all her equipment, Mario patted her shoulder. "Good luck tonight, Miss Malone."

"Thanks."

"Will I be picking you up after the game?"

"I'm not really sure. I'll text you." She walked off, heading toward the exclusive entrance. A wolf security guard was holding the door open for her when she suddenly stopped and looked over her shoulder.

"Everything all right, Miss Malone? Miss Malone?"

"Yeah, yeah. Thanks."

Cella took one more look around, but didn't see anything. It was just a feeling. Letting out a breath, she headed inside, smiling at the wolf still watching her. Once in the hallway, she put down her stuff and pulled out her cell phone. She hit her speed-dial and waited.

"Smith."

"It's Cella."

"Yep."

"I think someone's following me."

Smith was silent for a moment, then said, "You at the Sports Center?"

"Yeah. And my father and Crush are going to be here to-night."

"I'll be right over."

Crush impatiently stood in line with Conway. Usually he was impatient to see the game. But for the first time he could remember, he was impatient for the game to be over so he could see a woman. Not just any woman, either. But a foul-mouthed little feline with what his foster mother would have called "unsavory family connections." Like Peg Baissier was British royalty or something.

"You're really liking this girl, aren't you?"

"I specifically like her because she's not a girl."

"You mean because she's a feline?"

Crush remembered to hold his temper in. "Because she's a *woman*."

"Girl. Woman. What's the difference?"

"Ask your wife that. When the swelling goes down, let me know how well she took it."

Conway chuckled. "Chay's just glad you've found a girl-friend."

"Pretend girlfriend."

"Are you having sex with her?"

"None of your business."

"That's a yes, otherwise you'd just say no. You're one of those honest guys."

"You make that sound wrong."

"Depends. And if you're having regular sex with her, she's not your pretend anything."

"I don't know if we're that serious yet." Or maybe he just didn't know if Cella was that serious. She was not an easy woman to figure out; he at least knew that much.

While Crush was busy contemplating the extent of his re-lationship with Cella, he noticed that the crowd had grown disturbingly quiet. He looked at Conway, both of them frowning. Then he looked to his left—and into the cold blue eyes of the Marauder.

"Uh . . . hi?"

The Marauder looked him over. "What are you doing?"

Crush again looked at Conway, but his friend could only shrug.

"Waiting to get my seat."

"But this is the line for the shitty seats."

A bit insulted, Crush looked down at his season holder ticket. "They're a bit high up, perhaps, but I still see the game well enough." There. That was well put.

Well put for someone *not* The Marauder.

"But they're shitty seats. We call those the shit seats."

One of the males of the hyena clan standing behind Crush snapped, "Do you mind? We paid good money for these seats."

The polar bear–lion hybrid only turned his head, scowl turning him into something so fearsome Crush was glad the man had never become a criminal.

"Did you just interrupt me?" Novikov asked the hyena.

"What if I did?" the hyena demanded, and that's when Crush remembered the idiot and his Clan members had already had more than a few beers between them.

After years of being a beat cop, Crush went on instinct and grabbed Novikov seconds before those big hands were around the hyena's throat. Conway kept the hyenas back by flashing his badge and eventually his gun.

"You're gonna be late for the game!" Crush reminded Novikov and the hybrid immediately stopped fighting and looked at his watch.

"Shit!"

He grabbed his equipment and motioned at Crush. "Well, come on."

Figuring he wanted Crush and Conway to keep the fans off him until he got to the locker rooms, Crush pulled his buddy and the pair followed after him.

"What about our seats?" Conway whispered to him.

"They'll still be there when we get back."

"So what? We're doing protection duty now?"

"Stop whining."

"But it's Minnesota," he said about the team the Carnivores were playing against.

"If you say that one more time . . ."

They followed Novikov into the elevator. The doors closed and the hybrid shook his head. "Do you know who I blame for this?"

Crush was tempted to say, "Your bad temper?" but decided not to. The man was at least four inches taller and another sixty pounds heavier. Crush could shoot him, but what about the game?

As always, Crush's priority was his team.

"Because of her. Because of Blayne Thorpe." Novikov pointed at himself. "I'm never late. Never. And then I met her. And somehow she's managed to get me involved in her crazy timetable. I'm always here three to four hours early so that I can practice and avoid the crowds. But I had to wait for her to get back from Long Island. Do you know why?" Rather than verbally answer, Crush and Conway just shook their heads. "Because she had a surprise for me. Do you know what kind of surprise?" Again, they went with the head shake. It seemed the safest bet. "China patterns! Do I look like I give a holy fuck about china patterns?"

Still safe to go with the head shake.

"And it doesn't help she's all cute and adorable and sweet. Last week, do you know what she brought into my house? My nice, pristine, perfect house? An alley cat. Not a cheetah. Or some leopard. An actual cat that lives in the alley behind my building. She wants to keep it. A cat! She's a wolfdog and she wants to have a cat!"

"Crushek has a dog and he's a bear."

Novikov looked at him. "You have a dog?"

"It's just a foster."

"He's said that for three fucking years."

"I want to make sure she gets the right home!"

"Do you have other foster dogs?" Novikov asked him.

"No."

"Then she's your dog."

The elevator stopped and the doors opened. MacRyrie and Van Holtz stepped in with welcoming smiles. Then they saw Novikov. The smiling stopped.

There was some snarling as the pair got settled and the doors closed. Crush saw MacRyrie nudge Van Holtz, then casually say to Novikov, "You're kind of late."

Without missing a beat, Novikov threw down his equipment and the two bears went at each other. Crush and Conway grabbed Novikov from behind, trying to pull him off MacRyrie while Van Holtz did the same with the grizzly. The problem was, they were locked on and neither seemed ready to back off.

Then the elevator stopped and the doors once again opened. That's when Crush saw Cella standing there with Smith, Dr. Davis, and several of Cella's female teammates.

Smirking, Cella stared at the five males in the elevator before asking the women with her, "Show of hands for anyone else who's had this fantasy before."

He wasn't exactly surprised when all those hands went up.

Once off the elevator, Crush introduced her to his old partner. She was sure the man had a first name, but Crush only said, "This is Conway." She didn't bother busting his balls about it. She had the feeling it was a guy thing.

"Everything all right?" she asked him.

"Yep." He smiled down at her. "Actually it's better now."

"Awwwwww," said the entire hallway filled with shifters.

"He has a gun," she announced. "I'll let him use it."

When everyone went back to his or her own business, Cella went up on her toes and hugged the big bear. "I'm glad you're here."

"Uh-huh."

She leaned back a bit, looking up into his face. "You don't believe me?"

"I believe I just saw Smith sidle on outta here. Why's she lurking?"

"Wow." Cella was truly impressed. Most people, including Cella and even Van Holtz, never actually saw Smith go anywhere unless she wanted to be seen. The girl had a skill. Sissy Mae called her The Ghost. It was an accurate description.

"Are you going to tell me what's going on?"

"I'm probably just being paranoid."

"I've known a lot of paranoid people, Malone. You're not paranoid."

"I felt like someone was following me."

"Then they probably were. Don't worry. By the time the game's over, you'll have protection."

"But—"

"No. Don't wanna hear it." Crush leaned down and kissed her cheek. "I'll see you after the game."

"Okay."

Conway came over to them, holding up a Carnivores T-shirt. "Check it out. I got like six team signatures."

"I thought you were a Minnesota fan."

Cella looked the coyote over. "You're a Minnesota fan? Aren't they all like bears?" She glanced up at Crush. "No offense."

"I am a Minnesota fan. But I can sell this bad boy for a fortune."

"Where's the loyalty, canine?"

"He has none," Crush explained. "He's from Jersey."

"Ohhh."

The polar pointed at her. "Good luck."

"Thanks."

Crush turned to head off to the elevator with his coyote friend when Novikov walked up. "Where are you going?"

Both men stopped and slowly faced the hybrid.

"To our seats."

"The shit seats?"

Cella rolled her eyes. "Don't pick on him about his seats."

Now Novikov looked at her. "What kind of girlfriend are you?"

"A pretend one."

Novikov frowned. "You're so weird."

"This has been established."

"Here." Novikov handed over two badges hanging from chains.

Crush's eyes grew wide, his mouth dropping open. "I . . . I can't take—"

Before he could even finish, the coyote snatched the badges from Crush's hand and slapped him in the face with the game program.

"Thanks!" Conway said, grinning widely. "Really appreciate it, man."

"I don't know you," Novikov said. "It's for him. You just happen to be with him."

Yeah, Cella could see what Blayne Thorpe saw in the man. He'd never lie to you. He was too direct.

"Thanks," Cella said, winking at him.

"You should have thought of it yourself."

"Don't piss me off before we hit the ice, mutt."

Shaking his head, always looking a little disgusted by everyone around him, the hybrid walked off.

"I can't—" Crush began and Cella went up on her toes, placing her hand over his mouth.

"You can. You will. It's not like we just bribed you guys so we can bring in drugs or something. I'm just sorry I didn't think of it myself. You'd be all over me if I had," she teased.

And she knew that's what had him upset. "I don't need this stuff from you," Crush insisted. "I don't want it."

"I'm kidding," she told him.

"She's kidding," the coyote promised, not willing to give up those badges anytime soon.

Cella gave Conway directions to the owner's seats, worried that Crush would go back to his nosebleed seats out of some sort of Crushek-morality thing.

She kissed him once more. "Have fun," she ordered him. "Or Nice Guy Malone will hear about it."

"Oh, God," Crush said, appearing truly horrified. "Your father—"

"Is here and will be glad to see you." Laughing, she went to the locker room to get the rest of her gear on.

Jai stopped by on her way to check on everyone else she'd been caring for since the last game.

"Heads-up," Jai said, briskly writing damn notes on her damn clipboard.

"Heads-up on what?"

"That Minnesota team."

"What about 'em?"

"They have a reputation. So be careful. I'd rather not have to repair your arteries tonight."

"Got it." Cella winked at her and finished suiting up.

She met the rest of the team waiting in the hallway, where Van Holtz felt the need to say, "I like him."

"Who?"

"Your bear."

"He's not *my* bear. He's *a* bear that I happen to be fucking at the moment."

"Have you realized," MacRyrie asked her, "that you're just like Novikov but with more charm and no OCD?"

"The direct thing?"

"Yeah," both bear and wolf said at the same time.

"I like being direct. Then no one can hold shit over your head. Like when I got pregnant in high school. I ran around telling everybody. The nuns were horrified. But no one could shame me because I'd already put it all out there. For everybody!"

The team laughed until the announcer came on. That's when Cella motioned to Reed and the other rookies she'd been working with. "Remember what I told you guys. Don't panic, don't get pissed. Just play. Got me? Now get out there and kick ass."

CHAPTER THIRTY

Crush again looked at his friend. *This is your fault*, he mouthed at him, and all Conway could do was shrug helplessly.

"You know what I mean, right?" Cella's father asked.

"Uh-huh."

"Because if you kill them, how can you get your money? You can't. Every good bookie knows that, which is why they liked me. I knew how to break bones and heads without actually killing anyone. That's a skill, you know? A skill I have."

Crush nodded. "Uh-huh." He looked at Conway again. *Your fault!*

I'm sorry!

"She's out of the penalty box."

Thankful, because Nice Guy seemed to talk less when his daughter was on the ice, Crush focused on Cella. He'd have to admit, it was a tough game. The Minnesota team had a healthy mix of predators, but their best players were the hyenas. They were all from the same Clan and didn't like to give up their puck. They especially seemed to hate the Marauder. Must be the lion thing, because they kept going after him and Cella just kept getting in their way. There was a lot of blood on the ice and for once he couldn't just say it belonged only to the opposition. The team was fighting hard tonight to just keep the no-score going.

It was at times like this that Crush could see the benefit of Cella. She didn't back down, did she? And she always protected the Marauder. She kicked ass.

But as Crush watched the teams go at it, fighting for that puck, he noticed something right away. It was between the hyenas. Three of them. They skated around by their team's net, something silent passing between them. Then they shot off in three different directions.

Crush thought maybe it was his imagination, until Nice Guy stopped talking—the man rarely stopped talking altogether—and leaned forward, his elbows resting on his knees, fingers steepled together.

Focusing back on the ice, Crush watched the hyenas circle around and behind the Carnivores' goal. They were heading for the Marauder, again, and several players moved in to protect him. As they did, the hyenas broke off and went around them. It seemed normal. Until Crush realized that Cella was out on her own, away from the rest of the team, moving toward Novikov. She was focused on him, always watching out for her team more than herself. So she didn't see them coming. Didn't see them gunning right for her.

"Jesus—" was the last thing Crush heard from Nice Guy Malone seconds before two hyenas ran right into Cella. Hit hard from two sides, she went airborne, her body spinning up and over. Yet she was feline and when she landed, she landed on two legs. Crush winced, knowing her bad knee must have felt that.

But as soon as Cella landed, the third hyena was there, ramming into her, low and at an angle. Right into her lower body. Her legs collided with the rink wall. The entire crowd roared with rage and awe at the bold move, but Crush heard Cella's roar above everything else and he knew—*knew*—what had just happened.

He jumped from his seat, standing tall, not thinking of any poor sap that might be behind him. It took him a second to realize that Nice Guy was right by him, the father's horror palpable.

Together they watched Cella's body flip again and land hard. She wasn't knocked out. She was in too much pain. She'd still managed to hold on to her stick, but she finally dropped that and went for her left leg, now bent at an unnatural angle. The pain so bad, she couldn't even pretend not to feel it.

The hyenas, staring down at her, skated back as the rest of the two teams stopped completely. It was strange, how everyone just sort of froze.

The refs—a fellow polar and a lion male—skated between the two teams, pushing them apart while the Carnivores' team manager ran out on the ice and to Cella's side. A few seconds later the medical team came out, Dr. Davis with them. They surrounded Cella and Crush could only see the tops of their heads, so it was impossible to know what was going on. Although, on a gut level, he already knew. So did her father.

"I . . . I . . ."

He motioned to Conway, knew his friend would keep Mr. Malone calm. He was good at that. Crush patted the older man's shoulder. "I'll go check on her. You stay here."

Crush walked to the door and out of it. Once the security monitoring the door had closed it again, he ran.

Gritting her teeth, never having felt pain like this since the birth of her daughter, Cella tried her best to hold on. To not black out. But it was getting harder and harder. She was definitely out of this game. Fucking hyenas.

"Get the stretcher!" Jai ordered the techs. Then she was over Cella, hands on her shoulders, trying to hold her down, but the pain was too much to stay still. "Honey, you need to let me see."

"Fuck, Jai. Fuck!"

"I know."

Man, Cella would never hear the end of this. It would take at least a week for her knee to heal this time. Ice wouldn't do it. Not tonight, at least. But she could get through this. She would. She was a Malone. She'd force herself to stay off her knee for a week or so and that would be it. Then she wanted a rematch with those assholes.

Hands went under her shoulders and another under her waist. She was lifted/dragged onto the stretcher. The crowd didn't sound happy. They wanted blood. *Good luck getting out of the Sports Center, Minnesota.* Hell. Good luck getting out of the city.

Another bolt of pain hit Cella and everything went blank there for a bit. When she woke up, she was in one of the med rooms. God, how long had she been out?

"Cella? Hon? Can you hear me?"

She looked up at Jai. The pain was less. They must have shot her up with something. Good. That helped.

"Yeah. I can hear you."

"Okay. Great. We're going to be transferring you in the next few minutes."

"Transferring me?" Cella fought hard to focus. The meds were making her loopy. "Transfer me where?"

"To McMillian Presbyterian Hospital."

"But I'm Catholic." Oh. Wow. She was *high*. Cella shook her head. Tried again. "Why hospital? I can recover at home. I wanna go home."

Cella saw her friend's face. That expression. "What's going on?" Cella asked.

"Nothing. Let's just get you to the hospital."

Cella caught Jai's arm, and held her tight. "What's going on?"

Jai looked up at her techs, motioned them away with a hard jerk of her head. When they'd moved across the room, Jai looked back at her. "Your knee, hon."

"What about it?"

Jai stared at her, took a moment. "This has to be fixed. This won't heal on its own."

"What does that mean?"

"You know what it means."

"But—"

Jai's voice was no nonsense, strictly professional. "If we let this set, Cella, the way it is . . . you won't be able to walk on that leg, much less skate. But I've already contacted the specialist there. He's going to meet us at the hospital."

"To *fix* what I have."

"No," Jai said firmly. "There is no fixing what you have, Cella. We either replace or you start using a walker to get around.

"But don't worry. Once it's done, you'll be fine. This guy knows what he's doing. He's the best and no one will ever know you were ever hurt."

But that wasn't the point, was it? It wasn't that she'd walk or not walk again. It was that, in effect, her entire career was over. Just like that. There'd be no heroic tales of her working back to the team after lots of physical therapy and a miracle. Instead, Cella would get her knee replaced, her leg would be as strong, if not stronger than it had ever been before . . . and she'd never play pro sports again. Ever.

One of the techs moved up to Jai and whispered in her ear.

"Right. Okay." Jai looked down at her. "The ambulance is here, hon. We have to go." Because if they waited too long, her leg would heal on its own, but badly, forcing the doctors to destroy her leg again in order to repair it.

Taking her silence as some kind of agreement, Jai motioned for the techs to let in the ones who'd be taking her to the hospital.

But another bout of pain ripped through her before anyone could move her and Cella roared, her fangs and claws unleashing, ready to slash and rip and destroy. Big hands held her down and someone stuck a needle in her, more meds forced into her system.

And that was pretty much the last thing she remembered.

Crush impatiently waited outside the med offices, pacing. No one got too close to him. No one ever got too close to an anxious bear.

He was hoping to get in to see Cella, to find out what was going on. But then the EMS guys were taking her out, heading toward an ambulance parked outside the Sports Center. Dr. Davis followed behind them, rushing to keep up. Crush followed, calling out her name.

She looked over her shoulder. At first, he wasn't sure she even recognized him. Once at the elevator, she faced him, walking in backward, unwilling to waste precious seconds getting Cella to the hospital.

"We're taking her to McMillian Presbyterian Hospital. Get her father. He needs to be there when she wakes up. Understand?"

Crush nodded and watched the elevator doors close.

But instead of running to get her father, Crush stood there. He couldn't move. And he had no idea how long he stood there, staring at that closed door until he heard his name called.

Finally snapping out of whatever catatonic state he'd dropped into, Crush slowly turned. It was Van Holtz.

"Where is she?"

"Hospital."

"How bad is it?" When Crush could only shrug, Van Holtz turned to one of the med techs hanging around outside the room. "How bad?"

The jackal, using a towel to wipe blood off her hands, stated, "The knee's destroyed. They're going to have to replace it. They're waiting for her at McMillian."

Now Van Holtz looked like Crush was guessing he did.

Stunned and confused. But he couldn't help Van Holtz deal with it. Not now.

"I have to get her father," he said, walking past the wolf. "He needs to be there when she wakes up."

The second string was on the ice and Lock sat on the bench next to Novikov, who sat next to Reed, who sat next to Bert. They sat and said nothing, waiting for Ric to get back.

Something didn't feel right, but Lock couldn't put his finger on it. Yet he knew something was off. It was a sixth sense he'd picked up while in the Marines. To know when something that looks completely benign and merely an accident was anything but. And after a quick glance at the teammates sitting with him, he kind of knew he wasn't the only one feeling that way.

It just seemed like those hyenas had targeted Marcella. And maybe they had. She'd been on several other teams before she'd settled down with the Carnivores, recruited by Ric. She might have pissed off the Minnesota team or those hyenas specifically at any time over the last few years. Still . . . they hadn't just gone after her. Hell. *Lots* of players had gone after her. She was a well-hated woman in hockey because she was just so damn good at what she did. But this seemed so coordinated. So planned out. And they hadn't gone for her jugular. They'd gone for her legs. For her weak knee . . .

Ric dropped down next to Lock and Novikov leaned around to look at him.

"Well?" Novikov demanded.

"They're taking her to McMillian Presbyterian." An excellent hospital for shifters. Lock's sister was head of neurosurgery there. "Total knee replacement."

Novikov blinked, shocked and clearly upset. "Are they sure?"

Ric nodded. "They're sure."

There was silence after that. The entire first string just sat there, already missing Cella's "let's kill them all!" attitude.

Suddenly, Ric stood and put on his helmet. "First string in," he ordered. Normally something he left up to the coach, but he was the owner. He could do anything he wanted.

As one they all stood and skated onto the ice, the second string passing them on their way to the bench. With the puck in play, the opposition maneuvered it down the ice toward the Carnivore goal. Ric crouched, waiting, and Lock raced down as one of the opposition neared the goal, trying to get the puck in the net. Ric stopped the puck and Lock skated between his friend and one of the hyenas. Lock had just passed by when he saw Ric's stick flash out, slamming into the hyena's side.

Startled—Ric never fought anybody unless they started it—Lock spun back around just as Ric dropped gloves and he and the hyena rammed into each other. Another hyena was going toward Ric so Lock ran into him, grabbing him around the neck and yanking him by his head while Novikov picked up the third hyena and began bouncing him around the rink like he was a basketball player and the hyena was the ball.

Then both teams were on the ice and that was pretty much the end of the game. . . .

Chapter Thirty-one

The elevator doors opened and Dez stepped out, her husband Mace behind her. She stopped immediately, her gaze moving around the packed hospital hallway. She knew most of the people there, but she could easily spot Cella's family. They mostly looked like Dez's friend. Black hair with orange and white streaks, gold or green eyes; the women curvy, the men built like linebackers.

But what worried Dez immediately was the weight of tragedy she felt throughout the entire hallway. She had no clue what had happened, getting one of those short-worded Dee-Ann Smith messages on her voice mail. God, was she too late?

No, no. She didn't want to think like that.

After another quick look around, Dez saw Dee-Ann and she walked over to her. She stood next to a completely battered Ric Van Holtz, Lock MacRyrie, and Bo Novikov. They looked like they'd been through hell. Had they tried to stop what had happened to Cella? And if the guys looked like this . . . what did Cella look like?

"Dee—" Dez began, but then Blayne was wrapped around Dez . . . sobbing. Hysterically.

God, maybe I am too late.

Dee pulled Blayne off Dez and pushed her toward Novikov. "Come on." She grabbed Dez's arm and led her down another hallway and into an empty room, closing the door.

"What the fuck happened?" Dez got out before the door opened again and Blayne walked in.

"You can't stay," Dee told Blayne, "if all you're gonna do is cry like a baby."

Snarling, Blayne stepped into Dee, pointing her finger in her face. "She's my friend, too, Dee-Ann!" The tears started again. "I love her."

"Just yesterday you called her a bitch."

"*How can you bring that up?*" Blayne wailed.

Realizing that neither of these two would give her the answers she needed—one talked too much and the other not enough—Dez walked back into the hallway. "Stay here," she ordered before she went in search of Crushek. She knew the bear well enough to know he wouldn't be part of the crowd, but she also knew he was there. Somewhere. He wouldn't leave Cella alone.

And Dez was right. She found Crush at the end of the long hallway inside one of the rooms. He sat on the floor, his back against the wall, his knees raised, his gaze focused on the empty bed. She stepped up next to him and held out her hand.

Crush looked at it and up at her.

"Come on," she said.

He took her hand, but mostly got himself up off the floor. She led him back to the room where she'd left an eye-rolling Dee-Ann and a still sobbing Blayne.

"Oh, Crush!" Blayne cried before running into the startled polar, her arms wrapping around his waist. "You poor, poor man."

Dez closed the door, ignoring the look her husband gave her before she did.

"What happened?" she asked, figuring she'd at least get most of the story from the three of them together.

"Poor Cella's life is over!" Blayne sobbed into Crush's chest, but Dez decided not to take that at face value. Instead, she focused on Dee-Ann.

The woman shrugged. "She was hurt."

"How bad?"

"Bad enough."

See? That wasn't enough information. So Dez then moved her attention to Crush, who was awkwardly patting Blayne's back.

"It's my fault," he told her. "All of this. I think it's my fault."

Blayne looked up at him. "Your fault? How can you say that?"

"I should have known Baissier would do something. I just never thought she'd go after Cella like that."

Nope. Still not clear, so Dez went back to Dee-Ann.

"She called me earlier. Said someone was following her. It never occurred to either of us that they'd take her out on the ice."

The ice? Someone attacked her during one of those hockey games? With hundreds, maybe even several thousand shifters nearby? Then Dez remembered the way Ric and Lock had looked outside. They'd clearly been in a fight. But then . . .

Dez looked at the three shifters. "Was Cella shot?"

Dee-Ann shook her head. "No."

"They destroyed her leg," Blayne whimpered.

"Well," Dee corrected, "mostly just her knee."

"Her . . ." Dez scratched her head. "Was she kneecapped in the bathroom or something?"

"No. It happened on the ice."

Dez studied the three idiots. "Are you telling me you dragged me here for a fucking sports accident?"

"Figured you'd wanna know."

"I do want to know, Dee. Cella's my friend. But I want de-tails. Telling me 'You better come to the hospital. They got

Cella' implies something different to me than a sports injury."

"You don't undertstand, Dez," Blayne explained, pulling away from Crush as more tears flowed. "Her career is over. She'll never play pro hockey again."

"Is she going to be in a wheelchair?"

Dee pulled a piece of jerky out of her back pocket. Why it was back there, Dez didn't want to know. "Doubtful," Dee said. "Once she gets that knee replaced and all, she'll probably be back at KZS early next week. We're just waitin' for them to finish the surgery."

"Will she at least have a limp?"

"Nah. Our bodies take real well to replacement surgeries." Dee held up her arm, pointing at her elbow. "Got this blown off during a hunt. Docs replaced it . . . good as new." To illustrate, she bent what looked to be a mostly unmarred joint.

Dez pointed at the door. "Get out. Both of you. Out." She grabbed Blayne by the back of her jeans and dragged her to the door, opening it and shoving her out. "You, too, country. Out."

"You sure are moody," the wolf complained before she ambled out the door.

Slamming the door, Dez faced Crush. "What is going on?"

Cella opened her eyes and the first thing she saw was her mother . . . and tears. Then she looked around the room. All those Malones. All that crying. Men and women. She felt like she'd just woken up in a casket after being misdiagnosed as dead.

"Mom?"

"Oh! My dear sweet girl!"

Her mother hugged her and Cella could feel tears dripping against her neck. At least she hoped it was tears.

"It'll be okay, baby." Her mother pulled back and stroked

her hair. "You're going to be just . . . just . . ." Eyes wide, she looked at Cella's aunts who just days before she'd threatened to bare-knuckle fight. They all smiled down at Cella, then Kathleen began to cry, then Margaret, then . . . good God, even Deirdre. Then all of them were crying. It was pretty . . . strange.

In fact, Cella looked down at her leg to make sure she still had it and yup! It was there. It was bandaged and had a brace on it to keep it immobile while it healed. Cella could tell she was currently being pumped full of all sorts of painkillers because she knew her body was knitting itself back together and that often hurt. A lot. But she didn't feel a thing. So here she was. Breathing. Surviving as Malones liked to do. And yet her uncles couldn't even look at her. God . . . did she have scars on her face? Did one of those hyenas hit her with his skate? Was she hideous?

Then Cella remembered that this was her family she was dealing with. They were emotional basket cases on their best days. So rather than panic, she looked around the room until she found her daughter. Meghan stood in the back of the room, Josie next to her. What Cella loved was the absolute look of annoyance on her kid's pretty face. Okay. So if Meg was going to stay with the family, at least she had the potential to one day run this bunch. She had attitude to spare.

Even better, Meghan knew her mother. One look and she was pushing her way through the crowd of uncles, aunts, and cousins until she was by her mother's side. She took Cella's hand, holding it between both of hers. "Could you guys leave us alone, please? I need to . . ." She took a long, dramatic pause Cella was mighty proud of. She'd taught the kid well. ". . . *talk* to my mom for a bit."

"Of course, of course," Kathleen said, hustling all the aunts, uncles, and cousins out of the room. But it was Cella's dad who took hold of his wife's shoulders and, with a wink at Cella, led the still sobbing woman out of the room.

Once the door closed and Cella was alone with her daughter,

she let out a sigh. "No feline should sob unless she's been hit with a baseball bat."

"It's always gotta be so extreme with you."

Cella laughed, grinning up at her daughter. "It's in the DNA, kid. You might as well get used to it."

Still holding her mother's hand, Meghan sat on the bed. "Mom, I'm so sorry."

"For what? You didn't do anything."

"It's not about doing anything. It's about . . . empathizing."

"Empathizing?"

Meghan's eyes crossed. "Yes, Mom. Empathy."

"Sounds like weakness."

"It is not . . ." Meghan gritted her teeth. "Why do you make me crazy?"

"Isn't that my job? It's my mother's job, and as you can see, she does it well."

"All I'm saying is that I know how much hockey means to you. It meant everything—"

"No. You mean everything to me, baby. *You.* The rest is just gravy."

"So what are you going to do now?"

"Learn to knit."

"Mom."

"I'll figure out something. There's more to life than hockey."

"For everyone else, but not for you." Meghan thought a moment. "There's the female team."

"No."

"They don't have the same rules that—"

"Exactly." Cella gaped at her daughter. "Do you not like your mother's pretty face? Do you hope to see me missing eyes . . . teeth? Do you care so little that you'd suggest the all-female team?"

"You bare-knuckle box!"

"Men! Males, as you'll one day learn, are easy to manage. If the same shit that went down last night had happened while I was on the all-female team . . . I'd be missing legs. Both of them."

"I heard they're not that bad . . . anymore."

"They're that bad. Trust me. Coed, all male, or nothing. Because all-female is just painful trouble and suffering."

"Always with the drama."

"I'm a Malone," Cella explained again, making sure to let out a long sigh. "Once you grasp that, the drama explains itself." She thought a moment. "Any chance you can get everyone else to go away? Far away?"

"I can try. They usually listen to me."

"I know."

"No, Ma."

"What?"

"I see your mind turning. I will not be running this family anytime soon."

"Of course not. You're only eighteen. But another fifteen years or so . . ."

"Like you're ever going to let me boss you around." Meghan dropped Cella's hand. "You're so full of crap."

"Crap? Really?"

"Not everyone has to express themselves with profanity."

"No. But what fun is it *not* to express yourself with profanity?"

Meghan stood. "I'll get rid of everybody." She walked to the door. Stopped. "Your team's—"

"No," Cella said quickly. "I can't see them tonight."

"Okay. That scary She-wolf and Detective MacDermot?"

"First off, the She-wolf is Dee-Ann and she already said you could call her that."

Her daughter's lip curled a little. "Yeah."

"Forget it. Tell them to come by tomorrow."

"Okay." Her daughter glanced at the floor, then asked, "What about Mr. Crushek?"

"Crush is here?"

"Of course, he's here." Meghan nodded. "And he looks really upset."

"He does?"

"Uh-huh."

"Yeah. Let him come in."

"Okay."

"Are you going to go home with the family?"

"No," her daughter replied in her all-business tone. "And Mr. Crushek has until I get back before he has to leave, too. No canoodling."

"Canoodling?"

"You know what I mean."

"But do *you* know what you mean?"

"Of course, I do. I read."

Cella ordered herself not to laugh because her daughter was as serious as a heart attack.

"I'll ask Aunt Jai to stop in, too." Hand now on the door, Meghan warned, "And, Ma, do *not* move that leg."

Staring at her daughter, Cella sat up a bit and jerked.

Gold eyes narrowed on her. "*Ma.*"

The kid was so easy!

"I'm not moving my leg. Besides, right now I'm so high on whatever painkiller they're giving me that I feel like I'm floating anyway."

"I'll be back," Meghan threatened.

Once her daughter walked out, Cella relaxed back in her bed and stared across the empty room. After a minute, she announced to no one, "I am *so* high."

"So," Dez reasoned, "basically, her leg will be stronger than it was."

"Yeah."

"And she'll be, without even any physical therapy, back on her feet in like three to four days."

"Pretty much."

"And yet they're all acting like they're mourning her death."

"Just the death of her career."

"One of them. I mean she's in KZS. I'm relatively certain the half-a-mil they pay her per year—"

"Wait. How much?"

"Oh, yeah. KZS pays *really* well. They tried to hire Mace when he left the Navy but he had plans with Smitty."

"So even though we're paid better than any full-human on the force, no matter the rank, we're still paid less than everyone else?"

"Civil servants, baby." Dez stared at Crush for a moment and he tried not to hide from her straightforward gaze. Finally, after a moment, she told him, "It's not your fault."

"It is my fault. I should have known Baissier was going to do something like this."

"That she'd hire hyenas to break your girlfriend's knee at a hockey game? I don't think anyone would see that coming." She pointed her finger at him. "And you're not that guy."

Confused, Crush asked, "What the fuck does that mean?"

"I mean, you're not that guy who takes revenge on his foster mother by cutting her throat while she sleeps." She pointed at the door. "Dee-Ann's that guy. She'll do that shit in a heartbeat. Cella, too. Not you. You do that shit, you'll never live with yourself. And then you'll drive me, your partner, crazy with your Mr. Depression act. So let's not pretend that you're the guy who can hunt someone down and exact revenge."

"So just let it go?"

"Look, I get it. What happened to Cella sucks. And this . . . uncaring bitch deserves some pain. But I'm not sure what she did would be considered a mitigating factor for her eventual murder in a court of law. And, yeah, you have claws and fangs, you're a predator, yada yada—"

"Yada yada?"

"—but at the end of the day, my friend . . . you're still a cop. Old school. You'd never let anyone get away with exacting revenge, either, no matter who or what the hell they were or their perfectly good reasons."

"But I feel like I owe it to her. I feel I owe Cella."

"All you owe Cella is flowers, maybe some festive balloons, a ride home from the hospital, and nuzzling. You know, bear love."

"Bear love? Something else you saw on National Geographic?"

"Or Animal Planet. Both are very helpful in dealing with my husband and my new crop of friends that aren't canines."

"I just . . ." Crush stopped talking, lifted his nose, and sniffed. Reaching over, he grabbed the door handle and pulled it open. Cella's daughter stood on the other side, Dr. Davis's daughter right next to her. It looked like the two girls were in a heated discussion about something, but when the door opened, both froze. He felt like he'd caught them doing something, but he didn't know what.

"Hi, Meghan. Everything okay?"

Wide-eyed, the girl nodded while she shoved her friend away. The kid took off and Meghan stepped closer. "Mom's awake."

Cella yawned and looked up at Jai. Once again, she was writing on a chart attached to a clipboard. What was the woman's obsession with clipboards?

"Are you all right?" Cella asked.

"I'm fine."

"You don't look fine."

Jai lifted her gaze to Cella's and glared.

"I had no idea everyone was so invested in my career," Cella muttered. "That they'd all be so upset."

"Can't we just be empathetic?"

"What is that word?"

Before Jai could hit her with her clipboard—she was clearly thinking about it—the door opened and Josie ran in, stumbling to a stop by the bed.

"What is it?" Jai asked her daughter.

"Detective Crushek . . ."

"What about him?"

"Meghan and I went to find him and he was talking to Detective MacDermot and . . . he wants revenge."

Cella frowned. "Against the Minnesota team?"

"Huh?" She shook her head. "No, no. Against his foster mother or something?" She leaned in and whispered, "He's an orphan?"

"He is, baby, but he handles it really well."

"Not right now. He's really mad about what happened to you, Aunt C." Not surprising, really, if Baissier did have something to do with all this. Then again, Cella felt like she'd gotten off lucky. Fact was, if Baissier wanted Cella out of the way, she could have had Cella shot in the head while she was walking to the Sports Center. That was how KZS would have handled it.

"Where is he?"

"Meghan's bringing him in, but she wanted me to warn you first."

"Warn me?"

"You can't let him."

"I can't?" Cella asked, enjoying this, probably because she was high, but Jai slapped her shoulder anyway. "Ow!"

The door opened again and Meghan walked in, Crush behind her. At first, Cella smiled because it looked kind of comical. Her too-skinny, barely six-foot, very clean-cut daughter followed by a six-nine, three-hundred-pound cop wearing a black Black Sabbath T-shirt, and looking like he'd just been released from prison. Thankfully, he hadn't. Her daughter was perfectly safe. And realizing that made Cella's smile a little wider. She might be high, but she knew she trusted the bear. He cared, which meant little Josie was right. Crush would take the blame for this on his giant, bear shoulders. He shouldn't. None of this was his fault; this was just the world they all lived in. The cruel heartless games that they—the Group, KZS, BPC—all played. It really wasn't something he could control or manage and getting into it with someone like Peg Baissier would do nothing but get him seriously hurt.

And Cella cared! She cared if the bear got hurt. She cared if he was upset about all this. That made her smile even more. It was nice to care about someone who wasn't related by blood or the fact that they were pregnant the same time Cella was.

Frowning, Crush looked up, but when he saw her, he stopped, his hand on the door, his gaze on her, a small smile spreading across his face. And they stayed like that for a bit, both of them smiling at each other.

She was bruised and battered from the hockey game, her left leg in a brace that held it immobile, an IV attached to her arm, her black hair haphazardly piled on top of her head by a rubber band—but she was sitting up in bed and smiling.

God, she's beautiful.

Someone cleared their throat and Crush blinked, remembering they weren't alone.

"All right," Dr. Davis said while fluffing up Cella's pillow. "I'm going to take these two home."

"I'm not leaving Mom, Aunt J.," Meghan said.

"Yes, you are." Cella nodded at her daughter. "If you don't go home that means *my* mother will come back. Please don't do that to me. The mother you love. I can't take any more of the sobbing."

"What if you need something?"

"That's what a nursing staff is for." Dr. Davis pulled the pillow out from under Cella's head. "They'll take excellent care of her." She fluffed up the pillow again. "That's what they're trained to do." Then she put the pillow over Cella's face, pushing her back into the bed.

The two teenagers rolled their eyes, disgusted by their mothers.

"Mo-om," Dr. Davis's daughter whined.

Laughing, Dr. Davis pulled back, holding up that pillow. "I was just trying to help her get to sleep."

Cella slapped at her friend's arms. "You're an idiot. Go." She waved both girls away. "Go home. I'll be here in the morning."

"You shouldn't be alone, Ma."

"I'll stay." Crush stuffed his hands into the front pockets of his jeans. "I won't sleep anyway, so I might as well."

"Well, if Ma's okay with—"

"I am. Bye-bye." Cella waved them toward the door. "See ya!"

Crush stood back while the two girls kissed Cella good-bye.

"Do *not* move that leg," Dr. Davis warned her.

"I won't."

The doctor kissed her friend on the cheek and headed toward the door. As she neared Crush, he whispered, "Is she—"

"As a kite. So good luck to ya." She winked and walked out, the door quietly closing behind her.

The room was quiet and Crush stood there, staring at her until Cella warned, "Do not say you're sorry."

"Can I think it?"

"No. Trust me. I'm sure there will be lots of things that you'll need to apologize for as we go along . . . but this isn't one of them."

"I should have—"

"You're going to make me roar. And once I start roaring, I don't really like to stop." Cella rubbed her eyes. "You know what I don't want to do? Sit around and talk and analyze and, ya know, think."

"Okay. What do you want to do?"

"Play cuddle-bear."

Crush scratched his jaw to stop from laughing. "Cuddle-bear? And what's that?"

"That's where my bear cuddles me and tells me that I'm very pretty."

He nodded. "I think he can handle that." He took a step toward the bed.

"*Naked* cuddle-bear."

"No." Crush waved his hands. "No way."

"Oh, come on!"

"There will be no naked cuddle-bear. You're recovering, you gotta keep your leg immobile, and you're high."

"I am *sooooo* high." To illustrate, she brought up both hands, pinkies and forefingers raised, thumbs holding down the others, and rocked her head like she was at a Van Halen concert.

"Are you supposed to be enjoying it this much?"

"Look, I was sixteen the last time I . . ." She stopped, looked him over, and sneered, "Cop."

"I think you're past the statute of limitations on that, Malone. I must say, though, you are a hell of a mother because *clearly* your kid is on a different path."

She shrugged. "A boring path."

"Maybe, but not pregnant at fifteen either."

"First off, I was sixteen when I got pregnant and seventeen when I had that demon spawn." Cella looked off. "She's going to be a doctor."

"Were you hoping she'd join KZS?"

"I'd burn the main offices in Switzerland down before I'd let that happen." She scratched her forehead. "My kid wants to be a doctor, she's going to be a doctor."

Crush walked toward the bed. "Did you want to be in KZS?"

"Actually, yeah. I wanted to be a Marine, too. But like I said . . . that's not Meghan, that's not Josie."

"And Dr. Davis?"

"It's Jai. Jesus, just call the woman Jai. I hate this formal name obsession you have."

"Okay. Jai. Is she in KZS, too?"

"Just part of the medical team. I got shot in the neck once during a firefight. She was the one who fixed me up. But arterial damage is her specialty. Another doctor handled my knee." She looked down at her leg. "I'm going to miss hockey."

"I'm sorry."

"Again with the sorry?"

"I feel like I should say something."

"No. What you *should* do is come over here and be my cuddle-bear."

"You're whining."

"You're *making* me whine."

Crush sat on the bed beside Cella, his arm over her shoulder, moving as close as he could to her side so that she wouldn't try to stretch over.

"Better?" he asked.

"Much," she sighed out, her head resting against his chest.

"So what happens now?"

"When the brace comes off, we have sex."

"No." Crush briefly gritted his teeth and ordered his cock to control itself. "I mean, what happens now with all this?"

Her entire body began to relax, her eyes closing. "I have no idea. But I'll say one thing," she murmured before falling into a deep sleep, "I'm really glad I'm not Baissier tonight."

Crush frowned. "Why?" But it was too late. Cella was out cold.

Peg walked into her Brooklyn home with her two-man security team behind her. It was late and she was tired. Things were not going like she wanted them to, but she wasn't giving up. She'd never give up.

She quickly flipped through her mail. When she saw nothing

of consequence, she tossed the envelopes onto the silver tray sitting on top of the end table by her front door. With a sigh, she slipped off her shoes and headed through her hallway and toward her kitchen. She passed her living room, but stopped and walked back, gazing around the room. She felt rage inch up her neck at the sight of it.

"Someone's playing games," she muttered to her boys, taking in the carnage that had been left behind. Much of her furniture was antique, *all* of it was expensive.

"This is disgusting," one of them complained.

Reaching into her purse, she grabbed her cell phone and continued on toward the kitchen, wondering what had been done in there while the team went upstairs to check the rest of the house.

She walked in and stopped, her cell phone clutched in her hand. "Comfortable?" she asked the She-wolf sitting cross-legged on her kitchen table.

"Much. Thank ya kindly."

Peg swept her hand back toward her living room. "And was that your work, little puppy?"

"Nope. That was the cats. You know how felines are. And Malone is one of their own."

"Is all that supposed to bother me?"

"More like annoy. Figure you got homeowner's insurance. Although, doubt it'll cover what they did in your shoes and clothes."

"What did they do in my—"

"I'm sure you can smell what they did by now. You bein' grizzly and all."

And this was why she loathed felines. "So what? Is this where you threaten me, maybe slap me around a little?"

"Nah." The She-wolf shook her head sadly. "Can't. Momma always told me it was wrong to beat up the elderly."

Snarling a little, Peg snapped, "I am *not* elderly."

"As ya like."

"Then what do you want? To give me dire warnings?"

"Ain't much known for my warnings. Don't see the point." She slipped off the table. She was tall, but not as tall as Peg. Definitely not as wide. Just some little Group She-bitch. Like that alone would scare Peg?

The wolf headed toward the back door, but now Peg must admit, she didn't understand. The felines had done their little destroying furniture with their claws and desecration of her shoes thing and left, but the dog . . . she was still lingering around. Why?

"Why are you still here, canine?"

"Just a tad hungry was all."

Confused, Peg looked around, expecting to see used pots and pans in the sink. Maybe some dog shit in her refrigerator. But instead, all she spotted was the untouched food and water bowls on the floor. And right beside it, some blood.

Peg followed after the She-wolf, but the female stopped suddenly in the laundry room and faced her. Peg immediately flicked on the overhead light to keep the canine in her sights. There weren't a lot of people in the world who made Peg nervous, but . . .

Gazing at her with those yellow dog eyes, the canine scratched her cheek. At first, all Peg could see was the blood around the canine's mouth, but then she heard that soft tinkle noise and her eyes focused on what the bitch had wrapped around her thick, man-like wrist. It was a bright red collar, a small bell attached to it. That's what was tinkling as she scratched herself.

Livid, Peg roared, "*You disgusting piece of—*"

"Now, now," the canine easily cut in, never once losing her cool. She showed no fear, no anger, no hatred. Nothing. Nothing at all. "Let's not be rude."

"You ate my cat." The black-and-white tabby Peg had rescued two years ago to impress a cat-loving investor. A cat she'd become rather attached to!

"You know how it is." The canine's head tilted to the side, her forefinger wiping the blood off the corner of her mouth before sucking the digit clean. "You fucked with my pussy . . . and I fucked with yours."

Done, she tipped her baseball cap at Peg. "Y'all have a nice night now."

Peg's hands tightened into fists and she asked, "Exactly who the fuck are you anyway?"

"Name's Dee-Ann." She opened the back door and stepped out into the darkness, but when she looked back at Peg, yellow dog eyes glinted at her.

"You're Eggie Ray Smith's kid," Peg accused.

"That's right. I'll tell Daddy y'all said hi."

With that, the female disappeared into the darkness and Peg quickly closed the door, locking it. Then, with shaking hands, she speed-dialed her assistant. "Get a tactical unit over here now." She sniffed, the scent of disgusting canine female and, even worse, feline piss and shit, making her feel like retching. "And a goddamn maid service."

Chapter Thirty-two

A gentle pat on the shoulder woke Crush up. The smell of hot coffee actually got him to lift his head from the mattress. He wasn't, however, still in bed with Cella. He knew her family would be back and he just wouldn't feel right with them finding him in bed, cuddling up to Cella. So just before dawn, he'd reluctantly pulled away from her—God, she was so warm and smelled so nice—and sat down in the chair beside the bed. He'd put his crossed arms on the mattress and his head on his crossed arms. That was it until that gentle pat and the smell of coffee.

Rubbing his eyes and yawning, Crush sat up and smiled at the sweet face staring down at him.

"Morning, Mrs. Malone."

"Morning, sweetheart." Cella's mother held out the cup of coffee for him and he gratefully took it. One sip and he was already on his way to feeling better.

"How is she doing?" Mrs. Malone asked.

"Good. She slept well. But that probably had to do with the drugs they gave her."

"Pain meds, antibiotics, and something a little extra to ensure she sleeps, according to Jai," Mrs. Malone rattled off. "I guess they can't really afford for her to have a full-blown fever." No, they really couldn't. Although the fever helped badly wounded shifters to heal quickly, it also involved shifting back and forth from one form to the other, over and over, as well as a tendency to flail and jerk in one's sleep. Not the best thing for Cella's healing leg. So the doctors had doped her up more than they would most and hoped she'd quietly sleep through the night. Thankfully, she had.

Mrs. Malone walked around the bed and gazed down at her daughter.

"She's doing okay," Crush promised her. "She's amazingly strong."

"Just like her father."

Crush couldn't help but smile a little. "Just like her mother, I think."

The tigress blinked up at him in surprise, her cheeks getting a little red. "Well . . . thank you." Mrs. Malone cleared her throat. "Detective Crushek—"

"Call me Crush."

"Crush. Why don't you get something to eat?"

Crush looked down at Cella, still sleeping soundly.

"Now don't worry about Cella. I'm here and trust me when I say the rest of the family will be showing up very soon. Plus, I'll want you around to help with any visitors."

"Visitors?"

"One time her father was injured during a game. The hospital he was in had to call in extra security."

"Fan invasion?"

"Exactly."

"You have an excellent point."

"I know I do. It's my job to plan for the unforeseen." She waved him away. "Now go. Get something to eat."

Crush nodded, realizing he was starving. He'd been planning to get dinner after the game with Cella, so he'd only had one or two sandwiches, a steak, and a large pizza during the game.

Yep. Starving.

Standing up, Crush rolled his shoulders and nodded at Cella's mother. "I'll be back in fifteen minutes, Mrs. Malone."

"You just spent the entire night watching over my daughter, Crush. I think it's okay for you to call me Barb."

"Or Mrs. M., which still seems respectful."

"Barb is respectful enough if I tell you it is. Now go before my husband's idiot sisters get here and make me much less pleasant."

"Fifteen minutes."

Cella heard the bickering, but she chose to ignore it, keeping her eyes shut.

The meds had worn off, so she felt every moment of her leg threading itself back together, making the foreign object part of it. And, in a word, it fucking hurt. If everything went as planned, Cella knew the pain would lessen in another day, maybe two. But at this moment—it hurt.

And hearing her aunts bickering with her mother—again— was doing nothing but getting on her frayed nerves. But since Cella had been hearing her relatives argue since her first breath—rumor was that her mother got into a claw match with Aunt Deirdre seconds before Cella came out of the womb, which in retrospect kind of explained Cella's general personality—it was easy enough for her to tune them out and go back to sleep. Especially when she had something else to focus on. Specifically Crush. He was worth focusing on rather than the pain. She'd woken up here and there during the previous night and every time she did, he was still there, holding her. He snored a little, but nothing that made her want to cover his face with a pillow until he stopped altogether. And his arm was always around her, keeping her close and immobile all at the same time. Yet she didn't feel trapped by so much male holding on to her. Nope. She didn't feel trapped at all. Amazing. Because usually Cella felt trapped when one of the bathroom stalls at the Sports Center got stuck and it took her longer than two seconds to get the door open. Like five seconds. One time it took her ten seconds and she freaked out so badly, she just tore the door off the hinges, apologizing to the maintenance guy she'd passed on her way back to the gym.

Christ, was she really starting to like this guy?

Wait. No. She wasn't starting to like this guy. She already liked this guy. A lot. Again, surprising, because he was nothing like the males she was usually drawn to. Nope. Crush was excessively polite, quiet, well-mannered, and absolutely trustworthy. Although, when she thought about it, all those qualities were important for any male to have if they were going to be around Cella's daughter. Something she'd never really thought about because there had never been a male Cella had allowed around her daughter that wasn't the kid's father, a blood relative, or a schoolteacher.

Of course, it was too early to tell if all this thinking and analyzing about one bear was actually necessary, but it helped her fall back to sleep despite the continued bickering in the room.

Unfortunately, Cella didn't have the chance to really enjoy much of that sleep because someone decided to touch her leg. It was a light touch, but enough to have her reaching up and grasping the throat of whoever was touching her.

Cella opened her eyes and looked up into the face of a nurse. A tiny, itsy-bitsy bobcat staring at her with wide eyes and a rather daunting-looking needle.

After having what he could only say was an astounding meal in the shifter-only lunch room—shifter-only locations did like to provide the best food and supportive furniture for all the different breeds since it cut down on violent explosions of rage—Crush headed back to Cella's room.

The elevator opened on her floor and Crush stepped out,

stopping at the giant bouquet of flowers standing in the middle of the hallway. Leaning to see around them, he caught sight of what could only be called a mane of white and brown hair.

"Novikov?"

The flowers moved a bit and scowling blue eyes glared at him. "Crushek."

"Hi. Are you looking for Cella's room?"

"I don't know what to do with these."

Crush went around the flowers so that he could look directly at the Marauder. "Do with them?"

"Blayne said I had to bring flowers. I told her to come with me, but she said she'd be here later because there was yet *another* emergency with the wild dogs."

Wild dogs. What Crush deemed the chattiest of the shifter breeds. Mostly nice, though, unless their pups were involved.

"Okay."

"I told her I could go practice and we could go when she was done, but she said I had to go *now* so that Malone doesn't think all her friends are deserting her. I'm not deserting her. How can I be deserting her when we're not really friends? We're coworkers."

"Then why did you come?"

"Well . . . as far as coworkers go, she's tolerable."

Which probably meant Cella was as close to a friend as the Marauder was ever going to get from an actual teammate.

"Then I told her she should bring flowers from both of us and she said I should do it because it would be a nice gesture." His scowl grew worse. "I don't do nice gestures. I'm not a nice gesture kind of guy. Besides"—he looked the flowers over—"I think I may have gone a bit overboard."

And Crush thought *he* was awkward in daily, non-cop-related situations.

"I'm sure if you explain all that to Cella, she'd totally understand." And, even better, it would make her laugh her ass off.

"I guess. She gets me, ya know? She was probably one of the best enforcers I ever had. On most teams, I was not only the top scorer, I was the enforcer, too. But I didn't have to worry about that with Malone around."

"You should tell her that, too."

"Yeah. Okay."

Then the Marauder just stood there. The guy with the fastest reaction time on record just stood there, beginning to look mildly panicked.

Not one to leave a fellow bear just hanging—even one who was only half bear—Crush pointed down the hallway. "I'll show you where her room is."

"Okay."

They started walking, Novikov carrying that enormous bouquet of flowers.

"Speaking of enforcers," Crush said into their moment of non-talking, "who's going to replace Cella?"

"No one. Instead, I'm going to be stuck with a bunch of wannabes and MacRyrie, Van Holtz, and Bert."

"Probably. Or you could ask Cella to help you out."

"Help me out?"

"Let her pick out who should take her place. She's got a good eye and she'll worry if you don't have someone she approves of backing you up."

"Will that bother her? Asking her to do something after what happened?"

To Crush's surprise, he didn't think so. None of this would be easy for her, but for Cella, hockey went beyond just getting on the ice and playing. "I think Cella will handle whatever comes her way with great dignity."

The Marauder stopped, looked over at Crush. "We're talking about Cella Malone, right?"

"Yeah."

"Dignity? Really?"

"Well, yeah. I know on the ice she can be . . ." Crush's words faded away when he saw little Josie suddenly run out into the middle of the hallway. She turned in a circle, her hands flapping wildly. She was panicking.

Crush walked toward her. "Josie? What's wrong?"

Josie saw him and small hands reached for him, latching on to his forearm. "You've gotta get in there!"

She yanked him around the corner with an amazing amount of strength as Meghan ran to meet them.

"Thank God. I was just coming to look for you."

"What's going on?" Crush immediately thought of Baissier, worried she'd sent more trouble.

"Ma got a gun."

Crush stopped, Novikov right beside him and still holding those stupid flowers. "Excuse me?"

"Yeah," Dee-Ann Smith drawled, her back against the wall, an ice pack to her face. "My fault."

"You brought a gun to the hospital?"

"Hoss, I bring a gun everywhere."

Wait. Did she just call him "horse" or . . . forget it. He didn't have time for this.

"She'd already slapped around a couple of little nurses," the She-wolf went on, "so they sent for the bigger ones. I was trying to get her back into bed, when she snatched my .45 from my holster." She pulled the ice pack from her face, revealing a swollen eye, cheek, and jaw on the right side. "That's when the bitch clocked me with my own damn gun." She pressed the ice pack back to her wounded face. "That point, figured I'd better walk away instead of cuttin' her throat with my knife. 'Cause I was sorely tempted."

"Right." Crush looked at Meghan. "She didn't threaten you, did she?"

"No, no." She shook her head. "Of course not."

"Good."

"But she is holding a black bear hostage."

Crush rubbed his face with both hands. "I was gone fifteen minutes and there's now a hostage situation?"

Meghan patted his shoulder. "Welcome to my world, Detective Crushek."

The door opened and Cella snarled, "*Where the hell have you been?*"

"I went to get something to eat." Crush and a large moving crop of flowers behind him walked in. He rested his hands on his hips. "You're standing," the bear accused. "Why are you standing?"

"Calm down, I'm not putting any weight on my knee." Instead, she leaned against the wall and kept her brace-covered leg stuck out in front of her. It wouldn't be such a problem, either, if it wasn't for the black bear she currently had in a headlock who kept sobbing. Geez. Punch a big black bear in the nose, and he becomes all sorts of weak.

"Put the black bear down, Cella."

"He's in this position because he put his hands on me. I don't like to be bear-handled. Unless, of course, it's by *certain* bears." She grinned and winked at him.

Crush's face turned red and he glanced over at Cella's mother and aunts. They hadn't left the room, but they hadn't actually been much help, either. Then again, they knew how Cella was when she felt cornered, and why get into the middle of all this when they didn't have to?

"What do you mean he put his hands on you?"

"He tried to pin me to the bed. And not for what I'd call a fun reason, either."

"These people are trying to help you."

"Helping me is leaving me alone. Not ripping the bandages off."

"What are you talking about?"

"There's a bit of a problem," Cella's mother explained to

Crush. "While her knee still has some work to do before she can walk on it, her skin healed so fast that the bandages are sort of . . . attached now."

"They were trying to rip the skin off my legs," Cella clarified. "Without a painkiller."

"They were actually going to give her one." Barb smirked at her daughter. "But little Miss Overreaction decked the nurse before she had the chance to give her the shot. That poor bobcat."

"Where's Jai?" Crush asked Barb, which was starting to annoy Cella. Why was he talking to her mother?

"On her way."

"Hello?" Cella snapped. "I am right here. Mind not ignoring me?"

Crush glanced at her. "How much longer can you stand on one leg like that?"

"No idea."

"If you put weight on that leg too soon, Cella, you're going to risk permanently damaging it."

"That sounds like my problem, not yours."

"Good point. Besides, who cares? You're off the team anyway. Out on your ass. That's gotta hurt."

Cella's eyes narrowed, locking on the bear, while her mother and aunts backed up a little farther.

Crush jerked his finger over his shoulder. "Mr. Novikov brought you flowers."

"It's Bo, you geek. Bo. Not Mr. Novikov."

"He's planning to go without an enforcer now that you're out. I told him to go with Gene Martin."

"Are you insane?" Cella demanded, wondering what had gotten into the bear.

"What's wrong with him?"

"Everything! First off, he's second string for a reason. Second, he should still be in the minors. The only reason he's not is because his father pulled strings to get him in. And third, he gets even the tiniest cut and he's ready to go straight to a hospital bed. He's weak and kind of stupid. There's no way he can replace me."

"Who would you suggest?"

"The Reed kid."

The flowers were suddenly flung to the side, revealing Novikov. He'd brought her flowers? Really sweet, but she was sure he'd only done that because Blayne must have talked him into it.

"Reed?" Novikov growled. "Are you fucking kidding me?"

"The kid has real potential and wolves are great enforcers. Remember my Uncle Jimmy?"

"Uncle Jimmy?" Crush blinked. "Do you mean Jimmy Caufield?"

"Uh-huh."

"Jimmy 'I maul because it pleases me' Caufield? *That* Jimmy Caufield?"

"Well . . . I just call him Uncle Jimmy. He's one of my godfathers. He bought me my first car when I was stationed in Korea that year. Why are you staring at me like that?"

"Because I think part of me hates you right now."

"You had to buy your own first car?"

"Well, yeah, but that's not what I'm . . . forget it."

Novikov pushed past Crush. "You can't be serious about Reed."

"I'm completely serious about Reed. Don't let that hill-billy accent fool you—"

"Hey!" Dee-Ann complained from the hallway.

"—he's good. And he could prove that to you if you gave him the chance."

"No one gave me the chance and I proved myself."

"Only because you're a friendless loser who never worries about how he might come off to people."

"I am not friendless."

"Then name two friends you have that aren't Blayne Thorpe."

"Well—"

"And don't mention those two Eurotrash foxes you sometimes have hanging around."

"They're not Eurotrash. They're from Maine."

"Whatever. Here. I'll make it easy on you. Name *one* friend you have that's not a fox financially living off you or a crazed wolfdog who thinks her derby team is more important than my hockey team."

Novikov looked around, saw not only Cella waiting for his answer, but her mother and all her aunts. That's when he suddenly pointed at Crush.

"Him."

"Him? You don't even know his name."

"It's Crushek."

"First name?"

Watching Novikov try to remember what she was sure Blayne had told him, Cella bit the inside of her mouth to keep from laughing.

"Lou," he finally answered. "Lou Crushek. Crush for short." Novikov scowled at Crush. "Right?"

His mouth hanging open, Crush stared at his current favorite player. "Huh?"

"That's your name, right? And we're friends, *right*?" Novikov pushed between clenched teeth.

"Uh . . . yeah. Okay. Sure."

"See?" Novikov said to Cella, clearly feeling triumphant. "I have friends."

"Clearly. It must also help he's not really a threat since he doesn't play hockey professionally. Unlike Reed."

"Are you saying that some flea-bitten wolf referred to as 'one of the Reed boys' is a threat to *me*?"

"That's why you're not giving him a chance, right? Because you're afraid he'll make you look bad?"

"Like hell he'll—"

"Then give him a shot." Cella shrugged, trying to keep it all casual. "It couldn't hurt."

"He needs work."

"Cella can help him," Crush volunteered.

"I can?"

"You can. When your leg's healed."

"But I'm off the team."

"Doesn't mean you can't help the hillbilly."

"Perhaps I'm too devastated by this entire tragedy to—"

"Yeah. Blah, blah, blah," Novikov cut in. "The least you can do is work with the guy."

Wondering how the hell she'd gotten backed into this corner by two idiot bears, Cella dropped the black bear in her arms so she could cross them over her chest to show exactly how annoyed she was.

"Cella?"

"Fine! I'll do it. But give me a couple of weeks, okay?"

"Fine."

"Excuse me." Jai pushed her way into the room, her eyes going wide at the sight of Cella. "What are you doing out of bed?"

"I don't remember."

"Then get your ass back there. I swear to God, I leave you alone for five goddamn minutes . . ."

In the end, Crush sat with Cella while they removed the bandages from her leg and replaced the brace. He knew it was painful for her, but she handled it really well. It seemed that her issue was less about the removal of the bandages than about the way it was handled. Cella wasn't much for getting pounced on.

Once she was back in bed, her leg propped up again, a healthy lunch on its way to her room, her mother and aunts off to buy her magazines and candy, Cella finally looked at Crush and accused, "You set me up."

"No, I didn't."

"So is this some psychological thing? I'm supposed to help the team so that I can recover from my trauma?"

"I'm not really a therapist, Cella." He relaxed back in the chair and put his feet up on the bed. "I just don't think you should limit yourself."

"Limit myself to what?"

"Either you play or you're not involved with hockey."

"So what am I supposed to do?"

"You'll figure it out."

"Or you can just tell me."

"After-school specials always say you need to learn life lessons on your own."

"You're actually using after-school specials as a guide to how to manage me?"

"It's no stranger than Dez using National Geographic to handle her husband."

She chuckled. "That makes a little more sense, I think." She played with the blanket they'd put over her. "Are you heading home soon?"

"No."

"You're not?"

"Are you leaving tonight?"

"No. I'm not leaving until they're sure the knee has healed up properly."

"Then you have your answer."

"You're staying until my knee heals?"

"Pretty much.

"Think the hospital will let you stay?"

"No one's asking me to leave."

"Because you're a bear?"

" 'Cause I'm a cop. The benefits of the badge."

"Must be nice."

"I think so."

Dee-Ann Smith walked into the room and Crush watched Cella bite her lip to prevent her from laughing at the poor She-wolf's swollen face.

"Where's my gun, feline?"

"Your gun?"

"Yeah. The one you assaulted me with and then used on that black bear."

"I didn't use the gun on the bear. I just had him in a head-lock. He's lucky I didn't use a sleeper hold on him."

"Gun?"

Cella shrugged. "I don't know. Haven't seen it since I hit you with it."

"Trifling," Smith snarled before crouching down and disappearing under the bed.

"You shouldn't have gotten in the middle," Cella said.

"I was trying to help your dumb ass, you ungrateful heifer."

"Didn't need your help, backwoods."

Smith wiggled out from under the bed. She had her gun and tucked it back into its holster. "Don't make me cranky, whore, or I'm liable to break that knee of yours all over again.

"Blow me."

The She-wolf gave the finger and walked out. Two seconds later, she walked back in. "When you're feelin' better . . . dinner?"

"Sure. Can I bring Crush?"

"Sure. See ya."

"Yep." Cella reached for the newspaper someone had left on her side table, checking out the front page news. "Don't try to understand our friendship," she said to Crush without looking up from her paper. "Just accept it."

"I'm thinking that's a good plan."

Forced to stay in a hotel while a specialized crew cleaned up her house—they usually handled crime scenes—Peg was relieved to at least be back at her office. Her assistant told her she had lots of messages from "concerned bears," but

Peg was in no mood to talk to any of these people. She just had to get her paws on Whitlan.

For nearly fifteen years Whitlan had been one of the most important snitches for the FBI and NYPD. He'd ratted out his fellow scumbags with an almost childlike glee. And Peg had used him for almost the same thing. Only she hadn't been trying to stop drugs from being smuggled into the country or guns moving from one state to another. Instead she'd used Whitlan to tell her who the hunters were and exactly where they were hunting. BPC had shut down big-game hunters all over the Eastern Seaboard. It was something that had made her invaluable to the bear community and gave her a name to be feared and respected among the other species. But what she hadn't known, just like the FBI and the NYPD hadn't known, was that Whitlan was ratting out any fellow scumbag that got in his way or fucked with his business, while constantly moving his own product and doing his own deals. He'd made a fortune running guns, selling dope, and trafficking humans. But his hobby? That was hunting shifters. Especially male lions and bears. So while Peg and BPC were taking out some single, lowlife hunter in Jersey that Whitlan just didn't like, Whitlan was in Delaware or Connecticut or someplace else with a full hunting party, taking down some grizzly with four kids and a wife in Yonkers.

Unfortunately, by the time Peg had figured out what Whitlan was up to, he'd already hunted, killed, and stuffed one of the sons of Jebediah Meirston, patriarch of the Meirston bear clan, a very old and very powerful jewelry merchant family. Jebediah himself had come to Peg asking her to help him find the hunter who'd killed his boy, and considering how much money the Meirstons gave to BPC, her assistance was not in question. Yet the more Peg had dug into what happened, the more terrified she'd become, because she soon realized what a fool she'd been. Just like the FBI and the

NYPD. Only when the news got out that she'd let some full-human play her, there'd be no trial, no newspaper headlines. She'd be lucky if there'd even be a grave because bears didn't really tolerate stupidity. And God, she'd been so stupid.

Even worse was that as soon as she'd finally gotten a true lead on Whitlan, so had that goddamn boy. Anyone but Crushek. If it had only been one of the Group or those ridiculous cats, she wouldn't have worried. But Crushek . . . he was one of the few who could convince Meirston of her involvement because everyone knew Lou Crushek was "old-school honest." Whatever the hell that meant.

The door to her office opened and Gray and Chazz walked in, ignoring her assistant's requests for them to wait. Well, she'd known this would be coming. . . .

"How could you?" Chazz demanded. "How could you do that?"

Considering that neither of these idiots knew what was really going on, she could see why they didn't understand how Lou could bring her down. And although killing their brother would do nothing but make matters worse for her, she'd had to do *something* and she'd gone with crippling him. Not hurting his arms and legs because that wouldn't stop him, either, but his little feline girlfriend? That was his weakness. So she'd done what she'd had to do.

"Look, boys, I'm sorry about your brother—"

Chazz scowled. "Our brother?"

"Forget our brother," Gray snapped. "What about the goddamn team? How could you do that to the Carnivores?"

Peg sighed. Yeah, she'd been right from the beginning. Of the three, the contrary one got all the brains.

CHAPTER THIRTY-THREE

Three days after her career-ending injury, Cella returned to the Sports Center. Crush drove her over and walked in with her, but let her go into the locker room by herself to get the rest of her stuff. And she was grateful he was being so understanding because Cella just wasn't ready to face her old team yet. Her knee might be healed but her life still felt a little shaky.

But Crush . . . well, he was being amazing. So she'd rush through these five stages of grief thing that her family kept talking about and get Crush back to the hotel. There she could use some "sex treatment" to recover from her trauma. An excellent plan as far as she was concerned.

Yet as she stood there, staring at the old training jersey she held in her hands, she really wondered if she'd ever be "over" all of this. If she couldn't work for KZS anymore, she wouldn't shed a tear. Would she miss it? Yeah. She would. She loved hanging around cats. But hockey . . .

"Cella! Cella!"

Hearing her name bellowed, repeatedly, outside the locker room, Cella tossed her jersey to the bench and walked to the door, yanking it open.

"What?" she demanded, seeing that Crush had been doing

his best to keep Reece Reed from shoving him out of the way. Shame the bear really was a mess on skates because he seemed to have a healthy grasp on the rest of hockey's basics. "What the hell's going on?"

"You have to come to tryouts. Please."

Cella dropped her hand to her hip, lips pursed. "Are you *trying* to hurt my feelings? Are you trying to make me cry or something? Because if I cry, I'll make sure you cry with me, Reed."

"No, no. You don't understand—"

"Because I know that it must be fuckin' high-larious to you guys that big-mouth Malone is out of the league and now you can say all that shit to my face that you had to say behind my back, but let me tell you—"

"Novikov is handling the tryouts."

Cella's words stopped in her throat and she began blinking too much. Because she *must* have heard Reed wrong. She must have.

"I'm sorry. Did you say—?"

"He took over the tryouts. Insisted on it. Said you were the only one he trusted to do it and with you gone . . ." Reed took off his baseball cap, ran his hands through his hair. "I heard from one of the maintenance guys that you and Crush were in the building. I know you want to pack up your stuff and go, but you need to understand . . . he's destroying people's will to live. He made a hyena cry. A hyena. They laugh at everything, but this one was sobbing in the girl's bathroom and one of the lion male football players felt so bad for him . . . he went in to comfort him. Lion males don't do that."

"Why was he in the *girl's* bathroom?"

"Probably because that's where Novikov said he belonged. Because he was such a girl."

Cella's eyes narrowed. "That mixed-breed, misogynistic motherfucker."

"No one knows what to do and Van Holtz has already swung at him twice."

"Where the fuck is Reynolds?" The Carnivores' increasingly useless coach.

"In his office . . . drinking."

"It's eight in the morning."

"And I rest my case."

Cella looked at Crush, but he only shrugged. "It's up to you. But I should remind you that you invited Hannah to the try—"

"Oh, my God!" Cella pointed at Reed. "Round up a few of the guys and all of you get on your gear. I'll meet you in the rink."

"Okay."

Cella ran back to her locker and yanked out her equipment, quickly putting everything on.

Without opening her eyes, Sophie knew someone was in the Atlantic City hotel room with her, and even as she reached for the gun she kept under her pillow, she already knew it wouldn't be there.

It wasn't.

"Might as well get up, darlin'. Ain't got all day."

Her mind scrambling for a way out of this, Sophie sat up, her eyes straying to the two windows closest to her and the door. Maybe she could—

"You'll never make it out of here before I catch ya. We both know that."

They did. Sophie studied the tall, big-shouldered female sitting across from her. In the twenty-three years Sophie DiMarco had been on this earth, she'd learned how to read people. It was a skill that had kept her alive and relatively unscathed. When she'd picked up that bleeding guy, she'd known she was safe with him. Not just because he was bleeding out in the car, but because she could tell. She sensed it.

With this woman, however . . . she knew if she ran, the bitch would kill her and it wouldn't even cross her mind again once it was over.

"What do you want?"

Eyes like a dog's blinked at her. "I need you to show me where you picked up that boy."

"Can't I just give you—?"

"It's not that I don't trust you . . . I just don't trust anybody. So show me where it was."

"And then what?"

"Darlin', if I was gonna kill you, I'd have done it by now. But commitments were made and I hold to those."

"Yeah, but—"

"You want that boy safe, don't you?"

"I guess. I mean, I don't really know him or anything."

"You always pick up strangers bleeding out on the street?"

Realizing the woman was either going to kill her or not and there was nothing Sophie could do about it, she admitted, "That isn't what I saw. And we both know it."

"Help me," the woman said. "And I'll make sure no one bothers you." She leaned forward, resting her elbows on her knees, and added, "As long as you keep your mouth shut."

Crush followed Cella to the rink, then stood outside. A few seconds later, Reed and the rest of the players he'd managed to find at the Sports Center ran by, with their gear on except for their skates. Crush grabbed the handle and pulled the door open, allowing the team to charge inside. Reed stopped. "You coming in?"

"The sign"—he pointed at the big sign that had several stadium guards standing around it—"says only players and tryout invitees. I'm neither."

The wolf grinned. "Ain't you cute." Then he grabbed Crush by the shoulder of his sweatshirt and hauled him inside.

"Are you sure this is okay? I mean—"

"Quiet, son. And just watch your woman work."

Cella skated across the ice toward Novikov. Novikov, who was in the middle of a tirade against some kid that didn't even look eighteen years old.

Cella maneuvered between the two, coming to an immediate stop in front of Novikov. "What is wrong with you?" she asked him.

"Nothing. Why are you here?"

"I'm here to help."

"You can't. You're not on the team."

"I can't help, you idiot, during a game. There's nothing that says I can't help with tryouts."

"You're supposed to be getting me an enforcer from the losers we already have. I'll handle the new losers."

Cella closed her eyes, took a deep breath. "Can I talk to you for a minute?"

"Not if you're just going to yell at me about how I shouldn't call any of these idiots 'losers.' Especially when you're not even on the team anymore."

Cella opened her eyes, looking up at the seven-one hybrid through those black lashes.

"Uh-oh," Crush muttered.

"Yeah," Reed agreed. "I was thinking the same thing."

Cella skated off across the ice, stopped at one of the other exits, and walked out.

Reed looked at him. "That's it?"

"Doubt it."

Novikov was already back to destroying the hopes and dreams of complete strangers when Cella came in again. She skated over to him and stopped, gazing up at him.

"What? You're back? Why?"

"You did . . . didn't you?" a small voice said, and Crush and Reed leaned over to see who was standing in that entrance Cella had just come through.

"Oh, man," Reed muttered. "Malone is stone *cold*."

"I know."

Novikov glared at Cella, then faced his fiancée. "Blayne—"

"You!" the wolfdog exploded, "are a horrible, horrible man! How could you say that to Cella after all she's been through? I'll *never* marry you! *Never!*"

Blayne ran out and Novikov handed his stick over to Cella. "I hate you," he told her.

"Just be glad I didn't punch you in the face. *Again*."

Novikov went after his fiancée and Cella tossed the extra hockey stick to one of the regular players since she had her own.

With a smile, she skated over to the ones trying out. "Hi, everybody. I'm Cella Malone. First off—"

"Again with the first off," Crush said under his breath, unable to hide his smile.

"—how many of you were already told by Novikov that you're done?"

When all but three people out of the forty raised their hands, Cella shook her head and said, "Yeah. Let's start over."

Reed started walking toward the ice. "I think they're asking for you."

"Who?"

He motioned over to the players' bench where MacRyrie and Van Holtz were sitting with a few of the senior players. With a wave, they motioned him over.

Crush went to their side, figuring they needed something, but MacRyrie just made everybody move down on the bench. It took Crush a good sixty seconds of staring before he realized that they expected him to sit. With the team. On the bench.

Holy shit.

* * *

Cella skated over to where Crush was sitting with Van Holtz and MacRyrie. Novikov—after begging and receiving Blayne's forgiveness—was back out on the ice with Reed and several of the other players, but she'd forbidden him from speaking. She wanted to add "ever," but she thought that might be asking too much. So she'd ordered him to silence until after the tryouts.

"Where is she?" Cella asked Crush.

"Where's who?"

"Hannah. Blayne said she brought her, but she hasn't seen her since she changed in the locker room."

"I haven't seen her." When she sighed, he held his hands up. "I'll go look for her."

"Thank you."

After Crush walked out, MacRyrie muttered, "Nice guy."

"Uh-huh."

"Friendly," Van Holtz added.

Cella's eyes narrowed. "And?"

"Just an observation. No need to get testy."

Debating whether to yell at them just for the hell of it, Cella heard Novikov berating some poor kid who just wanted to live his dream. The kid had potential, too, which was why Novikov was bothering. She'd realized that the worst thing for any player was when Novikov completely ignored you. That meant you weren't a threat. As a player, you weren't worthy of his attention. But the poor kid he was currently yelling down to wouldn't know that.

Skating over, Cella slid between them. "Where's my silence?"

"He asked me a question."

"So you yell at him?"

"It was kind of a stupid question."

It probably was, but still . . . there were better ways to, oh, why bother?

"Go sit down, Novikov. Over there." She pushed him toward where MacRyrie and Van Holtz were sitting.

"I'm not done."

"Yes, you are."

"You're going to make me sit with *them*?"

"Be nice. They're your teammates and Van Holtz is your boss." She shoved, sending him gliding across the ice.

She faced the kid. "Okay." She smiled at him to put him at ease. "Why don't I have you work with Reed instead?"

Ric watched Cella Malone take the hopefuls through the paces. Unlike Novikov, she wasn't a ridiculous bastard about it, but she wasn't so nice that she was ineffectual. That was a great skill to have.

Novikov sat down next to him.

"I don't know why I have to sit here with you two."

"Because you're an asshole?" Lock asked.

Novikov leaned over Ric. "You got something to say to me, humpback?"

"As a matter of fact—"

"Hey!" Cella was in front of them. She raised her hands together, then pushed them apart. "Separate." She snarled and spit out between clenched teeth, "I said *separate.*"

Lock and Novikov sat back in their seats.

"I swear," Cella said, shaking her head. "You're worse than my baby brothers. You two—like cats in a bag."

Ric watched her get back to work. "Impressive, huh?"

"What?" Lock asked, using the handle of his hockey stick to scratch his forehead.

"Cella." Ric pointed at Novikov. "She handles this homicidal idiot quite well, wouldn't you say?"

"You do know I can hear you, right?"

"Know, but don't care."

* * *

Crush walked down another long hallway, letting his nose lead him. He eventually tracked the girl down by the soda machines. She was dressed in her hockey gear, skates included, but she was pressed between a Coke machine and a water cooler.

He knew that look on her face, too. He'd had it when he'd tried out for his school's hockey team—and failed miserably. In fact, Crush was mocked for a good six months—until the growth spurt. Amazing what an obnoxious fourteen-year-old left wing hanging from the school flagpole could do for a white-haired boy's rep.

"Cella sent me to look for you."

"I can't do it. There's like thirty guys out there."

"Some of them are female."

She blinked. "Really?"

"Don't judge."

"No, no. I wasn't. It's just . . ." Hannah shook her head. "I can't do it. I can't go out there and make a fool of myself."

Crush walked farther into the lunch room, closer to the snack machines. "Have you ever been on skates?"

She nodded. "I used to figure skate. It made sense when I was five. Then I was twelve and—"

"Suddenly five-ten?"

"Try six feet."

"Ouch."

"Yeah. My poor parents."

"Why were they surprised?"

She shrugged. "I was adopted. They were full-human. I didn't know what I was until my ninth grade English teacher told me. When she told me I was 'special,' I thought she was just hitting on me."

"Kind of a glass-half-empty girl?"

"It *is* half empty. Half full makes no sense."

Crush pressed his back into the wall, ducking his head so she couldn't see him smile.

"At the very least," he was finally able to tell her without laughing, "you can skate. You won't fall on your face. Some of the ones trying out . . . not pretty."

"I haven't skated in years. And I'm just not sure that I should be put into violent situations that involve sticks and big guys aggressively coming at me."

"Why not?"

Her eyes lowered and she seemed to suddenly close in on herself. Crush watched her, his head tilting to the side. The cop in him had a litany of questions to ask her, but that wasn't what she needed right now: a cop asking why she shouldn't be in violent situations. So Crush said, "Think of it this way . . . if you don't go to the tryout, Blayne will think you're still available."

Hannah's head snapped up, her eyes blinking wide. "Oh, God. I forgot."

"So you might as well give it a shot, right?"

She snorted, nodded her head. "Yeah. You're right. I might as well just get this over with."

She headed off and Crush followed, the pair walking back into the rink. Cella smiled when she saw them, and skated over.

"Am I too late?" Hannah asked.

"Nope. Not at all. In fact, I want you to hit the ice with these two ladies. They've been doing really well today." Cella motioned to two Arctic She-foxes. Sisters. No. Actually twins. They made their way over and stopped, grinning. "This is Nita and Nina Gallo."

"Hi!" the tiny foxes said in unison. Crush would guess they weren't older than nineteen. Maybe. They were cute, though, but tiny. Five-six, if that, and maybe a hundred pounds. He had to admit, he was surprised they were here. Foxes this age were usually off doing something that required Crush to arrest them. Or, at the very least, *try* to arrest them. The sole reason that he, unlike most polars, had no foxes to call his own.

"We'll meet you out on the ice!" these foxes chirped. Then they waved and skated off.

Hannah looked up at him. "Because it'll be so much fun for me to be the giant ogre standing over the little elf girls."

"Welcome to my world, kid. Now go out there and do some damage."

Cella saw the looks on the guys' faces and skated over to them. "Well?"

Van Holtz and MacRyrie shrugged, but Novikov . . . "She'll need work," he complained.

"I know."

"All three of them will."

"Uh-huh."

"Her skating is beyond rusty. And the other two have the attention spans of fleas."

"I know. I know." Cella didn't argue. She waited.

"She's fast, though," he finally admitted. "And the foxes, with some serious training, could be pretty good. Maybe."

Cella nodded. "I think you're right. Instead of putting them on right away, why not go your route? Start 'em off in the minors and let them work their way up." Of course, one of Cella's uncles was the assistant coach of the minors so Cella kind of worked with the minor team anyway, but no need to mention that.

Novikov looked off. "Well . . . that *might* work."

She glanced at Van Holtz and MacRyrie. They were staring at her, eyes wide, until Van Holtz mouthed at her, *How do you do that?*

They sat in Dee-Ann's car, staring across the street.

"That's a . . ."

"Yeah. A country club. For very rich people."

"Huh. Learn something new every day."

They hadn't driven all the way from Atlantic City to the Hamptons; they had taken Van Holtz's helicopter from AC to the Hamptons, a rental car taking them here. To a country club.

The girl pointed. "He came out of there."

"Past that hedge?"

"Yeah. But I think there's a door there."

"Okay."

Sophie briefly chewed her bottom lip.

"What?"

"I just don't know if you should . . ."

"If I should what?"

"Challenge these people."

"Because they're rich?"

"Look, I don't steal some poor guy's Prius or the Ford he inherited from his dad, you know? That's not my thing."

"You steal from rich people."

"And I know my targets. I know them really well. I make it my business to know. Although the town, in theory, owns the country club, there's a man who runs it. And he's not dangerous just because he's rich. He's dangerous because he knows how to play both sides of any situation. He practically makes me seem like Mother Teresa. Just . . . be careful."

And that was why Dee hadn't simply found out from the girl where she'd picked up the Callahan kid and let her go. That sort of information took time to pull from a person. "Thanks for the warning." Dee handed the girl a business card.

Sophie turned it over in her hand. "It's just a number."

"It's my number. You need me, you call. Understand?"

"Yeah. Sure."

"Good." Dee started the car. "Now, let's see if we can track down a White Castle before I let you go."

"You want to track down a White Castle in the Hamptons?"

Dee grinned. "I believe in livin' large."

"Yeah. I can see that."

Cella stood outside the locker room staring up at a bear-canine hybrid who could barely look her in the eye.

"You don't have to make any decisions now, Hannah. But you should at least think about it."

"Yeah, it's just . . ."

"Just what?"

"If I say yes, will they continue to follow me everywhere?"

Cella glanced over at the twin She-foxes. They waved, identical bright grins on their pretty faces.

"As it is, I can't get rid of this one."

She pointed at Abby, who'd been hanging out at the Sports Center all day, begging food off people.

"I don't know. No one follows me anywhere." Cella shrugged. "I'm a cat. This sounds like a bear issue. Ask Crush, I think he's getting coffee."

"Yeah, okay."

"But you'll think about it, right? Maybe go to a few practices just to see?"

"I'll think about it."

Cella nodded and watched the girl walk off, stop, glare at the foxes now following her, along with Abby, walk, stop, glare. Assuming it would go on all the way down the hall, Cella walked into the locker room to change her clothes and clean out her stuff.

This had been a good way to end it all. A good way for her to move on. What did they call that? Closure or something? Whatever. It worked out well.

But as Cella came around the corner, she found Ric Van Holtz standing there, waiting for her.

"What's up?" she asked, hoping he wasn't here to give her

some pathetic hug good-bye. Cella hated the hug good-bye unless it was from her kid or her father. Otherwise, it just annoyed.

"I've got your final player payout."

"Oh. Okay."

She took the manila envelope, opening the flap enough to look inside. She didn't let her eyes bug out at the size of the check, but honestly, she wanted to.

"Thanks."

"No problem. You earned it."

"I'll miss you guys," she admitted, opening her locker for the last time.

"Yeah, about that . . . I have a job offer."

"I don't need your pity job, Van Holtz. Thanks, but no—"

"For head coach."

Cella froze, eyes wide. "What?"

"Eventually," Van Holtz quickly added. "I mean . . ." He took a breath. "Coach Reynolds is retiring in a year. We haven't announced it to the team, but I'd already put out the word to a few agents I know and had gotten in some résumés from a few interested parties, including the coach for the Alaskan Bears. And he was my first choice, really. I mean, he handles a team full of bears and two foxes. There's gotta be skill there. But I'd forget him in a heartbeat if I could get you."

Cella ran her hands through her still sweat-drenched hair and slowly faced the wolf. "You want me to be coach?"

"Assistant to start and when Reynolds retires . . . head coach."

Cella just had to ask, "Why?"

"There's lots of reasons. I can sit here and rhapsodize about your skill on the ice, your ability to train and get the best out of the rookies, your amazing eye for talent . . . I mean, I love Hannah, but I would have never thought of her for the team. But really, it comes down to one thing . . ."

Cella couldn't help but smile a little. "Novikov?"

"You handle Novikov and he *lets* you. That alone is worth its weight in gold. Because if you can handle that man, you can handle *anyone*."

"That's true. I can handle anyone."

"And Novikov isn't going anywhere. Blayne wants to stay in New York and whether he disgusts me or not, he loves her. So he's not going anywhere. And even if I wanted to fire him, I can't because he flippin' wins."

"Yeah, but we're probably not going to quite hit the play-offs this year."

"I know, which means he's going to be hell to deal with next year. Which is the reason I'm sure Reynolds is getting out while the gettin' is good. You can't desert me, Cella. You can't. We're friends. You're friends with my mate. I'm a nice guy. And unless Bert's around, I have trouble separating that idiot and Lock. So you can't go. You might not be able to play on the team with your knee, but you can coach and you are probably the only thing that will keep us from ganging up on Novikov and beating him like they did to Vincent D'Onofrio's character in *Full Metal Jacket*."

Cella laughed, her body relaxing against her locker, her hand covering her mouth.

"Yeah. Sure. Funny to you. You're the only one I know, besides Blayne, who gets along with Novikov. And no matter what other offer you get, I'll beat it."

Cella held up her hand. "Other offers?"

Van Holtz rolled his eyes. "From the Philly team, the Boston team, the San Francisco team. I think there's a couple more. As soon as they heard you were out as a player, they began salivating." He placed his hand against his upper chest. "But you're *my* friend. You wouldn't betray me, would you?"

"You about to threaten me with your mate?"

"If I have to."

"Well—"

"Just think about it before you turn me down."

"I was just going to—"

"Think about your situation. Your daughter's staying in New York to go to school. So you'll be near her. And Crushek's here. He, for some unknown reason considering how much the rest of us like him, also gets along with Novikov. Maybe all his experience working with sociopathic drug dealers or something."

"Novikov is not that bad! He's just . . . myopic."

"Like a fighting dog?" When Cella rolled her eyes, "Hey, he was the one who threw bleachers at Reed and the other guys."

"I know, I know. I already talked to him about that. Told him it wasn't good for the team or morale."

Van Holtz smirked at her, one eyebrow up.

"All right, all right. How about I give you a tentative yes?"

"Will you sign something?"

"*No*. I gotta talk to my own agent and my kid and my dad."

"And Crushek?"

"Maybe."

"Because he's part of your life now?"

"What are you, Van Holtz? A girl?"

"According to Dee-Ann's father? Yes, I am."

Crush watched Cella skating around the rink. She was alone. Just her, the ice, her stick, and the puck. While she moved, he could hear her singing the traditional Irish song, "I'm a Man You Don't Meet Every Day," her voice sweeter than he ever thought it could be.

"She's in a good mood."

Crush shook his head and asked, "Didn't anyone ever teach you not to sneak up on bears?"

Dee-Ann Smith rested her arms on the low part of the training rink's wall and watched Cella skate.

"Y'all call it sneakin'. I don't call it sneakin'."

"What do you call it?"

"Amblin'."

Crush chuckled. "Good to know."

"New coach of the Carnivores, huh?"

"That's what your mate tells me."

"What do you think?"

"I told him it was about time."

He could see Smith look at him a few times before she said, "What about KZS?"

"What about it?"

"You going to talk her out of working for them now? So she can devote herself to all things hockey."

Crush laughed. A lot. So much so that Smith finally asked, "What's so funny?"

"That you think I can talk that woman out of anything she wants to do." He patted her back. "You're a funny little She-wolf."

Smith grinned. "You'll have to forgive me, son. I didn't realize you were one of those evolved males."

"I don't need to evolve. I'm a bear." He shrugged. "Bears are already perfect. It's the rest of you that need to catch up."

Cella turned and skated over to them. When she stopped, she looked past Crush and Smith.

"So I walked up to Crushek," Dez said from behind him, "and started telling him how Baissier took out the taxidermist not too long ago."

Wondering what she was talking about since MacDermot hadn't told him anything like that since the last time he'd seen her, Crush turned around and immediately snarled at the sight of his brothers.

"When," Dez continued, "*another* Crushek walked up to me and said to the first one, 'Who's the babe?' to which the other one replied, 'Don't know, but nice tits.'"

"It was a compliment," Gray stupidly stated, which got

him the punch to the balls from Dez that he so richly deserved.

"Why are you here?" Crush demanded of Chazz since Gray was currently on his knees, hands between his legs.

"Word is you're looking for that full-human . . . Whitlan."

"What? Are you here to warn us off for Baissier?"

"No. We're here to warn you that she's almost got him."

Crush glanced back at Cella. "That's why she took out the taxidermist. She knows where Whitlan is." Looking back at his brothers, he asked, "But why are you telling me?"

"Because of what she did," Chazz replied, his face solemn.

"What she did to me?"

Now Chazz looked disgusted. "You? Who gives a shit about *you*? I'm talking about what she did to . . . to . . . Bare Knuckles."

Crush's eyes crossed and Smith quickly ducked her head, her shoulders shaking.

"That was her going too far?" Crush snarled. "*That?*"

"You don't mess with the home team. You're a complete idiot, but even *you* know that."

Crush took a step toward his brother, but Dez got between them. "How does she know where Whitlan is?" she asked Chazz.

He shrugged. "I heard she got it out of some girl."

Smith looked up. "What girl?"

"Don't know? Some full-human."

Crush shook his head at Dez. "That can't be Sophie Di-Marco."

"It might be," Smith said and when they all stared at her, she added, "I tracked her down in Atlantic City earlier today."

Cella skated around and then walked over until she was in front of Smith. "You did what?"

"Why are you lookin' at me like that for?"

"Because," Cella snarled, "you goddamn hick! I promised the Callahans she wouldn't get hurt!"

"I didn't hurt her! I just wanted her to take me to where she found Callahan, and I'm thinking that's where Whitlan is. And when we were done, I put her back on the train to Atlantic City."

"Did you see her get on the train?" Crush asked.

"I did."

"Did you see the train leave the station?"

When Smith didn't answer, both Dez and Crush groaned.

Cella took off her helmet. "Oh, my God, Smith, what did you do?"

"I'm not likin' your tone."

"How would you like my fist?"

"Bring it, calico!"

"Stop it!" Dez snapped. "Both of you. We don't have time for this."

"She's right," Cella agreed. "Baissier's going to kill her."

"No," Crush corrected her. "She won't do that until she has Whitlan in her hands." He looked at Chazz, while Gray finally got to his feet behind him. "Where's Whitlan?"

Chazz and Gray gave identical shrugs and said together, "The Hamptons."

Crush looked at the three females, then said, "The Hamptons? Really?"

CHAPTER THIRTY-FOUR

The black Range Rover door opened and Peg stepped out. Her team surrounded her. She'd chosen only the most loyal for this, but was still disappointed in the Crushek boys. They were still whining about what had been done to that idiot cat all because of some stupid hockey team.

Whatever. They were of no use to her at the moment anyway. That was the girl. The full-human girl the Group and KZS had been busy trying to protect turned out to be the key. It's what Crushek and the others hadn't known about the little thief—it had been Whitlan's car she'd been stealing that day she'd rescued the cat. And what Peg had found out about Sophie DiMarco was how very good she was at her job. One of three thieving sisters, Sophie didn't just steal cars, she studied her mark. Learned everything about them. Who they were, where they lived, what their hobbies were. In the end, the girl had known more about Whitlan than any of them—including where he'd been hiding for the past couple of weeks.

"Bring the girl," she said, and walked into the country club. Another group of her men met her inside. "Well?"

One of the sows held up a full-human man by the neck.

His face was battered, his arms nearly pulled from the sockets, some of his scalp missing. But he was still alive.

Peg stepped closer. "Where's Whitlan?" she asked.

Shaking, his body slowly dying, the man stuttered out, "Base . . . basement."

"Good boy." Peg stroked his face with her gloved hand and turned away. "Let's go."

She headed toward the stairs, but stopped, looked back at her people. "And keep your eyes open. The boy might show up and try something stupid."

When she was confident that everyone understood, she walked on, heading to the basement.

Sophie heard the back door of the Range Rover open and she was yanked out. These . . . whatever the hell they were . . . they kept yanking her and dragging her everywhere. There wasn't a subtle one in the bunch. Not like that woman with the weird eyes. She'd been tall with wide shoulders, and you could smell the predator on her. These guys were *really* tall and wide, but they were like the mobsters she sometimes dealt with. Not big on brains and they thought their size alone gave them the only edge they needed.

Although her wrists were left bound in front of her, the blindfold covering her eyes was removed and she took a second to look around. "Yeah," she said to the guy holding her. "Really makes sense to make me wear that since I was the one who told you how to get here."

He tightened his grip on her bicep and Sophie had to grit her teeth together to stop herself from screaming.

"I can hurt you now," he whispered to her. "Or I can hurt you later. Your choice."

"That's not really much of one," she shot back. "But nice try."

He started to walk. When Sophie dragged her feet, he

swung his arm forward, yanking her around. Using the momentum, Sophie bent her knees and swung her tied fists up and into the guy's groin. He squealed, a sound that startled her, and then dropped to the ground, hands between his legs. Sophie took off running toward the other side of the road.

She made it to the line of trees and ran inside. But with her arms bound and the darkness of the night, the moonlight not helping much with all those trees, she kept stumbling. She could already hear at least one, probably more, of those guys coming after her. They'd be mad now, once they got her. But she couldn't have just waited for them to kill her. And they would kill her. She knew that.

A hand wrapped around her throat, choking off both screams and her ability to breathe. She was lifted off the ground, her feet dangling, and brought up to look the man in the eyes.

He stared at her, cold dark eyes studying her. She felt like a bug he'd found in his kitchen. A spider he was curious about. Or an ant.

His lips pulled back and she saw fangs. Not those stupid fangs she'd seen in even stupider vampire movies. But animal fangs. Just like the guy she'd picked up off the road. His had come out when she was driving him to that office and that's what she saw now. Even in this barely lit place, she could see them.

Panicked, she fought back, swinging her feet out, desperately trying to kick him away. Anything to get him to let her loose. She didn't care she couldn't breathe. She didn't care that he was really hurting her now. She just wanted to get away. Anything to get away.

Then there was a flash of silver.

Sophie blinked, blood slashing across her face and neck. The man holding her gurgled and dropped her. She hit the ground, but kept her eyes open. She crawled away, but watched that woman, the woman with the dog eyes, yank the biggest knife Sophie had seen out of the guy's neck. She wiped blood off on her jeans and tucked the blade back into the holster tied to her thigh. Then she pulled out the gun she had holstered to the other thigh, quickly fitted a silencer to the end, and walked around the man, gun down. Sophie thought she was coming for her. To finish what the man had started. But as the woman walked, she pulled the trigger four times, each bullet going into the man. One in his head, his face, his neck, his inner thigh.

She stopped in front of Sophie, crouching down. "You all right?"

Sophie nodded, but she still didn't know if she could trust her. If she should. Her eyes . . . as she moved, the moon reflected her eyes back to Sophie. Just like a dog's.

The knife flashed again and then Sophie's hands were loose. Fingers gripped her and helped her to her feet.

"I'm sorry," the woman said. "I promised to look out for you. Sorry I let you down."

Sophie hadn't wanted to admit it to herself. She wasn't much for fanciful flights of fantasy as her grandmother liked to call it. Reality had always made that impossible. But now she knew. That guy she'd picked up, he was one. The guys who took her tonight. That bitch woman who'd slapped her around until she got the answers she wanted. And this woman. They were all kind of the same. They weren't human. Not completely. Not like Sophie. Because no human Sophie knew, who could cut a man's throat, then shoot him in major areas and arteries on the body, would turn around and apologize for letting her down. And she'd meant that apology, too. Sophie could tell. Sophie knew liars and she knew truth tellers. This woman, or whatever she was, was all about the truth.

"What . . . what's your name?"

"Dee-Ann. Dee-Ann Smith."

"What now, Dee-Ann?"

"We get you someplace safe." With her arm around Sophie, Dee-Ann led her back to the road. "While my friends deal with Whitlan and Baissier."

Sophie stopped, forcing Dee-Ann to face her.

"What's wrong?" she asked. Sophie could see the concern on the woman's face, but it wasn't easy not to be completely freaked out by those eyes.

But Sophie choked back the fear. The woman had saved her life; she owed her this much. "Your friends are in there?"

"Yeah."

"Get them out, Dee-Ann. Get them out right now." Sophie licked her lips and admitted, "There's something I didn't tell the other woman."

So this is what a country club looks like from the inside.

Not surprisingly, most Malones were never invited to join country clubs. Although a few had worked in them and robbed several.

Following the scent of bears, Cella and her team worked their way down several flights of stairs, far under the club, until she hit the last floor. She and the two lions walked out a door and into a long and wide hallway with marble floors. There were animal trophies lined up on both sides of the hallway. It wasn't until she passed the first one that she stopped in her tracks, her body shaking. The two males looked at her, then at the trophies. They stepped closer, took a sniff, and immediately stepped back.

Every trophy in this hallway that had been stuffed and mounted—a male shifter. A couple of wolves, several panthers, but a whole lot of bears—grizzly and polar—and lions. The ultimate predators. Cella didn't see any tigers, but she had the feeling the pelts of her kind were decorating people's beds and floors.

Cella took several breaths. She had to keep it together. If she lost her control, got angry, and started killing everyone, this would not end well.

Cella gestured forward with two fingers and she walked

on, trying hard not to look or think about those who'd met what could only be called a cruel end.

They'd neared the end of the hallway when one male stopped, his hand raised to halt them. He lifted his head, sniffed. When he looked back at Cella, she let out a groan and pushed past him. She ran until she hit the last room. Stopping right inside, she closed her eyes and lowered her weapon.

"You need to pull them out."

Knowing his team had Baissier's men covered by their SUVs, Crush looked over his shoulder at Dee-Ann. She had the girl with her. The poor thing had clearly ended up on the wrong side of Baissier, but at least she was still alive. It seemed as if the sow had taken it easy on her. Surprising.

"What is it?"

But before Dee-Ann could answer his question, he heard Cella's voice over his earpiece.

He and Dee looked at each other and Crush said, "Repeat that."

"I said he's gone, Crush. Whitlan's gone. And you better bring everybody down here. Including Baissier's men."

Crush raised his arm and motioned to Dez, who had a spot on a nearby building.

"You better come with us," Crush said to the remainder of Baissier's team.

One of the bears laughed. "What? Are you arresting us?"

Crush shrugged. "I don't think there's a point."

"It was some kind of gas," Cella explained while turning her back to the room. The device that had been triggered had released a gas that had not killed Baissier or her team easily, their twisted and tortured remains littering the floor. "As soon as they opened this door. It went off and took 'em out."

"Dissipated quick, too," Smith muttered, walking around the room and coldly examining everything.

"And Whitlan's gone," Crush noted again, his gaze locked on where this room led . . . to a dock filled with lots of very fast and very expensive boats.

"Yeah, but he's got us looking for him. And the feds."

"And we have our own inside there. We'll find him, Crush."

"It better be quick. Whitlan enjoys killing our kind. He's not going to lose his taste for that anytime soon."

"So what do we do now?" one of Baissier's men asked.

"Call whoever is next in command," Crush told him. "Let him or her know about this."

"The trophies," Cella said. "We identify those we can, alert the families. The ones we can't, we give a proper burial."

Cella called in the cleanup team for assistance since they had to be done before the country club staff made it in for the morning shift. Knowing they were short on time, they all got to work.

Chapter Thirty-five

These days Cella didn't have time to be as exhausted as she felt. Why? Because she was a goddamn bridesmaid. Why? Why did she say yes to being a bridesmaid? Even worse, a maid of honor!

She could be such an idiot.

Between the bachelorette party, the bridal shower, and the never-ending dress fittings, Cella was goddamn burnt out. But she was almost done. Almost.

So, running down the stairs, lifting the hem of her five-thousand-dollar dress—only for a friend would she spend that kind of cash on a stupid dress—Cella yelled out, "Let's go, Malones! We've gotta get a move on!"

"Where's the kid?" she asked her young cousins, busy getting dressed up for the day.

"In back," one answered.

"All right. The cars will be here to pick you guys up soon. Do not keep the drivers waiting. And no whore makeup," she added before running outside.

Meghan and Josie, already dressed, with minimal make-up, and ready to go, sat at one of the tables and . . .

Eyes narrowing on her daughter and daughter-by-friendship, Cella demanded, "What is *that*?"

Meghan held the thing up, her grin wide. "It's a kitty! Miss Smith brought it over for me and Josie while you were in the hospital."

Cella studied the black-and-white tabby carefully. A bright red collar with an annoying little bell that kept making this tinkling noise was around its neck and it smelled distinctly of . . . well . . . of bear sow.

Josie reached over and took the tabby from Meghan's hands. What always amazed Cella about the pair of them was that they never fought over anything. They shared so easily. Cella would admit she didn't know any felines who could do that.

"Isn't she cute?" Josie asked, nuzzling her nose against the cat's.

"It's a cat. It's a *house* cat."

"And we're keeping her," Meghan told her mother, all haughty about it, too! "She was a gift to us and Grams said we can keep her. So we're keeping her."

"Whatever. But I'm not taking care of that thing while you're off partying with frat boys."

Her daughter shuddered in disgust. Knowing her kid, she'd spend her college years partying with the chess players' club or with the geeks who design lasers before returning home for a hot cocoa at eight p.m.

Cella stepped close, scrunching her nose at the cat. "What are you going to name it?"

"It's a she, and we're naming her—"

"Mrs. Fuzzybottom!"

"No," Meghan told Josie in no uncertain terms. "We will not give a cat a stupid name."

While Josie pouted, Meghan thought a moment and finally offered, "Cleo?"

"Over my dead body," Cella said quickly. "There will be no cliché cat names. No. Never."

"Well, since you're being so picky about it, She Who Will Not Take Care of This Thing, what would you suggest?"

The answer hit her so quickly, she was surprised she hadn't thought of it before. "Do you know what a really nice gesture would be, girls? Naming the cat Dee-Ann."

Josie grinned. "You mean in honor of Miss Smith?"

"It was her gift to you guys. I just think it would be a really sweet gesture."

"I like it." Josie stood, the cat in her arms. "I'm going to tell Mom. I'll let her know you're ready to go, Aunt C."

"Thanks, sweetheart."

Josie walked off to her house and Cella looked at her daughter. "What?"

"How do you live with yourself?"

"Very well," she told her. "I find myself quite entertaining."

It wasn't nearly as painful as Crush thought it would be. He'd never been to a Jewish wedding ceremony held by cats before, so it was new and interesting for him. And now he was back at one of the Kingston Arms' ballrooms for the reception. Although the ceremony was a little more serious, the couple wanted the reception to be a lot lighter and considering the dancing and laughing he walked in on, he could see they'd already achieved their goal.

"Hey, kid!"

Crush jumped a little, trying not to panic when Nice Guy Malone wrapped his arms around him in a big hug. "Hi, Mr. Malone."

"Butch, kid. Butch." He stepped back, grinned. "Did you hear about my girl? What the Carnivores offered her?"

"I heard." And he'd been bragging about it at the office so much that all his coworkers roared anytime it came up again. Including Dez.

Butch grinned. "*My* girl."

Meghan and Josie ran up, both looking beautiful in their bridesmaids' gowns.

"You came," Meghan said, going up on her toes to kiss Crush's cheek, Josie kissing the other one.

"Did you really think your mother was going to let me out of this?"

Meghan laughed. "Nope." She tugged at her grandfather's tux. "Grams is looking for you."

"As my wife or as—"

"Wedding planner."

"Crap. She wants me to move something."

"I can do it for you," Crush offered.

"Nah. She just makes me do it 'cause she likes to see my muscles ripple." Grinning, Butch walked off.

Meghan shuddered. "Ew." She jerked her thumb toward one of the doorways. "We better go, too. The bride and groom will be making their entrance soon."

"See you guys when you're done."

Meghan and Josie waved and rushed off. Crush looked around at the tables, debating whether he should go ahead and get seated now or wait a little longer when he realized Novikov stood beside him. Breathing.

He really liked the guy . . . but he hated when he did that.

"Hey."

Novikov nodded.

"Why are you here?" Crush had to ask.

"Blayne finagled an invite because she wanted to see how Barb runs her weddings."

"Is she happy?"

"Ecstatic. She really likes the cake."

"The cake?"

"It's Blayne."

"How have you liked the wedding?"

"Everything has been on time . . . so I love it."

Crush laughed, stopping when a woman in a full-length dress stopped in front of him and stared at him like she knew him. She seemed out of place because she was one of the few canines in attendance.

"What?" she finally asked.

Crush blinked, recognizing the voice. "Dee-Ann?"

"Who the hell did you think it was?"

"Not you," Novikov muttered.

"You look great," Crush told her honestly.

But her eyes narrowed and Crush held his hands up. "Forget I said anything."

Ric Van Holtz stepped in beside his mate, slipping his arm around her waist and kissing her cheek.

He smiled. "Crushek . . ." His smile faded and gave a barely there nod. "Novikov."

"Asshole."

The She-wolf snarled in warning.

"Gentlemen and She-wolf," Crush warned, "it's a wedding. Let's all be nice."

"Is that your cop tone?" Novikov asked.

"That's my cop tone. Don't make me bring out my cop fist."

"So—" Van Holtz began.

"I don't know anything," Crush cut in, knowing Van Holtz was about to ask him—again—about whether Cella would take his offer of becoming the Carnivores' assistant coach.

The wolf bared a fang. "What is taking her so long?"

"I don't know."

"Want me to talk to her?" Novikov asked.

"No," both Crush and Van Holtz immediately replied.

But Smith grinned. "Oh, Lord, please do."

Cella helped her mother adjust Rivka's gown. The bride and groom would be making their big entrance in a few minutes and everything had to be perfect. At least, as far as Cella's mother was concerned, it had to be perfect. Personally, Cella could give a shit. She was *hungry*.

"Your stomach is growling again," Barb sang at her. But

it was her trying-to-keep-the-bride-calm-while-telling-the-person-she's-singing-to-she's-annoyed voice.

"That's because I'm hungry," Cella sang back in the same tone.

"Where's Bri?" Rivka asked.

"He made a desperate run for it?" Cella teased, only to get a paw to the back of her head. An actual paw!

"Ow!"

"Go find out where Bri is," Barb ordered.

"Fine." Anything to get away from the dictator her mother became whenever she handled a damn wedding.

Cella went down the hall, her steps slowing when she saw Bri hugging Meghan. She smiled, her heart warming at the sight.

Bri caught sight of her over his daughter's shoulder and winked.

"Why don't you go make sure Rivka's doing okay. I'll be right there."

"Okay." Meghan kissed her father's cheek. "I love you, Daddy."

"You, too, baby."

Meg walked past Cella, stopping briefly to also kiss her cheek. "I love you, too, Ma."

"Tossing me a bone."

"I had to. I didn't want to hear the whining later." Grinning, Meghan walked off.

Smart. Ass.

"Where's Josie?" Cella asked her daughter's back.

"Getting Aunt J. for the entrance."

"Good. We'll be right there."

"How good did we do?" Bri asked Cella, taking her hand in his own.

"We did amazing."

"You okay about Hofstra?"

"I'm fine with Hofstra. I'm fine with her staying with the

family. God knows they need someone to manage their craziness."

Bri kissed the back of her hand. "Thanks, Cella."

"For what?"

"Giving me an amazing daughter and being you about it. You always worked with me about visitation, always made me feel part of the family."

"Because my kid is the most important thing and you are a great dad. I would never keep you away from her. Now go to your mate. Be happy." She hugged him.

"You be happy, too."

"I'm always happy," she told him honestly. "It annoys people."

Bri released her with a laugh, giving her one last kiss on her cheek before he headed back to Rivka.

Cella took a moment to adjust her dress, pausing when she saw her Aunt Deirdre heading from the bathroom back to the ballroom. Deirdre glanced at Cella, sneering a little at her without saying a word. Cella let her get a few feet before she said loudly, "I saw you sobbing at my bedside, old woman!"

"Shut up, heifer!"

Chuckling—okay, maybe it was a cackle—Cella adjusted her gown one more time and headed back to the rest of the wedding party.

Everyone was starting to line up and Cella walked toward her place at the head of the line.

"Everything all right outside?" she asked Jai, taking her bouquet from her mother.

"If you're really asking me if Crush showed up for the reception as he promised, the answer is yes."

"But?"

"But he's trapped between a bickering Van Holtz and Novikov."

Cella waved that off. "That doesn't bother him."

"He does seem to be enjoying himself. Oh. And that pit bull that hangs around you is in a designer dress."

"Yeah. I helped Smith pick it out, but Van Holtz paid because she refused. But the dress is great, though," Cella explained, "because she's got an arsenal under that skirt. Two nines, four full clips, and her bowie knife." She grinned. "Cool, huh?"

Disgusted, Jai shook her head and focused on the bride.

"What's the look for? For Smith that's like the equivalent of her being naked."

Crush looked up from the piece of red velvet wedding cake he'd been about to devour. "I don't understand. Why won't you just say yes? Why are you fighting this?"

"Isn't that my right?" Cella shot back.

"No! It isn't. Just say yes already."

"What I told him was that I had to take some time and talk to Meghan and Daddy . . ." Cella rolled her eyes and finally spit out, ". . . and you."

Crush dropped his head a bit. "You don't have to sound so angry."

"The fact that I care at all what you think irritates me."

"Okay, take out the fact that I'm a Carnivore fan on an astronomical scale and let's just look at this from a 'your best interest' point of view."

"Yeah?"

"Chance to coach a championship team with one of the best players since your dad—"

"Which, I guess, is still not me?"

"Do you want me to lie?"

"No, no. Go ahead and rhapsodize over your girl crush on Novikov."

"Thank you. As a matter of fact, I will." She let out a little laugh and Crush went on, "How about this? You've seen how Van Holtz works with Reynolds. You've seen how he works with you. Do you think he'll be one of those micro-managing bosses or big picture bosses?"

"Big picture."

"Which would you rather work for?"

"Big picture."

Crush figured that. He could tell Cella would kill a micro-managing boss in his or her sleep.

"Do you think he'll pay you well?"

"Extraordinarily well."

"Have a problem about you working with KZS?"

"He hasn't so far."

"Respect you as an equal?"

"He already does."

"Give you free rein on how you manage the team and its resources?"

She sighed. "Yeah. He will."

"Then what's the problem?"

Finally, Cella admitted, "I didn't want to look too eager to take this coaching job. My agent would have killed me if I'd looked too eager."

"That's valid. What about the rest of the team?"

"They're not supposed to know yet about Reynolds, but someone must have leaked something because since Van Holtz talked to me I've gotten twelve e-mails begging me to take the job, eighteen texts, and *more* damn flowers. And then there's Novikov, who for an entire day called me every hour on the hour, ordering me to take the job or he wouldn't be responsible for what he did to the hillbilly, which I assume meant Reed." Cella looked off and said, "He's a little obsessive, that guy."

"Ya think?"

"Aren't you friends now?"

"Apparently. Not sure how I feel about that, though. I mean on one hand, here's the player I really admire and like as a human being, and when you're talking to him one-on-one, he's really interesting. But while I was having lunch with him one day last week, I watched him take thirty minutes just to properly set his new watch. There seems to be a whole process involved. It was weird."

"God." Cella dropped her elbows on the table and cupped her chin in the palms of her hands. "So much change."

"I know."

"And my daughter informed me last night that now that she's made the final and unshakable decision to stay with the family and go to school locally, I should understand that it's time for me to move out on my own so that I won't cramp her studying schedule."

"You and your daughter have the oddest discussions."

"She's afraid I'm going to push her to go to frat parties and socially network."

"You will."

"Of course, I will."

"You know," Crush began, seeing his opportunity, "if you want to try this moving out thing without worrying about making a big decision too soon, you can, ya know . . . hang out at my house for a while."

Cella smirked. "Oh, really?"

"Just something to think about. No pressure. No ties that bind. Just you, hanging out at my house, coming and going as you like."

"Like a feral cat that lives under your deck?"

"I wouldn't have used that particular analogy, but okay."

"What about Lola?"

"She tolerates you well enough. And I'm still—"

"Looking for her forever home. Right. Sure."

"It's just a casual offer that shouldn't make you panic in the least."

"Uh-huh. So we'd be pretend living together?"

"Exactly. We can even start tonight since Meghan is flying to Israel for the second wedding. So you can see if staying at my place works for you in a completely non-pushy way."

"Cats hate pushy."

"Right."

Cella shrugged. "Yeah. I guess I could give it a try."

"Okay. Sounds good."

They sat silently for several long minutes until Crush said, "Cella?"

"Uh-huh?"

"I guess I should tell you . . . I'm in love with you."

"Pretend in love with me?"

"No, smart-ass. Really, seriously, *madly* in love with you. Borderline desperate but with enough personal fortitude to keep it under control."

"Oh. Okay." They fell silent again, Crush glad he'd gotten that off his chest. But it was when he looked over his shoulder to see if he could figure out which doorway led to the men's bathroom that he felt Cella Malone suddenly rub her head over his arm and across the left side of his face and neck.

By the time he'd turned back around, she was sitting in her chair, staring straight ahead, composed and completely unruffled.

"Did you just rub up against me?"

She blinked, looking at him as if he'd suddenly appeared. "Huh?"

"I said did you just mark me?"

She pursed her lips, shrugged her shoulders, and finally started blaming everyone else in the room.

"Look, if I'm going to stay at your house for the next couple of . . . whatever, I just thought it was prudent to make sure I warned off all these bitches who've been circling you since the reception started."

"Uh-huh."

"It's temporary."

"Sure."

"Just making sure things are clear."

"Of course, you are, brave Malone of the traveling Malones."

"All right fine!" she snapped. "I'm in love with you. There. I said it. Now get over yourself."

"You know, I think those are the words written on the Taj Mahal: 'I said it. Now get over yourself.' Some of the greatest love stories have started with those words."

Cella laughed so hard that Crush finally lifted her up and placed her in his lap, his arms loose around her waist.

"I'm sorry," she said. "I panicked. Besides, are you supposed tell a guy you love him when you're at your daughter's father's wedding? And you're not saying it to your daughter's father?"

"I think it would only be wrong if he wasn't actually marrying someone else. So I think morally, you're in the clear."

"You do understand that no matter where I go, the Malones will always be part of it?"

"Like a wolf pack?"

She shuddered. "If you need some words to describe it, at least use, like, a lion pride or something."

"That's fine and, yes, I know that. Just as you know every once in a while, you'll have to beat up my brothers when they break into the house."

"Since I enjoy doing that, I don't think that's a problem."

Crush pressed his forehead against Cella's. "Then I figure the rest we'll work out as we go along."

"Then I'm in," she promised, her eyes closing, her body relaxing into his. "And I really do love you, Crush. I really do."

"And can I just say, thank God," Crush murmured into Cella's ear. "Thank God, I can't handle Jell-O shots."

And her explosive laughter made everything for Lou Crushek absolutely perfect.

Keep reading for a very special look at The Unleashing, *the first in Shelly Laurenston's new* Call of Crows *series, featuring a band of tough-as-nails female fighters and the men who aren't afraid to stand up to them. Available now, wherever books are sold.*

The giant who'd gone off to retrieve the "scary" Rundstöm walked back out of the house, followed by another giant who had to dip down a bit to clear his own doorway.

He was a dark version of Giant Number One. Black hair that nearly touched his shoulders, a dark brown beard that covered the lower half of his face. He wore dark green jeans, a black, worn T-shirt, and thick black work boots.

"Now," Erin softly explained, "the thing to remember with Rundstöm is no sudden movements. No loud noises. Don't do anything that might freak him out. Just smile—but don't bare your teeth when you do—and let me do the talking. He tolerates me."

But to be honest, Kera could barely hear the directions. Her heart was beating too fast. And tears began to well in her usually dry eyes—a "flaw" that used to bother her ex-husband. Her lack of tears over anything.

What choice did she have, though? When she was looking at the man who'd saved her life?

So, ignoring all of Erin's warnings, Kera charged over to Giant Number Two and threw herself right into his arms.

* * *

Vig Rundstöm wrapped his arms around Kera Watson's perfect, *perfect* body and held her tight.

Tighter than he probably should. He couldn't help himself, though. She was alive.

Alive and well and in his arms. Hugging him back, and whispering, "Thank you!" over and over against his ear.

Kera finally pulled back a bit, her hands reaching up to grasp his face. She smiled and he saw tears in her eyes.

"I—" she began.

"So you two know each other?" Erin Amsel asked, the Crows having sidled their way up alongside them to get a closer look.

Kera blinked and immediately replied, "He's a customer."

"A customer?"

"Yeah." She looked back at Amsel and the other Crows. "A favorite customer. Used to come into the coffee shop I worked at. I always called him 'four bear claws and a black coffee.'"

"Really?"

Vig felt Kera's body tighten. "Yeah," she barked back. "Really."

"And you greet all your favorite customers with your legs around their waist?"

Kera unwrapped those legs from Vig—something he was not happy about—dropped to the ground, and turned to face Amsel.

"No," Kera replied. "Sometimes I just get on my knees and give 'em blow jobs in an alley."

"Did you learn that in the Marines, too?" Amsel asked.

A direct hit that Vig knew would turn ugly. He was already reaching for Kera as Stieg was going for Amsel. But Maeve beat them all, stepping between the two women and holding up her phone.

"I put my symptoms in . . . cancer. I have cancer."

"You," Amsel said, "do not have cancer. And," she added,

"if you keep talking about cancer you're gonna eventually get it!"

"Are you wishing cancer on me?"

"No. But now that you mention it . . ."

With a noise of disgust, Kera grabbed Vig's hand and led him back into his house, closing the door behind them.

She relaxed against the door and let out a relieved sigh. "I don't know what's wrong with me," Kera announced, "but all I want to do is beat that redhead. Beat her and beat her and beat her until she stops squawking at me."

Vig nodded. "That's not surprising. You're trying to get used to the new and improved you. It'll take time for your body to adjust."

Kera didn't seem to care about any of that.

"You saved my life . . ."

"Vig. Vig Rundström. And all I did was ask a god a favor. But trust me, if you weren't already worthy, Skuld would have completely ignored me. You're here, Kera, because Skuld thought you deserved to be."

"Put it any way you want. You saved my life."

"I couldn't. It was too late for that." When Kera shook her head, he explained, "Kera, you weren't already dying. You were on your last breath. Your soul was transitioning from this world to the next when Skuld took it. So I didn't save your life. I just gave you a shot at a second one. A brand-new life as a Daughter of Skuld. As a Crow."

She gazed at him, a wide smile suddenly breaking out across her beautiful face.

"What?" he asked.

"I don't think I've ever heard you say anything but"—she dropped her voice several octaves—"'four bear claws and a black coffee please.' Oh, and 'I'm fine . . . and you?'" She laughed. "I didn't know you could say more."

"I speak when I have something to say."

She nodded. "Your C.O.s must have loved you then."

Vig frowned. "My C.O.s?"

"Your commanding officers? In the military? What were you? ? God, please don't tell me you were Air Force," she teased.

"I'm not in the Army. Or Air Force. Or anything like that. I'm not even American. I'm Swedish."

She blinked. "You are?"

"I've been here since I was nine, but I've only ever been a Raven. A Swedish Raven."

"And that means . . . what? Exactly."

He gave a small smile. "No one's told you anything, have they?"

"There's been a lot of yelling. My God, there's been so much yelling."

"The Ravens, the Crows, the other Clans . . . we are the human representatives of the Viking gods on this plane of existence. We are the hammers of the gods. Some say fist of the gods, but . . . that always makes me think of that movie *Caligula*, and that makes me uncomfortable. So I like hammer. We are the *hammers* of the gods."

"We are?"

Vig nodded. "Oh yes, Kera. We are."

"Okay." Kera blew out a long breath. "I'll try not to freak out about that." Even though Vig sensed she was starting to freak out. He could see it in her eyes.

He decided to distract her. "So . . . what made you think I was in the military?"

She glanced off before lying. "Nothing."

"Kera . . . you're a very bad liar."

"Well . . . the hair . . . the beard . . . sometimes you wear that green jacket with the pockets that looks kind of military."

"Aren't I a little scruffy to be in your military?"

"True . . . unless you . . . ya know . . . snapped a little."

"Snapped?"

"You know." She suddenly rubbed her nose. "Had a little bit of a . . . breakdown."

Vig took a step back. "You thought I was insane?"

"No," she said quickly, moving closer. "I thought it was just a little PTSD with possible brain injury."

"Brain injury?"

"It's happened to a few of my buddies."

"Is that why you wouldn't take my money sometimes?"

She cringed. "I also kinda thought you were homeless."

Vig heard something coming from his back door and he turned to see Siggy trying to sneak back outside.

"What are you doing?" he asked his teammate.

"Trying to go away before you notice me."

"It's a little late for that."

"Yeah . . . I know." Then Siggy burst out laughing and ran out, slamming the door behind him.

Gritting his teeth, Vig turned back to Kera. "So all this time you thought—" A burst of laughter from the front of the house cut the rest of Vig's sentence off.

Vig blew out a breath. "Forget it."

"Vig—"

"No. You came here for a reason. Would you like to see the weapons I made for you?" he asked Kera.

"For me?"

"I just finished them. I knew you were going to need them."